# LOREMASTER'S MYTH

"Cawdor?" Eider laughed. "Cawdor doesn't exist, you fool. It's only a Loremaster's myth. It isn't a real place!"

"But it is!" Drib cried. "Silkstone says it is where the Nighthorses came from, beyond the wildness of Underfall, on the dark side of morning. The Nighthorses will take us there if we ride them on a loose rein and let them find the way. If you don't believe me, then ask the Battle Owl!"

Berioss hesitated, looking at the owl perched on the boy's shoulder. In his battle days he would have followed the owl's advice without question; so why did he now hesitate?

Was it because the bird spoke through a crippled boy instead of a Galloper captain? A boy whose head barely reached Berioss's belt?

Books by Mike Jefferies

LOREMASTERS OF ELUNDIUM
*The Road to Underfall*
*Palace of Kings*
*Shadowlight*
*The Knights of Cawdor*

*Glitterspike Hall*
*Hall of Whispers*
*Shadows in the Watchgate*
*Hidden Echoes*
*Stone Angels*

Available from HarperPaperbacks

# The
# KNIGHTS
## of
# CAWDOR
## Loremasters of Elundium

# Mike Jefferies

**HarperPrism**
*An Imprint of* HarperPaperbacks

This is a work of fiction. The characters, incidents, and dialogues are products of the author's imagination and are not to be construed as real. Any resemblance to actual events or persons, living or dead, is entirely coincidental.

HarperPaperbacks   *A Division of* HarperCollins*Publishers*
10 East 53rd Street, New York, N.Y. 10022

Cover illustration by Rob Alexander

First printing: June 1995

Printed in the United States of America

HarperPrism is an imprint of HarperPaperbacks.
HarperPaperbacks, HarperPrism, and colophon are trademarks of HarperCollins*Publishers*

❖ 10 9 8 7 6 5 4 3 2 1

*To my wife, Sheila, who stood beside me on the black marble cliffs of Cawdor listening to the thunder of the surf while we watched the new sun break free from the dark side of morning.*

# 1

## Daydreams in the Learning Hall

LOREMASTER GROUT SIGHED MISERABLY, SHAKING out the dusty folds of his gown as he signalled to the doorwardens that it was time to throw back the bolts on the doors of the Learning Hall and let the children in. He cursed, under his breath, the passing of the last Granite King and all the changes that he had been forced to endure since the Chancellors had fled. With a half-hearted hand he motioned to the throng of unwelcome faces that he could see lurking in the shadows beneath the archway and bade them enter. Grout wrinkled his nose in disgust as they swarmed noisily through the doorway, pressing a sweet-apple blended from rose petals, white sandal and camphor against his beak-sharp nose. "How I hate this new Elundium!" he muttered derisively, resting his bony elbows on the high lectern and watching the untidy, unwashed rabble push their way into the Learning Hall, searching for the best places to sit or crouch upon the floor.

King Thane's proclamation in Candlebane Hall had been made less than a dozen daylights ago; in it he had stated that learning was for everyone, no matter where or how they were born, and it had brought the scum of the Granite City clamouring to his door. Now wherever he looked all he could see were scullion boys, candlebrats, sweeps' boys and every common street-urchin imaginable. There was hardly a washed face or a combed head of hair amongst them

and he was at his wits' end to know what to do with
them. They didn't have the slightest interest in the
Lore of Elundium or the right and proper way of how
things should be done: all they ever wanted to hear
were stories of how King Thane had slain
Krulshards, the Master of Darkness, and how he had
ridden the great Warhorse, Esteron, upon the
Causeway Fields. They wanted to hear of the Battle
Owls and the Border Runners—useless, repetitive
stories of battles that had nothing to do with the cunning of barter, or lore, or the art of politics. And now
their heads were full of rumours of how the
Nighthorses were coming to the city escorting a pony
as a gift from Thunderstone, the Keeper of Underfall,
to Krann, Queen Elionbel's younger brother. Oh how
he wished for the return of the Chancellors, a return
to the old ways in which the common folk were kept
in their place. He longed to have his hallowed
Learning Hall filled once more with the studious
scratch of quills on parchment and to hear the steady
noonday drone of his favourite pupils reciting by rote
the age-old lore and customs of the kingdom.

There was so much knowledge itching at his fingertips, reams of lore and the art of counting, that
these new circumstances had forced him to lock away
to gather dust in the back of his mind. He longed to
impart knowledge of the important lines of title and
heredity, deeds of high breeding, etiquette and good
manners that King Thane had swept away with the
beginning of the new Elundium. All the finer things
of life that these ignorant urchins had no use for. The
lectern he was leaning heavily upon as he ruminated
upon the cruelty of his circumstances suddenly
rocked violently from side to side, threatening at any
moment to overturn and send him sprawling backwards onto the floor.

Grout, startled, uttered a curse, his dream of better
daylights shattered, and he grabbed at the lectern,

struggling to keep his balance. A ripple of childish laughter winged across the Learning Hall. His face darkened with anger. Two street-urchins, who had obviously been fighting for the same place to sit in his shadow, had almost knocked the lectern over as they tried to escape back into the crowd. His voice froze them where they stood.

"Come here, you two idle, loutish brutes! You will pay dearly for touching my desk—you know I will not tolerate such behaviour!"

His voice thundered, making the rest of his pupils shrink back as they realized what he was about to do. Grout reached down with his long, bony fingers and unhooked the ratstail flail that hung from his belt.

"I will not have your lowly, street manners in the Learning Hall!" he hissed, reaching out with his whip arm and preparing to set about them.

The boys cried out as the flail sang through the air towards them, and they flinched and cowered as its stinging tail cut raw, angry welts in their dirty skin.

"We meant no harm, Loremaster Grout, honest we didn't!" the small boy, a crippled sweep's scramble, pleaded. His crooked legs prevented him from dodging the flail as quickly as the other boy and its cutting edge twisted and snaked around his forearm, biting into his flesh, trapping him where he stood.

Grout gave a triumphant sneer that he had caught one of the wretches so easily and began to pull him roughly towards the lectern, demanding to know his name.

"Drib, master, my name's Drib!" he cried out, "I'm . . . I'm . . . I'm sorry I touched your desk, it was an accident, I only wanted to sit at your feet to learn everything about the Nighthorses that are coming to the city. Legends tell how they are gathered from the dark side of morning and . . . " his voice trailed off into sobs of terror as Grout pulled him closer.

"NIGHTHORSES!" The Loremaster laughed cruelly. "Why would the likes of you want to know about them? Perhaps you have an idea about applying to the Breaking Yyards to ride one?" Grout's voice grew silent as he looked down at Drib's crooked legs and his face hardened suddenly, clearly showing his contempt and hatred for all the common street-urchins. "All you're good for, boy, is scrambling up and down the chimneys and using those knees of yours to loosen the soot!"

Large tears welled up in Drib's eyes before spilling down his cheeks, scouring through the sooty grime that was ingrained into the skin of his face as Grout's cruel barb struck home. "I . . . I . . . I know I can never ride, but it doesn't do anybody any harm to learn all about them does it?" he tried to say through his sobs.

"You dare to answer me back?" Grout was almost speechless with anger as he jerked the child closer with a brutal pull on the handle of the flail. He leaned down, trying to catch at the insolence he was sure he could hear in the reply and raised his other hand to strike him. But he hesitated, momentarily distracted by an unfamiliar noise and a sudden murmur of wind that ruffled the parchments on his desk. The breeze had in it the echo of distant hoofbeats and the cry of the wild and it billowed around him before slowly subsiding and melting into the shadows.

Grout frowned as a cold shiver tingled his spine. He looked over the top of the urchin's matted hair and wondered what on earth it could have been. "A curse on all Nighthorses!" he muttered spitefully. The mass of his pupils crouched expectantly forward, watching him silently, waiting for him to vent his anger on Drib because the boy had expressed his love for the miserable creatures who had helped Thanehand seize the throne. But Grout wouldn't give them the excuse to report him for disloyalty. Slowly he let his hand fall to his side and eased his grip upon the flail. Much as he longed to beat the sweep's scramble he knew he dared not risk giving away his true feelings for this new Elundium. Anger was a dangerous luxury in these uncertain times. He had to be careful, he had to bide his time.

Forcing a glassy smile onto his face, he uncoiled the tail of the whip from Drib's arm and patted him, a little too forcefully, on the top of his head, sending him tottering to his knees. "Sit, my child, sit and do not touch my desk again."

Looking up at the other pupils he opened his arms and in a strong voice cried, "The gate-wardens informed me only this morning that the Nighthorses will arrive today, so this morning I will unfold the tales of all the glories of those proud horses, how they were gathered from the dark side of morning and how they helped our great King Thane in the battles he won to bring us this new Elundium."

Drib shook his head dizzily and squeezed in between two larger boys at the Loremaster's feet. He looked up, his eyes shining with tears, and let the master's voice flow over him, filling his ears with the thunder of the Nighthorses' hooves, the baying snarls and howls of the border runners, the savage dogs of war, and the shrieking stoops of Battle Owls as they hunted the Nightbeasts up across the steep shoulders of Manterns Mountain, relentlessly pursuing them towards the gates of the City of Night.

Grout, despite all his faults and the meanness of his nature, was a master story-teller and he had each pupil captured and entranced as he wove between them the story of King Thane's epic struggle to win the daylight. Drib imagined the wind ruffling through his hair and he was sure he could hear the rhythmic creak of leather and the jingle of harness as he rode upon one of the Nighthorses. The Greenway seemed to stretch away into a vanishing, hazy horizon, glistening with morning dew; he could hear blackbirds

singing in the hedgerows and the rays of early sunlight melted the mist between the trees.

The Loremaster suddenly lifted his arms, letting
his voluminous sleeves fall back in mysterious shafts
of light and shadow as he made the shape of a
gnarled old tree in the dusty rays of sunlight that
streamed through the windows. "Nevian, the Master
of Magic," he whispered conspiratorially, "told our
king to call out to the trees. King Thane, mounted
upon Esteron, had halted on the brink of the narrow
causeway that led down from the top of the Rising,
the last fortress to stand above the sea of shadow that
had spread across Elundium. Queen Elionbel sat
beside him, mounted on Stumble, the small relay
horse. She pressed Stumble close to Esteron's flank
in the chill, dawn wind—was afraid of the hopeless
battle that lay before them and reached beneath her
cloak for the precious bag of nightflower seeds that
Loremaster Pinchface had given her in the last few
moments of his life. She remembered his dying
words—"use them well, my Lady—they have a great
power against the darkness."

Grout paused, watching their faces, seeing the
effect of his story mirrored in their eyes. "Warriors!"
he cried, making each of them jump. "Warriors—I
have great need of all the warriors of Elundium who
love the daylight!" Thane shouted, standing in his
stirrups and looking around him.

Grout paused again, smiling and waiting as his
pupils crept a handspan closer. "Suddenly all the
ancient trees groaned and creaked and were still,
their whispering leaves falling silent. "Warriors!"
Thane shouted again. "Brave men who love the sunlight—I have great need of you." And all the trees
began to sway and crumble into hollow strips of
bark, their gnarled, old trunks broke and shattered
into a fog of splinters and in their place were thousands of grim-faced warriors with a glittering forest

of spearblades lowered against the army of shadows. Grout glanced at the hour-glass and stopped.

"What about Eryus? Tell us how Lord Willow rode Eryus out of the Rising to where Rubel struggled to carry the sword of Durondel to King Thane. Tell us that last story, please Loremaster Grout!" a small boy from the back of the hall called out.

"Oh no, please finish telling us about the Nighthorses! Where do they really come from?" Drib begged. It was the tale he loved best.

"Horses, always horses . . . " Grout muttered bitterly. "Oh, very well," and he lowered his voice to a theatrical whisper, making the urchins that crowded the Learning Hall fall silent as they hung on his every word. "Legends tell that the Nighthorses were wild and proud and fleet of foot and that they were gathered by the first Granite Kings in the shadows of Cawdor, the vast citadel that stands on the dark side of morning guarding the margins of the world. But this citadel's origins are buried so deep in those old legends that nobody knows for sure where it really lies, save that it must be somewhere beyond the last lamp that burns at World's End in the Fortress of Underfall, somewhere far beyond the Emerall Mountains and the forest of petrified, living stone. But stories also tell of frozen orchids and vines, and creepers of brilliant colours that climb the walls and towers of Cawdor, and of carvings of the purest black marble veined with silver and of the winged creatures and beasts that guard it. They tell how the walls rise sheer and terrible and how the wind cries eternally with a thousand restless voices that comb through its gloomy darkness; and of how the sharp tang of salt wets every warrior's lips who patrol its doors."

Grout suddenly clapped his hands, breaking the picture that he had painted in the still, dusty atmosphere of the Learning Hall. "Now, we've had enough of such tales for today: it's time you learned something of how Elundium was ruled during the time of the Granite Kings and the careful Chancellors who governed us then."

Grout put his fingertips together and slowly began to recite their names. "Chancellor Overlord, a wise and just Master of Barter. Chancellor Silverpurse, the Keeper of King Holbian's cloak of jewels. Lord Grasp, who oversaw the running of the Learning halls . . . "

"What of Loremaster Pinchface—you never mention him in any of the histories?" one of the taller boys at the back of the hall called out.

For a moment Grout's face darkened with anger. Of all the Loremasters who had ever served the Granite Kings, Pinchface had been the worst. To think how easily he had betrayed his exhalted position, how eager he had been to throw the responsibilities the Chancellors had awarded him back in their faces. And now Grout was forced to exonerate his crimes, to turn his treacheries into deeds of honour, to teach these unruly urchins that Pinchface was a good and brave Keeper of the Lore—here in the very place where his treacheries had begun!

Grout swallowed and tried to clear his throat in readiness to give substance to the common folk stories and wildly inaccurate rumours about Loremaster Pinchface's part in defeating the darkness. But the name stuck sourly. The stories were so ridiculous; Chancellor Silverpurse would never have turned against King Thane, nor would he have beaten and terrorized Pinchface, keeping him as a servant in the Fortress of Underfall while he conspired with Krulshards' vile offspring, Kruel, to spread the darkness of the shadowrats across Elundium. The very idea was unthinkable. And he would never, not in a thousand daylights, have kept Queen Elionbel prisoner along with King Thane's grandfather, Thoronhand, the horseman, Breakmaster and Tiethorm the archer, threatening to dishonour them all the while. It was all a gross and vile lie invented to tarnish the good name of the Chancellors. And he didn't believe for one minute that Breakmaster, while hanging bound in chains, had challenged Silverpurse, crying out 'how many times will you betray your true king?', only for the Chancellor to stab him in the throat with his dagger. No, it was far more likely that Pinchface was the culprit, that it was Pinchface himself who had held them all prisoner for some black purpose that filled his distorted, treacherous mind. And it was probably the innocent Chancellor who had called out to him, trying to make him see the wickedness of his ways. He could almost hear his words.

"Twice King Holbian, the last Granite King, forgave your treacheries. How many more times will you betray your new king?"

And for his boldness in speaking out against him the wretched Loremaster had plunged his dagger into the poor Chancellor's back, cursing Silverpurse and crying out to him, 'I am no man's slave!' which clearly wasn't true, since he was the slave of his own evil ways.

The mere thought of Chancellor Silverpurse as a traitor made Grout shudder and go quite cold. It shook the fundamental roots of everything written in the Lore, everything that he believed in. He shook his head, making a wet, clicking sound through his pursed lips. How could such a terrible, distorted lie have become the truth? What had happened in that bleak fortress at World's End to turn everything upside-down? He had taught Silverpurse all the Lore by rote here in this very Learning Hall and knew him to be a young man of high integrity, full of ambition, who would, in time, have trodden proudly in his father's footsteps in Candlebane Hall, turning good barter into profit.

A soft ripple of laughter at Grout's mutterings and his obvious discomfort at telling them about

Loremaster Pinchface ran quickly through the class. Each childish face lost its smirk seconds before the Master's eyes alighted upon him.

"My father is a friend of Archer Tiethorm who was a prisoner at Underfall and he told me that Loremaster Pinchface sacrificed his life so that our beautiful Queen Elionbel could escape from the shadow warriors that were guarding the fortress," Eider, Captain Greygoose's son, said proudly.

"No, no I'm sure he didn't . . . " Grout exclaimed, his eyebrows raised in disbelief, his eyes narrowing as he recognized the young archer.

"How can you be so sure he didn't? You weren't there were you?" Eider challenged him accusingly.

Before Grout could regain his composure and punish the insolent boy for speaking out of turn Eider laughed in his face: "Tiethorm said that our Queen urged the Loremaster to escape with them but he refused, telling her that he would only slow them down; he said that he could serve them better by staying to block the narrow causeway and buy them what time he could with his life. And that's the truth as my father tells it!" Eider's face grew pale and serious and his voice fell to a whisper as he told them the heroic story of the last few moments of the Loremaster's life.

"No, my Queen . . . " he said as he reached for the secret bag of nightflower seeds that he had gathered in the shadow of the wayhouse, Hut of Thorns, having carried them beneath his cloak, hidden from Chancellor Silverpurse's prying eyes. He wove the age-stained string of the pouch between Queen Elionbel's fingers as he told her that they had a great power against the darkness. "Give them to King Thane," he had urged. "Tell him to plant them where the night dwells longest, and beg him to forgive me for all those harsh daylights in the Learning Hall. Tell him that the Loremaster is once more strong and ready to defend the sunlight." And then, without another word, he turned proudly, to block the causeway as the first shadow-warrior charged at him with his spear lowered. Our Queen looked back once, lifting her hand to wave farewell, and as she escaped she saw the Loremaster stagger and fall with at least a dozen spears piercing his body."

Eider paused, catching his breath and grinning at the other pupils. Grout had been long overdue for a taste of the truth and he wasn't going to hang around in the Learning Hall to pay for giving it to him. He could see the Loremaster's lips trembling with rage and those tell-tale white flecks of spittle were forming in the corners of his mouth. Eider vaulted over the back of his chair and slipped out between the door wardens, making good his escape before anybody had the wit to stop him.

Grout's face tightened into a mask of disgust as the boy disappeared through the doorway, his knuckles whitening and trembling on the handle of the chair. "I will make you pay for that!" he muttered under his breath. How he hated these commoners' children that he had been forced to admit into his Learning Hall. "Yes!" he called out to the silent, shocked, waiting pupils. "Yes, I am sure Eider's father has told him some such tale and who am I, a mere Loremaster, to argue with a Captain of Archers? But . . . " He lowered his voice and leant down to stare at the class, his eyes hard and glassy, "you mustn't believe everything you're told from these fireside stories, for they change constantly with the telling. They are very unreliable messengers of the truth. You just remember that, boys. Now go and line the city walls and watch for the Nighthorses and forget these stupid tales about dishonest Loremasters. Go! Go!"

The noonday bell tolled out the hour and, with a clap of his hands, he dismissed any further argument on the subject. He was content. He had planted seeds of doubt in the boys' minds, so perhaps they would not be as quick to believe the stories about Loremaster Pinchface's part in the battle to win the daylight. He watched the unwashed rabble laughing and shouting as they ran out into the narrow, winding streets of the Granite City towards the outer walls and he began to think of a way to teach the insolent archer's son a lesson. An idea began to form and he rubbed his long, thin fingers together and smiled to himself.

The hollow tolling of the noonday bell struck panic and indecision into Drib. Normally the Loremaster wouldn't have kept them this long and he didn't know if he dared spend a few moments watching for the Nighthorses, for it would mean he would be late and then Sweepscuttle, the man his mother had been forced to barter him to or starve to death, would punish him. Sweepscuttle hated unpunctuality, but not as much as he hated Drib's love of horses and his attending the Learning Hall. Learning, he had told him more than once, was for the highborn, lordly folk, and was nothing but stuff and nonsense in the head of a sweep's scramble. His lateness was sure to be rewarded with three lashes from the buckle end of Sweepscuttle's belt and the chances were that Drib would be fed only bread and water for at least two daylights—but it would be worth it for one glimpse of those beautiful horses.

Drib scrambled awkwardly to his feet, his mind made up. He dragged his crooked leg behind him as he tried to run for the doors, stumbling over stools and benches in his effort to get out. "Let me past, please make way, let me through!" But his voice was lost in the rising mêlée of noise as the lesson ended and he was pushed and elbowed backwards out of the way by larger, stronger boys in their rush to be first out into the sunlight and away from Grout's sneering, crackling voice.

Breathless, bruised and close to tears Drib finally emerged into the autumn sunshine only to hear the last echo of the bell fade away and be swallowed by the rumble of the wheels of the market carts and the musical chant of the criers' voices calling out their wares from somewhere below him in the lower circles of the city. He caught the sound of fast-moving, iron-shod hooves clattering over the cobbles beneath the Stumble Gate. The noise swelled to a thunder: it had to be the Nighthorses arriving in the city! They were riding in from the Greenway that lay beyond the gate. His hopes soared above the towering houses with their steep, weather-bleached roofs and thousands of smoking chimneys as the echo of their hoofbeats grew closer. They would pass the end of the Learning Hall at any moment and he had to see them. One glimpse would be enough to fill a thousand daydreams. "Let me through!" he cried fiercely, looking down helplessly at the crowded street at the bottom of the Learning Hall steps.

"I'll miss the Nighthorses altogether if they don't let me through!" he thought, limping down the broad stone steps. "Let me past, please make way, let me through please, please!" he called out as he tried to squeeze between two thick-set, dusty masons' sons who were blocking his path.

Both of them paused and glanced down at the sound of his voice. It took them a moment to see where it came from; Drib's head barely reached their waists. "Well, look who we've got here!" one of them laughed loudly, making everyone in the slow-moving crowd stop and look round, craning their necks in curiosity. "It's our little horseman, the sooty one who always wants to know about the horses."

He grasped Drib by the elbows and lifted him up, forcing his legs apart and making him sit astride his brother's shoulders.

"Hold on, midget, here comes the ride of your life!" the boy shouted, shrieking with laughter as he grabbed hold of Drib's ankles, cruelly twisting his crooked leg until the small boy screamed. "Don't you dare touch my head with your filthy hands or I'll chop them off!" The mason's son leapt and pranced, imitating a horse bucking its way through the crowd of boys.

Drib felt his deformed bones creak and arrows of burning pain shot through his body until he was dizzy and sick. His hands were clenched so tight that his fingernails broke in the palms of his hands. Suddenly, with a shout, the boy let go of him and Drib was suddenly flying through the air, turning over and over above the upturned, startled faces of the crowd. His voice wailed thinly as, with a crash, he hit the smooth, granite wall of the Learning Hall and fell to the ground, all sense and breath knocked out of him. He lay there upon the cobbles, dazed and aching, his crippled right leg throbbing with pain. Dimly he was aware of a foot roughly prodding him in the chest, making him gasp and choke for air, and he looked up. Someone stooped over him but his vision was blurred and he couldn't see who it was.

"Next time I won't be so gentle," the mason's son laughed, and then his dark, bulky shape moved away.

Gradually the laughing voices of the other boys grew fainter as they moved away, leaving Drib lying alone in the gutter. His head sank down and his eyes closed in despair as he wept, beyond caring who saw him or what they said.

After a while he started to regain his senses and opened his eyes. Every bone and muscle in his small body was battered and bruised, his shins and elbows were grazed and raw, and blood from a large gash on his forehead was trickling into his eyes. Gingerly he moved his hands and feet, flexing his fingers and slowly crawled on his knees. Mercifully nothing seemed to be broken. He lifted his head and listened, but the sound of the horses' hooves was fading as they trotted into the upper circle of the city. He had missed them, he had suffered the beating for nothing and now his master, Sweepscuttle, would have his hide for being so late.

He scrambled to his feet only to stagger and clutch the wall for support. The crippled leg burnt with pain from where the bully had twisted it and he couldn't put the slightest weight on it. "I have to get back, I have to get to Chimney Lane, for Sweepscuttle will kill me if I don't!" he sobbed, lying in the centre of the lane and searching around for something to use as a crutch. Further down the street he spotted a broken broom and sinking back to his knees he began to crawl painfully towards it, his head hanging down, wincing each time his bleeding knuckles touched the road.

Suddenly the sharp clatter of horses' hooves was ringing in his head, the sound filling the narrow lane. He looked up, his eyes round and shining, the pain almost forgotten. A small company of horsemen, five or six, was riding slowly towards him, but it was the leading horse, its rider cloaked in a gown of bright violet, that held him transfixed. It was a King's Horse, the most beautiful creature he had ever seen. He had caught glimpses of King Thane riding this beautiful creature in processions but he had never been lucky enough to be this close to him before. He could see every muscle flex and shimmer beneath the skin and the horse's mane shone like threads of silk as he arched his neck, stretching down to snort and blow. Esteron's approach brought Drib to his senses and he blushed hotly, not daring to utter a word. He half-rolled, half-dragged himself out of their way and moved himself back into the gutter, cowering down and trying to hide amongst the sparse litter that lay there, hoping that the royal party would ride by without noticing him.

In all his secret daydreams he imagined he was with the horses, either mounted in a company of Gallopers patrolling the Greenways around the city or carrying messages as an Errant rider for the King. He walked straight in these daydreams without the slightest limp and nobody jeered or taunted him for being a cripple. He wore a shirt of mail made of the finest weave beneath a long, flowing cloak. He had fine breeches and boots of the softest leather reaching almost to his knees, and there were silver spurs strapped around his ankles and a metal helm with the King's sun-emblem upon his head.

The remnants of his childish daydreams fled as the laughter and easy talk of the King's company drew closer. He could have died of shame as he huddled there in his filthy, ragged chimney clothes and he tried to pull his twisted, deformed leg out of sight beneath his body. Yet despite his wretchedness Drib's heart was pounding with excitement. So many times he had tried to slip into the breaking yards in the first circle of the city to watch the horsemen working their mounts and breaking in young ones ready to serve the King only to be sent on his way with a cuff on the ear and now, quite by accident he was going to be able to watch the best, the most beautiful horse in the whole world. Soon they would be close enough for him to reach out and touch them—only he wouldn't dare. He was far too afraid of invoking the King's wrath to do such a thing, he hardly dared to breathe in case the King or anybody riding with him looked down and noticed him.

Drib suddenly froze as he heard the King call out, stopping the company. The horses' hooves clattered over the cobbles, striking up dancing sparks as they halted abruptly. Drib was paralyzed with panic. Oh how he wished he had two good legs so that he could have jumped to his feet and run away to vanish into the first alleyway before any of the King's company had time to see his face. But he couldn't: one limping stride and he would be given away as 'Crooked Drib.' There was no way he could escape: he would have to stay there and take whatever punishment was measured out for displeasing the King—for littering the street or getting in the King's way; it seemed that everybody was able to find something to punish him for. But this time, whatever the punishment was, it would be worth it. These few precious moments close to the horses, so close that he could hear their soft, nickering breaths and the creak of their harness as they fidgeted, was worth anything. Gathering his courage, he raised his head a fraction and opened his eyes. Esteron stood so close now that he could see where the skin of the coronet met the hooves and the soft, silky hairs of his fetlocks.

Thane had been laughing easily to Errant, first Captain of the Nighthorses, thanking him for bringing Thunderstone's gift all the way from Underfall, and he was about to turn to Breakmaster who rode slightly behind them and ask him what he thought of the new batch of unbroken horses that Errant had gathered on the journey and brought into the Breaking Yards, when a movement in the lane ahead caught his eye. He saw a small child roll and drag himself into the gutter. There was something about the movement that made him raise his hand and he called the company to a halt, reining Esteron to a standstill as he leaned over out of the saddle, resting his hand upon his knee for balance. He looked down at the child. There was something about the way he cowered, as if in fright, that troubled Thane. It prompted him to call out and ask the child to stand up and give his name.

"I . . . I . . . I'm sorry, my Lord, I meant no harm . . . " Drib cried out in a small, terrified voice. He knew he had to obey his king and he tried to rise to his feet, only to fall back onto his knees, his eyes full of pain.

"The boy is injured, my Lord, look: there is blood on his face and his arms are cut and bleeding. And there's something wrong with his leg, look how it is twisted. I will tend to his wounds," Breakmaster murmured with concern, spurring his horse forward.

But Thane reached out a hand and stilled the old horseman. "No, dear friend," he smiled. "If I am to become a true shepherd to my people now that the battles for the daylight have been won then I should be the one to tend him."

"But sire—you are the King!" Breakmaster exclaimed in horror, trying to stop him.

Thane laughed easily, shaking his head and swinging his leg over the high cantle of Esteron's saddle as he jumped lightly to the ground. "You of all people, Breakmaster, should be the last to forget my humble beginnings, or have you forgotten already? Don't you remember that night all those suns ago when I fled from the Chancellors' wrath, and crawled out of the buriers' tunnel at your feet? What would have happened to me if you hadn't reached out a hand to help me then? What would have happened to me if you hadn't hidden me in the Breaking Yards?"

"That was different . . . " Breakmaster scowled, but he shrugged his shoulders, knowing from experience that once King Thane had set his mind on something there would be no changing it. He was just like his grandfather, Thoron.

Drib cowered in horror as the King bent down over him, fearing even greater punishment if but a speck of soot should touch the sovereign's clothes. Every moment his predicament seemed to become worse. "No . . . no, Lord, you mustn't touch me. Please, I beg you. I beg you come no closer, I didn't mean to get in your way. My master, Sweepscuttle, will flay me alive if you dirty your hand by touching these rags, I know he will."

The words came out in a small, frightened, tumbling rush that made Thane hesitate, the laughter in his eyes dissolving suddenly. Clearly the child was really afraid. "No one is going to harm you, child: you have the King's word on it. You have nothing to fear, now give me your name." He reached down and gently lifted Drib up with his strong hands.

"Drib, my name's Drib, my master's Sweepscuttle."

Thane could see at a glance that the boy had received a severe beating but it was the deformed right leg that made him frown with concern. "Did the shadow rats bite you, Drib? Did they bite you when Kruel's shadow-warriors overran the city?"

Drib shook his head miserably. He would dearly love to be able to say that before the rats had bitten him his leg had been as perfect as all the other boys'. He would love to be able to tell the King that his leg had been bitten out of shape while he had been defending the Stumble Gate. He would never forget those times when the shadows of darkness had rampaged through the city, crippling and deforming everyone they touched; even now, whenever he closed his eyes, he could still hear the sounds of the people screaming, crying out in terror as the black shadowrats swarmed through the streets. Yet for him it had only been a brief time when he had been no different to everyone else and it had quickly passed. When the King defeated Kruel at the last battle on the causeway of the Rising, plunging the broken sword of Durondel into Kruel's footsteps to give him a shadow, it had all passed. The sunlight had returned and everybody else's deformities had healed magically—except his. He still limped and dragged that cursed foot behind him, so victory had held little joy for Drib. Everybody he knew, even strangers in the street, seemed to suddenly curse and shun him, even going so far as to stone him, and he couldn't understand it, for he hadn't done anybody any harm.

He blinked back the tears that were brimming in his eyes. Much as he was tempted he couldn't lie to his King. "No, my lord," he whispered. "I was born with my leg deformed, that's why everybody calls me Crooked Drib. But I truly love the sunlight and I would have fought against the shadow rats if only they'd have let me. I tried . . . " his voice trailed off wretchedly and he dissolved into sobs as he hung his head in shame.

There was confusion in Thane's eyes as he looked down at the ragged youth. He couldn't understand why there was so much fear reflected in his eyes, unless he had done something really bad. And yet he seemed so small, so vulnerable: surely nobody would want to punish him simply because he had a deformity or persecute him because he was different. "What is it, Drib? What is it that you are so afraid of? You haven't offended the Loremaster or this Sweepscuttle in some terrible way have you?" Thane paused as another thought suddenly occurred to him. Gently he lifted the boy's chin with the first finger and thumb of his right hand until their eyes met and he smiled as he asked, "You're not afraid of me are you?"

"Lord, whatever I do seems to get me into trouble . . . " Drib whispered, but there was something in the King's smile—a kindness and a patience that he had never seen in anybody before, that made him blurt out all his troubles.

"Honestly, I didn't mean to get in your way, Lord, any more than I meant to touch the Loremaster's desk this morning—it was an accident. I deserved the beating he was going to give me for daydreaming, I know that, and if he hadn't kept us till the last peal of the noonday bell and I hadn't tried to see the Nighthorses go past I wouldn't have been bullied by the mason's son and my master, Sweepscuttle, wouldn't have to beat me for being late for work . . . " Drib suddenly blushed hotly as he caught the sound of his own tongue running away with itself.

"Nobody should be punished for waiting to see the Nighthorses, for they are a proud and beautiful sight." Errant frowned, spurring Dawnrise towards the boy so that he could caress his neck.

"Daydreaming!" Breakmaster laughed. "We've all done that in the Learning Hall, my lad, the trick is not to let the Loremaster catch you!"

"He was going to punish me for dreaming about riding the Nighthorses. He said I wasn't good for anything except scrambling up and down chimneys with this crooked leg and he's probably right."

The laughter died in Breakmaster's voice. "I think it's time I had a word with this Loremaster and reminded him that some of the best Gallopers in Elundium, and their horses for that matter, fought and died bravely despite being cruelly crippled by the bite of the shadow rats. I am surprised that he hasn't told you the story of their valiant defence of the Granite City—that's another matter I intend to take up with this Loremaster."

"No, wait, Breakmaster," Thane murmured, lifting his hand to halt the horseman as he dismounted stiffly. "There's more to this than tales out of school. Tell us, Drib, why would this Sweepscuttle beat you for being a few minutes late?"

"Lord, he is my master, he only took me in barter as an act of charity after my father was killed by the darkness as it swept through the city. He's always complaining that I'm slower than the buriers' cart with my crippled leg and now I've made matters worse by coming to the Learning Hall in the mornings. Sweepscuttle's completely against it, he says it won't do me any good burdening myself with a head full of useless knowledge about Battle Horses and their likes. But I don't care, the beatings are worth it. I want to hear everything there is to know about those beautiful horses—everything!"

"Do you now?" Thane smiled. "Then it's high time

you really started to learn." He lifted the boy up and
sat him sideways upon Esteron's saddle, carefully setting his crooked leg up against the pommel and making him hold the cantle with his left hand while he
placed the reins in his right hand.

Whispering softly to Esteron he let the boy go and
the warhorse proudly arched his neck, snorted and
trotted slowly up the narrow lane with Drib sitting
upright in the saddle, a look of sheer astonishment
and delight in his eyes. Thane laughed as he called
out to him, "You need have no fear, Drib: Esteron is
a Warhorse and he will not let you slip or fall."

"Lord, oh Lord, I do not know what to say. This is
the best—the most wonderful thing that has ever happened to me in my whole life. It's better than in my
dreams!" Drib cried out in joy, but he had to cling
onto the saddle really tightly and concentrate hard on
trying to keep his balance as the horse strode forwards. Riding didn't feel anything like he had imagined it would, but he barely had time to wonder how
the Gallopers he had seen cantering out of the
Stumble Gate had made it look so easy before Esteron
was checking his pace to turn at the top of the lane
and trot back to where the King's company waited.

"Speak to Esteron, lad, pat him on the neck. Use
your voice: you're so light in the saddle he hardly
knows you're there!" Breakmaster called out with
laughter in his voice. "It is the first, and the most
important, lesson that a horseman must learn. If you
can communicate with your mount it will form a special bond with you that neither of you will ever forget. Go on, ask him to canter—don't be afraid, he's a
Warhorse and he will understand every word you
say. He won't let you fall."

Drib leant forward awkwardly. It all sounded so
easy, but it wasn't, and he only managed the briefest
caress of the horse's powerful shoulder before he had
to grab at the saddle again. "Canter, Esteron, canter.

You're the most beautiful, the bravest, horse in all the world and I love you so much . . . " his voice ended in a cry of surprise as Esteron snorted, arching his neck before sitting back on his hocks and breaking into a slow, measured canter. Drib had never experienced anything like it. The sensation was wonderful—and frightening; they seemed to be going so fast. The wind ruffled his hair and the beat of the horse's hooves echoed around him in the narrow lane, louder than thunder in his ears. The windows and doorways seemed to rush past in a blur and he swore afterwards that he saw a shower of bright sparks dance briefly across the cobbles beneath them before Esteron stopped in front of the King.

"Of all the things I could ever wish for—I would never have dreamed of sitting on Esteron—to have cantered on him, to . . . to . . . " Drib was breathless and babbling with excitement as Breakmaster moved in close beside the horse and lifted him easily down from the saddle to stand, as best he could, in front of Thane.

"Well, Drib, do you fear me now? Do you still think I am going to punish you for no just purpose?" Thane asked solemnly.

"No, Lord, it's just been the most wonderful moment of my life and I will treasure it always, but . . . " He hesitated, shyly digging in the bottom of his torn breeches' pocket. His fingers emerged holding a tiny lump of grey, sooty sugar. "Please, my Lord, can I give this piece of sugar to Esteron? I know it's not much for letting me ride upon his back but it's all I have. I've been saving it for ages."

Breakmaster frowned as he saw the grubby offering and he reached for the small leather pouch that hung from the pommel of Beaconlight's saddle. It was full of fresh haycake made from new-mown grass and molasses, pressed into dark, sticky slabs; he always carried some to reward the horses during their training, but Thane caught the old horseman's eye and shook his head. He smiled down at Drib, "If it is all you have it will indeed be a great gift, but it is to Esteron you must offer it, not to me, because he is a Lord of Warhorses and he serves no man, not even the King."

Drib turned clumsily, dragging his crooked leg behind him, and looked up at Esteron, holding out his open hand with the tiny piece of sugar in the centre of his palm. Esteron lowered his head, brushing his velvet-soft muzzle on Drib's hand and took the tiny offering. For a moment he stood there, towering over the small boy as he crunched it between his teeth, and then he lifted his head and roared out the Warhorse challenge that set Drib's heartbeat pounding and brought a cry of joy to his lips. It echoed through the narrow streets, bringing the old warriors to their doorways, archers reaching for their bows and spearmen for their pikes, as it reverberated through each circle of the city. It cut right through Loremaster Grout's thoughts as he sat, hunched and brooding on his misfortunes in the empty Learning Hall and brought him running to the window.

"By all the strings on a Chancellor's purse!" he hissed in alarm, the colour draining from his narrow face as he craned his neck and looked down into the narrow lane, seeing to his horror that the King and all his company of horsemen had stopped only a dozen paces from the entrance to the hall. To make matters worse that wretched young sweep's boy, the one he had almost beaten only that morning, was standing in front of the King. A cold shiver of apprehension ran up Grout's spine as he saw the King bend forward and speak earnestly to the boy and Grout would have given almost anything at that moment to have been able to hear what was being said. He could only imagine what lies, what treacherous slander, the boy might be telling the King about his lessons in the Learning Hall.

"There is no dishonour in your deformity, Drib, I want you to remember that, no matter how much others may cruelly taunt you, it is their ignorance they most exhibit. To me, and to all those who ride beneath the emblem of the sun, you are as whole as any other boy. I know you love the sunlight, it shines and reflects in your eyes, and one day, who knows, with time and patience you may be able to ride as well as any of the horsemen you see with me today."

Thane paused, a smile softening his eyes as he remembered the rough and tumble of his days of learning to ride Esteron in the sand school. "It is not a crime to dream, Drib," he continued, seriously, "but I do not hold with you answering the Loremaster back. He is there to teach you about more than horses: remember that. Nor do I look kindly on your lateness, much as I deplore the idea of your master beating you."

"Lord, Loremaster Grout is a great teacher, and I truly deserved to be punished for answering him back, and yet he spared me; I will try never to do it again, I promise. And without the food my master, Sweepscuttle, gives to my family they would starve, and I will make every effort never to be late again."

"Then away with you, Drib, and King's speed. I think we have kept your master, Sweepscuttle, waiting long enough, don't you?" Thane felt there was something about the boy that mirrored his own humble beginnings. "Go on, be off with you!" he laughed as Drib tried to bow awkwardly. Esteron whinnied and struck up sparks from the cobbles with his iron-shod foreleg but he lowered his head and let the boy stroke his muzzle before the child limped off towards a narrow alleyway further along the lane.

"Come over to the Breaking Yards whenever you have a moment that doesn't belong to your master, lad, I'll make a rider out of you. But be warned, there will be lots of hard work cleaning with a bucket and broom, fetching and carrying with the other boys before your foot is set in the stirrup!" Breakmaster called after him.

"Dawnrise will welcome you to visit him, call any time you can, boy, in the short time before we return to Underfall," Errant smiled.

Drib paused in the entrance to the alley and looked back, hardly able to believe what he had just heard. Then a huge grin of delight spread across his face as he lifted his hand to wave at the old horseman. "I'll be there, Breakmaster sir, I promise I will, even if I have to run up and down chimneys night and day to earn the time," he answered before hurrying away as quickly as he could down the thousand steep, twisting steps that led into the lower, crowded circles of the city.

"Nobody's going to believe a word of what has just happened," he laughed to himself, his voice echoing between the smooth granite wall of the houses that hemmed him in, but he didn't care, for Breakmaster had promised to teach him to ride!

The laughter on the old horseman's face dissolved as the boy disappeared from sight. "Now I'll deal with this Loremaster!" he muttered grimly, but Thane put a restraining hand upon his arm.

"No, old friend, I think it would be better to let him fret and worry over what he imagines the boy might have said to me," Thane murmured. A movement in the high window of the Learning Hall had caught his eye as Drib hurried away and he'd had the briefest glimpse of the Loremaster's face, white and pinched, looking full of anxiety as it pressed against the glass while he tried to listen to their conversation. Thane had seen him duck back out of sight, thinking his spying had gone unnoticed.

Grout wrung his hands anxiously as he paced backwards and forwards causing the scrape of his quick footsteps to echo in the empty hall. He expected the doors to be thrown open at any moment and to see the King striding towards him ready to confront him with whatever lies that wretched boy had told him. He expected to have to give an explanation of his loyalties and have questions asked of him as to what he was teaching those miserable children. Why had he been so foolish as to voice his doubts over Pinchface's part in the victory over the darkness so openly, or to mutter so loudly against the Warhorses in front of those gutter-urchins? He regretted letting them goad him so easily. But children lied and exaggerated: everybody, even a king, would know that. Grout's eyes narrowed; perhaps he could convince the King that the boy was an habitual liar, that he always painted the truth a different colour, surely . . .

The noise of horseshoes clattering over the cobbles from the lane outside made him jump and catch his breath. He hurried back to the window just in time to see the King's company riding away. The noise of the hoofbeats didn't fade away altogether, but seemed to stay with him, to swirl around him, stirring up particles of dust in the shafts of sunlight that streamed in through the window. And there were other noises, whispered voices, the cry of eagles and the rustle of leaves, and then slowly, gradually, the faint, indistinct figure of a man wrapped in a rainbow cloak started to manifest itself, seeming to hover on the edge of his sight. It appeared to reach out a hand towards him and then vanish in the swirling dust. Grout let out a breath of light-headed relief, he had thought for a moment that it might be Nevian, but the magician was long gone from Elundium. He hated magic.

Grout gripped the stone casement for support and let his eyes travel past the weather-bleached rooftops of the city out across the fields and hedgerows that were cloaked with the colours of autumn. His gaze flowed past the rolling hills and on to the dark forest that lay far away along the hazy horizon. "Where are you, brave Chancellors?" he called out bleakly. "Why don't you return and seize the crown from this candleman who would be king? Come back and bring some order, some dignity and sense of purpose back into our lives."

# 2

## Old Hatreds Lie Hidden

CHANCELLOR IRONPURSE SHIVERED FROM THE BITING cold and hunched his wet shoulders beneath the coarse sacking cloth that circumstances now forced him to wear. He was thinking murderous thoughts as he glanced up through the dense tracery of branches, pulling his hood down hard over the top of his head in a futile attempt to keep out the driving rain.

"I will make you suffer, throne-stealer!" he spat bitterly as he searched for a moment through the winter-black branches and bare tree-trunks ahead, searching for the Greenway in the gloomy light. He didn't want to be blundering around in Meremire Forest after dark, not in this atrocious weather.

"You will keep nothing, Thanehand, nothing that you stole from the last Granite King. I don't care if you still have the help of all those cursed Warhorses and Battle Owls, or all the magic of Nevian's cloak: mark my words, candlecur, I will find a way to turn all your victories against you, I swear," he hissed, lashing out blindly with his vicious flail at the mule which was struggling to pull the heavily over-laden cart of firewood along the muddy track beside him.

"Pull, damn you, pull harder, you miserable, wretched creature or I'll whip your hide raw! Get moving, faster, or it will be pitch-dark before we get to the village of Deepling."

The imagined injustices and persecutions that he felt were heaped upon his shoulders boiled up into a

blind rage that made him strike out at the helpless
animal, the iron-tailed flail cutting red weals into its
neck and muzzle. The mule bellowed and shied away
from him, floundering in the traces as the mud made
it slither. The cart lurched sideways, its offside wheel
riding up over a tangle of tree roots, pushing the
other wheel into a deep, muddy rut. Logs and bundles of kindling began to roll and fall off the cart into
murky puddles.

"It's no good, father, you should know by now that
beating the beast in fury always makes it shy. We
always spill the logs we've just loaded," Snatchpurse,
his son, called out as he hurried past the cart, reaching out to take the flail from him. "Come on, let me
have it," he coaxed, his voice falling to less than a
whisper. "You know it will be quicker if I do it."

Ironpurse reluctantly loosed his grip but the look
in his eyes was glassy with hate and his mouth was a
sour, bitter line as he relinquished it. His son was so
clever at handling the mule, so clever at this and that,
but he hadn't thought to use the sense he was born
with and kill Thanehand in the Learning Hall when
he'd had the opportunity. Oh no, he'd been far too
full of himself, far too clever to slip a silent strangle
around the cursed candlecur's throat and pull it tight,
or use a quick dagger-thrust between the crowded
desks.

Snatch knew that look of accusation all too well
and his ears had grown weary from the recrimina-
tions. His father always seemed to forget he had only
been a boy, barely two or three suns older than
Thane: how was he, or any of the other Chancellors'
sons, supposed to have known that Thane would
catch King Holbian's eye and beguile him with
Nevian's magic? It wasn't his fault that the wretched
candlecur had given them the slip when they had
chased him out of the Learning Hall; and he was
growing tired of taking all this blame, tired of being

wet and cold as they trudged deep into the forest to cut firewood, and he was sick of listening to his father's incessant mutterings. It was time to start taking revenge, if only he could think of a way. He shrugged his shoulders as if to dismiss that look in his father's eyes but his narrow, weasel-like face hardened with contempt. He'd had to listen all too often to the Chancellors bemoaning their lot; they had become weak and indecisive, frightened of their own shadows.

Snatch couldn't resist returning his father's glassy glare or muttering loudly enough for him to hear, "Chancellors! Call yourselves proud men? You seem to have forgotten that you did nothing but run and hide when the Nightbeasts attacked the Granite City. No wonder Thanehand stole everything from you!"

Ironpurse's face darkened with rage at the intended insult. He clenched his fists and rose, ready to strike Snatch down, but then he hesitated and let his hands fall to his sides. He knew in his heart there was a whisper of truth in what his son had said.

Snatch grasped the mule's bridle with his free hand, but as he raised the whip he paused, catching a glimpse of his father, a pathetic, dripping figure between the trees, and a thin smile wrinkled his mean lips. "You need not fret forever, father," he whispered. "We'll seize it all back one daylight—it's just a matter of finding the right lever to tip Thanehand off the throne."

He laughed harshly, shaking the raindrops out of his eyes, before returning his attention to the mule, bringing the flail down brutally across its flanks, cursing and pulling at the bridle, changing the angle of each cutting lash and making the animal bellow with pain before it threw its weight against the collar. The cart rocked violently and lurched forward, scattering more of its load of logs across the track. The wheel rode free of the muddy rut and Snatch hauled

on the animal's bridle until it pulled it away, sweating and snorting with fright. Neither man spoke or
looked at one another again as they struggled to
reload the cart before continuing slowly along the
narrow track to where it joined the Great Greenway.

It was getting dark and the lights of Deepling were
still far-off pinpoints showing through the overhanging canopy of trees. Ironpurse hated being outside
once the nightshapes brought the silent darkness, for
everything changed and he saw a threat in every
shadow. He was forced to light a spark to give himself courage, shielding it from the deluge underneath
his cloak as he trudged along beside the mule. To
complete his misery the water from the sodden
ground was beginning to seep through the rush and
ferns he had packed inside his rotten boots and to
ooze icily up between his toes with each step. He
bowed his head, pulling his hood down over his forehead, and wrapped himself in secret mutterings to
shut out the world.

A movement deep amongst the trees, a silent, half-
seen shadow in the twilight, caught Snatch's eye and
made him drop back a pace behind the cart to scan
the forest. He had sensed before that they were being
watched; as if something had followed them as they
cut wood, travelling behind them on the Greenway.
Many times he had stopped suddenly, thrown down
his axe and spun round to search the undergrowth,
but whatever it was had always vanished, melting
away without the slightest flutter of a wing or tell-
tale crack of a twig underfoot. The sensation of being
watched with such stealth unnerved him, sending a
cold shiver of apprehension down his spine. What in
all Elundium could it be? The Warhorses, the border
runners and the battle owls had been set free from
their pledge to serve Thanehand. He had been at the
back of the crowd at the ceremony and had watched
the owls fly away; he had seen the great crescent of

horses disappear across the rolling countryside. It couldn't be any of them spying; nothing would come back to serve such a king once he'd set them free. He had seen the magic fade from Nevian's rainbow cloak and he wasn't afraid of magic any more: there *was* no magic in Elundium. The nightbeasts were all dead: he had come across hundreds of their rotting carcasses deep in the forest. They didn't frighten him at all.

He took a step towards the dark, impenetrable forest and hesitated to wonder if it could be a nightboar. Then he laughed and shook his head; they might be the most dangerous creatures still roaming the woods but they made enough noise crashing and barging through the undergrowth to wake the dead. It was certainly no nightboar stalking them. Curling his lips, he called out to the silent trees, "I'll catch you, whatever you are. Nothing's clever enough to escape me for very long!" Then he turned quickly on his heel and ran to catch up with the cart.

With each squelching footstep leaving a slight imprint between the deeper wheelmarks in the sodden turf, Snatch huddled beneath his cloak and didn't look back as he followed his father. He didn't see the white magpie detach itself from amongst the shadowy branches above his head and flutter down to land silently in his footprints. For an instant the bird searched the ground, scavenging, combing its sharp beak through the wet grass, before strutting and hopping after them, mimicking Snatch's hurried gait.

"Father—watch out—the mule's wandering off towards the trees again!" Snatch shouted, running past the cart to make a grab at the animal's bridle.

Startled by the sudden commotion, the bird rose from the ground and vanished in a blur of white feathers to be lost amongst the trees.

"Always so quick to criticise; always so alert," Ironpurse muttered under his breath, barely bothering to give his son a second hate-filled glance as he hurried through the rain.

The lights of Deepling grew steadily closer. Now he could make out the Wayhouse Inn and see it standing on the Greenway's edge, its steep, weathered roofs towering over the straggle of village houses around it. He could imagine the roaring fire in the hearth, the hot, smoky atmosphere and the frothy jugs of ale and he quickened his pace.

Masterwort, the landlord, stood just inside in the kitchen doorway, his arms folded across his enormous stomach and a scowl of dissatisfaction on his heavy jowls. He watched as Ironpurse and his son unloaded the cart into the log shed. "Mind you stack the wood properly or it will never dry," he demanded.

Ironpurse spat at the ground in the shadow of the cart, "I'll teach you to order us about. One daylight I'm going to make you stack logs until your fat arms fall off! I'll make you . . . "

"Father, we'll never get finished if you stand there mumbling to yourself all night!" Snatch whispered, giving him a sharp nudge with a piece of kindling as he gathered up another armful from the cart. Ironpurse sighed and glared at him but he helped to clear out the rest of the logs and had almost finished stacking the kindling when the landlord's voice brought him to a halt.

"If that's a full load then I'm a two-headed nightboar! I've been counting and it's a good five armloads short!" He accused, shielding the lantern from the rain with the tail of his apron he crossed the innyard and peered into the woodshed.

"Yes, I was right!" he exclaimed indignantly as he prodded at the neatly-stacked, dripping logs with the toe of his boot. "And what's that yellowing, rotten wood I can see at the bottom of the pile? I've told you before I'll only pay for the best cut oak, black-thorn, beech or elm; that other rubbish you are trying to pass off on me will crumble and burn away to nothing in no time. I won't have it, do you hear? There's plenty of other woodcutters who will jump at the chance to supply the Wayhouse. Everybody warned me not to do business with the Chancellors!"

His voice subsided as he turned on his heel and hurried back into the kitchen out of the rain, keeping a tight hold on the strings of the barter-purse that he had tied around his waist. Ironpurse fought to swallow the murderous rage boiling up inside him. Never trust a Chancellor indeed! They were the only ones with any honour in this miserable world. He had no intention of cheating the landlord—it was too wet to fully load the cart—anyway he always kept such a sharp eye on them. He sensed Snatch close beside him and a glance showed his son's hand closed around the hilt of his dagger.

"No, not now," he whispered. "There are too many eyes watching."

He forced a smile to his lips and nodded greeting to the servers and kitchen-boys who had stopped whatever they were doing to stare at them. "But Landlord Masterwort, I would never cheat you. If you had given me but a moment to get my breath after unloading all that wood I would have explained to you that the ground in the forest is too wet to fully load the cart, and you should know I would have willingly offered to take short barter."

Masterwort hesitated, puffing out his cheeks as the fingers of his right hand fidgeted with the drawstring of the barter-purse. "And the rotten logs you tried to hide at the bottom of the pile? How are you going to explain those away?"

"They are not rotten, landlord," Snatch quickly answered, using his sharp wits to invent a lie. "They are cut from a rare storax tree."

"Storax tree? I've never heard of such a thing," Masterwort murmured, his eyes narrowing in disbelief.

"Oh, yes, they're very rare, landlord, and there are only a handful of them still standing in the depths of the forest. Their leaves are so fragile they shimmer like beaten silver and the wind sounds like sweet music when it stirs them. The wood feels soft, almost spongy, when it's wet but it hardens when it dries and burns with a white-hot flame. Wait, I plucked a leaf to take home." Snatch paused, reaching beneath his cloak and feeling in the bottom of the pocket of his leather jerkin amongst the broken twigs and rinds of mouldy bread. "Yes, I've found it, here it is." He smiled as his fingers found a bunch of small, shrivelled leaves. Deftly, he chose one, rubbing at its brittle surface with his fingers as he withdrew it, shredding away everything but its fragile network of veins, making sure it touched the shiny husk of a rotten forest-apple he had forgotten to throw away. The remains of the leaf glistened with the fermented slime of the forest-apple as he held it up. Each tiny vein caught and reflected the flickering candlelight that illuminated the vast kitchen.

"Storax tree—I've never seen anything like it before, it's beautiful, really beautiful," Masterwort gasped, reaching out to touch the leaf but Snatch was quick to crush it between his fingers and drop it back into his pocket, telling him how they shrivelled into nothing in no time at all if they were exposed to too much light.

"And it burns well you say?" Masterwort asked, loosening the strings of his barter-purse and tipping its contents out onto the stone-scrubbed central table. He began to count out the barter carefully, marking off the twists of tallow, new sparks, silver stones, threads of copper and all other devices to pay for the firewood.

"Brighter than the sun in the sky, landlord!" Snatch assured him in a soft, convincing voice.

Ironpurse rubbed his hands together as he watched the barter mount. The landlord was so taken with the story of the storax tree that he was being over-generous but he hooded his eyes to disguise the cunning gleam in them as he glanced across at Snatch, well-satisfied, for once, that his son had used his quick wits. He caught a rare glimpse of the qualities that would one daylight make him a good Chancellor.

"Will you drink from the finger-bowl, as is the King's custom, and seal the barter?" Masterwort asked, pulling a fine, silver chain attached to his belt and fishing a small, crystal bowl from his pocket.

Ironpurse frowned and patted at the pockets of his soaking jerkin beneath his cloak in mock-dismay, indicating that he must have left his cup at home. He would never adhere to the King's custom if he could avoid it.

"Never mind, let us seal the barter with a jug of ale by the fire in the long hall instead. Boy, be quick, bread and ale for the woodcutters!" The landlord cuffed one of the ale-boys across the top of his head and sent him scuttling with two tankards to the huge barrels set in the stone wall at the far side of the kitchen.

"That was very clever, my boy, but what happens when he comes to burn that rotten wood?" Ironpurse whispered, leaning across the table so that none of the other people in the inn heard him.

Snatch smiled, his lips curling back across his teeth. "He's so stupid he only remembers his own name because people are snarling it at him all day long. Don't worry, he'll have forgotten all about it long before he gets to the bottom of the pile. And if it looks as though he's going to remember we'll get rid of the rotten wood. Stop worrying."

"That's easy for you to say but it's me he'll berate if he finds out," Ironpurse grumbled, but he couldn't resist a ghost of a smile from crossing his pinched

and sour face. He had to begrudgingly admire his
son's guile and allow himself the luxury of a gloat
over cheating the innkeeper into giving them more
than the full barter with that ridiculous story about
the storax tree.

But the moment was quick to pass and he shivered
with dissatisfaction as he glared at the crowds that
filled the great, smoky hall of the wayhouse. It would
take a lot more than cheating that fat fool
Masterwort to restore his dignity. He began to mutter
under his breath, picking at the raw wound of his disgrace, his voice rising as he became more agitated.

"We should be treated with honour—not reduced
to cutting wood in the forest and sitting in this common inn, soaked through to the skin. We shouldn't
be forced to eat stale, mouldy bread and drink sour
ale with vulgar folk. We were not born to feed from
the trough: we should have honour and respect. We
are Chancellors!"

"Father, be quiet! Your cursing is drawing attention to us!" Snatch hissed, gripping at his arm and
shaking him fiercely. People in the crowds closest to
where they sat were turning their heads in curiosity,
and the noisy hum of conversation and laughter was
beginning to crumble into silence.

"It is nothing that concerns you, my father is wet
through and cold to the bone. Leave him be, his mutterings are no concern of yours." Snatch's voice cut
through the spreading silence and the hard, cold look
in his eyes made the onlookers shuffle uncomfortably
and turn away. The ordinary village people still held
an inbred fear of the Chancellors despite the knowledge that all their powers had been stripped away.

"Honour!" Snatch ground the word between his
teeth as he held his father's face close to his own and
spat the word at him. "All you ever talk of is the
'honour and respect' that the Chancellors squandered
so freely squabbling amongst themselves. Well it is

gone, gone forever, so why don't you face up to it and stop this infernal muttering?"

Ironpurse shrugged his shoulders bleakly as the truth in his son's words struck home. He turned his head and stared into the crackling flames of the fire, remembering the echoes of those daylights of power in Candlebane Hall when the reins of the whole kingdom rested in the Chancellors' hands.

Snatch touched his arm lightly and whispered, "I will give you back honour. I will make the people respect you, father, but you have got to help me. You've got to stop making such a spectacle of yourself and reminding everyone of what you have lost. Nobody will give honour to a weak man."

Ironpurse blinked and looked hard at his son. Excitement reflected in his watery eyes. "How? How would you do such a thing?"

Snatch's eyes narrowed cunningly as he leaned across the table. "I'm going to turn the people's fears against them, and use them for our profit. All I need is some way to begin."

Ironpurse frowned as disappointment dimmed the spark of excitement in his eyes. He wouldn't show any excitement if this were the case.

"We'll make them pay dearly. There's no honour without profit!"

"Yes, of course you will, and I'll become King of Elundium. Now drink your ale and we'll get out of this miserable wayhouse," Ironpurse muttered, raising his jug to his lips.

"No, wait a moment, listen to the people talking around us and you'll see what I mean," Snatch urged, restraining him by the arm. "Go on, listen, these people aren't rejoicing in the new Elundium that Thanehand has given them. They might sing his praises on the surface but listen more carefully to what they are really saying. They constantly resurrect old fears. They're more afraid of the dark than you are if the truth was known, and they are afraid that the Nightbeasts will come back to terrorise their lives again. Afraid that when the sun comes up tomorrow they won't have a shadow—or worse, the magic of Nevian will suddenly reappear and turn them into something unpleasant. And there's another thing I've been noticing lately: people may shun us but they steer well clear of those warriors that Nevian once turned into trees. I think they're afraid that something bad will rub off them if they get too close!" Snatch paused and hunted the crowded hall before pointing away to his left.

"Look! If you don't believe me look over there, those two warriors Ustant and Berioss have a whole table and more to themselves. They never need worry about anybody stealing their ale. You see, father, old fears die hard and those fears are what we've got to find a way of using, I know that's what we have to do!"

Ironpurse sat back and turned his head slightly. The fine hairs in his ear rustled as he eavesdropped on the crowd of travelling merchants sitting at the next table.

"I tell you, I preferred it when the Marchers and Gallopers patrolled the Greenways and these way-houses were safe-houses, not inns where the riff-raff could congregate. You never know who is listening to your business these days. I know we had to kick our heels and wait until an escort could be found before we could travel to the next village, but it felt safe somehow," one of the merchants grumbled before burying his mouth in his ale.

"I had a real fright only yesterlight," cried another merchant waving the roast leg of a forest fowl towards the others sitting at the table and sending hot globules of fat scattering around. "Somehow I wandered off the Greenway and lost my way—I don't know how it happened—anyway the next thing I know I get this feeling that something's following me. I began shouting and hollering for help and sent my pony cantering as fast as it could when I suddenly came upon a strange clearing in the trees. It was full of broken, moss-covered rocks and bent, withered blackthorns but there was something else in there, something that leapt up on the far side of the clearing the moment I appeared . . . "

The merchant paused and opened his mouth to take another bite of the forest fowl but someone grabbed his wrist to stop him. "Get on with it, we're waiting. What was it?"

"I'm not sure," he continued, slowly wiping at the dribbles of fat on his chin. "I'd swear it wasn't human but I didn't get a chance to see more than a glimpse because it vanished quicker than I could blink—you know the way a shadow does when the sun moves behind a cloud—but it left a vile stench behind it in the clearing. And there were flies, clouds of them, that rose up as I entered. I didn't want to see if anything else was about to move in the rocks and bushes—I turned my pony and fled."

"It must have been a Nightbeasts' camp. You were lucky it was daylight and they didn't attack you," somebody murmured in the shocked silence that followed.

"We had better start locking our doors at night," another voice warned.

"I told you King Thane was over-hasty in disbanding the Gallopers and Marchers!" Masterwort added from where he had been carving the fowl at the head of the table.

Snatch caught his father's eye and covered his mouth to disguise his grin. They knew that clearing very well. Despite his father's protests he had cut away a piece of armour from one of the five rotting Nightbeast carcasses that lay among the rocks and had taken it home as a trophy. He knew they were never going to get up and threaten anybody again.

"There, you see how easily their imaginations run away with them!" he whispered behind his hand. "It's just a matter of finding a way to use it to our advantage."

"Look, there's old Whitlowgrass, the Marcher captain, putting his coat on near the door. He used to keep the wayhouse out at Larach Way. Let's catch him before he leaves: he'll know what we should do about the Nightbeast camp." Masterwort ignored the merchants' reluctance to share what he had seen with the old warrior. "Captain Whitlowgrass—over here—a moment of your valuable time if you please."

Masterwort caught his attention and beckoned him over, dispatching the serving-boy who was waiting on the merchants' table and sending him to fetch a fresh jug of ale for the captain. Captain Whitlowgrass listened seriously, his bushy eyebrows raised at the tale that the merchant told him. Snatch felt his ears buzz with interest and he held his breath, leaning as close as he dared, to eavesdrop as the merchant finished his story and the landlord asked the Marcher, "Well, what do you think of that, Captain? Should we send a messenger to the King to warn him?"

Master Whitlowgrass could hardly believe what he had heard. He looked slowly at each of the journeymen and merchants who were sitting around the table and then shook his head, lifting the jug to his lips to drain it down in two enormous swallows.

"Do?" he shouted as the implications of what the merchant had said sank in, and he slapped the jug down so hard upon the table-top that it made the table jump and the jug shatter into a dozen pieces. Everyone in the inn turned sharply towards him. "Do? There is nothing you need do save apologise for daring to doubt your King. The Nightbeasts are all dead, merchant, I should know—I saw them dying by their thousands in the great battle on the Causeway

Fields. I should not think our King would be too pleased to hear you doubt his victory."

"But what if some of them escaped, or fled unseen from the battle?" the merchant tried to argue, but Captain Whitlowgrass would have none of it. His cheeks were mottled with anger as he leaned across the table and gripped the merchant's velvet coat with both hands.

"Would you dare to challenge the King's word, merchant? Are you telling me that King Thane did not rid us of the Darkness—that he did not kill Krulshards and bring his head down onto the Causeway Fields for us all to see? Or that he did not sew a shadow into Kruel's feet at the battle of the Rising and reduce him to innocence, to be an infant again, as pure as the driven snow he fell upon?"

"No, no, of course not, I would never suggest such a thing," the merchant stuttered, his teeth chattering in terror of the old warrior, who released him with a shake. He almost fell of the bench he had been sitting on. "I must have been mistaken, it must have been a shadow, a trick of the light caught between the trees. It could have been nothing more than that, certainly nothing to worry the King about."

"That's better." Marcher Whitlowgrass nodded as he straightened up and prepared to leave. "Remember, merchant, there's nothing out there on the Greenways to be frightened of. You can travel freely now without an escort. Why, it's so safe I don't even carry my sword."

Captain Whitlowgrass motioned Masterwort to accompany him to the door and as Snatch listened to the last piece of conversation it brought a thin smile to his lips. "You must nip these fears in the bud, landlord, and put a bridle on those merchants' tongues. There's no knowing what trouble they will stir up if they let their imaginations run away with them—Nightbeasts roaming in the forest again, whatever next!"

"It's easy for him to talk," the merchant grumbled as the Marcher left the inn. He straightened his coat and tried to smooth his ruffled dignity. "Nobody's going to try to rob him on the Greenway are they? Oh no, it's the likes of us those thugs will pick on once they get bold enough. Mark my words, we've not seen the last of those Nightbeasts, I know what I saw!"

The others around the table shifted uncomfortably and nodded silently to one another. They had all overheard the Marcher's words and nobody mentioned the Nightbeasts again as Masterwort bustled back to their table. He was out of breath and had barely picked up the carving knife to lay it upon the forest fowl when the inn door swung open. A gust of wind sent the candle-flames dancing on their wicks and smoke billowed from the hearth, clouding the low-beamed room as a chilling squall blew in across the threshold. A small company of tunnellers hurried in out of the rain, shaking the weather out of their cloaks and calling for the landlord.

The thin smile on Snatch's lips soured instantly. The noisy hum of conversation died away as grim faces turned towards the newcomers. Begrudgingly the villagers, travellers and merchants moved aside to give them space.

"Now, what in the King's name do they want at this hour?" Masterwort grumbled, throwing down the carving knife, "If it's not one thing it's another tonight. I'll be run off my feet into an early grave at this rate."

He shuffled around the table and threaded his way through the crowds, forcing a smile onto his fat face and rubbing his hands together in an effort to put a little warmth into his greeting.

"There's another ragtail rabble that the folks hate, and I would be glad to see the backs of them," Snatch muttered in disgust. "It's not too difficult to see why people don't like them, is it? Look at them: they're barely taller than goblins and they're so ugly with their bulging eyes and those queer shell-shaped ears. I can't for the life of me understand why that throne-stealer gave them the freedom to roam Elundium. They come and go as they please with their high and mighty ways."

"He did it to spite us, that's why," Ironpurse hissed, his fingers clenched tightly around his jug, the dregs trembling in the bottom of the glass.

Oaktangle, the leader of the small group of newcomers, hesitated and brought them to an uncertain halt a dozen paces inside the door of the inn. It wasn't difficult to sense the hostile atmosphere, for sudden silence had muffled the noisy hum of conversation the moment they had entered and they received dark, unwelcoming glances from every side. If it hadn't been for the appalling weather he would have had them leave immediately. He couldn't understand what troubled these people of Elundium, or why, whenever they stopped their labours to seek shelter in any of the small villages scattered along the Greenways, they always seemed to meet this same hostility. It was almost as if the people feared them and begrudged the work they did gardening and mowing the Greenways, pruning and trimming and keeping everything beautiful in the sunlight. It wasn't as if they were a burden or demanded anything in return. King Thane paid them royally for keeping the Greenways open, and would greet any of their wandering groups with open arms on their rare visits to the Granite City. He always publicly reaffirmed his pledge that all Lord Willow's people had the freedom to wander the length and breadth of Elundium in payment for the loyal service they had performed in helping to destroy Krulshard's darkness and to help to make amends for everything that was taken from them during the rule of the Granite Kings.

Oaktangle had sought an audience with Lord Willow on his last visit home to the Rising and had asked him if *he* could explain the hostility they experienced everywhere. Lord Willow had thought long and hard on the question before beckoning Oaktangle to follow him out of the long hall. He had spread his arms to encompass the vast expanse of Elundium spreading away beneath the Rising to the hazy horizon-line on the edge of vision and told him that sometimes people are so set in their ways that they become afraid of change. He said that there were many changes taking place in Elundium and he urged Oaktangle to remember that the age of the Granite Kings had gone forever and because of this the ordinary folk of Elundium had become suspicious of everything they saw as different.

Willow had laughed as he gripped Oaktangle's arm in parting, "Look no further than the glass, my handsome young lad, and have patience. Time will eventually rub away all things that separate us."

"Really, Oaktangle, you might have sent word. Calling this late has put me in quite a muddle. Can't you see how crowded this inn is tonight?" Masterwort muttered through his false, exasperated smile, wringing his hands together as he hurried up to them. "Now, quickly, how many of you are there? How many do I have to feed and find beds for? I must ask now as I'm run off my feet."

"There are seven of us but, if it's too much trouble, we will willingly leave and pitch our camp in the forest. It was only the bad weather that drove us to seek shelter," Oaktangle replied, pulling up the collar of his cloak and turning towards the door.

"No, no, we can't have that can we?" Masterwort

cried, bustling around them to stop them leaving the inn. "No, that wouldn't do at all would it? Only the best will do for the King's friends in the Wayhouse of Deepling. We couldn't have you complain of rough treatment here could we?" Masterwort was well aware of where his duty lay. Like it or not, along with every wayhouse keeper in Elundium, he had received explicit instructions sent under the King's seal of a battle owl holding the sword of the realm after the great battle at the Rising. Lord Willow and all his people had the freedom of Elundium and the right to wander as they pleased: and the King had pledged them food and shelter whenever and wherever they asked for it. The last thing Masterwort wanted to do was to upset the King, what with all these rumours of Nightbeasts and the like wandering in the forest.

"Servers—bring jugs of mulled ale to thaw our guests out and the best roast forest fowl, the one turning over the fire. Prepare beds of the warmest down above the trophy room. See to it, see to it! Now, let us find you a nice warm table near the fire, I'm sure nobody will mind moving . . . "

Masterwort hummed tunelessly to himself as he scanned the crowded room. It was going to upset somebody wherever he put them. "Aaah, there's just the place for you," he beamed suddenly, spotting Ustant and Berioss sitting hunched and gloomy on their own at a table near the fire. They were another two trouble-makers he would willingly throw out of the inn, but like all the villagers, he feared to cross them just in case some of that bad magic that had once turned them into trees rubbed off. "I'm sure these two old warriors won't mind sharing their table. Ustant, Berioss, these friends of the King would like to sit with you. Make room and I'll bring them over." Masterwort rubbed his hands energetically; the problem was solved to his satisfaction and he had a genuine smile on his face as he threaded his way through the crush.

Every footstep that Oaktangle took following on the landlord's heels caused mutterings. His sharp ears caught whispered curses against his people, which sent a warning chill up his spine but it was too late to turn back now though the comments burned into him.

"Those tunnellers are ugly—uglier than goblins."

"Somebody should teach those wandering bands of gypsies not to come begging amongst honest folk."

"If I had my way I'd send them all packing—send them back to where they came from."

"King's folk indeed—coming in here with their high and mighty ways!"

"I call it living off the backs of decent folk."

A huge ironmaster gave one of the smallest tunnellers a hard dig between her shoulder-blades, making her stumble and almost fall, much to the amusement of the watching crowd. Oaktangle half-turned, his anger rising, but Lord Willow's words echoed in his head and cautioned him to be patient. He gritted his teeth, keeping his eyes fixed on the broad apron-ties knotted across Masterwort's back.

A flicker of interest and welcome crossed Berioss's eyes as the tunnellers settled themselves around the table. He had no axe to grind against them but he knew their presence in the inn would aggravate the ordinary folk. Ustant held Oaktangle's gaze and lifted his cracked, earthenware drinking vessel to his lips. "To the King and all those who fought with him against the darkness," he murmured softly so that only the tunnellers could hear his words.

"To true friends who wait beneath the Greenways' edge, to the battle owls and border runners and the proud Warhorses wherever they roam," Oaktangle answered in a whispered breath, his lips scarcely moving. At least at this table he felt as if they were amongst friends.

Gradually the crowds seemed to lose interest in the

tunnellers and the conversation around them returned to normal. Masterwort carved the forest fowl and oversaw the serving before hurrying away through the warm, smoky atmosphere of the inn to attend to a boisterous group of weavers who were visiting the village bartering their wares.

"It's a foul night out there, a bad time for honest folk to be abroad," Ustant muttered over the top of his tankard at the tunnellers as they hungrily attacked the steaming bowls of food that were set down on the table before them. "I've never know it rain like this," he continued, nodding his head at the rivulets of water trickling down their cloaks and dripping off the hems to form widening puddles on the stone-flagged floor beneath the benches they were sitting on.

"We do not shun the weather," Oaktangle laughed softly. "We are glad of Landlord Masterwort's kindness and hospitality: there is no doubt about that, but we would never wish to escape the beauty that is to be experienced in all the elements. But how could you understand it? It has never been denied to you has it?"

"I can't see any beauty myself. How anybody who wears cloaks as finely woven as yours, even though their boots are greased with swans' fat, could enjoy standing out in the rain on a night like this beats me. I wish I could see the beauty, I really do!" Berioss frowned and fell silent, slowly scratching his head. His memories of being transformed into a gnarled old oak tree by Nevian's magic were still so fresh. It wasn't that he hadn't deserved it, along with all the other warriors who had refused to pledge their loyalty to Thane, when Nevian had made him King on the death of old King Holbian, the last of the Granite Kings. He had never seen the Master of Magic so angry, and when they refused to pledge he had thrown the rainbow cloak from his back and cursed them, binding them with a spell so powerful that when they set foot on a Greenway they were turned to trees. Nobody believed it would really work, of course, and had turned their backs on King Thane, leaving standing there on the Causeway Fields; but they had been fools to think they could cross Nevian. The spell had overtaken them all in time and they had been condemned to stand, parched and thirsty in the hot sun or shivering in the bitter winter blizzards on the Greenways edge, waiting for King Thane to call for them and break the spell.

Berioss looked down at his crooked knuckles that had never quite straightened when the spell was eventually broken and murmured, "No, I would much rather be here in the warm."

"But there is so much you miss," cried Sloeberry, one of the younger tunnellers at the far end of the table. "The joy of combing your fingers through the wind, the feel of the hot sun scorching your back as you mow the grass, the thrill of watching a storm boil up upon the horizon as the clouds pile one atop the other."

"Have you ever tasted rain, or let a snowflake dissolve upon your tongue?" asked Master Mistletoe who sat beside her waving a gnawed leg-bone from the forest fowl.

Sloeberry spoke breathlessly, "And sometimes, if we're lucky, we see the battle owls hunt and the wild Warhorses moving silently through the forest as the early-morning mist melts. It is such a magical time before the first blackbird sings and the dew still glistens like a vast, shimmering carpet of diamonds on the Greenway—and the new sun is born wreathed in fire—and . . ."

Ustant glanced anxiously along the table past her youthful outburst of enthusiasm to where Snatch and his father sat glaring sullenly at their places. He reached out his hand and touched Oaktangle lightly on the arm, warning him to make his people guard their tongues. "That Chancellor's boy, Snatchpurse, the weaselly one sitting at the next table, is in an evil humour tonight. I was watching him earlier and I should be careful if I were you, he's spoiling for trouble."

But it was already too late, for Snatch was rising purposefully to his feet and the crowd fell silent as they turned to watch.

Snatch had listened with sharp ears to the cursing and muttering against the tunnellers as they came in. But the tunnellers didn't seem to care who they upset and their strange voices, the way they looked and their fine clothes, along with the fact that the landlord had to feed them so freely while honest folk had to pay, began to rub at Snatch's temper. If another one of them laughed or mentioned those cursed horses and owls he swore he would snap its ugly neck. He felt his fingers twitch convulsively and his thigh muscles were tense as he rose to his feet. He couldn't help himself: the buried anger that he felt for everything the Chancellors had lost consumed him and he hated injustice. His self-control snapped and propelled him across the room.

Sloeberry's voice was rising in soft, silver tones, echoing first the songthrush and then the skylarks as they lift effortlessly above the rolling grasslands. She threw out her arms, unaware that everyone was watching her and not noticing the silence that was spreading throughout the inn as Snatch approached her chair; she was so intent on trying to express the sheer beauty and the vastness of the great wilderness they travelled through. Her voice melted into laughter and at moments shrunk into whispers as she imitated the secret sounds of the woods, painting pictures in the air with her fingertips of the Warhorses as they moved between the trees with sunlight dappling their coats in the cool, resin-scented shadows. She clicked her tongue to the rhythm that their muffled hoofbeats made on the thick carpet of leaves and pine needles that covered the forest floor.

"They move with such grace, such elastic ease . . . " She stopped as her hand struck Snatch's arm and warm droplets of mulled ale from the earthenware cup she was holding splashed across her hand.

"Shut up, you vile hobgoblin! Your whining voice is souring the ale we drink!" Snatch's voice snarled immediately behind her.

Sloeberry gave a small cry and glanced up at him, her face colouring scarlet. Suddenly she was aware of the unnatural silence that had spread through the room and saw the mass of hostile, angry faces staring at her. As Snatch cursed her a whispered ripple of hatred seemed to echo through the crowd, making him grow bolder.

"Isn't it enough that you steal our food, you ugly dwarf!" His voice grew wilder as he raised his clenched fist above her head.

"I'm . . . I'm so sorry . . . " she tried to cry out, her eyes full of panic as Snatch loomed threateningly over her. She flinched, instinctively raising her arm to protect herself but his fist hammered brutally down onto the top of her head.

There was a sudden explosion of light and pain inside her skull as the blow struck. The sound of Snatch's voice seemed to roar in her ears abruptly cutting short as she felt her jaw snap shut with a sharp stab of pain and the hot, salty taste of blood flooded her mouth as her teeth cut through the tip of her tongue. She felt herself falling, surrounded by a roaring sea of noise. Her head hit the hard edge of the table and a well of darkness folded over her. The earthenware cup flew from her hand, scattering its dregs of ale across the table before smashing as it hit the wall in the back of the chimney. She slid off the bench, collapsing into a heap on the cold stone floor.

Oaktangle leapt to his feet as Snatch struck her but he was too startled by the sudden, unprovoked attack to do any more than rush to where Sloeberry lay. Snatch heard a rising murmur of approval from the crowd behind him and it fuelled his anger, making him step in front of Oaktangle to prevent him from reaching the young girl he had just struck down. Snatch's face was a tight mask of hatred, his eyes glittering slits, their pupils shrunk to pinpoints of madness in the firelight as he roughly grabbed at the tunneller's jerkin.

"How dare you come amongst us like wandering gypsies, living off the backs of honest folk?" he snarled, lifting Oaktangle off his feet.

"Tear his ugly little head off his shoulders!"

"No, slit his throat and let him bleed to death! It's time these dwarfs were taught a lesson!"

Voices from all over the inn goaded Snatch on, prompting him to draw his dagger.

"Snatch, stop it! Stop this madness at once and come back here: you'll get us into no end of trouble!" Ironpurse cried in alarm, spilling his ale as he rose to try to get his son's attention before he did something really stupid. He caught sight of Masterwort, his face as black as thunder, forcing his way through the crush of onlookers who were closing in around the table where the tunnellers were sitting, but the landlord's look of anger turned to one of fear as strong hands reached out to restrain him.

"Shut up, you old fool, and watch the fun. We've been waiting a long time to see this!" a voice hissed in Ironpurse's ear as he was forced back into his seat.

Ustant and Berioss tried to rise in Oaktangle's defence only to find a dozen strong arms holding them down. "You'll keep out of this if you know what's good for you," a burly ironmaster warned them, his large, calloused fingers gripping their shoulders painfully.

Snatch threw back his head and sneered cruelly at Oaktangle, "See! See how these people welcome you with open arms!"

"We mean no harm. We come in peace—the King himself allows us the freedom . . . " Oaktangle gasped as he struggled to break free but Snatch tightened his grip, his face contorting with rage and hatred.

"Oh, the King doesn't care how much you steal from us, but then it isn't his food you're cramming into your ugly little faces is it!" he spat, raising his dagger and pressing the point of the blade into the soft flesh, a finger's span behind the angle of Oaktangle's jaw. The crowd fell utterly silent. A bead of blood swelled up out of the wound in his neck and trickled slowly down the blade.

"Leave him alone—he hasn't done anything to you!" one of the tunnellers cried angrily, leaping to his feet only to be knocked down instantly as the crowd surged forward and a shout went up. Blows began to rain down on the rest of the tunnellers who cowered down, trying to protect themselves from the vicious onslaught.

Oaktangle desperately tried to break free, kicking at Snatch's shins, trying to prise apart the fingers of the hand that was gripping the front of his jerkin, but the Chancellor's son was far too strong for him and he jeered and laughed at the tunneller's puny efforts. He repeatedly lifted Oaktangle up above his head, making him dance as he trod the empty air to the delight of his audience. But he didn't notice that each time he threw him up so roughly the tunneller's jerkin rode up higher and higher, gradually bringing his hand closer and closer to Oaktangle's mouth. Dizzy and gasping for breath the tunneller waited his chance. Snatch's clenched fist struck the side of his jaw propelling him up towards the low-beamed ceiling. Oaktangle opened his mouth as the hard knuckles grazed across his nose and the heel of Snatch's hand brushed his lips, and snapped his jaw shut, biting as hard as he could on Snatch's hand.

Snatch screamed and let go as a red-hot stab of

pain shot up his arm. He made a furious lunge at the
tunneller but his bleeding hand swept through empty
air. Oaktangle stumbled as he hit the ground but he
scrambled quickly to his feet; he knew his life and
the lives of the other tunnellers depended on how
fast he reacted. He dived between Snatch's legs,
hooking his right foot around his ankle, and gave him
a firm push from behind that sent him sprawling
onto his knees. Oaktangle grabbed the dagger from
his belt and threw it into the fire where it landed
amongst the crackling flames in a shower of sparks.

"Get out of here, all of you—run for your lives!" he
shouted at the cowering tunnellers as he caught
Sloeberry's wrist, hauling her unconscious body over
his shoulder. "Run, Mistletoe, run, run!" he urged,
almost colliding into the Chancellor's boy who was
only just recovering from the blow he had taken.

"Keep beneath the tables, it will be more difficult
for them to catch us."

Pandemonium erupted in the inn, but Oaktangle
vanished with the still body of the girl almost before
anybody had the time to realize what was happening.

Berioss and Ustant were quick to act. Grabbing the
ironmaster's arms, they threw him over their heads
and he landed with a crash amongst the jugs of ale
and half-eaten plates of food that lay upon the table.
"You should be ashamed of yourselves for picking on
these defenceless tunnellers. You're almost three
times their size!" Ustant shouted, the light of old battles shining in his eyes as he took a wild, defiant
swing at the angry mob that surged in around him.

The tunnellers used that moment of confusion to
make a rush for the doorway, disappearing beneath
the tables and chairs. For once their diminutive
stature helped them, enabling them to duck and
move as quickly as elusive shadows between the legs
of their attackers. One by one they ran out through
the doorway of the inn, barely noticing the pouring

rain as they dashed across the Greenway towards the dark line of trees.

"Wait!" Oaktangle called breathlessly when he reached the trees. "We can't leave those two old warriors, Ustant and Berioss behind."

"What do you suggest we do? Go back in there and rescue them? We're not warriors you know!" Blackthorn muttered, only too glad they managed to escape with their lives.

At that moment the door of the inn burst open and the light from the lamps flooded across the wet grass. There was a commotion in the doorway as Berioss and Ustant were thrown out, pieces of broken jugs and plates raining down on them, driving them away from the threshold.

"Get out! Get out and stay out! We don't want your kind in here any more!"

A chorus of voices were screaming at the old warriors through the doorway. Snatch pushed his way through the crowd and was briefly silhouetted against the light. His eyes narrowed as he hunted the dark eaves of the forest on the far side of the Greenway.

"I know you're hiding out there, you miserable, ugly creatures. This is your last warning—if you ever dare set foot in this wayhouse again I will kill you!" He took a step out into the pouring rain and raised his clenched fist. "Do you hear me, tunnellers? I will skin you alive one by one, and then I'll nail your vile little hides onto the chimney beam!"

He laughed, a harsh, cackling, self-satisfied sound as he rubbed away the raindrops that were streaking his forehead, and then he whispered softly into the darkness, "And this is only the beginning!"

# 3

# Dark Beginnings

BERIOSS AND USTANT FLED FROM THE ENTRANCE OF the inn beneath a hail of missiles and angry shouts. Running across the Greenway they vanished into the undergrowth, cursing as they collided blindly with tree-trunks and branches until they ducked down and tried to crawl on their hands and knees, only to feel the sharp stab of thorns as they became entangled with a blackthorn tree.

"It's no good, we can't go any further," Ustant cursed, trying to free the hood of his cloak from the spikes it had snagged upon somewhere above his head when he had tried to pull it over his head as protection against the deluge. With each movement it only became even more entangled.

"Don't make so much noise, you'll let them know exactly where we are. Come on, we've got to get further away!" Berioss hissed.

"No, we're better off staying where we are: these thorns are dangerous in the dark. Nobody's going to follow us, especially on a night like this. They are all much too afraid of the dark to come looking for us," Ustant muttered in disgust.

"Hush, listen, I don't like the sound of what the Chancellor's boy is shouting," Berioss whispered. "There's so much hatred and malice in his voice."

Ustant nodded bleakly. "Things are coming to a sorry state when decent folk are swayed by the likes of him."

"I'm not sure that's what's happening," Berioss

murmured slowly, tilting his head on one side to try
and catch snatches of the last whispered threat. "I
think that the boy has touched on something that has
been lying just beneath the surface ever since Thane
became king. But what has surprised me is the feroc-
ity of the attack on those poor tunnellers. I wonder
where they've got to . . . "

The door of the inn slammed shut, making both of
them jump. It seemed darker without the light that
had been streaming out through the entrance.

"Oaktangle, Mistletoe—where are you?" Berioss
called through the dense tangle of thorns that surrounded him and made him afraid to move.
"Oaktangle, where are you? Did all your people get
out safely?" he called again, more urgently.

The bushes rustled directly behind them and the
branches above their heads scattered ice-cold droplets
of water onto the two old warriors. "Yes, we all got
out safely, don't worry, we're here, right behind you,"
Oaktangle's voice was closer than either of them had
imagined was possible.

"We're stuck, I'm afraid. We seem to have crawled
into the middle of a thorn-bush in our rush to escape
and we can't find a way to get out in the dark,"
Ustant muttered, cursing the thorns that were pricking his arms as he tried to turn towards the tunneller's voice.

"Sometimes the ability to see in the dark has its
uses. Stay very still and Mistletoe and Damask will cut
a path through the thorns to where you are trapped."

Berioss and Ustant kept their faces protected by their
hands and let the two small tunnellers guide them out.
Breathing a sigh of relief, they climbed to their feet on
the Greenway's edge and dabbed gingerly at the
scratches on their hands and arms as they thanked the
tunnellers for their help.

"What can we do? Sloeberry is still unconscious
and blood is seeping from the wound on top of her

head where that brute hit her," Oaktangle asked in a worried voice.

"Let me have a look." Ustant murmured with concern as he searched in his pocket for the worn, old spark he always carried. When he found it he had to shield the flame with his cloak to hide it from any prying eyes that might still be watching them from the inn. It crackled between his fingers and his wrinkled brow drew into a worried frown as he looked down at the unconscious girl cradled in Oaktangle's arms. Her face had gone deathly white and her shallow breaths barely ghosted the belt-buckle he held towards her lips.

"We must get her into the dry and out of this atrocious weather: there isn't a moment to lose. My hut is only a short distance beyond the village. Quickly, follow me. Berioss—go and find Inva, the healer, but tell him nothing of what happened in the inn. Bid him bring his bag of oiled cottons and brews to infuse warmth and vigour back into the blood."

"But he's bound to ask who needs him. What shall I say?" Ustant thought for a moment, blinking as a trickle of raindrops ran into his eyes. "Tell him that one of the tunnellers who garden the Greenways has had an accident. Yes, that will do, tell him that we found her injured on the Greenway's edge and that she's close to death."

"You say a branch of a tree fell onto her? How extraordinary, I would have thought that with your people's ability to see in the dark and your sharp sense of hearing she would have heard it falling or else one of you would have sensed it."

There was an edge of doubt in the healer's voice and he held the silent group of tunnellers with penetrating and suspicious eyes for a moment before returning his attentions to the girl's injuries. "Yes, most extraordinary, and there's not a trace of bark

from the branch," he murmured as he cleaned the
ugly wound on top of her head and dressed it with an
oiled cotton soaked in juniper and calamine, dipping
the tip of his little finger into the cauldron that hung
over the fire to test the heat of the vile-smelling infusion that he had set to warm. He filled an earthenware cup with the glutinous brew and passed it
slowly backwards and forwards beneath Sloeberry's
nose. She stirred, her eyelids fluttering, her lips trembling as her nose wrinkled at the stench. Inva carefully cradled her head in his arm and pressed the cup
to her lips. She swallowed a sip and coughed, gasping
for air as she sat upright, blinking and staring at the
unfamiliar surroundings of the old warrior's hut.

"What . . . what happened?" she cried, her eyes
wild and staring as she shrank back from the healer.

"It's all right, everything's going to be all right, you
didn't have a chance to get out of the way and a
branch fell on your head. It knocked you unconscious," Ustant quickly interrupted.

"We were lucky these two warriors found us and
sent for the healer. I don't know what we would have
done without their help. Don't try to say anything
now, just rest and take the healer's medicine,"
Oaktangle added, taking her hand gently.

"But . . . but . . . " she frowned, falling silent as she
saw the anxious looks on her friends' faces and
Mistletoe put his finger to his lips.

"Drink, drink," Inva insisted and she reluctantly
swallowed the evil-tasting infusion from the cup he
was holding.

Sloeberry sank back against the coarse bracken-
filled pillow in confusion; her head was dizzy and
throbbing with pain. She watched the healer gather
up his bag of oiled cottons and his assortment of
small, pot-bellied jars of ointments and spirals filled
with evil-coloured cures and remedies. She couldn't
understand what was happening. A branch couldn't

have fallen on her head, they had all been sitting in the inn—that much she did remember. Yes, she had been telling Ustant, the one with the white, curling whiskers, all about the beauty of Elundium. She had been singing when somebody had shouted and cursed her. She distinctly remembered looking up to see him towering over her—and then everything went black. How had her clothes got all wet?

"You're lucky the branch didn't break your neck, my girl," a voice broke into her thoughts, making her look up. The healer was standing in the open doorway, his bag slung across his shoulder, looking curiously at her. "Rest easy for a daylight or two and you'll be none the worse . . . " he sighed, casting a sideways glance at the rest of the tunnellers as he bid Ustant and Berioss farewell and pulled the door shut behind him. "Extraordinary, most extraordinary," he muttered to himself as he hurried away.

"It wasn't a branch, I know it wasn't a branch!" Sloeberry cried out, only to be urged into silence by the old warrior as he peered out through a crack in the shutters at the departing healer.

Inva had stopped a few paces from the door and turned back to stare at the ramshackle hut. Something wasn't quite right, it wasn't something he could put his finger on but he could have sworn there was an odour of intrigue in that hovel. He wondered what the tunnellers were doing there, they normally stayed at the inn. And he was sure that ugly wound on the girl's head was never caused by a falling branch. Inva didn't trust those two old warriors, they had never been quite the same since that magician, Nevian, had turned them into trees—but what could they possibly be up to? Inva rubbed his hand thoughtfully over the sparse stubble on his chin. Perhaps he ought to pay Landlord Masterwort a visit before returning home. If anybody in the village could cast some light on what was going on he could. He wasn't sure whether to

trust those wandering tunnellers and he thought he
had better warn the landlord that they were in
Ustant's hovel. Yes, it would be safer to get to the
bottom of this just in case there was something under-
hand going on. Grumbling under his breath at the
atrocious weather, he trimmed the wick of his lamp
and pulled his hood down over his head against the
driving rain before hurrying through the village.

"That can only mean trouble for us. The healer's
heading straight for the inn, I'll bet he's going to
inform Masterwort that you're here with us," Ustant
frowned, pushing the door shut and turning towards
the others.

"I think we had better get well away from here
while we still can. I'm pretty sure that mob will come
howling for our blood again now that they have a
taste for it, especially if the Chancellor's boy is leading them," Berioss warned, getting out of his chair
beside the fire where he had been sitting as he tried
to dry his clothes.

"But all I did was sing about the beauty of
Elundium!" Sloeberry cried in despair. "I never meant
to cause all this trouble."

"It wasn't anything you did, child," Berioss smiled,
taking her tiny hand in his.

"Then what was it? What have we done that was
so terrible that they wanted that brute to slit
Oaktangle's throat?" Mistletoe demanded.

"It's because we're different. Lord Willow coun-
selled me once that it would take the people a long
time before they accepted us," Oaktangle answered,
touching his neck where Snatch's dagger had punc-
tured the skin.

"Yes, and in a way that is true," Berioss tried to
answer. "People fear what they do not understand, but
it doesn't excuse that ferocious attack. No, the fault
lies with them because they have refused to accept the
changes that are taking place around them . . . "

"But King Thane gave us the freedom to wander the length and breadth of Elundium. He said we would be welcomed wherever we stopped to rest and that he would provide our food and shelter for the work we do gardening the Greenways. Surely these people know that!" Damask interrupted, his hands on his hips.

Ustant looked anxiously out through the crack in the shutters, he could see lights approaching. Berioss threw up his hands in a gesture of helplessness and replied, "We're a long way from the Granite City, Damask, and the old ways die hard here. I don't think the villagers have any idea what's going on in the outside world or how much King Thane has done . . . "

"Berioss—quickly, we've got to get out now! They're surrounding the house!"

Ustant leapt back as a hail of stones and clumps of wet earth struck the door and shutters. They could hear the angry shouts of the mob from the inn outside and Snatch's voice was the loudest as he demanded that they send out the tunnellers. Sloeberry cried out in terror, scrambling dizzily to her feet and clinging to Oaktangle. Ustant crossed the room in three giant strides and took down two of his rusting swords from where they had hung forgotten since the last battle on the Rising. Their blades were blunt and chipped and the point of one of them had broken but the hilts felt familiar in his hands.

"They won't take us easily," he growled, throwing one of the swords to Berioss.

"No, I won't have the blood of these people on my hands! They are caught up in a madness they don't understand and we must escape. Is there a way to get out of this house without them seeing us?"

Berioss backed away from the door as heavier barrage of rocks and branches was hurled at it and it began to splinter on its hinges. Ustant took a quick look through the shutters at the mob outside and nodded. "There's a small window in the scullery at the back beside the log shed. Quickly, follow me!" he urged as chairs were upturned and an earthenware jug crashed to the floor.

Oaktangle jumped down after Ustant, landing lightly amongst the debris of the half-sawn logs and kindling that had spilled untidily out of the log shed. He could hear the voices of the villagers getting closer as they spread out to circle the hut. "Be quick, there isn't a moment to lose. Get out all of you and run for the shelter of the forest," Ustant cried as he waited for the others crouching beside the shed. Oaktangle reached up and almost dragged each tunneller down as they scrambled through the window.

All at once the door of the hut creaked and splintered beneath the violent assault and finally crashed to the floor as the mob swarmed in over it. As Berioss, who was bringing up the rear, swung his feet through the window and tried to jump out he felt his jerkin snag and tear and his broad shoulders became stuck in the small opening. He could hear footsteps and shouts inside the house behind him and he tried frantically to free himself. Oaktangle grabbed his feet and pulled. He could see the lights of the villagers' lanterns surrounding the house and realized they were almost upon them.

"Run, run for your life, Oaktangle, save yourself!" Berioss shouted as hands clawed at his head and pulled painfully at his beard.

Ustant, seeing that his friend was stuck, ran to Oaktangle's side and with a mighty pull they freed Berioss's shoulders. "Run, run you fat old fool!" Ustant gasped, grabbing his friend's arm as they fled for the cover of the forest. For an instant, the crowd seemed to close in on either side of them, shouting and hurling stones at them as they ran, but nobody made a move to follow them as they passed between the first line of trees. Ustant cursed as he collided with a tree-trunk and Berioss stumbled and fell over an unseen tree-root, knocking his breath out of him.

He felt Oaktangle's hand under his arm as he helped him up and heard him whisper in the inky, rainy darkness, "Go more slowly and let us be your eyes. We can see in the dark."

A sudden blaze of light and wild shouts through the trees made them all pause and turn back to see flames crackling and leaping up through the roof of Ustant's hut. Illuminated by the fire they could see the crowd from the inn, led by the Chancellor's boy, dancing and chanting around the blaze.

"That's everything I own!" Ustant cried angrily, taking a step back through the trees, his face streaked with tears and his sword arm raised in anger.

Berioss restrained him. "It will do no good: you cannot stop what is happening. Your memories are safe, they are here with us, we carry them in our hearts." He paused, glancing back at the small group of tunnellers who were waiting for them and lowered his voice. "I fear news of what has happened here tonight will travel faster along the Greenways than fire through dry bracken. We must stay with Oaktangle to protect his people and try to get them back to the Rising."

Ustant thought for a long moment, watching the silhouettes of the villagers in the flames that were devouring the only place he had ever called his home. It made him realize that the villagers were people he had never really known. The roof collapsed suddenly, sending up a brief shower of sparks before the fire began to die down.

"Yes, you're right," he muttered bleakly, turning his back on the glowing embers of his home and following Berioss into the darkness.

Snatch grinned and licked his lips; he was so well-satisfied with the unexpected turn of events that he hardly noticed the chill downpour as it hissed and spluttered on the dying embers of the old warrior's burnt-out hovel. "This is just the beginning!" he laughed, his mind alive and dizzy with possibilities after the success of his attack on that group of tunnellers.

Who would have imagined that the crowd would egg him on so eagerly—that they actually hated those miserable creatures even more than he did; and they had made him their hero, calling for more jugs of ale than he'd seen in a whole sun. They had slapped him on the back and promised to buy their firewood from nobody else but him. For a moment, in the smoky, noisy atmosphere after they had stoned those two interfering old men and driven them away, he had felt a sense of respect and importance for the first time since his family had been driven into exile. People wanted to shake his hand and call him their friend. Of course his father had done nothing but sit there with a long, miserable face, wringing his hands and muttering a lot of incoherent nonsense about him being the death of them all, and that dull-witted landlord, Masterwort, was no better, for he had tried to put a damper on the whole affair, berating him the moment he had driven those ugly little creatures out into the night. He had stood there and cursed him and his father, threatened to have them both thrown out for good. He had started to threat them with the King's wrath, imagining there would be a squadron of Gallopers at the inn by morning with a troop of Marchers close on their heels. But the crowd had shouted him down and chased him back out into the kitchen, demanding more ale to celebrate their triumph.

Snatch had sneered and shouted after him, "The King's the only one who might care, you fat fool! The Gallopers, the Marchers and everyone else for that matter are glad to see the back of those wretched tunnellers—you see if I'm not right!" Snatch was about to raise his jug brimming with fresh ale and toast the death of those ugly dwarfs, when the door of the inn had burst open and Inva, the healer, had bustled in, full of a story about what he had just seen in that treacherous warrior's hovel. It hadn't taken him much more than a moment to stoke up the crowd's anger against Ustant and Berioss for harbouring the tunnellers. Sparks were struck, lanterns lit and cloaks thrown hastily about their shoulders before they marched on his house at the end of the village.

"Now look what you've done, you stupid, irresponsible boy!" Ironpurse hissed in his ear, shaking his arm fiercely.

Snatch blinked, his eyes sharpening into focus as he turned from the hot embers of the fire to look blankly at his father. "What? What have I done?" he frowned, irritable with his father's persistent mutterings.

"You've attacked those tunnellers and chased them out of the inn—well, that was bad enough: but it was utter madness to burn down Ustant's house and chase those two warriors into the forest. Don't you realize they'll go straight to the King? They fought beside him at the Rising, they're what he would call his friends, if he had any. He's bound to send somebody out here to investigate, you stupid fool! What will you say then?"

Snatch merely laughed in his father's face. "I'll tell them nothing happened, of course. Everybody who was here tonight will back me up. I'll say that the silly old warrior probably dropped his spark while he was trying to light his lamp—accidents happen all the time don't they?"

"What makes you think that anybody will believe you instead of the tunnellers or those old and respected Marchers?" Ironpurse snapped, enraged by his son's insolent behaviour. "It would have been different when the Chancellors ruled, you might have got away with what you did then."

"You don't see it, do you?" Snatch interrupted in a mocking whisper. "It wasn't what I did that was important, it was the way everybody reacted to it that mattered. I tell you this, I could have murdered that ugly little dwarf, cut its head clean off its shoulders, and the crowd would have carried me around on their shoulders. Everybody's sick of them and people don't want their kind barging in here any more, stealing the food from their mouths, lording it over ordinary folk, pruning and gardening the Greenways as if they own them."

"But you can't go taking the law into your own hands, that candleman of a king will send out the Marchers and Gallopers to stop you. We will be powerless to help in this miserable exile," Ironpurse tried to remonstrate as they left the embers of the fire and started to walk the short distance to the inn to collect their cart.

Snatch threw his head back and laughed. "Sometimes, father, you're so blind, so wrapped up in how things used to be, that you don't see what's going on right in front of you. You don't listen to anything except your own incessant mutterings about what you have lost!"

Ironpurse turned sharply on him and raised his hand to strike him but Snatch stepped out of the way, sneering. "I'll prove it to you: listen. Tell me what that group of travelling merchants sitting at the next table were talking about."

Ironpurse frowned, trying to remember, letting his hand fall back to his side beneath his coarse, hessian cloak.

"They were going on about travelling, or something, but I don't see what's so important about that."

"And that Marcher what's his name—Whitto something or other—what was he going on about? Perhaps you can remember that?" Snatch pressed as they reached the cart.

"He was angry at something—said something about the Greenways not being safe to travel or something."

Snatch sighed and muttered, "There, I told you you weren't listening, didn't I?" He lowered his voice so that none of the villagers could hear him as they left the inn and made their way home. "The whole point of those travelling merchants' conversation was that they don't believe the Nightbeasts are dead. One of them swore that he had stumbled upon one of their camps. We know the place he described—that hollow with the rotting carcasses lying in it, about a league east of the village . . . "

"But we were cutting firewood near there in the spring! You and I know they're nothing but fly-infested corpses."

"Yes, but that merchant was so frightened of what he had discovered that he imagined he saw some of them move, and everybody at the table was ready to believe him. That proves what I'm trying to tell you: nobody really believes in half the claims King Thane makes—they're just too afraid to stand up and say so. I wasn't surprised when that pompous Marcher shouted the merchant down and threatened him with treason for daring to doubt that the King might have failed to destroy all the Nightbeasts. No—what did surprise me and started me thinking before those wretched tunnellers burst in was the look in the eyes of everybody else sitting around that table. They really did believe the merchant despite what the Marcher said—because they're still living in the shadows of their old fears, only they have become too frightened to admit them openly."

Snatch paused, shivering as the damp seeped through his clothes, and looked out into the rainy darkness. "All it needs is somebody who is prepared to do something about it, who can use these fears." He grinned to himself as he gave a vicious pull on the mule's bridle.

"Do? What can you do?" grumbled his father in reply, scrambling up onto the cart.

Snatch shrugged the question off as he trudged through the rain beside the labouring creature, not yet quite sure, though images were forming in his mind, prompted by what that merchant had said—dark, shadowy visions of Nightbeasts lurking between the trees which made the people huddle together, too frightened to travel alone; images of those miserable tunnellers being stoned and driven off wherever they tried to seek food and shelter, bearing the brunt for everything that had ever gone wrong; images of himself in the centre of it all, manipulating everybody's fears and prejudices to his advantage.

"Tonight," he whispered to himself as he turned the mule off the Greenway onto the muddy, rutted track that led to their hovel, "tonight it's all just beginning, we just have to find a way of using it."

"The boy's been possessed with a madness—he'll be the death of us all!" Ironpurse cried as he threw the door open, making his heavy-jowled wife, Banashe, scowl and roll up her sleeves. The rest of her ill-assorted children and the animals that shared their mean abode vanished beneath the broken chairs and rickety table. They had seen the sharp edge of Banashe's temper too often to want to stay in sight.

"You wouldn't believe it, wife, but he nearly killed one of those tunnellers in the inn with one blow from his fist. He picked another one up and hurled him out of the door. I'm telling you he'll bring us nothing but trouble once that candlebane King gets to hear of it. And then—to make matters worse—he goaded the crowd into burning down old Ustant's hut. I don't know what's come over him, I swear I don't . . ." Ironpurse sucked in his shallow cheeks and threw his dripping cloak aside as he stalked across the room to dry out in front of the meagre fire flickering in the hearth, blinking as his eyes watered from the smoke. "Of all the things for a Chancellor's son to do—the disgrace of it!" he muttered under his breath, raising his hand for silence as Snatch tried to defend his actions.

Banashe watched him with contempt from across

the shabby, threadbare room. There was barely a
shadow of the proud Chancellor she had married all
those suns ago in Candlebane Hall. His sharp cunning and clever politics were all reduced to self-pity
and bitterness. "Well, boy, you've got a tongue in
your head, haven't you?" she scowled, turning on
Snatch and pushing him towards the scullery, but
there was a flicker of interest in her eyes as she followed him out of the room.

"Everybody cheered me. They wanted me to kill
the ugly, little creature, but I didn't, I controlled the
urge, I just humiliated him instead," the grin widened
across his face as he told her everything that had happened. "Do you know the best part of it was that
everybody in the inn would have done anything I had
wanted them to do at that moment. I felt a sense of
real power—it was incredible!"

Banashe reached out and gripped his arms, at least
one of her children had some backbone. Her eyes
shone with pride. "You must be very careful, my
child, you are a true Chancellor's son but you must
use all your cunning to exploit that power and . . . "
she paused, glancing back to where Ironpurse was
hunched mumbling to himself over the fire, warming
his hands, oblivious to anything going on around him,
"say nothing more of it to your father lest his pitiful
mutterings betray you. Now eat and grow strong."

Snatch frowned, moving his weight from one foot
to the other as his mother hurried past him back to
the fire, pushing Ironpurse out of the way as she bus-
ied herself ladelling a bowl of black gruel from the
cauldron for the boy.

"But I don't know how to use that power. I don't
know what to do now, mother, that's the problem,"
he whispered to her as she returned with the food.

Banashe cursed one of the younger children who
had crept out from beneath the table and sent him
out for more wood for the fire. "Let me think," she

grumbled, thrusting her jowl forwards in concentration and folding her thick-set arms across her chest. Clearly the villagers hated those tunnellers more than she had thought, and from their behaviour they were becoming dissatisfied with this new king. "Of course, it's obvious what you have to do, boy," she laughed suddenly, exposing a mouth of missing teeth in a wide grin. "You've got to make everyone more dissatisfied with the way things are. You've got to blame every mishap, every setback, in fact everything that goes wrong in any way on those tunnellers. And make it clear that it's the King's fault for letting them wander wherever they please, and then cunningly remind them how much better things were when the Chancellors ruled."

"But won't the tunnellers just vanish if everybody starts blaming them for everything?" Snatch frowned, licking out the bowl.

"It doesn't matter what they do, you fool! That is the beauty of this plan; once you've planted the idea in people's heads and perhaps coaxed it along a bit, it will give them something to focus their dissatisfaction upon. Before you know it they'll be blaming the King for letting those ugly midgets roam wherever they please and then it won't be long before they're blaming everything on that candlebane King himself!" She laughed, thoroughly pleased with the plan.

Snatch nodded eagerly, his eyes narrowing with cunning, "Yes, yes of course, the next time they come barging their way into the inn . . . "

"No, things need to happen now—little accidents, unfortunate incidents that will allow you to point your finger directly at the tunnellers," Banashe murmured.

"Yes, but all those wretched creatures do is to wander along the the Greenways, gardening, mowing the grass, planting flowers and pruning back the trees—when they're not demanding to be fed," Snatch frowned.

"Gardening? Gardening . . . " Banashe murmured to herself as she paced slowly backwards and forwards. "Of course, the answer's simple!" She grasped the boy's arm, throwing a cloak over her shoulders as she took him out into the rainy darkness and whispered quietly to him so nobody else could hear her. "I think it's time the Chancellors' children did a little gardening themselves—only you'll do it in secret in the dead of night when nobody can see you," Banashe paused, listening for a moment to the rain drumming on the roof of their hovel.

"Gardening?" Snatch shrugged his shoulders. He didn't like the sound of that.

"Yes," his mother answered firmly. "Only you'll be chopping the heads off people's cabbages, trampling down their vegetables, pruning their fruit trees down to the stumps, digging up the Greenways instead of mowing them. You'll be making as much mess of everything you possibly can and you are going to start tonight!"

"But why? I can't see the point in all that, and anyway it's raining out here," Snatch tried to argue. He would much rather do something to frighten the travelling merchants: this kind of gardening sounded like hard work.

"Because people will think the tunnellers have done it, you fool! They're bound to think it's been done in revenge for being thrown out of the inn tonight. Now, take the mule and rouse everyone you think you can trust to help you."

Snatch grumbled as he pulled on his soaking-wet cloak. He didn't think this sort of revenge was such a good idea.

Banashe gripped his arm as he was about to leave, "Say nothing to any of the elder Chancellors, it will be our secret, our way of getting back at that candle-cur of a King who drove us into exile!"

\* \* \*

"Gardening!" Snatch cursed under his breath, wishing he had never mentioned the rotten word to his mother. That wasn't his idea of increasing the power he had felt, momentarily, in the inn, but he knew better than going against her once she got her mind fixed onto something. Shivering, he bent forward in the saddle to keep the worst of the deluge out of his eyes and lifted the lantern he was trying to shield beneath his cloak, but its flickering flame was too feeble to illuminate much beyond the mule's ears. He was afraid of the dark; not in the way most of the villagers were but it gave him an uneasy feeling when the nightshapes that carried the darkness each night across Elundium silently brushed against his skin and touched his sodden clothes as they melted and mingled together. Being alone in the dark always seemed to sharpen his senses and make him even more aware of them, filling his imagination with half-heard sounds, whispering voices, footsteps. Night had always been the time when the Nightbeasts roamed, when magic moved between the trees; a time when you stayed indoors with the shutters locked up tight.

Snatch laughed and tried to shake off the feeling that there were other noises out there beyond the squelch of the mule's feet in the mud and the constant hiss of the downpour falling through the trees. Nevian, the magician, had faded away and the Nightbeasts were all dead, he knew they were, he had poked about amongst their rotting carcasses looking for a trophy to bring home. There was nothing to be afraid of any more.

The white magpie that had followed the cart to the inn suddenly alighted on his shoulder, making him jump as it seemed to appear from nowhere. The bird squawked shrilly into his ear and Snatch tentatively stroked its feathers and laughed. The warriors might have their owls to warn them of danger but he had a far better ally: a thief and scavenger of the air that watched out for him while he sought his revenge. He reached the huddle of huts where the other Chancellors' families lived and eked out a subsistence and he slipped out of the saddle with his spirits lifted.

"Girrolt, come out here—Uxoit, come quickly," he hissed, scratching at each of the doors, calling out the names of his friends and asking them to follow him into the shallow pit beneath the grain-store.

"You'll never guess what happened tonight!" he whispered dramatically as the group gathered around the flickering lanterns, and he proceeded to tell them the whole story before outlining their parts in the future troubles.

"I can't wait to chop down Masterwort's apple trees after the beating he gave me for stealing his apples! I've been longing to get even," Kush sneered, rubbing his hands together almost before Snatch had finished telling them what he wanted them to do.

"Wait! Not so fast!" Snatched hissed, stopping the group as they rose to crawl out beneath the silo, eager to create as much damage as possible in the name of the tunnellers. "I don't think persecuting those ugly little dwarfs is enough—I want to have real power."

"But it's a start isn't it?" Huxort questioned. "Surely anything that turns the people against King Thane is worth doing, even if it's only digging up a bit of turf or trampling down some vegetables? We've got to begin somewhere, that's what my father is always saying."

"Well, yes, yes of course it's a start, but I want to do something more . . . more . . . " Snatch threw up his hands in frustration. "You know there was a moment in the inn tonight when everybody was looking up to me, when they would have done anything I asked. I could see their fear, their distrust and hatred of the new ways, it was in their eyes, and when that healer burst in and told us that those tunnellers were hiding in that old warrior's hovel it didn't take me long to fan the flames of that fear and make them march on Ustant's hut and burn it down. It's that power I want again . . . "

"Yes, but how? King Thane has banished all those old fears," Girrolt frowned, impatient to do a little damage in Deepling and get back before his father noticed he was missing and he couldn't see what Snatch was trying to get at.

"No, wait a moment, listen to me. Before the tunnellers barged their way into the inn I overheard a travelling merchant telling his friends how he had stumbled on a Nightbeasts' camp, you should have seen the look of fear in their eyes."

"But the Nightbeasts are all dead, everybody knows that," Kush laughed, making a move to leave before Snatch grabbed his arm.

"That's where you're wrong, you stupid fool, that's where we've all been wrong. The ordinary people don't really believe it, not deep down inside, that's where our real power lies—in feeding their fear of the Nightbeasts!"

"But how?" Huxort asked in a voice that filled the silence that followed Snatch's outburst. All eyes were watching him, waiting for an answer.

Snatch looked 'round his friends as they sat, anticipation holding them silent in the darkness. "By making them believe the Nightbeasts are still alive! By resurrecting them from where they lie rotting in that shadowy hollow to the east of the village, by cloaking ourselves with their armour and spreading terror along the Greenway's edge!"

"You must be mad—stark, staring mad!" Thoragrasp whispered from the back of the group.

"What are you afraid of?" sneered Snatch. "Are you afraid of going into Shadow Hollow?"

# 4

## No Welcome Beside the Greenway's Edge

"**I** MUST STOP AND REST FOR A MOMENT. I CAN'T keep up with you," Berioss gasped, his red cheeks puffed out in his efforts to keep with Mistletoe who was guiding him through the forest. He could hear the tunnellers' soft voices whispering and laughing, and sometimes as he stumbled he could feel their gentle touch urging him, trying to help him, but he couldn't see them in the pitch-darkness. He couldn't even see his hand if he put it up in front of his face. "Damn my dim eyes!" he cursed as he snagged his toe on what seemed like the thousandth tree-root since they had fled from the mob besieging Ustant's hut. He would have fallen onto his knees on the slippery, silent leaf-mould but Mistletoe caught his arms and steadied him.

"It's no good! I'm getting too old for this—you'll get along a lot quicker on your own," he grumbled at the darkness, regaining his balance and wiping his hand across his rain-streaked face where it itched and stung from the countless unseen thorns and branches that he had blundered into as he tried to pull free the tangles and knots in his beard.

"Some warriors we make!" he heard Ustant complain through laboured breaths as he stopped somewhere close to him.

"Wait, don't move, I think we must be far enough from the village—I'll light a spark," Berioss called, fumbling in his damp pocket. "Come on, come on," he muttered, repeatedly crackling the spark between his fingers, but it only flickered once and went out. "It's no good, the wick's too wet," he called out miserably, thrusting it back into his pocket and preparing to feel his way forward again.

Something moved quickly through the undergrowth, so close to where they had stopped that they felt it rustling the bushes. "What in all Elundium was that?" Ustant gripped the hilt of his sword. He had sensed strange noises and movements in the darkness around him ever since they had entered the forest, and twice he had felt a cold draught of air against his cheeks as if some huge bird were fluttering its feathers and hovering in front of his face. He had reached up to fend it off but had only found thorns and branches above him.

"It's nothing to be afraid of," Oaktangle answered.

His voice made them jump; Oaktangle had returned so silently that neither of them had heard him approach. The tunnellers moved so lightly and nimbly over the ground that they barely left a footprint in the wet earth.

"There's a ruined hut only a little way ahead in a clearing. We can rest and shelter there until morning—it's not far now. Sloeberry and some of the others have gone ahead to light a fire and forage for something to eat," Oaktangle said lightly.

"Somewhere dry would be a real blessing, but I doubt you'll find very much to eat in this dismal weather," Berioss agreed with Ustant on this: he was cold and soaked through to the skin. If he'd had the slightest idea that he would be spending the night out in such atrocious weather, living rough as he had in his marching days, he would have worn his old marching cloak. It might be threadbare from use and peppered with moth-holes but it would still have kept out the worst of the deluge.

"You will be surprised what the forest will yield," Oaktangle laughed. "Now take a grip of Mistletoe's hand and don't forget to duck when he gives you the signal, so that you'll keep your head out of the low branches. But keep your other hand up in front of your face just in case he forgets he's leading such a giant." Oaktangle moved off noiselessly ahead of them.

"Whatever made that rushing noise just then? It wasn't a nightboar was it? It felt so close, I could almost have reached out and touched it," Ustant asked, catching up and keeping his hand on Berioss's shoulder.

"No, it certainly wasn't a nightboar," Mistletoe smiled. "If a nightboar had been that close it would have turned and charged at us; no that was old Whisper, one of the Warhorses. He always seems to follow us when we're travelling near the Deepling Gorge."

"Warhorses? Where are they? I haven't seen a single one since the Battle of the Rising. They never come into the village," Berioss exclaimed, hunting the darkness, listening intently as he tried to catch the sound of a footfall above the monotonous hiss of the rain falling amongst the trees. His heartbeats always quickened at the sight of those beautiful creatures.

"I can see the light of the fire through the doorway of the hut. Come on. Let's get in out of this weather," Ustant urged, quickening his stride and forging past the other two. The flickering firelight picked out the mass of low branches, undergrowth and twisted tree-trunks ahead of them, showing them in silhouette and making it possible for Ustant to find his own way, but Berioss hung back, searching the shadows, listening. A smile twitched his lips as the Warhorse appeared between the trees, it stopped and stood quietly, watching him, the firelight illuminating the dapples on its coat and shimmering on its silken mane.

"Berioss, come on. You'll catch your death out there!" Ustant shouted from the doorway.

Berioss half-turned, distracted by his friend's voice, but although he looked quickly back, the horse had vanished into the shadows.

* * *

Ustant stretched out his legs to ease the cramp that came from having to sit awkwardly on the cold, earth floor, shifting his weight to try to get as comfortable as he could amongst the ring of tunnellers around the fire. He looked across at Berioss and smiled as he watched him chew on the tough, fibrous roots of ruggedwort and squinawth that Sloeberry had roasted on sharpened sticks over the fire. It had a smoky, bitter, earthy taste and seemed to be full of fragments of grit and dirt that kept getting stuck between their teeth, but it filled a hole on a cold, wet night.

"Yes, I was wrong, I don't mind admitting it," Berioss laughed, brandishing the half-chewed root he was holding.

Oaktangle nodded, "The forest is more than just trees and undergrowth, earth and sky: it is a garden full of so many wonderful things—if you know where to look for them."

Sloeberry smiled and her voice began to rise in a song that echoed with stories of the wind in the trees, of the heaviness of blackberries ripening on the bramble, the rattle of the woodpeckers busy in the spring and the cooing of the doves in the misty evening light. Berioss yawned and settled back, drowsy in the warmth of the fire. He glanced across to see Ustant's head nod forward onto his chest as he fell asleep. Berioss blinked and rubbed his eyes as he tried to stay awake; there was so much he wanted to ask the tunnellers, so many old stories to retell, but the flickering flames were throwing too many dancing, mesmerizing shadows up across the hut and Sloeberry's soft, melodic voice was lulling him to sleep. She had seemed to sense his love of the warhorses and was weaving them into her song.

"So beautiful, they are so beautiful . . . " he murmured as the ring of faces in the firelight slipped gradually out of focus. The thin wreathtails of steam rising from the tunnellers' drying clothes seemed to make translucent pictures in the smoky room, blending and twisting together with all the colours of the rainbow cloak.

"Nevian? Is that you Nevian?" he whispered.

Faintly, from somewhere on the edge of the enfolding darkness that was closing in over him he heard Oaktangle calling to him and pointing towards something up in the gloomy rafters. There was soft laughter in his voice.

"Look, old friends are gathering to seek shelter from the storm with us."

Berioss tried to rouse himself and look up but Sloeberry's haunting lullaby lay heavily on his eyelids. "Owls . . . " he murmured. "Is that a stoop of battle owls?" The words were slurring together as he caught sight of a row of eyes above him in the smoky shadows. His head slipped sideways as sleep overtook him and he rested against Mistletoe's shoulder.

Silverthorn, the battle owl, dropped silently from his rafter perch to hover a handspan first from Berioss and then from Ustant as he searched their faces. He reached out with outstretched talons and touched the rusty swords that rested haphazardly against their knees. The draught from his outspread wings ruffled white whiskers and greying hair as they beat the air and he rose to alight upon Oaktangle's shoulder. Flexing his talons and turning his head he spoke to the tunneller in quiet hoots and whispers.

"Why are those two old warriors here? Why are they armed and abroad on such a night?"

"They were the only ones who came to our aid when the people of Deepling turned against us. They are travelling with us to protect us, but I think it is us who are now looking after them," he answered, smiling at Berioss and Ustant who were now covered by the tunnellers' cloaks and snoring loudly.

"The people of Deepling attacked you?" Silverthorn

shrieked, spreading his wings and drawing himself tall. Hoots and whispers erupted from the other owls perching amongst the rafters.

"Yes, there seemed no reason for it. We were merely seeking shelter from the storm and . . . " Oaktangle tried to explain but Silverthorn lifted from his shoulder before he had time to pause for breath and called to the other owls gathering them into a council at the far end of the hut.

"We must fly high and watch the Greenways with sharp eyes. We must find the truth behind this dreadful matter," Silverthorn hooted above the noisy debate. "The King's peace has been broken, there is the scent of trouble and unrest in the air."

"We must warn the Warhorses to be on their guard," hooted a small owl, puffing out its feathers.

Oaktangle rose quickly to his feet, took a hesitant step forward and stretched out his hands towards the noisy council of owls. "We did nothing to break the King's peace, nothing that could have provoked those people's anger, I promise you. You must believe me."

The council fell silent as each feathery head tilted downwards and they held him with their piercing, blinkless eyes. "It is the truth we must find: there are always two sides to barter," Silverthorn hooted coldly and one by one, without another sound, the owls stopped down through the broken doorway to fly out into the rainy darkness and seek shelter elsewhere.

"You have to believe me—we did nothing!" Oaktangle cried, running after them to the doorway, but they had vanished as silently as they had come and he saw only darkness outside.

"We must hurry back to the Rising. Lord Willow will know what to do—he'll believe we didn't start the trouble," Sloeberry whispered and the others all nodded in agreement.

"What about Berioss and Ustant?" Mistletoe asked. "It is our innocence, not theirs, that has to be decided. It would be unfair to make them accompany us all the way to the Rising—look how just one night has tired them out. We should leave them here."


Berioss awoke with a grunt; it took him a moment staring up at the derelict surroundings to remember where he was. "Ustant, Oaktangle," he tried to call as he struggled to rise, but the words came out as a choking rasp, his mouth was so dry and filled with a foul taste of earth and smoke. Rolling over, he managed to scramble up onto his knees only to stagger and almost fall back, his hands and feet numb and his legs and arms so stiff he could hardly move. Cursing and grinding his teeth as arrows of pain shot through his old joints, he stretched his limbs flexing his fingers slowly. That would teach him to spend most of the night out in the rain and then to sleep on a damp, earth floor.

"Ustant! Where is everybody?" he called out crossly as he climbed painfully to his feet. "I am even getting too old to keep a decent fire!" He stirred the cold ash with the toe of his boot. He heard Ustant call out to him and walked stiffly to the door, blinking and raising his arm to shield his eyes from the bright morning sunlight that was streaming through the trees on the edge of the clearing. He frowned and looked slowly around him before asking Ustant where the tunnellers were.

"I don't know; they seem to have vanished," Ustant answered with an edge of worry to his voice as he searched the undergrowth.

"But that's impossible, they wouldn't just have gone off without telling us, would they?"

"Well, I'm not sure . . . " Ustant answered slowly, scratching his head as he returned and sat down on a broken stone bench close to the door.

"It doesn't make sense does it—they knew we were going to accompany them to the Rising didn't they?"

Berioss shrugged. "But then, everything happened so fast last night I'm not really sure."

"Something disturbed me in the night. I'm sure I woke up to hear the strangest commotion going on; as if a whole flock of Battle Owls were hooting and shrieking all at once up in the roof—you know the way they used to hold their battle councils high up in the trees in the old daylights. And the other odd thing was the tunnellers were huddled up together all talking at once, and then I remember it getting very quiet, but of course it could all have been a dream couldn't it?"

Sunlight reflecting on a small bubbling fountain near the corner of the hut caught Berioss's eye. He walked across to it and cupped his hands to drink deeply and wash away the bitter, earthy taste in his mouth, and then he plunged his head into the icy water. Shivering and gasping from the shock of it, he scattered droplets of icy water all over the floor. "That's better, I can think more clearly now!" he said, inhaling a deep breath and stretching out his arms to the sun.

"I really can't imagine what has happened to them, can you? It's so out of character, vanishing like that." Ustant sighed.

"But is it?" Berioss asked slowly. He was drying his face with the dirty cuffs of his shirt, leaving faint smudges of dirt on his ruddy cheeks as he came back to where Ustant sat on a broken stone bench. "Tell me, exactly how were you expecting the tunnellers to behave?"

Ustant looked up sharply. "Well . . . well . . . as they always do, of course. I would have thought we knew them better than most: Landlord Masterwort sits them at our table often enough when they stop at the inn. They're always so polite, aren't they, never short of a please or a thank you—and they leave the Greenways so neat and tidy."

"Yes, yes, but do we really know anything about them? Do we know anything beyond common gossip and that polite face they always present to us when they stop in the village?" Berioss pressed.

"Of course we do!" Ustant retorted. "We were there at the Battle of the Rising and we both watched King Thane give Lord Willow and his people the freedom to roam Elundium as they pleased in exchange for their help in destroying the darkness. What else is there to know about them?"

"But they're so different from us in so many ways. They can see in the dark and travel quickly, leaving barely a trace of where they've been. Perhaps they thought they had already been too much trouble to us."

"I . . . I . . . I don't see what you're getting at, unless you're trying to excuse their behaviour, Ustant interrupted crossly. "You seem to be forgetting that they vanished into thin air without saying so much as a goodbye, and my house was burnt to the ground for trying to help them. Now it seems we did it all for nothing."

"No, I'm sure you're wrong, my old friend," Berioss smiled, taking Ustant's hand in his and gripping it firmly. "You know in your heart that what we did wasn't for nothing. We're Marcher-born, King's men, and neither of us could have stood by and watched those louts attack the tunnellers without doing anything to help, now would we?"

Ustant nodded slowly and climbed to his feet. "I know, I know," he muttered bitterly, looking past Berioss's shoulder to the faint blue-grey line of the horizon he could just see between the trees. "I think, deep down inside, I know why they disappeared while we slept."

"What on earth do you mean?"

"It's because we've got too old to be of much use as fighting men; because they were worried we would slow them down and become a burden, and they were far too polite to tell us."

Berioss stared at him for a shocked moment and then threw back his head and laughed. "But that's absurd, what nonsense! Standing on the Greenway's edge beguiled by Nevian's magic may have weathered us a little over-soon and lined our skin with leather creases but too old to fight! Too old to defend them! Why they don't know the half of it, we'll show them! Come on!"

"But will we?" Ustant's voice brought Berioss to a shambling halt. "I don't think we made much of an impression last night. We were chased out by the mob; we didn't stand our ground. We would never have run away in the old daylights. And then, to add insult to injury, we were reduced to stumbling blindly through the forest clinging on to the very people we were supposed to be protecting. To make matters worse we forced them to stop and seek shelter because we were soaked through and too exhausted to go any further. Warriors! Marchers! Look at us, we're two bedraggled old fools, lost in the forest with dirty faces and rusty swords."

"Lost? I'm not lost, and I'm no fool, I know exactly where we are!" Berioss thundered angrily, his face darkening as he swept his sword round in a savage arc. He spun round, searching the edge of the clearing. "The village is that way—no, that way . . . " His words faltered and the anger dissolved. "It all looks the same." Hesitantly he pointed his sword first north and then north-east, was forced to raise his free hand to protect his eyes from the glare of the sun's rays as he turned due east. Gradually he let the blade dip and trail uncertainly along the ground. "It's got to be somewhere in that direction: it's only a matter of finding our way through the trees until we meet the Greenway. There must be a path."

"Yes, but which Greenway? Go on, admit it, Berioss, we're lost: we can't even find a way out of this clearing, so how are we ever going to find the tunnellers?"

Berioss sighed and nodded, reluctantly. "But we're still Marchers, Ustant: we've got to find them somehow. We have to protect them on their journey back to the Rising."

"But the Rising is beyond Underfall, beyond the endless grasslands: we will be worn away to shadows long before we are even halfway there!"

Berioss laughed, a deep, rumbling sound that made his shoulders shake. "Now that is the talk of an old man! Hold still a moment, I have an idea that may set us on the right road."

He cupped his hands to his mouth and shouted, "Can any of the King's friends hear me? This is Marcher Berioss and Marcher Ustant. We are lost in the forest and have great need of your help to find our way!"

"What now?" Ustant frowned as Berioss's voice died away amongst the morning chatter of blackbirds and wild doves from the undergrowth and trees around the clearing.

"Wait and listen" Berioss whispered.

"I can't hear anything! If we're going to find those tunnellers we're wasting precious time," Ustant muttered impatiently gathering up his sword.

The undergrowth rustled immediately ahead of him and the grass parted. A huge, ferocious-looking dog broke cover, the sunlight catching on its sable coat and glinting on its rows of teeth as it leapt forward. Suddenly another burst through the dense bushes, and Ustant backed away hastily as more and more of the creatures began to appear making barely a sound. His fingers tightened instinctively around the hilt of his sword, the muscles tensing in his forearms as he looked for a way to escape.

"Stand still, don't make any sudden movements! You know the border runners will not harm you," Berioss warned in a whisper. He knew how much Ustant feared the dogs of war and he could see the rising panic in his eyes. He had called out in the hope that the Warhorses would hear him and had never imagined any of the Border Runners would respond to the sound of his voice, for they were wild creatures, free to roam the forest and rolling grasslands.

Ustant was paralysed with terror. He had never managed to overcome his childhood fear of dogs: no matter how many times the Border Runners had run beside him and fought in the battle crescents against the darkness, he had always shrunk away from touching them and making much of them the way the other Marchers had. Cold sweat trickled between his shoulderblades as Magadas, the leader of the small pack, padded forward and circled once around him. His head was almost level with the Marcher's chest and he could sense the man's fear oozing from every pore as he sniffed at his clothing, his hands and then his face. Magadas curled his lips back as he growled a soft greeting.

Ustant swallowed, dizzy and sick with panic. He could feel the dog's hot breath ghosting his cheek, its fangs a mere finger's span from his nose. He could see all the way down its throat as it snarled. He screwed his eyes tightly shut and waited for those vicious teeth to snap shut on his face and claws to maul and tear at his skin. Then through his terror, he became aware of Berioss's voice talking softly, calling out the lay of old battles, telling of the time when Granogg had run at the King's stirrup. Then his voice rose urgently as he told them of the attack on the tunnellers and how they must find them quickly before they were attacked again.

Magadas snarled, the hackles rising along his back as he moved closer to Berioss. His head was tilted to one side and his ears were pricked as he listened and let the Marcher caress his powerful neck and shoulders before lifting his head to howl. The scent of old battles was sharp in his nostrils and one by one the pack lifted their heads and the cry of their voices travelled far across the tree-tops.

\*　　\*　　\*

Oaktangle was about to leave the cool, quiet shadows of the woods and step out onto the busy Greenway when he caught the faintest echo of the Border Runners' voices on the morning wind. There was a warning, an uneasiness in the sound that made him hesitate and become wary of joining the groups of travelling merchants and the noisy, talking journeymen on the road. The alarming howl in the wind made him pause and listen carefully to the voices of the passing travellers.

"I tell you, Mearsnart, those tunnellers have had it coming to them for a long time . . . "

"It's a pity nobody's put them in their place before . . . "

"You should have seen that boy, Snatch, holding that ugly little creature in the air and making it dance—I nearly died laughing. Ask anyone—it was the best evening's entertainment there's been for ages."

Oaktangle drew back, his face white and anxious. Surely not everybody was against them. What had they done to stir up this much resentment? He retraced his footsteps thoughtfully and went back to where the others waited. "It seems the road is full of stories about last night's attack on us. I think we'll be safer if we keep to the woods. Meremire will hide us for today, at least until we get to the village of Larach."

"But Larach is not on our way home. It will take us an extra three daylights if we go that way!"

"I know, but it will be safer to keep off the main Greenways, at least until we are well away from here."

One by one the tunnellers nodded in agreement and silently melted back into the shadows beneath the trees.

Magadas reared up on his hind legs and planted his forelegs firmly on Berioss's shoulders, making the Marcher stagger beneath his weight. He barked in his face, pledging his help, and then closed his teeth lightly on his sleeve to pull him away from the hut. Then Magadas released him from his jaws and growled softly before running across the clearing, repeatedly stopping and crouching to scent the wind. He barked furiously as he caught a trace of the tunnellers' scent and followed it, vanishing into the undergrowth. The pack surged around the two Marchers, sniffing at their clothes before turning and following on Magadas's heels. The bushes on the edge of the clearing rustled and shook as the dogs passed through them and then were still, leaving no trace of their passing.

"Thank goodness they've gone at last!" Ustant's voice was tight and trembling as he sucked in a shallow breath and sank down onto the broken bench to recover his composure, his legs as weak as jelly.

"There's no time to rest—come on, get up!" Berioss urged sharply. "I think those dogs are going to lead us, or at least show us the way the tunnellers went. But we'll have to be quick or we'll lose sight of their trail. It should be easier to follow once we're through this dense undergrowth. Come on, there isn't a moment to lose!"

"No, it's utter madness rushing off into the wilderness after a pack of savage dogs! You never know what they might do to us."

"They won't hurt us: the Border Runners are our friends. You should know that better than anybody, the times they've fought beside you. I know they're going to help us—I can hear it in their voices."

Berioss ran impatiently across to where Magadas had disappeared into the tangle of bushes and then he stopped and turned and shouted at Ustant, "I thought there was more Marcher beneath that cloak! I never imagined you were this frightened of anything. They're dogs, Ustant, just dogs!"

Seeing Ustant huddled, refusing to move, he threw

up his hands in exasperation and plunged into the undergrowth, shielding his face from the thorns with his arm and shouting over his shoulder, "Come with me or stay here! Do what you like but I'm going to try to find those tunnellers and protect them!"

Shamed by Berioss's words Ustant climbed reluctantly to his feet, cursing and muttering under his breath as he tried to give himself courage. He shouldered his broad marching sword and hurried after him. He would rather face a Nightbeast than the marauding pack of dogs he was now following.

All morning they followed the Border Runners through the undergrowth until finally they slithered and slid their way down a steep, tree-filled bank before coming to a stop on the Greenway's edge. It was long past the noonday hour and the road lay deserted in either direction. Berioss puffed out his cheeks, gasping for breath as he sank down on his haunches, glad of the moment's rest while he patted the closest dog. Ustant stood with his back to a gnarled old oak and his feet deep in damp leaf mould. He had a tight grip on his sword and he, too, was breathing hard as he watched the pack anxiously while they milled around his feet, casting wider and wider as they scented the ground.

Repeatedly Magadas and three of the largest dogs criss-crossed the close-cropped turf searching for where the tunnellers should have emerged. "I think their tracks must have got mixed up with everybody else's. So many people use this Greenway," Ustant muttered, watching the border runners move further and further away in their hunt.

Suddenly furious barking erupted away to the left and Berioss climbed to his feet. "They've found the scent! Look, over there!" he cried, pointing away to his left as the border runners ran back into the trees.

"Why didn't they take the Greenway? It's got to be the quickest way to the Rising."

But the dogs streamed past him, vanishing noisily amongst the trees and gradually the sound of their barking grew fainter as they ran hard on the tunnellers' scent.

"You're right, they must have come down here almost to the Greenway's edge and then turned back. What on earth made them keep inside the forest? Perhaps word of last night has travelled faster than I thought: perhaps somebody frightened them off the road." Berioss frowned, shouldered his sword and scrambled back up the bank as fast as he could, searching for a path. "Come on, we've got to find them as quickly as we can!"

"This is going to kill me, I know it is," Ustant panted as he clambered after him.

Nightshapes were gathering together the shadows, silently weaving them into the fabric of night as twilight deepened across the wooded valleys of Meremire Forest. Ustant leaned wearily against the trunk of a towering oak on the Greenway's edge, his sword trailing along the ground, hunting for breath as he watched the lamps of the village spring on below him making small pinpoints of light in the encroaching darkness. He felt a dog's cold nose brush against his hand as it slipped past him and ran along the Greenway towards the village. He was to tired, too exhausted even to flinch.

"I think that must be the village of Larach below us," Berioss whispered.

Oaktangle hesitated on the threshold of the Wayhouse inn, his hand upon the latch. He had kept the company hidden in the trees until darkness fell for instinct had warned him to keep well away from the village. The others crowded anxiously behind him.

"All we want is something to eat, a crust of bread, a rind of cheese, the people here have always been friendly to us, surely they won't harm us now?" Sloeberry whispered hopefully.

"Wait a moment," Oaktangle whispered. "I don't want us to go in there until I'm sure it's safe."

"But I'm tired and really hungry," Mistletoe cried, pushing against Oaktangle as he waited.

"All right—but remember, all of you, don't do anything to upset anybody—no singing or talking too loudly, or answering anyone out of turn: we don't want a repeat of last night do we?"

Taking a deep breath, Oaktangle lifted the latch and pushed the door open. He paused slightly and then stepped in over the threshold followed by the rest of the company. The hum of conversation, the laughter and clatter of knives, the scrape of wooden bowls, the clink of glass and jugs of ale stopped abruptly. Everyone in the inn turned to stare at them.

Landlord Caskplenty's sharp ears pricked up, alerted by the sudden silence in the inn. "Now, what's the matter?" he grumbled. "As if we don't have enough trouble to contend with, what with these rumours about Nightbeasts roaming through the forest again—and then those tunnellers picking a fight in the inn at Deepling and then rampaging through the village, setting light to folks' houses! Nobody will be safe in their beds soon. Make way, make way!" He pushed and elbowed his way through the crowded room. "Of all the cheek!" he exclaimed. The loose folds and wrinkles of skin that hung down around his mouth formed into a sullen scowl as he spotted the small group of tunnellers standing a few paces inside his door.

"We . . . we . . . we hope we haven't left it too late to ask for food," Oaktangle asked in a small voice. He could sense the hostile atmosphere and he regretted entering the inn but he smiled nervously and opened his hand in a gesture of friendliness, hoping the others standing behind him had the good sense to retreat while they still had the chance.

"That's him! That's the one who picked the fight with the Chancellor's boy!" somebody whispered from the crowd, pointing at Oaktangle.

"Yeah, that's the one. Ugly little creature, isn't he?" added one of the travelling merchants. "Perhaps we should teach them some manners!"

The crowd began to push forward but Landlord Caskplenty held his arms out, keeping them back. "No! Wait and be quiet, all of you. Let me give them a piece of my mind first and then you can do whatever you like with them."

He turned back to the tunnellers. "You've got a nerve showing your faces here after the trouble you caused over in Deepling. Don't you think we haven't heard all about it. You're not welcome amongst honest folk, not here, not anywhere!"

"Catch this, you ugly little dwarves!" a forester cried impatiently as he threw his ale at them.

The crowd surged, sticks, fists and knobbly cudgels raised above their heads.

"Get out! Run for your lives!" Oaktangle cried to the others, trying to make his voice heard above the shouts and curses of the crowd as he raised his hand to ward off the blows that were about to rain down on him. But then the advancing mob hesitated and anger froze into gasps of fear. Faces stretched in startled surprise at something that had come into the inn behind the cowering group of tunnellers.

Oaktangle spun round, not knowing what to expect, his own fear turning into a cry of delight as he saw the open doorway crowded with Border Runners. The flickering light from the hanging lanterns and the flames from the fire in the hearth reflected from their pale yellow eyes and their rows of white fangs and sent huge, grotesque shadows leaping up the walls and across the low-beamed ceiling as they advanced over the threshold, fanning out, keeping close to the ground. They were snarling and growling, ready to attack, and the crowd retreated hastily.

Magadas ran through the tunnellers to Oaktangle's side, his hackles raised along his back, his lips curled back to expose razor-sharp fangs in a menacing snarl. He paused for a moment beside the tunneller, letting him rest his hand upon his back before he advanced, step by step, towards the landlord. Caskplenty felt his legs turn to water as the monstrous beast singled him out. He had never stared so closely into the face of death before. He waited in terror and a thin, reedy scream escaped his lips as he stumbled backwards and tried desperately to force his way into the crowd, but there wasn't a finger's space between the scrambling, frantic bodies of the crowd as they all tried to find a way of escape. Tables and benches were overturned in the panic; jugs, glasses and plates were sent crashing to the floor to be trampled heedlessly underfoot.

Magadas snapped and clawed at the landlord's fleeing heels. His teeth tore through Caskplenty's breeches before he leapt, his powerful forelegs striking the man's chest, sending him sprawling helplessly into the mêlée. The Border Runner's jaws opened in a roaring snarl and his hot breath made Caskplenty choke and gasp for air as his teeth closed around his throat.

"No! Stop, stop it! You mustn't hurt him, all we asked for was some food!" Oaktangle cried, rushing forward to try to pull the huge creature off the landlord as he savaged at the crying man's throat, shaking him as easily as a ragbarter doll.

"Magadas, leave him, in the King's name put him down—there must be no blood shed here tonight. Call off the pack, be still all of you!" a deep voice called out from the doorway.

The leader of the pack snarled fiercely. He had the taste of blood in his mouth as he shook the man again before letting him go. He knew the tunnellers to be kindly, gentle folk of the forest who harmed nobody and had come at the Marchers' bidding to protect them, scenting the hatred and anger directed against them from the crowd in this room. Reluctantly he opened his jaws and let go of the innkeeper who collapsed in a terrified, shivering heap on the floor and he barked to the rest of the pack who retreated and formed a circle around the tunnellers. A whisper of relief rippled through the mob as the dogs backed away from them.

"Berioss! Ustant!" Sloeberry cried in surprise as she turned towards the familiar sound and saw the two old warriors standing in the doorway, their swords held high.

"There will be no killing in this inn tonight! And there will be no violence against Lord Willow's people: they have the protection of the King, and the right to ask for food and to seek shelter at any way-house in Elundium—or have you, in your haste to swallow every wild rumour that has been set against them, forgotten your duty?"

Berioss's voice was grim and forceful as he stepped in over the threshold and crossed the room slowly to where Magadas was crouched watching Caskplenty.

"You should be ashamed of yourselves" attacking these innocent tunnellers with no good reason!" Ustant cried out, accusingly, his sword held ready as he followed Berioss into the inn to face the silent, hostile crowd.

Some of them were beginning to shuffle and edge forward now that the dogs had pulled back around the tunnellers and their faces were hardening with distrust.

"Marchers!" somebody spat. "You can't trust anybody these days!"

"You can't blame us for not wanting their kind in here—stealing the food from our mouths, demanding the best beds in the house! And after all the trouble they caused over Deepling way last night I'm surprised you're supporting them!"

"We don't hold with louts who start fights and burn down people's houses!"

A murmur of agreement rippled throughout the crowd. Two of the Border Runners snarled and stepped forwards a pace and the crowd shrank back, falling into a sullen silence.

"But we didn't start the trouble, we . . . " Mistletoe began, only to have Oaktangle motion him to be silent. He could sense from the hostile reaction that it didn't matter how much they tried to protest their innocence, the people were turning against them, and they had already judged them guilty of something.

"I think we had better get out of here as quickly as we can," he urged, reaching out to touch Berioss's sleeve.

Berioss frowned and shook his head. He had no intention of letting the hysterical mob intimidate him: he wasn't running away so readily a second time. "These people are innocent of what you accuse them of. They didn't attack anybody last night, they were sitting at my table, breaking bread and describing all the beauty they saw in their travels through Elundium when that Chancellor's boy, Snatch, suddenly attacked them. If you don't believe me then ask Ustant!" he called out, angrily shaking his fist at the mass of hostile faces glaring at him.

"People!" a voice mocked from the back of the crowd. "You can't call those ugly little dwarves people!"

A snigger of laughter swelled as they saw the tunnellers' obvious discomfort and one of the merchants suddenly pushed his way through the crowd despite the snarling Border Runners and pointed his finger accusingly at Berioss and Ustant. "I though I recognized these two the moment they burst in here. Yes, I've seen them both before in Deepling—and I've heard some strange stories of how the Master of Magic, Nevian, turned them into trees. Yes—trees!

The folk of Deepling say that some of that magic is still trapped inside them, that on dark nights they go off into the forest and get up to no good. Nobody trusts them in Deepling so I'm not at all surprised to see them turning up here like bad barter taking the side of those wretched tunnellers. They're almost as bad as they are!"

"Yes, you're right, they were in the inn at Deepling last night—I saw them with my own eyes! They were whispering and plotting with those tunnellers. They are probably the ones who put them up to it—and I've heard the old landlord, Masterwort, say they've been nothing but trouble since that cursed magic touched them!"

"What utter nonsense!" Ustant exploded. "We are Marcher-born and pledged to protect the King's peace. How dare you suggest such a thing! It was my house that was burned to the ground by that mob last night!"

"More lies," sneered a small, sharp-faced tallow-maker. "You probably set fire to it yourself so that you could blame the honest folk. That's what comes from consorting with those thieving tunnellers and running with a pack of wolves. We want none of your kind in here: it's unnatural, that's what it is!"

Magadas snarled and turned threateningly on the tallow-maker. Ustant's face darkened with anger and he raised his sword to strike the man down. "Wolves! The Border Runners are not wolves!"

Berioss gripped his arm and stopped him. "There will be no shedding of blood, it will only confirm the vile lies they have been told. Let me try and make them see how wrong they are."

He lowered his sword and faced the crowded room, watching their hardened, hostile faces for a moment before he demanded, "Which of you are prepared to stand before your King in Candlebane Hall and say that you broke the pledge he made to Lord Willow's people at the Battle of the Rising? Have you forgotten so quickly how they were given the freedom to wander the length and breadth of Elundium in return for their service to the King? Have you forgotten how he promised that they could freely ask for food and shelter in return for gardening the wilderness, keeping it back and mowing the Greenways? I am ashamed that after all King Thane has done for you, how he destroyed Krulshards' darkness, that you disgrace him so easily and break all his pledges!"

The crowd shuffled uncomfortably and none would look up and hold the old Marcher's eye until somebody muttered, "It's all right for you, you're a Marcher, the King makes bold promises but it's us who have to pay for them and we're sick of it!"

"And another thing—what about those rumours about the Nightbeasts? We've heard they're roaming through the forest again. Who's going to look after us now that the Wayhouses have been turned into inns? Who's going to look after us now that the Marchers and Gallopers have been disbanded? All this gardening that those tunnellers insist on doing will only make it easier for the Nightbeasts to get at us!"

"Nightbeasts? That's ridiculous . . . " Ustant began.

"If it's food you want then take it—take anything you want and get out!" Caskplenty stuttered from where he still knelt nursing the scratches and gouges at his throat.

Berioss sighed and shook his head: it obviously wouldn't matter what he said—the people of Larach were as set against the tunnellers as the people of Deepling. "Go through to the kitchens but take only what you need for the road—and be quick; nobody will harm you," he advised Oaktangle.

Berioss stood for a moment on the threshold, holding the mob at bay with the point of his sword after the others had hurried away into the night surrounded by the Border Runners.

"Your King will hear about this—you have my

word on it!" he shouted at them angrily, aware that
the mob were beginning to shuffle closer as they
grew bolder.

"He's on his own now those mangy dogs have
gone. Go on somebody, make a grab for him, stop
him escaping!" urged Thatcher.

Berioss retreated quickly, slamming the door in
their faces as they surged towards him. He turned and
ran as fast as he could after the others, behind him he
heard the crowded room erupt into an uproar. The
door was thrown open violently and light streamed
out across the Greenway, filling it with a muddle of
lengthening shadows as the mob chased after him,
shouting and cursing, demanding his head for daring
to defend the tunnellers. Gradually they slowed and
hesitated, crowding together on the edge of the light,
shaking their fists and calling half-heartedly for lamps,
afraid to follow him into the darkness.

Berioss stopped, his lungs burning, his heart pounding in his chest. He leaned heavily on his sword, gulp-
ing in the cold, night air. He took a moment to catch
his breath before shouting back, "Come on, what are
you afraid of—Nightbeasts in the dark?"

A stone whistled past his head, followed by
another and another, making him raise his arm to
defend himself and hurry away to get out of range.
"You're not so brave now, are you?" he shouted in
disgust. Then he paused, wondering which way the
others had gone. He wasn't afraid of the dark but he
was blind and as helpless as any other man in it.

A cold nose brushed against his hand and he heard
a soft growl of welcome.

"Magadas, is that you?" he whispered, crouching
down and feeling for the familiar bulk of the dog in
the darkness. Magadas barked and rubbed against
him, gripping the edge of his sleeve with his teeth and
leading him in amongst the trees that grew along the
Greenway's edge. "Not so fast, I can't see a hand in

front of my face!" Berioss cried as the stars were blotted out by the canopy of branches overhead and the leaf mould on the forest floor deadened his footsteps.

For what seemed like an age he scrambled, puffing and blowing over the hidden tree-roots, colliding with unseen branches, as they forced a path through the thorny undergrowth. The moon rode clear of the wooded hill-tops, casting fingers of eerie, silvery light amongst the trees, owls hooted and nightjars sang in the branches above his head. A herd of grazing deer, startled by the blundering noises he made as he ploughed through the undergrowth, scattered from beneath his nose making him cry out as their silent, leaping forms vanished between the ancient oaks.

"Magadas, I must stop now, I'm so out of breath," he gasped, stumbling exhaustedly to his knees in the centre of a steep, mossy clearing. The huge dog of war tugged and shook at his sleeve, but Berioss lay where he had fallen, his chest heaving, the sound of his heart thundering in his ears. The stars that spangled the sky above him seemed to spin and blur dizzily together. Magadas barked furiously at him, licking his face and pulling at his collar. Slowly Berioss climbed onto his knees, using his sword for support, and struggled to his feet. "All right, all right, I'm doing the best I can," he muttered testily as the dog lolloped easily away across the clearing and disappeared between two jagged rocks.

Berioss took a moment to recover his breath. He hadn't reckoned on all this running about when he had insisted they escort the tunnellers back to the Rising: it was testing his creaky old bones to the limit, but he was far too proud to turn back now. He wasn't about to admit defeat: it was bad enough to be the one left straggling so far behind, but he would catch up.

He gazed up at the sparkling canopy of stars as he climbed up the slope to the edge of the clearing where the dog had disappeared. "Beautiful! It's so beautiful,"

he murmured before suddenly crying out as he lost his
footing and had to clutch at one of the jagged rocks to
stop himself from falling. The ground beyond the
clearing dropped away so sharply he was almost level
with the swaying tops of the tall pine trees that grew
amongst the litter of misshapen, weathered rocks and
spindly rowan trees on the steep slope. "That will
teach me to pay more attention to where I'm going!"
he cursed as the loose stones he had dislodged echoed
and clattered into the valley below. He realized he
was standing upon a high ridge, the moonlight illuminated the undulating canopy of the forest below him,
stretching into the distance. Looking back he could
see the lights of Larach in the valley, mere pinpoints
riding in a vast mantle of darkness. He smiled and
wiped the back of his hand across his sweating brow.
He had travelled a lot further that he had imagined,
running and scrambling along at Magadas's side.

He moved tentatively forward between the two
jagged rocks, prodding the steep slope with the point
of his rusty sword as he searched for a way down.
Below him to his left he heard the dog growl softly and
for a moment he thought he could see a dark shape
amongst the rocks, then Magadas looked up and his
eyes reflected in the moonlight before he barked and
ran swiftly up to where Berioss stood, revealing the
narrow, twisting path that he was to follow.

Slipping and sliding, clutching at the rough sur-
faces of the huge boulders that lined the winding
track, he descended, trying to keep Magadas in sight.
He stirred up a small avalanche on the way down and
caught momentary glimpses of silver moonlight on a
river that meandered through the denser trees in the
valley's bottom. He was sure he could see the flickering light of a camp fire in the trees beside it.
Gradually the steep, treacherous scree began to flat-
ten out and the track became easier to follow with
soft, springy moss and wild grasses growing beneath

his feet. The tall, whispering pines and rowan trees gave way to groves of silent oaks and elms. It was darker between the trees but the path was lined by deep banks of small flowers that seemed to shimmer with an almost magical, white light and the sweet, heady scent of nightflowers filled the air.

Berioss yawned, his eyes felt heavy and his footsteps began to wander, making him stumble sleepily. "Nightflowers? Why are there so many nightflowers?" he mumbled, resting wearily against the gnarled trunk of an ancient oak, barely aware of Oaktangle and the others as they gently grasped his arms and led him into the clearing beside the river and sat him down on a moss-covered stone at the fireside. The sweet scent of the nightflowers was receding and his head was beginning to clear. He could hear the soft, musical voices of the tunnellers talking around him, and Ustant grinning at him from across the dancing flames of the fire. Dribbles of grease from the roast leg of a forest fowl were trickling down his chin as he devoured it eagerly.

"I was wondering if you were going to take all night to catch up! We thought you may have thrown your lot in with the villagers in Larach!" Ustant laughed as Sloeberry offered him a bowl of food and a small earthenware cup of wortle wine.

Berioss scowled and shook himself fully awake as he took the bowl and cup. "You should have set a watch instead of lolling there by the fire. Call yourself a Marcher! Anybody could have crept up on you!"

"But there is no need," Oaktangle explained, sitting down beside him. "Wherever we stop and rest on our journeys we plant nightflower seeds: they have a great virtue against evil and the Border Runners were among the trees keeping a watch for you."

"Nightflowers? Yes, I was wondering why there were so many beside the track. It never occurred to me that anybody had planted them there," Berioss murmured, glancing at the small patches of shimmering light from the flowers planted amongst the trees around the clearing. "But why did you do that? There's nothing in Elundium for you to be afraid of—well, there wasn't until that Chancellor's boy stirred up everybody's hatred against you and I'm not sure the nightflowers can stop them."

Oaktangle laughed softly and spread his hands. "There are so many creatures in the forest that care little that we have the right to wander as we please—nightboars and wolves are but two who would prey on us while we sleep if we give them the chance. But the nightflowers give off a bitter, acid scent and their sharp thorns grow rapidly at their approach and tear and lacerate their skin, driving them off. Lord Willow ordered us to harvest the seeds from the flowers as they grow on the causeway of the Rising from the very spot where Queen Elionbel hurled the precious seeds Lord Pinchface had given her into Arbel's face, blinding him momentarily during the last battle against the darkness."

"I think you are going to need a lot more than nightflowers to protect you in the future, a lot more," he warned, sipping thoughtfully at the dry, fragrant wine that had the taste of bilberries and wild flowers in it. "This is an unusual taste, you didn't take it from the Wayhouse at Larach did you?" he asked.

"No, of course not," Sloeberry laughed, filling his cup from a large earthenware bottle slung across her shoulders. "We have used this clearing many times on our journeys through the great forest of Meremire. You mustn't forget we harvest as well as garden when we travel and we make preserves and liquors from the berries and fruits we find, ales from the wild hops and wines from the ripening vines. This one is from the wortle vine which grows in profusion along the river banks."

"And you had some hidden here?"

Sloeberry smiled and was about to answer but Ustant laughed, "They have a whole larder of delicacies hidden in a cool cave they've dug in the river bank. Try some of that wild saffron jelly on the meat: it's delicious, far better than anything I've ever tasted from Masterwort's kitchen. Now eat up before the food is spoilt—we can talk later over the embers of the fire."

Berioss smiled at the waiting group of tunnellers, carefully licking the last of the sticky, saffron pickle that had trickled down between his fingers as he ate. "Yes, it's good, very good—no, it's delicious." But his smile turned into a questioning frown as he wiped his fingers clean on the long hem of his cloak, sipped from the earthenware cup and asked the tunnellers what they thought would have happened to them in the inn at Larach if the Border Runners hadn't led them to the door in the nick of time. "Next time it won't be so easy, you know, people will be ready, they'll be expecting you, and you won't have that element of surprise."

"I'm surprised you vanished last night without so much as a goodbye, or telling us which Greenway you were taking to travel to the Rising. We could have been wandering around for daylights looking for you if the Border Runners hadn't come to our aid," Ustant added in a serious voice.

"I'm sorry, we never meant to cause you so much trouble," Oaktangle answered in a small, apologetic voice as he stared down into the shrinking flames of the fire. The other tunnellers looked away, guiltily.

"You thought we were too old to be of much use, didn't you? With our blunt and rusty swords, stumbling along blindly behind you in the dark, shivering and soaked to the skin and far too tired to stay awake to finish the food you had cooked for us. It's not difficult to see that you think we are a couple of worn-out, old Marchers best left behind where we won't slow you down, but you're not strong or big enough to defend yourselves are you?" Berioss observed.

"No, it's not like that at all!" Mistletoe cried, jumping up, his face flushed. "You were a little slow and needed a lot of help to travel in the dark but we would never have thought you were too old to help us. You defended us so bravely in the inn, and without your help Sloeberry's head would never have got better, and we would never have escaped from the village."

"Mistletoe, be quiet and sit down!" Oaktangle interrupted, crossly. "We never meant to offend you by leaving the hut as the grey hours were breaking," he apologized, "but the burden of our innocence must rest squarely on our shoulders; it is us the people of Elundium have come to hate, and we felt it was unfair to make you travel as our protectors all the way to the Rising. You had already done enough."

Berioss rose to his feet and laughed as he grasped the little tunneller in his strong hands and lifted him up. "But we are Marcher-born and pledged to serve the King. It is our duty to protect you, to see that justice is done."

"But it goes deeper than that, far deeper," Ustant murmured, staring out into the silent trees that ringed the clearing. Berioss put Oaktangle down carefully and turned to look quizzically at his friend.

"Don't you sometimes feel a part of it?" Ustant asked, sweeping his hand vaguely out across the dark landscape woven with the silvery fabric of night.

"What?" Berioss frowned, taking a step towards him.

"I don't know if I can explain, but it was something Sloeberry said last night in the inn: it brought back those memories I had while I was beguiled by Nevian's magic. It wasn't all shivering in winter blizzards or standing parched and thirsty on the Greenway's edge—I do remember the beauty of combing my fingers through the wind, of tasting the rain, of listening to the first blackbird of the new morning. We're not just protecting these tunnellers, we're protecting the beauty and the wildness of Elundium, which everyone seems to have lost. We're protecting the freedom to touch that beauty and to be a part of it."

"That's a bit deep for me," Berioss answered slowly, "but I'll go along with the bit about protecting their freedom, and I'll go one better by suggesting we teach them to protect themselves before this hatred gets out of hand and people start trying to kill them."

"You mean you'll teach us to use swords and spears—real ones just like the ones in the elders' stories?" Mistletoe cried in excitement.

"But we are gardeners, people of peace, we don't want to fight. The only time we lift a blade is to prune or mow," Oaktangle protested making Mistletoe and two of the other younger tunnellers sit down.

"You would turn Lord Willow's people into warriors!" Ustant laughed. "But they are far too small, they would be swept aside, killed at the first sword thrust. If we armed them it would certainly provoke the villagers to attack, remember how uneasy everybody becomes if we carry our swords about the village, and they know us to be Marchers."

"No, I am set against it. We will not bear arms against the people of Elundium!" Oaktangle cried.

"Not even if they attack you first?" Berioss questioned. "Surely you have the right to defend yourselves? What will happen when this canker of hatred has spread far and wide across Elundium and you have done nothing when your people are stoned and driven out from wherever they travel? Will your people starve to death walled up within the Rising or creep with stealth in the darkness, scavenging for food, afraid to show their faces?"

Oaktangle shrugged and walked away from the circle of firelight with tears in his eyes, seeing the truth in what the old Marcher said.

Ustant followed him and touched him lightly on the shoulder. "You know Berioss is right, don't you? You know you can't run away and hide from this hatred."

"No!" cried Oaktangle fiercely, shaking off the Marcher's hand and making the other tunnellers turn anxiously to stare at him. "You don't seem to understand, we cannot fight, we were given the freedom to wander, to garden and nurture the beauty and wildness of this land, not to raise arms against its people at the first stone that is cast in anger against us. I will not have us betray the King's trust! I will report everything that has happened to Lord Willow, and he will decide what must be done. We will not talk of it again while we travel, but to avoid any further trouble I think it is best if we keep away from the larger villages and the busiest Greenways as much as we can. The journey shouldn't take us longer than six daylights."

"That's all very well, but what will you do when the food you took from the inn at Larach is gone? You certainly didn't take enough to last all the way to the Rising and I know you are gardeners, not hunters. What are we going to eat?"

"In summer, the roots and berries are plentiful: I'm sure there will still be more than enough to feed us on the way," Oaktangle answered, but Ustant sensed the doubt in his voice.

"If we are forced to stop at another Wayhouse Berioss and I on our own would be no match for an angry mob," Ustant warned.

Sloeberry tilted her head, catching the faint, faraway sound of a border runner hunting in the dark. "I'm sure the Border Runners will protect us on the journey home."

Berioss followed the faint sound of barking on the wind, letting his eyes climb the steep, moonlit slopes of the valley that hemmed in their refuge by the river. "I'm sure they will, if they're close by, but just because they helped us find you today doesn't mean they'll be near tomorrowlight. Remember, they are wild and free and serve no one, not even the King."

Oaktangle knew Berioss was speaking the truth and he left the circle of firelight and walked down to the river to stand, staring through the moonlit ripples into its swirling depths. He felt helpless: what had they done to make the people of Elundium hate them so much? Even the owls had flown away, seeking truth rather than believe that they had been wrongly set upon in the Wayhouse of Deepling. What if the King also blamed them out of hand? What if he banished them in his anger? What if he decided that they had abused his offer of freedom and denied them the sunlight, what if he set his Marchers and Gallopers to drive them back into the darkness of Manterns Mountain? What if nobody but those two old Marchers believed their side of it?

Slowly Oaktangle sank down onto his knees in the dew-wet grass of the bank, his head in his hands as fresh tears of despair brimmed in his eyes, blurring and softening the liquid reflections of the moon and stars upon the water. "What can I do? I feel so helpless, so alone! Tell me what to do!"

The silvery ripples closest to the bank began to change, breaking into small, swirling eddies that spread out in widening circles, smoothing the surface of the water into a still, burnished mirror of light. Silent shoals of swordtails and rainbow fish were drawn by the light, wheeling and turning, diving through the tangled weeds and rising to the surface to catch and reflect the brilliance of the moonlight on their phosphorescent scales. Slowly a shimmering, swaying image of a man was created, an old man, old beyond the time of the Granite Kings and shrouded in the melting colours of the rainbow that eddied and flowed with the current of the river. He seemed to reach out a hand towards the tunneller and

Oaktangle gasped in wonder as he caught sight of the beautiful colours just beneath the surface. He leaned closer to the mirrored stillness of water and reached out with trembling fingers to touch the hand that was moving towards him. Somewhere in the darkness a voice carried on the wind seemed to whisper his name, seemed to counsel him to trust in true friends and listen to their wisdom.

The moonshadow cast by his hand suddenly passed across the shoals of fish disturbing them, and they scattered, darting away amongst the weeds and rocks. The image dissolved and moments later the shoals reappeared, gliding and swimming effortlessly through the watery shafts of moonlight, stirring up new shimmering, images that appeared and disappeared so quickly that he hardly had the time to see what they were. A cloud drifted silently across the moon, shrouding its light, and the fish began to jump, chasing the insects that were hovering just above the river's surface, sending widening ripples across the dull, broken surface of the water. The magic vanished as mysteriously as it had appeared. The voice he thought he heard in the wind was gone, no more than the rub of one branch against another.

Oaktangle climbed shakily to his feet and stared down into the murky depths of the river, trying to recapture the moment, trying to remember what he had seen. Was that ancient figure shrouded within the colours of the rainbow beneath the surface of the water really Nevian? He felt both a cold tingle of fear and a hot flush of excitement run up his spine. Had he really glimpsed the Master of Magic? But why? What could he possibly want with him? He couldn't do anything to stop the people of Elundium hating his people: he wasn't brave like Lord Willow.

Oaktangle wanted to hide in the darkest corner he could find, but the magic woven in the air around him held him prisoner. Images from the stories he had listened to as a child whilst sitting at the elders' feet in the long hall on top of the Rising on wild, winter nights flooded back. He saw again those pictures that had been so carefully painted with the tiny speck of light in the flickering darkness. He saw his people, lost and forgotten, born without names in the City of Night, slaves to Krulshards, the master of Nightbeasts. He heard the cries of their pain and torment and watched them being trampled into the dust on the ground. Suddenly a single point of light, no larger than a pin prick, blazed for a moment and sent shimmering reflections out across the water. Oaktangle gasped as the surface frothed and boiled with brilliant colours. The darkness was shattered, the cruel images of the Nightbeasts tormenting his people were snatched away by the current of the river; now sunlight dappled and danced on the ripples and he saw a reflection of himself and his friends laughing, careless and happy as they mowed the Greenways and pruned back the wildness. But a dark shadow gradually spread across the surface of the water threatening to engulf them and deny them the sunlight. It seemed to be full of sinister, malicious figures whose voices were poisonous whispers that scratched painfully at his ears. The darkness seemed to become thicker and even the stars grew dim. The point of light blazed briefly again and there, in the water, he saw the figure of Nevian wrapped in the soft colours of the rainbow.

"Trust to wise counsel and look inside yourself, Oaktangle: you will find the courage you need. But without it your people will vanish back into the shadows of night."

The figure disappeared and in its place he saw himself dressed in the strangest armour and mounted on a beautiful, grey horse with the dapples of summer shadows ghosted upon its flanks.

The moon rode clear of the clouds and silently bathed the river bank in a cold, silver light, casting his shadow out over the eddies and ripples in the swift-flowing water. Oaktangle blinked and took a hesitant step to the river's edge. "Nevian, Nevian, are you there?" he called out, crouching down and trailing his fingers in the water, scattering the shoals of swordtails and rainbow fish.

"Was that a vision of the future—tell me, please tell me!"

A noise behind him made him quickly stand up and spin round as he searched the undergrowth.

"Sloeberry, is that you?" he called out as he saw a slight figure emerge into the moonlight.

"I was getting worried," she whispered as she hurried to his side; "I thought I saw flashes of bright-coloured light down here by the river."

Oaktangle frowned and led her away from the water, drawing her closer before he asked in a whisper, "Do you believe in magic?"

"Why yes, of course I do, everybody does. We've all watched the elder paint stories in the dark; and we've all listened to the tales of the rainbow cloak; that's magic isn't it? And there are the tricks that the travelling magicians perform at the mid-winter feast, vanishing in puffs of smoke and producing singing doves from their sleeves . . . "

"No, I don't mean that sort of magic, I mean real magic . . . " Oaktangle hesitated, frightened to put into words what he had just experienced, afraid that it would make it more real, but he had to tell somebody. Gripping Sloeberry's arm he glanced back to the river and whispered fiercely, "Nevian isn't only a part of the elders' stories, he's real! I swear on my life that I saw him a moment ago. Those flashes of light were the Master of Magic appearing right there in front of me. I . . . I . . . I could have reached out and touched him—he was standing so close that the rainbow colours of his cloak floated out across the water. No, he was more underneath the water, amongst the shoals of fish and in the ripples on its surface . . . "

He paused and shook his head in confusion. "That isn't right either. He was all around me, his magic was woven into everything—the water, the wind in the trees—it trapped me so tightly that I couldn't move and he created pictures in the water, pictures that were far brighter and more terrifying than anything the elder ever drew in the firelight."

"Nevian? He appeared here? But why, do you think he has come for those two old Marchers? Or do you think . . . ?" Sloeberry fell silent, her eyes round and frightened. She had spent a dozen sleepless nights as a child worrying that the Master of Magic would come to the Rising and turn her into something unpleasant for disobeying her mother after listening to the elders' story of the Marchers who would not pledge themselves to King Thane.

Oaktangle shivered as an echo of the image he had glimpsed welled up in his mind. "I think he appeared because I called him," he uttered, wretchedly. "I would never have said a word if I had realized what would happen. I didn't mean to: I only came down to the river bank to think, to try and work out what to do after Berioss said that our people will starve and be driven into hiding if we don't learn to fight for our place in the world. I know there's a lot of truth in what he said and running away isn't going to solve anything, that's why I called out for help. But I never expected an answer like that, never!"

Controlling the sobs in his voice he told Sloeberry everything that had happened on the river bank, from the stark images of their people, slaves in the City of Night, to the joy and laughter they shared together as they wandered in the sunlight. And then he described how they went from joy to the gradual desolation and darkness that Nevian revealed to him would eventually overshadow and smother their lives unless they stood up for themselves.

"It was a warning—an omen—I know it was," he

frowned, "and I saw myself mirrored in the water clothed in bright armour and sitting upon a dapple-gray Warhorse."

"But that's ridiculous, you've never ridden a horse. None of us have, except Lord Willow," Sloeberry interrupted, glancing back into the whispering shadows of the river and silently wondering if he hadn't dreamed up the Master of Magic and woven him into his nightmare.

"I know, I know, that's why I can't understand why Nevian chose to appear to me. Surely if he's so powerful, so magical, he should have chosen someone else, somebody who could fight—a Marcher or a Galloper. He must know I hate violence, that I can't do what he wants me to!" Oaktangle cried, his voice rising in helpless frustration, his fists clenched so hard that his nails bit into the palms of his hands.

Sloeberry pressed her finger to his lips and whispered him into silence, warning him that he would wake the others. Oaktangle looked past her to the sleeping forms huddled beneath their cloaks around the dying embers of the fire; he had completely forgotten about them.

"Say nothing to the others—nothing at all," he insisted as they walked slowly back towards the fire.

"Perhaps it was a dream," she suggested softly but Oaktangle shook his head fiercely.

"No, it was no dream, it was too real, much too frighteningly real. There was even a ruined Wayhouse, a sort of enormous fortress in the background with battlements and collapsed towers, it was where we lived and it was so overgrown with creepers and ivy that I could barely see it. Dark clouds and mists kept billowing up and it seemed to be silhouetted against a shimmering lake. I know I could recognize it if I ever saw it again. I could hear the rattle of armourers' hammers and the clean swish of sharp stones honing swords and lances to a razor's edge. And there was a peculiar figure clothed in armour sitting crookedly upon a dark bay horse, someone I don't recognize at all—you were there, you were on a horse beside him, and . . . " Oaktangle's voice trailed off as the fragments of his vision became blurred and muddled together.

Sloeberry glanced anxiously at him, saw that his suntanned face looked deathly white and drained of colour in the moonlight. "Lord Willow will know what to make of Nevian's appearance," she whispered, trying to comfort him in a sisterly way. "Remember, the Master of Magic was always appearing in those stories that the elder told us from the time before the great battle of the Rising." She couldn't imagine riding a horse and sitting close to some crooked stranger, it sent shivers up her spine.

"But will he?" Oaktangle muttered bleakly as he lay down and wrapped himself in his cloak, shutting out the darkness, afraid of what impossibility he might see lurking in every shadow.


Oaktangle woke the company early the next morning before the dawn had chased the grey hours away, urging them to make haste and barely giving them time to break a crust or rake over the embers of the fire to warm themselves before he hurried away between the trees. Berioss sensed a change in the young tunneller. Something had happened in the night: the lad had become quiet and serious, with a haunted look in his eyes, as if he was trying to escape some unknown fear, but he couldn't keep pace with him long enough to draw him out. For two daylights Oaktangle kept up a punishing pace. Stumbling and exhausted the two old warriors sank down in the eventime of the third daylight, leaning against the smooth trunk of a spreading beech tree. The last of its falling leaves made a crisp, crackling carpet beneath them and they welcomed the rest.

"Tight belts make smaller bellies. We'll be nothing but walking skeletons as this rate," Ustant grumbled as he picked through the last of the meagre crumbs of food that Sloeberry had offered him.

"I know, but something is driving Oaktangle, I can see it in his eyes," Berioss muttered. "I just wish he would share his fears with us."

"It's food we need. If I had any idea where the nearest village was I would raid it on my own, I'm so hungry," Ustant cursed. He frowned and glanced up through the tracery of branches above his head, wiping the back of his hand absently across his forehead as he felt the first, irregular prickles of cold raindrops. "There's a storm brewing. Look at those black clouds boiling up: we'll be soaked to the skin if we have to spend the night here in the open. Damn it, where have those tunnellers disappeared to? They're going to ground, I suppose at the first sign of bad weather. It's all right for them, they're small enough to squeeze into any nook and cranny."

Berioss nodded gravely. The last two nights had been bitterly cold and despite sleeping as close to the dying embers of the fire as possible they had woken shivering and numb with a stiff layer of hore-frost on their cloaks. He wasn't sure they could survive many more nights outside especially if it poured with rain. "It's no good sitting here complaining, we've got to find somewhere to shelter."

He climbed wearily to his feet and moved through the trees onto higher ground, looking for a fallen tree or an overhang of rocks to crawl beneath. "Look, there's a light in that valley away to the right. I can see more between the trees. I wonder what village that is."

Ustant hurried to his side and stood on tiptoe to peer through the branches. "There must be a Wayhouse—and food!"

"It's the village of Sowerweed, we always used to call in there on our way back to the Rising, but I think it is better to avoid it this time." Oaktangle's voice directly behind them made them both turn quickly to find him and the rest of the tunnellers, their arms loaded down with long, slender saplings.

"But we need food, none of us will reach the Rising if we don't have something more substantial than crumbs or sour roots to eat. We're all exhausted, look at us!" Ustant cried, angrily.

"It's not only food we need, we'll perish for sure if we have to spend the night out in the open with this storm," Berioss warned, pointing up to the low thunder-black clouds that were rapidly darkening the last of the evening light.

"You needn't worry about keeping dry, we have been collecting these saplings to build a shelter against the storm. You are right, though, we cannot go on much further without some proper food, but I'm torn between risking entering Sowerweed or trying to travel on for another daylight. It would be easier to make up my mind if I knew if those vile lies about us have already reached this village," Oaktangle's voice echoed his indecision.

"Wait a moment, there isn't any need for you to risk going into that Wayhouse, I've just thought of a way of getting us the food we need," Ustant laughed. "It's so easy. Berioss and I will go into the inn: we're not tunnellers, just two old Marchers travelling home and stopping to barter for our needs. Nobody here is going to recognize us. Mistletoe or Damask could lead us down to the village and then hide in the trees and wait to show us the way back."

"It's a good idea, but I haven't got much on me to use for barter and a King's promise won't get us much these days. I'm afraid we don't carry much."

Berioss frowned and turned out the meagre contents of his pockets as Ustant rummaged through his leather jerkin and breeches but all they had upon them were two worn-out sparks and a handful of broken copper threads, dulled and stained with age. Oaktangle and the others piled everything they had into their broad palms but Ustant shook his head as he carefully picked through their possessions.

"No, I'm afraid these won't do at all. They are beautiful, especially these woven copper bracelets and the tiny silver necklaces, but they are far too small to belong to the people of Elundium. Even the sparks are crafted to fit between your tiny fingers. If we try to barter with them I'm sure somebody in the inn will smell a rat, especially if the rumours of what has happened in Deepling *have* travelled this far."

"There's got to be something we could barter," Berioss muttered to himself, pacing backwards and forwards between the trees, trying to ignore the steady patter of the rain on his cheeks. As he turned and pulled up his collar, the finely engraved finger-bowl hanging by a heavy silver chain from his belt rattled against the hilt of his sword. Pausing, he closed his fingers around the cup and unfastened it, reluctantly holding it up to the light. It was the one thing he treasured above all else and the memories of that feast in the dancing shadows of Candlebane Hall came flooding back. He remembered how he had waited nervously amongst the ranks of Marchers to kneel before King Thane and how he had received it for his valour in the Battle of the Rising, how on each feast night he lifted it to his lips and how possessing it separated him from ordinary men.

"No, there is nothing in the whole of that village worthy of bartering for the King's cup!" Ustant cried, gripping his own finger bowl protectively. "I would rather starve than part with mine!"

Berioss merely laughed but he couldn't disguise the regret he felt as he tossed the small, beautiful cup into the air. "You have forgotten too easily, Ustant, how need once drove our King far further than a simple act of barter. Everything he possessed lay in ruins before he was able to destroy the darkness. Anyway, we can always barter them back in better daylights."

Ustant sighed and nodded before he followed in Mistletoe's footsteps as he led them down through the trees. Berioss glanced back and frowned as he saw the tunnellers hard at work. "I can't imagine what sort of shelter they're going to build out of sticks, it will never keep out the rain no matter how tightly they weave them together!"


"Act naturally!" Berioss hissed as he followed Ustant in over the threshold of the Wayhouse at Sowerweed. "Whatever you do you must not tell anybody we're from the village of Deepling. If they ask then tell them we're travelling from Underfall to the Granite City and we've lost our way."

The noisy hum of conversation fell silent as they stepped into the low-beamed inn. Chairs and benches scraped on the stone-flagged floor as the inhabitants of Sowerweed turned to stare at the newcomers. It had become so quiet in the hazy, smoky room that Ustant could hear the rattle of the rain on the windows and the hiss and crackle of the flames in the hearth. Berioss laughed loudly, rubbing his hands together, anxious to break the uncomfortable silence.

"Is there food and drink here for weary travellers?"

Berioss sensed a growing hostility in the atmosphere of the inn and shuffled his feet uncomfortably in the lengthening silence.

"Perhaps if we find somewhere to sit down, out of the way in a corner, everybody will begin to ignore us," Ustant murmured, searching for an empty table.

"Travellers? What kind of travellers?" somebody in the crowded room questioned loudly.

"I would have thought these were dangerous times to be out wandering far from home, especially now it's getting dark," another voice added and a murmur of agreement spread through the smoky room.

"I don't recognize your faces and I know everybody who lives around here. Where are you from?" demanded another drinker, standing up to confront Ustant.

The landlord, alerted by the disturbance, armed his serving boys with kitchen knives and set them to guard the kitchen doors before bursting out into the crowded room. "All right, all right, what's all this commotion?" he grumbled, stopping abruptly in front of the two old, dishevelled Marchers and eyeing them up and down suspiciously. "What business brings you into Sowerweed? Strangers are not welcome here!" he demanded, his hands firmly planted on his hips.

"Sowerweed? I wouldn't have thought we could have wandered this far from our road, but it's only food and ale we trouble you for," Berioss answered, thinking quickly as he spoke and spreading his empty hands in a gesture of friendliness. "We are journeying from Underfall to the Granite City, but I'm afraid we argued over the shortest route and must have taken a track into the forest instead of following the Greenway. We had just made our camp for the night in a clearing in the trees when we spotted the lights of your village . . ."

A roar of laughter erupted in the room. "Marchers losing their way? Now I've heard everything!" cackled a wheelwright sitting close to the fire.

"Marchers from Underfall you say?" the landlord questioned, his eyes still sharp and suspicious. The rest of the crowd were leaning forward waiting to hang on every word that Ustant and Berioss might utter.

"Yes, that's right, and we've been wandering around in circles, lost in Meremire Forest for more daylights than I care to remember. I dread to think what punishment awaits us for being so late with the messages we're carrying for Thunderstone, the Keeper of Underfall."

The lies were running easily from the tip of Ustant's tongue but a telltale trickle of sweat escaped from his matted hair and ran down the side of his grimy temple.

"A company of Nighthorses passed this way a few daylights ago heading for Granite City. You're nothing to do with them are you?"

Berioss was about to nod his head when somebody cried, "I'll bet it's a message about those wretched tunnellers you're carrying."

"You should know better than to pry into the King's business but what's the matter with the tunnellers? Has there been an accident?" Berioss asked, his forehead creased into a feigned frown of ignorance.

"So you've not heard, news hasn't reached Underfall yet? That surprises me," the landlord exclaimed, the suspicion fading but not entirely vanishing.

"They can't have anything to do with it. These Marchers can't be those two burly villains who have thrown their lot in with that gang of rampaging tunnellers, the ones who are burning every village in their path. These ones are much too old and too small from the descriptions we've heard," a wizened charcoal burner insisted, burying his face in a frothy head of ale.

"What on earth has been happening? Tell us!" Ustant cried.

"It all started over Deepling way only a few daylights ago," the landlord answered. "One of those tunnellers, a particularly large and ugly one, picked on young Snatch, Chancellor Ironpurse's boy. By all accounts he beat him half to death and the rest of those revolting troublemakers smashed up the Wayhouse and burnt down half the village before escaping into the forest."

"There are two enormous brutes with them, hairy giants with arms as thick as tree trunks. Some say they're Marchers or Gallopers turned bad but I think they're from the darkness, that they're related to Nightbeasts: after all they came from the same place as those tunnellers didn't they! They say there is a pack of savage dogs running with them. They're terrorizing the villages around Larach and they've killed a dozen sheep, bit their heads clean off with their powerful jaws, scattered their carcasses all over the Greenway! That's why everybody was worried when you walked in here a few moments ago. That's how their attacks are always supposed to start, then the whole mob of them burst in with their dogs. But, as I said, it can't be you two can it!" the charcoal burner added dismissively, smacking his lips together.

"Well, I would never have believed the tunnellers could turn bad if I hadn't heard it with my own ears. They're always so polite and peaceful whenever they call at the fortress at Underfall. It just goes to show doesn't it!" Berioss exclaimed in mock surprise.

"You don't know the half of it," muttered a thick-set blacksmith into his ale. "Nobody's safe in their beds any more. I've heard tell they suddenly appear in the dead of night, howling and screaming enough to terrorize a village, tearing up the Greenway and trampling everything to ruin, smashing windows and setting honest folks' homes on fire!"

"And they steal everything they can lay their thieving hands on. It's high time the King, or somebody, did something about it!" demanded the landlord, beckoning two of his serving boys to attend to the Marchers' needs.

"You're just not safe anywhere now!" a merchant protested, mopping at his glistening forehead. "Those Nightbeasts in the forest aren't just a rumour either. I was set upon by three of them, monstrous creatures. It was about six leagues west of here. They swarmed down out of the trees and attacked me, knocking me to the ground and trampling all over me. My mules were so frightened they fled into the forest taking everything I own with them. I'm ruined, but at least I escaped with my life!"

Voices rose in murmured sympathy as the merchant paused for breath. They were indeed living on the edge of dark times where nobody was safe any more.

Berioss used the moment to touch the landlord's

arm lightly and ask him if they could barter for enough food for the journey to the Granite City. "It would save us having to stop along the road and then we could carry the news of these disasters faster to the King."

"Fat lot of good that will do!" grumbled a journeyman from the far side of the room. "We're a long way from the Granite City out here in the wilds of Meremire Forest. Much too far away for the King to be bothered with the likes of us. He won't do anything to help us, you see."

Berioss's face darkened with anger to hear the King's name spoken of with disgust. He began to turn towards the journeyman but he felt Ustant's restraining hand upon his arm and saw a warning look in his eyes.

"That's right!" the merchant answered hotly. "Why, only yesterlight I was talking to a fellow traveller on the road who has a relative who serves in Candlebane Hall and he says the King laughed out loud when news reached him of the Nightbeasts re-awakening. He said it was impossible, that he had destroyed them all in the Battle of the Rising, but he's wrong! I know he is because I've seen them with my own eyes and . . . and . . . " he paused for breath as the crowd waited in horrified silence as he dabbed at the beads of perspiration on his forehead and lowered his voice. "Those tunnellers are the King's favourites. They can do no wrong in his eyes. He thinks their ugly uprising is all stuff and nonsense and he doesn't care what they do to us. I'm telling you, he won't have a word said against them."

"What we need is a proper King," the landlord muttered. "Someone like King Holbian who was as hard as granite and ruled with an iron fist. He would never have taken any nonsense from that ugly rabble!"

"If the Chancellors still governed us we would have protection, we wouldn't have to put up with those tunnellers. The Chancellors would have driven them back into their dark beginnings in no time at all!" cried the wheelwright.

"Chancellors or no Chancellors we'll protect ourselves! Those ugly vermin will get what they deserve if they try to steal food from Sowerweed, we'll kill them if they try anything here!"

An enormous Ironmaster crashed his fist down so hard on the tale where he was sitting that the earthenware ale jug leapt into the air.

"I think we had better get out of here before they turn on us!" whispered Berioss from behind his hand.

Ustant acted quickly, raising his hands to quieten the mob. "You seem to have forgotten, all of you, that the King pledged Lord Willow's people the freedom to wander unmolested throughout the length and breadth of Elundium. I'm not so sure he will take too kindly to you taking the law into your own hands and breaking his pledges."

Mutters and grumbles of dissent began to rise from the crowd.

"I would warn you that as King's men and Marchers pledged to serve him we must advise you to do nothing until the King has passed judgement on these wayward tunnellers. He will not be pleased if you take matters into your own hands!" Berioss warned them gravely, letting his cloak fall open to reveal his sword.

"We will travel with all haste to inform the King of the tunnellers' uprising and we will tell him that the good people of Sowerweed await his urgent judgement whether you provide us with food for the journey or not," Ustant added, taking a step towards the door, fearing that the crowd might try to overpower them and stop them reporting what they intended to do to the tunnellers.

"Wait! You're right, these troubles should be reported in the proper manner. We'd be fools to take the law into our own hands as we threatened!" The landlord motioned to the crowd, demanding their

silence as he stopped the two Marchers from leaving.
Smiling and rubbing his hands together he beckoned
them back into the room, all too aware of what might
happen if he were to be summoned to Candlebane
Hall accused of breaking the King's pledge.

"Of course, we all love the King. Why don't you
spend the rest of the night here, you'll be safe and
secure in your beds: we wouldn't want you to be able
to complain about our hospitality, now would we?"

Ustant shook his head as he turned down the landlord's kind offer, insisting that they feared nothing in
the dark and had already made camp.

"Very well, servers, bring two sacks of food for
these good Marchers to eat upon their journey," he
cried, snapping his fingers at the gaggle of serving
boys crowding the kitchen doorway.

"You will, of course, leave barter for the food: it is
the custom," the landlord said as they shouldered the
heavy sacks.

"Our barter is in our camp, but we will leave you
these," Berioss passed over the two tiny, silver finger-
cups to the inn keeper.

The landlord barely gave them a second glance as
he tossed them into his barter pouch. "It isn't much
for all that food. May your journey be safe and free
from Nightbeasts," he added as they hurried away
into the rainy darkness.

"You're a fat fool to waste good food on the likes
of them, landlord. You should have let us slit their
throats while we had the chance. Things are bad
enough without those two old Marchers meddling in
our business. They're sure to report everything we've
said to the King." The Ironmaster snarled as the landlord slammed and bolted the door of the inn.

"It would have taken braver men than you lot to
kill those Marchers."

The landlord frowned, cut short by a savage laugh
from the Ironmaster. "No, you are wrong: it would

have been easy, they were only puffed up with piss and wind. We could have killed them and tossed their bodies into the pit. Nobody would even have known . . ."

"Oh, that would have been very sensible, wouldn't it!" the innkeeper cried, throwing his hands up in exasperation. "And tell me, what do you think would have happened when they didn't deliver their messages from Thunderstone? He wouldn't have just dismissed their loss would he? No, he would have been sure to send a squadron of Gallopers here nosing around, prying into our business as he looked for them. And you can bet all of next sun's barter somebody would have seen them coming into the village, even if nobody here gave you away. Then there are those wretched Battle Owls, they befriend the Marchers and Gallopers don't they, and nothing ever escapes their blinkless eyes. I'll bet one of them, or one of those Warhorses who roam through the forest saw them enter this inn and they would tell Thunderstone exactly where they were. My kitchen boys know the signals, they didn't take anything of value. Sending them off with two sacks of kitchen scraps means we're well rid of them, and they'll be leagues away from here by this time tomorrowlight. We can carry on as we've planned. If those tunnellers dare to show their ugly faces around here we'll be ready!"

# 5

# A Harsh Judgement at the Rising

"THIS WAY, MIND YOUR HEADS, THE BRANCHES are very low at first," Mistletoe warned over the dull, persistent roar of the rain amongst the trees. He reached out to grasp at their hands and guide them as they tumbled blindly off the Greenway following his voice into the dense undergrowth.

"I was getting really worried, I heard angry voices coming from inside the inn. You seemed to be in there for ages and I didn't know whether to wait a little longer or go and fetch the others. I decided to count to twenty—I'd reached fifteen when you suddenly reappeared in the lighted doorway," Mistletoe whispered with relief.

"Thank goodness you had the sense to stay put! We would have been in a fine old pickle if you or the others had burst in through that door. The crowd in there were in a murderous mood," Ustant replied seriously, blinking and wiping at the trickles of rainwater running down into his eyes. "Damn the weather!" he muttered, pulling the collar of his cloak tighter as they climbed up through the trees and away from the village.

"Surely it can't be much further," Berioss cursed a while later, his breath coming in short gasps as his boots slipped continuously on the wet leaves and earth. The heavy sack of food that was slung across his shoulders seemed to snag on every thorn and bramble in the undergrowth. The rain was getting heavier and had begun to soak through his clothes, making him shiver.

A brief glimpse of firelight through the trees ahead of them told him that they had reached the camp.

"One thing at a time!" he cried, as the tunnellers clustered around, asking a dozen questions. "Wait until we are out of the rain. I thought I saw firelight as we approached; where's the shelter you said you would build while we were gone?" Ustant fished his damp sparks out of his pocket and tried to crackle it alight between his fingers without any success.

"The shelter's right in front of you!" Damask laughed. "And the fire's set back a little inside the entrance so the rain will not put it out and unwelcome visitors won't see it in the dark. Here, take a look!" She bent down to pull a lit branch out of the fire and held it up. It hissed and spluttered as the flames illuminated the clearing.

"Of all the wonders! I'd probably have walked right into it without realizing what it was in broad daylight! It looks like a small hillock!" Berioss exclaimed, handing the sack of food to one of the tunnellers who staggered slightly beneath its weight while he bent down to examine the shelter.

"I wouldn't have believed it possible to build anything like this so quickly," Ustant murmured in admiration.

The long saplings had been notched and formed into a curving shelter, the thinner ones woven tightly through them to make the shape of an upside-down boat that was open at the front. The thicker ends of the saplings at the back and sides had been sharpened and driven into a shallow horseshoe trench that had been filled in with loose earth and stones to hold it into place. The woven lattice-work of the shelter had then been smeared with moss and earth to seal it before it had been covered with layers of turf and moss that slightly overlapped one another and were held in place by small, sharpened twigs.

Ustant dropped to his knees to crawl inside the shelter and squeeze himself into a place the others had left for him. He grinned across at Berioss who held his hands out towards the fire. There was something ingenious about these tunnellers, something so wonderful and inventive; they would have completely missed it if they hadn't taken this journey to protect them. Berioss smiled and nodded; he understood exactly what was going on in Ustant's mind. Together, somehow, they had to find a way to make the tunnellers fight and defend themselves. They had brought so much beauty into the wildness of Elundium it would be a tragedy if their uniqueness were lost, like the fairies and the goblins, into the mists of legends, trampled into the ground for no other reason other than that they were different.

"What did you find out? Tell us, have those terrible rumours about us reached Sowerweed?" Oaktangle asked, breaking into his thoughts.

The old Marcher blinked and looked around the ring of eager, waiting faces. "It's worse—far worse than we'd imagined," Ustant answered seriously. "Those stories of what happened in Deepling and the village of Larach seem to have taken on a life of their own and they are growing out of all proportion to the truth."

"But it's lies—all lies! We've never done any of those terrible things!" Oaktangle cried in despair as Berioss finished telling them everything they had learned in the inn.

"And that's not all . . . " Sloeberry interrupted from where she was kneeling, tending to the fire with Damask's help in readiness to prepare them a meal from the food. "Those people have cheated you. There's nothing but gnawed bones, stale crusts and mouldy rinds in these food sacks."

"What!" Berioss cried, trying to leap to his feet only to bang his head on the low roof of the shelter and dislodge a fine trickle of stones and cold, damp earth. He sat down heavily and his hands knuckled into fists of anger. Then he unsheathed his sword and began to crawl towards the entrance of the shelter.

"I did not barter that cup lightly, Ustant; I swear upon my life that the people of Sowerweed will pay in full what they owe us! Are you coming with me? They won't treat us like fools a second time."

Ustant prepared to follow but Sloeberry barred their way; she had heard Mistletoe's description of the angry crowd at the inn and didn't want to risk them going back. "I didn't say we couldn't turn their leavings into something wholesome did I?"

"If you go and fight who will protect us and teach us to bear arms? What chance do you have, two against so many? Those villagers will overwhelm you and kill you!" Oaktangle called out.

Both Marchers hesitated and turned awkwardly back to face the crowded shelter. "But I thought you said you would never take up arms?"

Oaktangle shrugged and tried to avoid Berioss's gaze, afraid of revealing the agony of conflict he had suffered since witnessing the vision of the Master of Magic on the riverbank. "If Lord Willow decrees that we must defend ourselves against these lies and ugly rumours then I will have no other choice but to fight," he answered flatly, looking away.

Berioss laughed, a deep gravelly sound, and gripped the tunneller's hands. There seemed to be magic dancing in the flickering, smoky firelight and he was glad in his heart that Oaktangle was beginning to see some sense at last, although how and with what he was to transform these people into warriors he could not begin to imagine.

"Where would we get arms and armour forged and fashioned to fit such small stature?" he murmured to himself.

"What was that? What did you say?" Ustant frowned, but Berioss shrugged.

"Oh, it was nothing, I was just thinking out loud that's all," but as he gazed out into the darkness and listened to the whispering patter of rain on the roof of their crude shelter he had the oddest sensation, as if somebody he couldn't see brushed up against him, and he shivered as he felt cold fingers lightly touch his knee and comb through his beard. Then a voice whispered to him.

*"You need not worry, there will be arms and armour enough."*

He had the briefest impression of a soft glow of all the colours of the rainbow as they blurred on the edge of his sight. Berioss frowned and moved a little further back into the shelter.

Ustant turned his head, wrinkling his nose and sniffing at the night air and Sloeberry smiled up at him, pausing for a moment from stripping the remnants of the flesh from the bones as she threw it into a shallow, bubbling cauldron that Damask had suspended from a hook in the roof of the shelter.

"It won't be the first time we've been served with kitchen scraps in an unfriendly Wayhouse, but you'll be surprised what difference a little preserve or pickles, or maybe a sprinkling of herbs and berries with some wild onions will make.

Some while later, she tapped him on the shoulder. "Would you like to taste it?" she laughed, passing him a brimming, steaming spoonful of the broth.

"You are a marvel; it's delicious, better than anything I've been served in all the Wayhouses on my travels!" he cried, and all thoughts of returning to Sowerweed to seek revenge for bad barter vanished as Sloeberry ladled the broth into small, wooden bowls.

Berioss settled back after his third helping of the stew and sighed, letting the soft, whispering voices of the others wash over him.

"Have you burnt your lips on the broth, Berioss?" Sloeberry's voice, full of concern, made him jump. He looked across to where she was holding out a handful of crushed leaves. "Rub them with tormentil leaves; they will soothe and take away the pain."

Berioss thanked her and took the leaves but he only

half-heartedly dabbed them on his mouth. Turning away he frowned. He knew he hadn't burnt his lips but he must have been repeatedly rubbing the back of his hand across his mouth, touching his face where he had felt that invisible touch, without realizing it. Thinking about it began to stir up disquieting memories of those seemingly endless daylights when he had stood, trapped and beguiled by Nevian's magic, turned into the shape of a tree. He remembered now: it all came flooding back: he had felt that same, cool touch from the flowing rainbow cloak as the Master of Magic had moved silently between the trees. The magician must be somewhere very close by.

"Ustant—Ustant!" he hissed, anxious to warn him and moved his hand in an effort to catch his friend's attention while he was deep in conversation with Damask. Ustant frowned and turned to look across at him and each of the tunnellers fell silent, one by one.

"Just now . . . I thought . . . " Berioss began to hesitate. Something warned him to keep silent but now he realized that everybody was looking at him. It wasn't the moment, not here, in the wildness of Meremire Forest, to reveal that the Master of Magic was close to them. "I . . . I was thinking about what those villagers were telling us in the inn . . . " he began again, shifting to safer ground. "Something's happening that I don't understand, rumours and stories always become exaggerated with the retelling: that's common knowledge, but the stories of what happened in Deepling and our brief visit to the inn in Larach are being exaggerated out of all proportion. Each time I hear them new atrocities are being added in places we haven't been anywhere near!"

"Yes, you're right," Ustant agreed, nodding slowly. "It's almost as if the tunnellers are being blamed for every mishap or disaster that occurs."

"But why? Why do they hate us so much? We haven't done anything to them!" Mistletoe cried.

"I don't think that's the issue," Berioss frowned, "and I don't think that digging up the Greenways or trampling down everything that grows in the vicinity of the villages is a rumour. No, I think someone is using you to stir up trouble and what happened in Deepling is making it look as though the tunnellers are on the rampage. But who is it and what could they possibly gain from it?"

"Yes, I agree, and there's another thing that's been bothering me now I've come to think about it," Ustant added. "Something doesn't ring true about those Nightbeast attacks the merchants told us about in the inn. The Nightbeasts hardly ever appeared in the daylight and never behaved like common robbers as far as I can remember. There's seems to be something very strange about the whole nasty business," Ustant yawned, "but worrying about it now isn't going to get us very far is it?"

"Lord Willow will know what to do," Oaktangle offered, "and we could be at the Rising in two daylights."

"Yes, I suppose you're right, and it will be a long daylight tomorrow so I think we had better get some sleep."

Berioss made himself comfortable. It was warm and dry in the shelter and the hazy, thin curls of smoke rising from the fire smelled of peat as they drifted across the low, curved roof, seeking a way out. His eyelids felt heavy and began to close and the soft drumming of the rain on the turf above his head lulled him into sleep. A silent shadow woven with muted colours seemed to paused momentarily in the entrance of the shelter, an owl hooted from somewhere very close by and the shadow melted into the night. Berioss's eyelids flickered and his lips trembled on the edge of sleep. "Nevian, is that you?" he whispered. But the words collapsed into a grunting snore.

\*     \*     \*

"We must be safe now," Oaktangle called to the others, leaving the cover of the trees to scramble down onto the Greenway. But he only took half a dozen, hesitant steps before stopping and bringing up his hand silently to motion the others to halt.

"There's something wrong—it's too quiet!" he murmured to the two old Marchers as they hurried to his side.

"Wrong? What could be wrong? You're almost home!" Berioss frowned, instinctively closing his fingers around the hilt of his sword and loosing it in its sheath as he glanced anxiously at the fortress that lay ahead of them.

The Rising filled and straddled the Greenway ahead of them, overshadowing the village of Wood Rising with its steep, thatched roofs and tall chimneys that had sprung up on the lip of the dyke surrounding its base. It seemed much larger than he remembered from the last time he had seen it at the great battle. For the whole of yesterlight they had been able to see it, at first no more than a distant, hazy mound that peeped above the trees, but with each hurrying footstep it had grown until now it seemed to fill the landscape. A huge, dark fortress of earth and bones it glistened and reflected the evening sunlight. Ustant shivered, remembering the stories he had heard of how it had been built; how Lord Willow's people had been bound in chains by the first Granite Kings to raise the bones of Elundium into great cities, to make spires of sheer stone and places of beauty for others to wander in. How they had been enslaved and passed on from king to king, knowing nothing of freedom. He remembered how their last great task before Krulshards' darkness came was to build the Rising, chained together, trampling the soft earth layer by layer, dying in their thousands until it rose above the shadows. He remembered, too, how Krulshards had condemned them to live in his darkness, tunnelling and enlarging the City of Night, as punishment for building such a fortress.

"It is a place of great beauty now, and such peace since the King released us from bondage," Sloeberry whispered softly, seeing the fear in Ustant's eyes.

Ustant looked up and nodded. Its sheer sides rose in countless, narrow, flower-decked steps and deep banks of blue and white nightflowers grew all along the side of the steep spiralling ramp that led from the causeway bridge which spanned the dyke all the way up to the broad plateau on its summit where Lord Willow had built his long hall.

"Standing here worrying about nothing isn't going to do us any good—or get us a full belly—I'm hungry, come on!" Mistletoe urged, hurrying towards the village.

"Wait! Wait a minute all of you!" Oaktangle called out to Mistletoe and the others, but they were deaf to him and evaded his outstretched hands.

"I can't see what you're so worried about—everything looks quite normal to me. There's smoke curling up out of the chimneys of the houses in Wood Rising, and I can see people congregating on the summit of the Rising, quite a gathering of them by the look of it," Berioss observed cautiously.

"I hope they're gathering in welcome." Ustant frowned.

Oaktangle shrugged in answer and glanced around him. A second sense, a warning of danger was gnawing at the pit of his stomach. "I don't know: there's something missing, something I can't quite put my finger on."

Reluctantly he followed the others adding, "It's much too quiet: there should be the sound of children playing and people out here on the Greenway enjoying the last of the evening sunlight. There should be the smell of new-mown grass and . . . " his voice fell away to nothing as they caught up with the others who had stopped, their way barred by a high banner made of birch twigs woven through stout

upright saplings that had been erected across the
Greenway at the entrance to the village.

"This wasn't here when we left was it? What do
you think it's for?" Damask asked, looking up at the
wattle fence and pushing her hand against it. The
barrier moved slightly at her touch, the birch twigs
rubbing against one another with a dry, whispering
sound that echoed in the unnatural silence.

"I have seen wattle walls just like these built
around villages in the grasslands for defence against
roaming Nightbeasts, sections of the wall overlapped
leaving narrow gaps for the villagers to pass
through, too narrow for marauding Nightbeasts who
tried to enter, so that they had to force their way
through and make the fence rattle which warned the
villagers; and sometimes they would even weave
windbells into the fence to give them extra warning
of attack." Ustant was thinking out loud.

"Come over here: I've found a gap just wide
enough to squeeze through," Mistletoe called out
impatiently, barely waiting for the others before he
slipped through the fence.

The rest of the tunnellers followed by Berioss and
Ustant had to push and force their way through the
small opening as their clothes snagged and caught on
the sharp-cut ends of the birch that protruded from
the fence.

"Oaktangle's right, we should have taken more
precautions before blundering in here. We haven't a
clue what we'll come up against," Berioss cursed, his
arms and hands scratched from the sharp twigs as he
squeezed through the fence and stumbled into the
muddy village street. Ustant emerged behind him and
both Marchers came to a shambling halt.

Oaktangle and the rest of the company were huddled nervously together only a pace away, unsure of
what to do. To the left and right the narrow street
was lined with silent, angry-faced tunnellers all the

way to the Causeway Bridge. A voice shouted at them from the crowd.

"How dare you come back here! You've brought nothing but shame and dishonour upon us!"

The cry was taken up with a roar of hatred that erupted along the silent line, knuckled fists were shaken at them and a hail of mud and stones began to fly.

"But we've done nothing—nothing I tell you," Sloeberry tried to cry out, but the roar of anger rose and drowned out her voice and she had to raise her hands to protect herself from the hail of missiles that came raining down on her.

"Shame! Shame! Shame!" the crowd began to chant: "Shame! Shame! Shame!" And they began to close in, shaking their fists, revealing threshing sticks and clubs.

"We're under attack! Quickly, Berioss, defend the left flank!" Ustant shouted, trying to make himself heard above the din of the crowd. Drawing his sword, he brandished it above his head and swept out the tail of his cloak with his other hand to try and shield Sloeberry and the others as best he could from the onslaught of mud and stones.

"Get back! Get back, all of you or I'll take off your heads!" Berioss snarled at the shifting, surging crowd, unsheathing his sword and sweeping it in a low, humming arc a mere finger's span above their heads to make them hesitate and mill in fear and confusion.

"No! You must not kill anybody: I won't have my own people harmed!" Oaktangle cried out, making a desperate grab at Berioss's sword arm

The old Marcher shook him off, angrily, shouting back in answer, "I will not stand here and do nothing while this ignorant, heedless mob kills you and tramples you underfoot—I don't care who they are: I will see true justice done!"

"But I would rather die than be responsible for shedding one drop of my own people's blood!" Oaktangle wept, falling to his knees.

Sloeberry and the others cried out together, "What you have heard is all lies—why don't you listen to us?"

And they began to sink down onto their knees, their heads bowed in submission, beside their leader.

Berioss felt his face darken with anger. He hadn't run his boots to ruin and come all this way just to see the company of tunnellers they had protected, stoned and trampled by their own people within sight of the Rising. He knew they had but moments to act before the advancing mob overran them. Reaching down, he grabbed at Oaktangle's sleeve and roughly hauled him to his feet. "You will not dishonour us by dying here in the dirt like a common thief!" he hissed. "We know you are innocent of all those vile rumours—to die here would prove nothing—nothing at all. Now run! Run as fast as you can and go for the Causeway Bridge when I let go of you—throw yourselves on Lord Willow's mercy—tell him everything and let him decide your fate—not this disorderly rabble!"

Berioss glanced across at Ustant and braced himself for the onslaught of the mob. He lifted Oaktangle up for everyone to see and cried out for silence in a strong, deep voice. The noise of the crowd gradually fell away.

The Marcher then spoke: "I am Berioss, Marcher-born and pledged to serve my king. I was in the inn at Deepling on the night when the first atrocity was supposed to have happened and I say that Oaktangle and the company he leads are innocent of all the foul lies and rumours that you have heard. But it is your Lord Willow and the King himself who should judge them, not you or me."

Berioss paused, holding the restless mob with his steady eyes for a moment before adding, in a more menacing voice, "And you have my promise—I will kill anybody who tries to stop them reaching the Rising, for Ustant and I are not afraid to die!"

"Now run!" he hissed as he let Oaktangle drop to the ground.

Oaktangle sprinted, head down, through the sullen crowd and, one by one, the others followed him. The people closed into a narrow corridor and spat at them, throwing clumps of mud and refuse, but still they let them pass without laying a finger upon them as they ran through the village.

Berioss and Ustant followed and the crowd fell back, keeping a respectful distance from their swords, but the Marchers twisted and turned to keep an eye on the people who closed in silently behind them, cutting off any hope of escape.

"I don't think we're going to have an easy job convincing Lord Willow, or anybody else for that matter, about what really happened," Ustant murmured as they reached the Causeway Bridge and began to climb the spiralling ramp to the entrance of the fortress, leaving the mob behind.

"Everybody seems determined to judge them guilty, no matter what the truth is," Berioss nodded gravely, resheathing his sword.


"Of all the stupid things to do—I can't understand what has got into you!" Lord Willow's voice exploded, echoing through the long hall on the top of the Rising. He raised his hand to silence Oaktangle's explanation every time he paused to take a breath.

"There is no justification, and never can be any, for your wild rampage through the countryside. To betray the pledges and trust of King Thane, to jeopardize our friendship with the people of Elundium— why? Haven't they always given us everything we have ever asked for? Why didn't you think for one moment about what you were throwing away? What damage you have done to all of us with your actions! This . . . this . . . this rampage of violence will isolate us, it will prevent us from travelling . . . "

"It's the senseless killing and stealing I can't understand," Lady Oakapple, Lord Willow's wife, interrupted from her seat in the window. "Your mother was here yesterlight begging for Lord Willow to be merciful. She said she couldn't understand what had got into you—you never wanted for anything, you have never gone hungry . . . "

Oaktangle hung his head, his cheeks flushed scarlet. It didn't seem to matter what he said, everybody was convinced of his guilt. He was almost beginning to believe it himself.

"But surely you don't believe these wild rumours, my Lord? We were there in the Wayhouse in Deepling and we have accompanied Oaktangle and the others all the way here. We can tell you exactly what happened and which villages we stopped at to ask for food. It's all lies, all . . . " Berioss began to protest in their defence only to fall into silent confusion beneath Willow's withering, doubting gaze.

Berioss felt a cold knot of fear tighten in his stomach and he glanced anxiously across to Ustant as he realized that nobody wanted to listen to them, nobody wanted to hear the truth or even to give them a moment to tell their side of it.

"Rumours! There's more to this outrage than mere rumours! Didn't you see the wattle fence my people have had to erect to protect this village? Do you want me to send for the mutilated carcass of the sheep that was hurled into the village this morninglight—torn to pieces by the pack of marauding dogs that run at your heels!" Willow answered angrily. He watched the old Marchers warily, remembering them from the Battle of the Rising; the forest of trees that had gathered, grove upon grove, around the base of their fortress. He remembered how, when King Thane had called for all those warriors who did not pledge themselves upon the Causeway Field, the trees had swayed and creaked before shattering into a fog of splinters and falling branches. These two old Marchers had been

two of the thousands of grim-faced warriors who had
emerged with a roaring shout to clear a broad path
through the shadow warriors who had been closing in
about the King. Yes, he remembered them only too
well. Treacherous men that Nevian, the Master of
Magic, had been forced to trap and transform into
trees, to hold them prisoners upon the Greenway's
edge until they saw the error of their ways and learned
to love the King. He may have forgiven them after the
battle and welcomed them back as proud warriors,
but Willow had never wholly trusted them and whenever any of them had broken their journey to seek rest
and shelter in the Rising he had half-expected to catch
that same bitter odour of bark and earth, oak and
crushed mulberry leaves upon them that had hung in
the air for many daylights after the great battle. He
frowned, turning away from Berioss as he caught himself sniffing, hunting for that same smell to confirm
his conviction that they couldn't be trusted.

The door of the long hall suddenly burst open and
the cold draughts of twilight air that invaded the hall
made the candle flames dance and sway sending
smoky, elusive shadows leaping away across the low-
beamed ceiling.

"Lord, there are riders approaching on the road
from the Granite City. A squadron of Gallopers riding hard beneath the King's emblem of the sun!"
called out a doorwarden.

"You will await my judgement!" Willow frowned
at Oaktangle and his company as he hurried to the
open doorway, arching his eyebrows and searching
the gathering darkness he peered through the silent,
gliding nightshapes that filled the air.

After a moment he caught sight of the fast-moving
ribbon of light cast from the flickering stay-safe
lanterns the Gallopers were carrying to light their path.
Willow smiled: it always seemed so magical watching
the column of bobbing lights appear and disappear as

they followed the Greenway up and over the hills, down into the shallow valleys, never slowing or quickening the pace, each rider keeping his place, carrying the pennants that crackled and flowed in the wind.

Fast-moving hoofbeats thundered on the steep ramp that led up to the top of the Rising. Rays of lamplight shone across the plateau as the Gallopers breasted the top, sending long, twisting shadows fleeing up the walls of the long hall. Horses whinnied and snorted, misting the night air with clouds of vaporous breath, their flanks heaving and glistening, white with sweat from their journey as their riders brought them to a halt on the cobbled floor.

Gorass, the captain of the squadron, leapt lightly to the ground from Argo's saddle, caressing the horse's shoulder and whispering his thanks for a safe road. His armoured boots echoed on the cobbles and his long Galloper's cloak flowed out behind him as he strode to where Willow waited on the top step before the entrance of the hall. Drawing off his calf-skin battle gloves he gripped Willow's hands in greeting saying, "Lord, our King has sent me with grave tidings. There is unrest and a strange disorder spreading throughout Meremire Forest!" Gorass paused, glancing around before continuing in a hushed whisper, "There is even a rumour that new Nightbeasts are roaming through the forest!"

"I know—I know . . . " Willow replied, urgently, drawing Gorass and the rest of the Gallopers into the hall and dispatching the doorwarden to organize grooms to tend to their horses and bring food for his guests. "I have the culprits right here with me. They gave themselves up earlier this evening, and a sorry sight they look. I was about to pass judgement but perhaps you should help me, especially while I judge what to do about the two Marchers."

"Marchers!" Gorass exclaimed, coming to a sudden halt, his face hardening as he caught sight of Berioss

and Ustant standing with the small group of tunnellers huddled together like common criminals in
the centre of the hall.

"You . . . you are a curse on honour, both of you, a
disgrace! To think that the King forgave you for not
pledging yourselves to serve him upon the Causeway
Fields. He called you Marchers once again after the
battle here upon the Rising—he gave you each a finger bowl to seal the new pledges you offered—and
yet still you blacken his name and everything he
strives to do for the people of Elundium!"

"It is a lie! A foul lie, all of it! We have been trying
to protect the King's name but . . . " Ustant tried to
argue in their defence but Gorass would hear none of
it. Turning to Willow he asked his leave to take the
tunnellers and the two Marchers to the Granite City
to be tried in Candlebane Hall.

Willow nodded silently: much as he would have rather
judged them himself here in the Rising he knew he had
no other choice. They had betrayed the King's trust and
now they must stand alone in Candlebane Hall.

"You two shall be judged separately for the treachery and the evil that you have incited in these young
tunnellers. You will be judged for all the trouble you
have stirred up in Meremire Forest—and don't think
we don't know about it. The city is alive with gossip
and rumour." Gorass spoke angrily as he returned his
attention to Berioss and Ustant.

"Rumours are a poor cloak for the truth!" Berioss
tried to say, but he was shouted down.

"Call yourselves Marchers! Call yourselves King's
men! You are a disgrace; surrender your sword and
the finger-bowl our king gave you. You are not worthy of them!" one of the Gallopers cried, his hand
upon the hilt of his sword.

"We had better do what they say. It's no good
protesting; anything we say only seems to make it
worse," Berioss muttered, unsheathing his sword and

kneeling to offer it, hilt first, Ustant beside him. The Gallopers who took them laughed and sneered at the rusty blades.

"And now the finger-bowls," Gorass demanded impatiently holding out his hand.

Ustant reached back to the place where it normally hung from his belt and found the empty chain. Then he remembered the barter in the inn in Sowerweed. "I . . . I . . . I haven't got it!" he stammered, searching for a half-truth as Gorass turned his attention to Berioss who was holding out his empty hands.

"We were forced to barter them for food in the inn in Sowerweed," he offered.

Gorass looked at the two old Marchers with a sense of loathing and disgust that they could have bartered something so precious. The atrocities these two had indulged in proved how right he had been to doubt the sincerity and honour of the Marchers who had refused to pledge their loyalty to King Thane upon the Causeway Field. He had known that it would only be a matter of time before they revealed their true nature.

"You have no honour! None at all!" he cursed at Berioss and Ustant. "And *you* should have known better than to disgrace your people!" he glared at Oaktangle and the small company of tunnellers who were huddled together awaiting their fate.

"Secure them and lock them up: we travel by first light!" he ordered the Gallopers standing close to him before turning on his heel and beckoning Willow and Oakapple to accompany him.

"The air here is tainted with their lies and treachery. Let us walk a while beneath the stars and talk of better times."

Gorass sighed and inhaled a deep breath of the cold night air. It crackled with hore frost and was heavy with the scent of nightflowers. Far away he could hear an owl hooting in the darkness. The canopy of peace that had been theirs for so long was beginning to shatter.

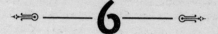

# The Seeds of Doubt

EVENING WAS DRAWING ITS SHROUD OF DARKNESS down over the Granite City. Nightshapes wove and slithered silently over the steep, weather-bleached roofs filling the narrow lanes and alleyways, gliding and swirling around the candlemen who sang and called out the hours as they moved from lamp to lamp trimming and lighting the wicks.

*"Who calls the candlemen to light them to bed?*
*Who calls the candlemen to weave dreams in*
*their heads?"*

"I just can't understand why those tunnellers have become so wild!" Thane muttered, absently reaching up to caress the chest feathers of Mulcade, the Battle Owl and chief loftmaster who perched silently and unblinking, ever watchful, upon his shoulder as he paced restlessly backwards and forwards between the tall, fluted candlesticks that thronged Candlebane Hall and descended in concentric circles from the high throne to fill the hall with shifting, smoky light.

"Tell me, why—what madness has possessed this band of tunnellers? What is making them destroy the very things they love? Why, Breakmaster? Why, Errant? Can you cast any light on it before beginning your long journey back to Underfall? I can see no reason for what they are doing!" He turned and made his shadow leap out with giant strides before him as he hurried back across the hall to where Breakmaster and his few trusted friends, friends who fought at his side to defeat the darkness, waited beside the throne.

"You are my council, my ears amongst the people. Can you tell me what has brought on this madness?"

Arachatt, the master mason, frowned and shook his head, at a loss for words. "If you ask me, they're an untrustworthy bunch."

Gray Goose, Captain of Archers, muttered under his breath. He had enough problems of his own to deal with without taking on the burdens of Elundium as well. He was an archer born and bred, not a councillor or a man of politics.

Errant overheard the mason's words and turned angrily on him. "Untrustworthy are they? Well, that's easy for you to say, mason, I don't remember seeing you at the battle before Mantern's Gate where the tunnellers fought with picks and shovels and their bare hands against the Nightbeasts. Neither were you standing in the front rank at the Rising to take the shock of battle where thousands more of Lord Willow's people died that we might win the daylight!" The horseman scowled angrily.

"I'm sure there are a dozen explanations," Breakmaster intervened quickly, trying to pour oil onto their argument before Thane reached them. Bickering and squabbling amongst themselves wasn't going to get them very far.

"From what I've heard from the travelling merchants who barter tallow in the shadow of the Stumble Gate it's only a handful of the younger tunnellers, no more than twenty or so, who have turned truly bad and they've been led astray by two enormous, ugly villains—giants of men they took up with in Deepling," observed Cherus, Lampmaster of the Hall, his ears twitching to catch every word, as he paused to trim the wicks closest to the throne.

"But that's exactly what I feel!" stuttered Gray Goose, elbowing his way into the debate. "It's the younger generation who is at fault: they always think they know better than their elders, and you can't tell them anything. I'm at my wits' end to know what to do with Eider, my son: he always seems to be in trouble in the Learning Hall or with the merchants, stealing worthless things just for the fun of it. Beating him doesn't seem to do any good—he merely sneers and says I don't understand. He says that all the glory, all the challenge, everything worth striving for has gone now that the battles are over. But I . . . " Breakmaster coughed loudly, catching the Archer's attention and making him glance around, red-faced, as he swallowed the rest of his words while Thane returned to where they stood.

Mulcade hooted softly and rose from Thane's shoulder to alight on the kingpost beam in the smoky rafters high above the hall from where he looked silently down, tilting his head to one side, listening with sharp ears as Thane's council reported the rumours and stories that were daily being brought into the city by the journeymen and merchants.

"There is unrest everywhere, my Lord, and it's spreading like a black tide. We must do something to stop it!" Arachatt warned.

"That's easier said than done!" Breakmaster frowned, glancing at the mason. "You see, nobody seems to know where they are going to strike next. Why, from the rumours I overheard in the Breaking Yards from a drover who arrived this morning, only two nights ago those tunnellers tore up the Greenways in the villages of Featherwrinkle and Thistleford, and they made a terrible, howling din as they broke windows and terrorized people, stealing everything folks weren't quick enough to hide or lock away."

"Wait a minute! Are you sure it was those villages

that were attacked on the same night?" Thane asked, turning towards the huge, black, ebony map chest that stood in the shadow of the throne.

"Why, yes, my Lord, those were the villages the drover spoke of. He was in Thistleford when the attack happened, he said that the howling sounds made his blood run cold and he feared for his life!"

Thane selected a parchment map of Elundium that had been illuminated with hammered silver and indigo hues. He instructed Arachatt and the Lampmaster to unroll it on the floor and weight its edges with heavy candlesticks.

"Now, look carefully at the map all of you," he murmured in the guttering candlelight, using his dagger to point out the two villages and the tracery of Greenways that separated them. "How could those tunnellers have attacked both villages on the same night when so many leagues lay between them? Well, can you explain it?" He looked around at the others.

"Perhaps there are secret paths, or . . . or . . . or something . . . " Arachatt mumbled helplessly as Thane's eyes came to rest on him.

"It is more likely that more of those tunnellers are turning against us now they've got a taste for it!" Greygoose spat darkly.

"But why?" Thane asked impatiently, turning away from the maps. "I gave them all they desired. They garden and travel, enjoying the beauty of Elundium in the sunlight. Why would they destroy everything they love: it doesn't make sense."

"Lord, there seems no rhyme nor reason to it." Breakmaster shrugged his shoulders heavily; he had no explanation as to why these gentle people had suddenly turned bad. If he hadn't heard so many vivid descriptions he would have thought that the villagers must have been mistaken.

"People say it's because they're jealous, my Lord, and they want what they don't have."

The Lampmaster's voice made Thane turn and stare at him as he continued. "Yes, lord, there's talk in the tallow houses that it is because you have been so generous to the tunnellers, with all the feasts and banquets, that it's made them greedy and lazy and they want more than ordinary folk. They're different to us, that's plain to see, and they're too idle to work like the good, honest people they're stealing from."

Thane's face darkened with anger. He had not expected to hear such a slanderous lie spoken against Willow's people so easily. Lazy? Greedy? Nothing could be further from the truth. "How much the truth gets twisted and teased out of shape by ignorance and envy. Tell me, Lampmaster, do you or the people you gossip with really know the measure of my generosity? Do you know what the tunnellers give us in return? Well, answer me, man!"

"It . . . it . . . it's common knowledge, my Lord. They may wander where they please and they live off the fat of the land, sleeping in the softest featherbeds; and they can have, by your royal pledge, the best food any wayhouse has to offer," the Lampmaster stuttered, seeing the king's jaw tighten with anger at each word he spoke. "Well, that's what I hear everywhere, Lord." His voice trailed away into a frightened silence.

Thane laughed suddenly, a hollow, bitter sound that made the candle flames illuminating the throne dance and sway. "How wrong you are, Lampmaster!" He sighed heavily and turned towards the council. "Have the people really forgotten so quickly how Elundium was overtangled with wilderness, how the great Greenways were choked with weeds, nettles and briars for suns beyond counting while the black shadow of Krulshards haunted them? Have they forgotten that in those dark daylights the people were too afraid to travel more than a dozen paces beyond the safety of their own villages where they eked out a living on the edge of starvation? Oh yes, and they have forgotten only too quickly how they cowered even here in the Granite City, terrified of the creatures that roamed through the night, afraid to journey far without an armed escort. Willow's people helped us to rid the world of such fear."

Thane paused, turning sharply on the Lampmaster, his eyes hard and accusing. "So, the good people of Elundium are envious of the meagre handfuls of food and shelter that I offered to Lord Willow's people in return for their labour in clearing the ruin and wilderness, in mowing the Greenways and tending to the neglect that has choked our beautiful land for so long? Well you tell them, Lampmaster—illuminate their greed and jealousy—the tunnellers' labour comes cheap. There isn't barter enough in this city to pay them the true value of what they do for us!"

"Yes, yes, my Lord, I'll tell them everything. I meant no offence, I was merely repeating what I had heard," the Lampmaster apologized, hastily retreating towards the doors of the Candle Hall.

"And you can tell your gossiping friends another thing!" Thane called out after him. "The tunnellers have no need to steal from us, the daily clutter of our lives means nothing to them and would only burden them as they travel. It is their freedom they value above all other things having been kept imprisoned, slaves to Krulshards' darkness for suns beyond counting. The things they treasure most are to see each new sunrise, to feel the wind and rain upon their faces and to hear the first blackbird burst into song along the Greenway's edge. Tell your friends this—there is no barter great enough to set against releasing them from the darkness than to give them back their freedom. That was the real measure of my generosity!"

The fierce echo of Thane's voice lingered in the hall as the Lampmaster's hurrying footsteps shuffled into silence.

Breakmaster coughed quietly to catch Thane's attention. "I'm sure he meant you no offence, my Lord, but was only trying to inform you, to assist the council by putting his finger on the pulse of the people and relaying the things he hears as he goes about his business in the tallow houses."

"Yes . . . yes . . . I know, and I flare up too quickly, but sometimes I despair at the ugliness, the meanness that always seems to dwell in people's souls just below the surface. And I grow weary of the politics of government. It doesn't seem to matter how much we strive to make the world better; jealousy and envy always rear their heads. What, I wonder, would the Chancellors have done in my place? Would they have put every tunneller they caught to death? Would they have banished them to the wilderness beyond World's End or burnt their village of Wood Rising to the ground and staked Willow's and Oakapple's heads above the Stumble Gate as a warning and a lesson to the others?"

"One thing's for sure," Errant laughed. "They would never have given them their freedom in the first place!"

The hollow toll of the bell summoning everyone to evening fare rang through the great banqueting halls, the high chambers and the endless, winding stairway of the citadel that rose sheer and powerful above the Granite City.

"Come, walk with me to table and we will discuss this problem further," Thane smiled at his council as he called Mulcade down from the kingpost beam to his shoulder.

"Lord, I beg you to excuse me, only I have told the masons who are to help me rebuild the fountains of Swanwater to meet on the steps of Candlebane Hall so that we may go over the drawings. I am due to be with them at the last sound of the evening bell. We begin work on the fountains tomorrowlight," Arachatt said.

Thane clasped the mason's dusty arms, a broad

smile breaking out on his face. "Go, with all speed, Arachatt, everything must be ready for the swans' return. Winter would be dull and dreary without the company of Ogion and his Queen Ousious. Yes, everything must be ready to welcome them back with much honour," he murmured, his eyes softening and a faraway look coming over him as he remembered how the two beautiful swans had led him through the wilderness in search of Elionbel, his Queen, when she was Krulshards' prisoner.

Ogion and Ousious had known of the old legends foretelling how they would be driven into silence if they aided him and yet still they had offered their help. Thane could still hear that last, far-off echo of Ousious's voice when she found Krulshards, a tortured cry that chilled his heart. He remembered how she had returned, cruelly wounded, flying low across the last tumbled ridges of the ice field beside the lake, Ogion flying beside her and two swans supporting her tired wings. How they had eased her exhausted body down into the icy-cold water with Krulshards' black, broken spear blade protruding from her chest. Thane smiled and lightly touched the scar on his wrist where he had slashed his arm to use his own blood to save her when she had almost died as they took the blade out. And the legend came true, from that daylight the grey swans had become mute. They could no longer speak.

"It isn't just the damage the tunnellers are causing that is stirring up this wave of unrest, my Lord," Errant ventured as they left the Candle Hall and walked through the maze of corridors and courtyards towards the banqueting halls. "The villagers are blaming the re-emergence of the Nightbeasts on the tunnellers. I have heard many rumours during my short stay here in the city telling how they have joined together and attacked the villages and even companies of travellers."

"But that's ridiculous! It's utterly ridiculous!"

Thane cried. "The tunnellers were kept as their prisoners, slaves—they were tortured and murdered by the Nightbeasts. No, they would never take up with them. Anyway, the Nightbeasts are all dead, you know they are, only Kerzolde and Kerhunge survived Krulshards' death and that was only to serve his bastard offspring. Even they perished with Arbel, Elionbel's black-hearted brother, at the Battle of the Rising. You know they did, you saw them shrivel to nothing when I stabbed Durondel's sword bound up in that remnant of Krulshards' black malice into Kruel's footprints and gave him his shadow. You saw Kruel reduced to an innocent baby. You, and all the warriors gathered there saw me lift him up and name him Krann—a helpless, innocent child. You know the shadows of that fear have fled forever."

"Yes, Lord, I know you're right, but there's many who didn't see it happen and probably have never heard it told properly," Breakmaster ventured.

There was the slightest hint of doubt in the old horseman's voice that betrayed his own conviction. Thane was about to question him about it when he heard the sound of Elionbel's voice and Krann's childish laughter floating up to them from a lower courtyard. He beckoned to the others and they came to a halt to look down over the ornately-carved balustrade. Elionbel was sitting beside a fountain with Krann on the ground beside her, she was telling him the story-rhyme of the clever giant and he was laughing and joining in with the verses he could remember. Mulcade hooted softly and left Thane's shoulder to swoop silently down, circling the courtyard once before settling beside Krann, hooting and squawking noisily as the boy ruffled and stroked his feathers. Krann looked up and jumped excitedly to his feet to wave to the company above, calling out to Errant, demanding that he wait for him, and ran towards the stairs that would lead him to where they stood. Elionbel looked up, her face breaking into a smile as she caught sight of her husband.

"It is time for evening fare, my love, and those at table await us!" Thane called out to her.

Elionbel rose gracefully to her feet and crossed to the stairway. Thane watched until she disappeared from sight at the twist in the stair and then turned seriously to the old horseman.

"I sensed doubt in your voice just now, Breakmaster, but look at the way Mulcade flew to the boy. Remember, old friend, Battle Qwls have hunted Nightbeasts since the time of Holgranos, the first Granite King. If there was the slightest trace of Nightbeast or the merest echo of Krulshards left in the boy, Mulcade would know."

"Then who, or what, are those creatures that are attacking travellers on the Greenways? They can't simply be the people's imagination: it's happening far too regularly." Breakmaster frowned. Then his face creased into a wide, weatherbeaten smile as he watched Krann reach the stairhead and run to Errant.

"Fleetfoot's so beautiful! When can I ride him?" he cried with excitement.

Errant picked up the boy in his strong hands and swung him easily around to sit upon his shoulders. "You must have patience. He is not yet broken, Krann, but tonight you shall ride to your table." He laughed as he strode ahead of the others.

"Perhaps I should send a Galloper out to the Rising tomorrowlight and see if Lord Willow can throw any light upon these wild rumours. I need somebody I trust to get to the bottom of it," Breakmaster offered.

"Yes, that's a good idea," Thane agreed. "But send a squadron of Gallopers, all you can muster from the Breaking Yards, and if they come across these troublemakers, whoever they are, they can round them up and bring them back here. Let them cry for justice here in Candlebane Hall!"

"I could take the Nighthorses, my Lord: they are fleet of foot, we could be at the Rising in no time at all," Errant offered, but Thane shook his head.

"No, Errant, your journey back to Underfall will be hard enough to complete before winter closes the roads. No, rest the Nighthorses a while longer: there are horses and Gallopers enough for the task here in the city."

Thane suddenly strode ahead of Errant and Greygoose, his hands outstretched, laughter on his lips as Elionbel reached the stairhead. She ran to him, entwining her fingers with his to walk with him to the banqueting hall.

"Drib, Drib, come down here at once you useless, idle boy. The good landlord Swatheplenty's customers will starve and freeze to their deaths in the length of time it's taking you to sweep this chimney. Come down I say, come down now!"

Sweepscuttle, Drib's master was shouting up the chimney from where he stood amongst the kindling and logs stacked on the edge of the hearth of the cavernous inglenook of the Prancing Warhorse Inn in Pudding Street that stood in the third circle of the city close to the Learning Hall.

"A curse on his idleness!" Sweepscuttle muttered, his mean, grimy face blotched with livid spots of anger as he shielded his eyes from the trickle of smuts and soot that were falling down the chimney and scattering across the hearth, caught in the swirling eddies of chill, evening draughts.

"They are all the same, these useless boys!" the landlord grumbled impatiently as he glanced up the chimney: "I don't know what the world's coming to, do you? You can't seem to get decent help these daylights. It's the same with my servers: nobody wants to do the fetching and carrying any more, or spend the time learning their trade. All they want to do is sit with my customers and idle away the time talking about the troubles those tunnellers are stirring up out Meremire way." Swatheplenty spat on his fat hands, and continued, "I don't know where it's going to stop."

He picked smuts of soot out of the mountainous lump of dough he had on the table before beginning to knead it impatiently. Then he started to divide it into segments ready to place upon the long-handled iron peels beside the pies and pastries that would be pushed into the bake-ovens lining the chimney. He glanced anxiously over his shoulder at the grumbles of discontent and saw the sour faces of the merchants, burymen, chandlers and street hawkers who filled the inn and were waiting for him to light the fire beneath the black-bellied cauldrons suspended upon the trammels and chains that hung down from the thick, fire-scarred beam of ironwood that spanned the chimney. Cooking pots were brimming with the cold, wholesome broths and pottage that were to be their supper, if only that cursed boy would finish his work.

"Drib used to be a good boy. Slow, yes, and a dreamer, but those crooked legs of his get into all the awkward nooks and corners of a chimney and do a proper job of knocking loose the soot. But he's not been the same since he fell in with that old fool who breaks horses and makes them fit for the Gallopers to ride. The boy says his name is Break . . . Break-something or other. Well, I'll teach him a thing or two about breaking things if I ever get my hands on him! It's bad enough with this King's proclamation that lets Drib waste half his day in idleness in the Learning Hall without this horseman filling his empty head with ideas far above his station. Riding horses indeed! Whoever heard such nonsense!"

"You don't mean Breakmaster do you? The big,

strong fellow who always accompanies the King when he rides through the city? The master of the Breaking Yards?" the landlord exclaimed, his bushy eyebrows raised in surprise and disbelief.

Sweepscuttle nodded morosely. "Yes, that sounds like the measure of him. Drib came home with some wild story of how he had met the King riding with Captain Errant—the one who brought the Nighthorses to the city—and this horseman outside the Learning Hall one day. Of course I didn't believe a word of it at the time: I thought it the best of his excuses and lies that he tells me to avoid me beating him for being late, but I now know there must have been some truth in it, curse him. From that daylight on he vanishes from the moment he finishes the work I've set him and when he reappears there's the reek of horses about him. And he daydreams now like a boy in a trance. I say curse this horseman for meddling where he shouldn't!"

Swatheplenty dropped the lump of dough onto the kneading board in front of him, alarmed as Sweepscuttle's voice rose in anger. Heads began to turn in their direction. He grasped at the mastersweep's arm, hissing at him to keep his voice down. "You fool! You want to be more careful who you berate in public, especially when you talk of the King and his favourites. There may be some of them in here tonight. Be warned, sharp ears are always listening!"

The landlord released the sweep's arm and glanced casually around the room before plunging his plump fingers back into the dough. But his eyes were keen as he searched the faces of his customers for any listeners.

"Friends!" Sweepscuttle spat derisively into the soot that Drib had dislodged and which had piled up into a soft, black mound over the ashes. "Friends— this King would be lucky to find enough friends in this city to fill this chimney-hole. There are rumours of discontent everywhere, what with the taxes on even the simplest barter—how are we supposed to pay them, I ask you, when he sends our apprentices to the Learning Hall for a half of every daylight? Who is going to do the work? And then there's all those Gallopers and Marchers he disbanded and sent home—who is going to defend us now those new Nightbeasts have appeared in Meremire Forest? I tell you it won't be long before they are hammering on the gates of the city and he will be hard pushed to find . . . "

"Keep quiet!" the landlord warned. "There's a crowd from the Breaking Yards sitting at the table next to the Loremaster. I think they overheard what you said."

Sweepscuttle looked anxiously around him and saw a huge, sullen fellow slowly rising to his feet from a table near the ale barrel.

"Are you going to keep us waiting all night, sweep?" he demanded, advancing towards the inglenook.

"We're almost finished. I'm sorry for the delay: it's that idle boy, Cripple Drib's fault, daydreaming again I'll be bound. I'll call him again. Drib—Drib—come down this minute!" Sweepscuttle's voice echoed up the chimney.

"Is that Drib? The same crippled creature who plagues us in the breaking yards—that good-for-nothing boy?" the rough rider cried angrily. "If I haven't had enough of him getting under my feet and upsetting the horses to last a dozen daylights—and now he's making me wait for my supper!" The horseman roughly pushed the sweep aside and shouted up the chimney, "Come down here now, you wretched nuisance!"

"It's high time somebody gave that boy the thrashing he deserves for always poking his nose in where it's not wanted. He's always asking questions and interrupting our work," grumbled another of the riders, wiping his lips with the back of his hand after draining the last dregs from his tankard. "And now he's here, spoiling our supper. Wait until I get my hands on him!"

Loremaster Grout's ears pricked up at the horsemen's grumbles. He would dearly love to punish that wretched boy himself for a long string of insolences, but he knew he dared not lay a finger on him, not after seeing him talking with the king outside the Learning Hall. Grout smiled suddenly, his lips stretching into a thin, bloodless line, his eyes narrowing angrily, as an idea began to form inside his head. He might not be able to punish the boy himself but there was no reason why somebody else couldn't do it for him. Snapping his fingers he beckoned one of the servers over and ordered him to refill the horsemen's jugs with fresh ale.

"I'll drink a toast to that boy getting the hiding he deserves. I'd do it myself but my hands are tied . . . " Grout smiled apologetically to the horsemen at the next table as he raised his own tankard.

"So would we, but we dare not. He's Breakmaster's favourite and he lets him do what he likes. He comes and goes as he pleases and follows the old man about asking an endless string of questions. And he is always getting in amongst the Nighthorses loosening off their picket ropes and making a thorough nuisance of himself. I don't know why he puts up with it."

"I can't see what our boss sees in the wretched, filthy boy," grumbled the breaker sitting at the furthest end of the table. "He leaves more muck in the stables than he takes out and he spills most of the water out of the buckets when he tries to carry them with that limp of his. And he drops hay everywhere and leaves the stables in a terrible mess for us to clear up."

"I'm having to wear my fingers to the bone clearing up all the dirty soot marks he leaves on everything he touches. And you know how particular Breakmaster is! I've had enough of it, everywhere I go he's there under my feet, getting in the way!"

"But surely there must be a way of getting rid of him? Surely you can think of some way of making your master displeased with him?" Grout lowered his voice, watching carefully as a flicker of interest kindled in the horsemen's eyes.

"Perhaps you could set a little trap—you know, arrange for your master to catch him doing something he dislikes . . ."

The rough rider's voice from the inglenook made everybody in the inn look around in alarm.

"If you don't come down immediately I'll toast you alive, you miserable creature!" He crackled a spark alight between his fingers and kicked a bundle of kindling.

"No, you can't do that—you'll burn the poor boy!" cried a merchant in dismay, but the burly rider merely laughed at him and pushed him back out of the way as the bright blue flames crackled and leapt up from the kindling, burning fiercely as the curls of smoke began to rise and vanish up the chimney.

"Can't I? And who is going to stop me?" the horseman sneered, knuckling his fists.

Grout wrapped his cloak up high around his shoulders and tried to disguise the grin of delight that had spread across his face. He rubbed his bony hands together at the thought of Drib getting the toasting he deserved: he hadn't felt this happy for a long while. Times were indeed changing; there were rumours of discontent everywhere with these stories of the tunnellers' revolt. And best of all, only that morning he had heard a whisper from a true and trusted friend that the Chancellors were behind the unrest. But how they were causing it he couldn't imagine.

\* \* \*

Drib paused from brushing and scraping at the thick,
soot-encrusted bricks, shielding his mouth with his
filthy hand as he inhaled a shallow breath of the foul,
dusty air inside the chimney. He was tired and his
head ached; the higher he climbed the more difficult it
was becoming to find a purchase: the bricks were so
old and fire-scarred that the crevices between them
crumbled at his touch. Reaching up, he found a shallow ledge on either side and forced his sore elbows
into it. Gritting his teeth, he braced himself as he
knocked his crooked legs on the sides of the chimney,
pulled himself up and felt with his toes for a better
hold. He knew he was nearly at the top: he could see
the first evening stars glistening and twinkling in the
darkening sky above his head beyond the last, narrowing twist in the chimney. Below him in the sooty
blackness he could hear his master, Sweepscuttle,
cursing him and telling him to hurry but he couldn't
work any faster: he was doing his best.

"Not far now," he whispered to himself, filling his
head with clear images of the beautiful horses he had
seen in the Breaking Yard, imagining the soft, silky
touch of their skin as his fingers and toes scrabbled
and clawed at the soot-encrusted, crumbling bricks.

The snarling shout of the rough rider, Hinch, calling for his blood and threatening to roast him alive
from the inglenook below sent a shiver of fright up
his spine. He had seen the looks of hatred and jealousy in many of the eyes of the grooms and riders
that first morning when he had accompanied
Breakmaster into the stables, and since then he had
heard them whispering and cursing him behind his
back, hating him for being their master's favourite.
He saw how they sneered and laughed at him, tripping him up or pushing him over the moment
Breakmaster's back was turned. He heard their cruel
taunting as they tapped their whips on their long,
leather boots and hummed that persistent tune—

"Cripples can't ride, cripples can't ride." But none of that mattered: he could take it all if he had to just so that he could be close to those beautiful horses.

Drib saw the bright flash of a spark in the darkness which lit up the inside of the chimney. He heard Hinch laugh and sneer.

"Can't I? And who's going to stop me?"

Panic seized Drib as the first waft of hot air warmed his heels and the wisps of smoke from the fire below stung his nostrils. He knew he couldn't go down: the only way for him to escape before the smoke and fumes of the fire overcame him was to climb. He dropped the brush of crested porcupine spines, and heard it spin and clatter its way down to the hearth, where it was consumed in clouds of sparks as it burnt up in the fire. He scrambled frantically for the narrow opening above his head. He fought to hold his breath, his lips clamped tightly together. His eyes were streaming from the hot, acrid smoke and the tears scoured white streaks down his filthy cheeks. Drib's fingers and toes bled from kicking and clawing at the sheer, crumbling walls. His head was dizzy, swimming from the effort, his lungs burned and screamed out for air. He knew he couldn't hold on much longer.

The fingers of his right hand suddenly found the cold, flat, moss-covered bricks that lined the top of the chimney. He reached up above his head, caught hold of the rim with both hands and with a last, desperate effort he hauled himself out into the cold, evening air and stood trembling on the roof. His bare feet slipped and skidded on the steep, frost-covered, weather-bleached tiles of the inn and he had to hang on tightly to the chimney to stop himself from falling to his death on the cobbles lining the dark alleyway below. Choking and sucking in lungfuls of air he tipped his head back away from the plume of thick smoke and fumes that were now belching out. Faintly, mingled with the sound of the crackling flames in the hearth below, he could hear Sweepscuttle cursing his ill luck to have the slowest boy in all Elundium and demanding that the horseman find him another lad to take his place. He could hear Hinch laugh as he dismissed the sweep's ravings and they had a wager that the wretched boy had survived.

"Nobody who is that much of a nuisance can be got rid of that easily. Mark my words, sweep, Crippled Drib will turn up none the worse for his little warming. We were just hurrying him along. He'll be back before the night is out and he'll be pestering anybody silly enough to listen to that endless stream of stupid questions, and he'll still be getting under everybody's feet no matter which way they turn. You just stop your carping and see if I'm not right!"

"I'm not a nuisance! It's not my fault if there is so much to learn about horses!" muttered Drib indignantly, edging his way cautiously along the ridge of the roof.

A cold draught of air touched his cheek and ruffled his hair. He frowned and glanced up to see a huge bird, an owl, hovering just above his head. The owl hooted softly and stooped silently away between the forest of tall, smoking chimney stacks that peopled the steep, frost-glistening rooftops. The bird reappeared moments later, retracing the route it had taken and settled on a stack close to him, strutting backwards and forwards, its voice rising to shrieking hoots.

"Thank you, but it's all right, I can find my way down. I know my way about up here almost better than the lanes and alleyways below!" Drib laughed, and then he suddenly stopped and frowned as he stared across at the owl. It had spoken to him. Well, not exactly in words but he had understood what it had said. He felt a sharp tingle of excitement run up his spine. He remembered listening, entranced, to the

stories of how Mulcade, the Battle Owl, had saved the
King's life. How he had swooped low across the sand
school between Esteron's hooves when he was young
and wild and the owl had called out for him to spare
Thane's life after two of the rough riders had thrown
him into the school. He remembered hearing how the
King had understood every hoot and shriek of the owl
and the great Warhorse's thundering hooves had
come to a stop almost touching his outstretched fingers.

"You spoke to me! You spoke to me exactly as
Mulcade once spoke to the King. Why?" Drib whispered in startled amazement.

"Esteron bade me watch over you, chimney boy,"
the owl hooted, spreading its wings and vanishing as
silently as it had appeared.

"Esteron!" Drib smiled, half-closing his eyes as he
remembered, savoured, that wonderful moment
when the King had come upon him lying hurt and
bleeding in the gutter in front of the Learning Hall.
Drib remembered cowering down, terrified of being
in the King's way, never expecting him to stop and
lift him up to place him upon Esteron's saddle and let
him ride the horse up the lane and back. It had been
the most magical daylight of his life, an experience
far beyond his wildest dreams, and ever since he had
begged and pleaded with Sweepscuttle to let him
earn an extra scrap of barter. He had promised to
sweep six extra chimneys every daylight and do anything else that would give him enough to buy the left-
over fragments of the sugar cones the sweetmeat
merchants bartered from their stalls at the bottom of
Chimney Lane so that he had a gift for the Lord of
Horses whenever he had the chance to spend a few
precious hours in the Breaking Yards.

Most of the time he was kept far too busy fetching
and carrying, mucking out, polishing and scrubbing
floors or raking the sand school where the young

horses were broken to saddle to get near any of the horses, let alone visit Esteron's stable. But whenever chance allowed and there weren't a dozen demanding voices shouting and cursing him, shouting at him to be quicker, he would slip into the quiet, shadowy stable for the briefest of visits, whispering Esteron's name as he breathed in that special rich aroma of hay-cake in the manger and the smell of harvest in the deep bed of golden straw. Esteron would arch his neck and snort a nicker of greeting, brushing his velvet-soft muzzle across his cheek, crunching at the tiny offering of sugar that he held out.

Drib shivered with cold and begun to work his way down onto a lower roof, searching all the time for the sight of the owl between the chimney stacks, wondering if he hadn't dreamed it up after all. He laughed softly and shook his head, his white teeth gleaming in the darkness: of course he must have dreamed it— owls don't talk to the likes of him—they had much more important things to do. But he paused as he reached the ornately-chiselled gable end of the rambling inn where he knew he could scramble down the rough-hewn granite wall to the ground without too much difficulty. He looked out across the rooftops of the lower circles of the city, towards the flickering lamps that illuminated the Breaking Yards and something caught his eye away to the left, a momentary glimpse of a dark shape. Perhaps it was a large bird gliding away, its silent shadow smoothing effortlessly over the tiles between the chimney stacks, but it vanished before he had time to blink. Drib pinched himself and grinned: perhaps it hadn't been a dream after all. Perhaps the great Warhorse, Esteron, hadn't forgotten all about him. Scrambling from ledge to ledge and humming softly to himself he quickly descended into the alleyway and limped to the door of the inn. There he hesitated, screwing up his courage to take the beating he knew would be awaiting him, and took

a deep breath as he pushed the door open and
stepped in over the threshold.

"You are the most useless, slow, idle boy I've ever
had the misfortune to own. Now stand still and take
your punishment!" Sweepscuttle snarled in fury, his
face purple with anger as he raised his leather belt to
thrash Drib.

The jeers and the shouts of encouragement from
the crowded room fuelled his rage. He brought the
belt down brutally hard across the helpless boy's
shoulders, making him cry out and stagger towards
the roaring fire in the inglenook where the cauldrons
hissed and bubbled as they hung from their trammels
and chains in the thick smoke that curled around
their fat, black bellies.

"Master—I was being as quick as I could. I didn't
mean to drop the brush: there's a difficult twist in the
chimney and . . . " Drib tried to cry in his defence but
Sweepscuttle was deaf to him.

"Stand still, you wretched, crooked boy, and stop
your whining or I'll double the punishment!"

He raised the belt again, this time high above his
head, but as he went to bring it down he felt a strong
hand gripping his wrist. Grunting and turning his head
in surprise, he found Landlord Swatheplenty, red-
faced and flustered, standing close behind him.

"That's enough!" he demanded over the shouts and
jeers of the crowd. Slowly he released his grip on the
sweep's arm. "I don't care what this rabble is urging
you to do: we're not in the practice of beating our
apprentices in public, not in the Prancing Warhorse.
Do it at home if you must—but not in here!"

Drib cowered, his eyes screwed tightly shut, as he
waited for the full force of the blow and when it
didn't come he opened his eyes cautiously and
looked up. He could hardly believe his luck when he
saw that the landlord had intervened to save him.
He took a quick sideways, limping step closer to his

protector, looking past his voluminous, ale-stained apron tails at the crowded room. The shouts and curses for his punishment were beginning to subside as the merchants and traders lost interest in him and returned to their earlier talk. Drib breathed a sigh of relief, only to stifle it as he caught sight of Hinch and a table of men from the Breaking Yards glaring sullenly at him. Then he noticed the thin, sharp face of the Loremaster watching him from the next table. Grout leaned across, drawing the riders into a conspiratorial huddle as he whispered something. One by one they glared across at him, laughing and nodding. Hinch sneered and spat at the floor then climbed to his feet and left.

"Get out, you wretched creature. Get out of my sight before . . . " Sweepscuttle was barely able to contain his anger and as he spoke white specks of spittle were gathering in the corners of his mouth.

Drib didn't need to be asked twice and he made a welcome dash for the door, stepping sideways and ducking quickly as Sweepscuttle threw the studded belt after him. It clattered harmlessly to the floor. The sounds of laughter and cat-calls faded but Drib didn't stop running until he reached the narrow, gloomy entrance to Chimney Lane, where he paused to catch his breath and wonder if he dared risk a quick visit to the Breaking Yards. He knew he might not get another chance for quite some time and his master probably wouldn't arrive home from the Prancing Warhorse until the grey hours had touched the sky, but his punishment wouldn't be forgotten no matter how late the hour, that was for sure. Drib knew his master would be in his favourite corner seat in the inglenook of the inn by now, complaining bitterly that the world was going to ruin and how you couldn't get a good apprentice for love nor barter. He would tell anybody who would listen what an utterly useless, crooked boy Drib was, describing blow by blow what form his punishment must take because, as everybody knew, he must be punished for dropping a brush, especially one as new as the one he had dropped down the chimney; it was the most serious crime a boy could commit.

Drib sighed as he looked up at the glittering canopy of stars above his head, wishing there was some way he could escape, some way he could pay back the barter Sweepscuttle had given his mother to buy him. He wished there was a way he could be free from the miserable life he was trapped in but in his heart he knew that it was impossible. Sweepscuttle would own him to the day he died. He scraped his twisted foot across the frosty cobbles and dug deep into his pocket. Amongst the dust and soot he found a few small crumbs of sugar he had been saving to give to Esteron but there wasn't even enough to cover the centre of the palm of his hand. The cold night air made him shiver and he pulled up his ragged collar, deciding that he would put off going home for a little while longer. He would hurry down to the Breaking Yards and, although he had never been there this late, he hoped the doors were still open so that he could slip unnoticed past the door wardens. It was the one place in all Elundium where he felt really happy and tonight he didn't want to ask anybody a question or fetch and carry; tonight he just wanted to be close to the horses, to whisper his thanks to Esteron just in case he really had sent that owl up across the rooftops to watch out for him.

Drib hesitated when he reached the lower end of Tallow Finger Alley. His sharp instincts warned him that something was wrong; it seemed far too quiet in the lane ahead and the bright lamps set in their firebaskets above the high-arched gateway leading into the Breaking Yards across the lane were guttering and threatening to go out at the slightest breath of wind for the want of trimming. Drib knew that this was something the door warden never allowed to happen until the grey hours had lightened the sky close to morning. Oddly, there wasn't any sign of the door warden sitting in his niche or patrolling slowly between the two huge iron-studded doors as he called out the hours, stamping sparks off his boots as he tried to keep out the cold.

Cautiously Drib crept forward, feeling his way along the rough granite wall until he reached the low entrance to the disused buriers' tunnel that had once led under the lane into the stableyard. In the day-lights of the Granite Kings it had been the pathway of the dead and rumour had it that on dark nights the echo of the buriers' bell could still be heard. Customs and superstitions might have changed with the passing suns but Drib still shivered nervously and felt his dirty scalp prickle as he crouched down, pressing himself into the inky shadows that dwelt in the bricked-up entrance of the tunnel. He was unsure of what he should do and he was trying to ignore the small voice inside his head that was urging him to go back to Chimney Lane and await his master; it was reminding him that he was already in enough trouble for dropping the brush down the inn chimney without making it worse by trespassing in the stables at this late hour. But there was something wrong: he was sure of it, and he couldn't go back without trying to find out what it was.

He tried to peer across the lane through the mass of swirling nightshapes that lazily drifted around, threading their darkness through the city.

"Damn it, let me see what's happening!" he whispered fiercely, shaking his head and rubbing his fingers across his face in an effort to brush them aside as they glided smoothly and silently across his skin. The Nightshapes swirled faster, scattering at his agitated touch, momentarily thinning and drifting apart. Drib craned his neck, moving a step closer to the gate arch, frowning as he saw that the huge, unguarded doors stood unlocked and slightly ajar. This was something he knew Breakmaster would never allow. Suddenly he caught the sound of voices and running footsteps in the stableyard beyond the doors. Drib caught his breath as he realized that there must be intruders, Nightbeasts or something, in the stables. They must have broken into the city under the cover of darkness. He'd heard the rumours of the creatures roaming through Meremire Forest and everybody said it would only be a matter of time before they were hammering on the gates of the city again.

"Esteron! They mustn't hurt Esteron!" he gasped in panic, running and limping across the lane towards the entrance as fast as he could. He had to raise the alarm: he had to warn Breakmaster.

He was about to slip through the gap between the doors when a tall figure, hooded beneath a heavy door warden's cloak, emerged directly in front of him, blocking his path. The figure stooped, caught hold of Drib's sleeve and demanded to know what he wanted at this late hour.

"I . . . I . . . I thought Nightbeasts had broken into the city—you . . . you . . . you weren't out here patrolling or sitting in your niche—I heard voices, I thought they'd broken in. I was going to wake Breakmaster and warn him."

Drib was breathless with fear. Suddenly he was lifted up roughly, and felt himself twisted and turned as if the hooded figure wanted to examine him and make sure of who he was in the flickering lamplight.

"I . . . I'm sorry—I came down to see if you would let me into the stable yard to say goodnight to the horses—I know it's late but . . . "

He was cut short by the man's laugh, a harsh, crackling sound that sent a warning shiver up Drib's spine. This wasn't the usual door warden, Drib was sure of that: he had caught the rough edge of the warden's tongue and a clip behind the ear often enough to recognize him.

"Were you now, Drib? Well, in that case you had better go in and say your goodnights!"

There was almost a veiled sneer in the man's voice as he set Drib down, but he kept a firm, almost painful, grip on his arm as he looked past him through the gap in the doors, tilting his head as if he was listening, waiting for something.

"It's late—I'd better be going home. Yes, perhaps it would be better if I came back tomorrowlight rather than risk disturbing the horses now. I don't want to wake everybody up, and my master will be worried: he'll be waiting up for me . . . " Drib cried out, squirming and wriggling against the strong fingers that were clamped around his arm. Something was desperately wrong in the stables: he was sure of it now, and he knew he had to get away and raise the alarm.

"Keep still, you wretched, crooked creature. Sweepscuttle's too drunk by now to care where you are: he'll never come looking for you!" the figure snarled as he manhandled him through the doors and pushed them firmly shut behind him, cutting off Drib's escape.

Drib looked up at the hooded man helplessly and felt a knot of panic tighten in his stomach. There was something very familiar about his snarling voice: he was sure he had heard it before. Yes, he remembered: he'd heard it cursing him for his slowness whenever he ventured into the stables—it belonged to one of the horsemen, the tall one who had been sitting at the end of the table in the inn. He was almost certain it was him, but why?

Drib suddenly heard the rattle of a stable bolt being pushed home and a low whistle, followed immediately by a startled, neighing shriek from the inner stableyard. Drib's captor laughed and shook him fiercely before letting him go. "Get along, Drib, go and see your precious horses. Go on!"

Drib stumbled and limped forward, almost falling, catching at the cold, stone wall to save himself. The horse in the inner stable screamed again. Drib took a running step towards the vaulted corridor that led to Breakmaster's rooms only to find his captor had beaten him to it and was blocking the way.

"Call one word for help and I'll kill you where you stand, sweep's boy!" he hissed, giving Drib a brutal push towards the stables, almost sending him down onto his knees. "Move! Get going, you miserable creature!" He drew a dagger from beneath his cloak and prodded it threateningly at his back. The needle point sheered through Drib's ragged coat easily, making a hole between his shoulder blades as he staggered forward.

"The horses, Drib, go quickly—one of them is in trouble!" the man sneered.

The muffled, neighing shrieks of pain and the sound of a whip lashing across flesh grew louder as Drib ran as fast as his crippled legs would carry him past the shadows beneath the archway that led into the inner stableyard.

"Why? What are you doing? Why do you want to hurt any of the horses?" he cried out in dismay, hoping his voice would raise some of the riders and grooms sleeping in their quarters in the hay-lofts.

All around him, the other horses were becoming agitated in their stalls and stables and had begun to snort and neigh in alarm, lashing out at their stable doors and kicking-boards, tossing their heads. The whites of their eyes showed in the gloomy, flickering light of the hanging lamps. Esteron had heard the cry of distress from his open stable beside the sand school and his ears were flattened as he roared out the Warhorse challenge and leapt over the high barrier fence of the school. Sparks flew from his iron-shod feet as he galloped through the breaking yards while lanterns were being lit and voices began calling out in the darkness. Suddenly everyone in the breaking yard began tumbling out of bed and the Nighthorses were rearing and plunging, breaking their picket ropes.

"Because we hate favourites! We'd sooner be rid of you now and forever!" the voice behind Drib hissed as he ran out into the centre of the inner stableyard. He turned his head from side to side, trying to pinpoint exactly which stable the muffled, neighing screams were coming from, confused by the other sounds of alarm erupting all around him.

"Ahead on the right—third box from the end—go quickly before it's too late, boy!" the voice goaded him.

Drib ran towards the stable where Fleetfoot, the small, dark bay pony that Thunderstone, the Keeper of Underfall, had sent as a gift for Krann was stabled ready to be broken to the saddle.

Drib heard the sickening sound of an iron-tailed whip sing down through the air and strike the pony as he reached the stable door. "Leave him alone! Leave him alone, you cowards!" Drib shouted, boiling with anger as he reached the stable door and threw back the bolts. As he pulled open the heavy, wooden door the two shadowy figures laughed at him and one of them threw the iron-tailed whip in his face, almost knocking him off his feet as they ran past him and vanished. Drib caught the whip and rushed forward into the darkened stable, falling to his knees in the bloody, trampled straw beside the pony where it lay, trembling, its nostrils flared in terror, its shivering flanks and neck a mass of long, bloody, open weals where the iron-tailed whip had cut through its flesh.

Drib had heard all the dark rumours that surrounded Krann. How Queen Elionbel had rescued

him but how he had really come from the darkness, a
bastard offspring of Krulshards. There were rumours
of a powerful magic that turned the boy into a helpless, innocent baby at the Battle of the Rising and
told of how King Thane had given him a shadow: but
there were plenty of people who believed that King
Thane was a fool to care for him. Word was that the
magic spell could always be broken, but Drib did not
have the faintest idea what that would mean.
Curiosity had meant that Drib had stopped more
than once to look at the pony on his way through the
Breaking Yards and had seen that he was going to
make a beautiful riding pony one daylight, or would
have done before this atrocity.

"Fleetfoot, oh Fleet, what have they done to you?"
he cried, leaving the flail hanging forgotten over his
shoulder as he gently lifted up the pony's head and
cradled it in his arms. Drib sobbed, tears coursing
down his cheeks, as he stroked the pony's velvet-soft
muzzle and the white terror around Fleet's eyes
began to lessen as the boy whispered and soothed
him.

Light suddenly flooded the stable and Drib cried
out as strong hands lifted him up and pulled him
away from the stricken animal. He looked up at a
crowd of angry faces crowding the stable door.
Suddenly Esteron burst through them, snorting and
whinnying at the pony, nuzzling its wounds before
turning on Drib with his ears flattened along his
head. He struck the boy in the chest, sending him
reeling backwards across the stable towards Errant
and Breakmaster who now stood filling the doorway
staring down at the injured pony. Drib stumbled
against the horseman, blood from the whip wetting
his arm.

"Boy—what have you got there?" Breakmaster's
voice had the rage of thunder in it as he spotted the
whip and plucked it from Drib's shoulder, grabbing

him by the scruff of his neck with his other hand. He lifted the boy clean off his feet and shook him so violently that he would have broken his neck if Hinch hadn't intervened from beside the stable door.

"Easy, master: he should be tried by the law in Candlebane Hall for what he has done this night. Clearly he is guilty and the King will have him flogged in public until his skin hangs from him."

Breakmaster hesitated, his face red with anger, his body trembling with the effort to contain his rage. "To think I befriended you, boy. I lifted you from the gutter and trusted you. I nurtured your dreams and let you come unhindered into the Yards among my beautiful horses . . ." his voice trailed off in bitterness and regret. He thrust Drib into the waiting hands of two of his riders and dropped to his knees beside Fleetfoot.

"Take him away from my sight forever. Lock him up in the darkest hole you can find until he is tried in Candlebane Hall. Take him!"

"But Breakmaster, I am innocent. The warden forced me in here at dagger-point, I swear. I could never hurt Fleetfoot, I would never harm a hair . . ."

Breakmaster looked up at Drib and for a moment their eyes met and Drib almost quailed beneath the withering, accusing gaze.

"I . . . I . . . I am innocent—I swear it!" he tried to whisper, but the horseman was deaf to him.

"No, wait!" Errant frowned as he searched the faces of the crowd that filled the doorway. "Let the warden speak, let us see if there is any truth in what the boy says."

"Well, warden, what say you to the boy's accusations?" Breakmaster asked as the warden stepped forward into the light.

"It is a mystery to me, master: I don't know how the boy got past me on the door. The first I've seen of him tonight is here in the stable when you caught him red-handed with the whip across his shoulder. The bare cheek of him—trying to accuse me!"

"There, you see, he lies. Take him away. Get him out of my sight!" Breakmaster demanded.

Drib looked desperately around the sea of hostile faces as he was taken from the stable. Surely somebody must know the truth? Surely somebody must realize he could never do a terrible thing like that? The helpless animal must have been nearly beaten to death. He caught sight of Hinch and two of the riders from the inn and when he saw the look of triumph in their hooded eyes he realized in an instant that they must have planned it. He was half-carried, half-dragged away across the cobbles and made to stagger and crawl up through the seven circles of the city, his crippled knees a raw and bleeding mess before he was thrown into a damp, filthy cellar beneath Candlebane Hall to await his trial.

"But I didn't do it—why won't anybody believe me? I didn't do it!" he cried in despair as the cellar door was slammed shut and the key turned.

Drib sank down upon a mouldy scattering of damp, evil-smelling straw in the darkest corner of the vast, vaulted cellar beneath Candlebane Hall. He buried his head in his hands and wept hot tears of despair as he tried to shut out the cursing shouts that had followed him while he was being dragged out of the stableyard. Cruel, taunting jeers and curses that still scratched painfully at his ears: so much hatred against him that still echoed inside his head. People had accused him of beating the pony out of jealousy because, with his crooked legs, he would never be able to ride. Voices that cursed him and called him a treacherous liar who had wormed his way into Breakmaster's affections, beguiled him with his cunning, just to get close enough to hurt the horses. They had sneered and spat at him, deriding and cursing his dead father, calling him a coward who had let the shadow warriors into the city; they had accused his mother of lying with Krulshards, Master of Nightmares, to spawn such a crooked, ugly, spiteful creature.

"But I didn't! I couldn't have! I would never have hurt any of the horses. Why, oh why doesn't anybody believe me? Why do they all hate me so much? I can't help the way I look, I didn't ask to be born this way!"

Blind misery overwhelmed him and smothered him in a blanket of black despair so that he was unaware of the swarm of large, spiny rats that infested the cellar and were scuttling towards him, drawn by the noise of his sobs. Their black eyes gleamed in the feeble light that filtered down through the barred grille high up in the wall and they closed in, pausing to stand up on their hind legs, their sharp noses twitching, scenting an easy kill. The leading rats moved faster, their claws scraping and slipping as they swarmed over the piles of refuse that had been spread across the shiny floor. Suddenly they stopped, cowering and squealing as they scattered, running for the cover of their underground nests. The spines along their backs prickled in defence, their long tails snaking and thrashing the ground behind them.

Drib heard their high-pitched squeals and instinctively drew his legs up underneath him as he searched the gloomy cellar. "Rats! I hate rats!" he hissed in alarm.

Ever since his second daylight in Sweepscuttle's service when he had been forced up the chimney of a rat-infested hovel in the poorest part of the weavers' section of the city he had loathed rats. The whole area had been overrun with the creatures and he had been warned to watch out where he trod for fear of being bitten. They could be seen everywhere: feeding in the gutters and alleyways, scavenging in every dark corner, and there were thousands of their nests in the bales of wool and rags. He had watched a weaver break open a bale once, beating it with a stick as he cut the ties, and hundreds of them had run up the walls in a grey, shrieking tide as the others scuttled away across the looms. The weavers cursed and hit them with anything they could lay their hands upon. Everybody who worked at the looms wore thick leather boots, trousers and jerkins to keep them safe and the caps they wore upon their heads had a broad flap sewn across the back that came down below their shoulders to prevent the rats that dropped on them from the ceilings biting their necks or getting inside their clothes. Once, an old weaver had taken him into the store houses and made him stand very quietly to listen; he had heard the sound of the rats gnawing their way into the new bundles of rushes and reeds that had just been piled up after the harvest.

"You can always smell them: that's the first warning that they're near you," he had warned Drib.

Sweepscuttle had laughed at him, deriding his fear as he pushed Drib into the chimney hole, but he had given him a stick and told him to beat the walls as he climbed. Drib shuddered: the memory of that climb was still so vivid, the taste of soot, the choking, dusty darkness that had filled his eyes as he'd scrabbled for a hand-hold, and that dreadful moment when he had blindly put his hand into that rats' nest halfway up the chimney. He would never forget the soft, warm touch of their bodies, their sudden, squealing shrieks and the shearing pain as a row of sharp teeth bit at his fingers. He could feel their claws as they had swarmed along his arms and up across his chest. He had screamed and fallen with the vile things clinging onto him, but all Sweepscuttle had done was to laugh and curse his slowness, telling the startled weaver to stay put in his chair as the boy landed in a billowing cloud of soot and scattering rats. He had said that a nip or two from the vermin would make the idle lad all the quicker and more careful where he put his hands the next time he sent him up a chimney. He had ignored Drib's screams as he had fought to tear away the creatures whose claws were caught in his ragged clothes.

Drib frowned and looked carefully around the gloomy cellar. Rubbing his sleeve across his nose, he wondered why the rats hadn't attacked: he knew they were there—he could smell them and hear them scuttling through their underground tunnels. Gradually he became aware of a faint glow in the room, a thin, translucent aura of light that shimmered and curled around the corner like mist and spread up to where he lay huddled on the ground. He looked up and could just see a tiny, fingernail moon riding the black night sky high up beyond the bars in the grille but it was too weak to cast more than thin shadows on the floor of his prison. He shrugged and let his head fall back into his hands. What did it matter where the light came from? Nothing mattered any more: the rats might just as well kill him now and end his misery; they might just as well gnaw his bones into dust because he was never, ever going to be allowed near the horses again. All his fragile dreams were broken and lay in ruins. Nobody was ever going to believe he hadn't hurt that pony: nobody cared about the truth. His shoulders trembled and shook with grief and new tears welled up to blur his eyes. He was so alone, so utterly alone and helpless.

"Truth, Drib, truth is a precious flame that you must never allow to be extinguished," a soft voice whispered from the darkness close to his ear.

Drib blinked and looked up, startled by the voice. He stared around him to see where it had come from while shrinking nervously back against the wall. The thin beams of moonlight seemed to strengthen and change, converging into a swirling, rising cloud of bright, transparent colours of a rainbow cloak that seemed to fill the vaulted cellar with a soft, beautiful light.

Drib's teeth began to chatter with fear as a tall, translucent, fragile figure began to appear cloaked by the shifting light. It was an old man, old beyond the time of the Granite Kings, bowed and heavy with the wisdom and cares of the world that hung about his shoulders. "I heard you, Drib."

The figure smiled gently, moving slowly towards him, reaching out long wrinkled fingers that had the touch of summer warmth in them as he took hold of Drib's dirty hands. He fixed the boy with a penetrating gaze that Drib felt searched into every dusty, sooty corner of his soul.

"I heard you cry out in the dark hopelessness of your despair: you are crying for the truth to be heard, child. Now, tell me, what has reduced you to this? What cruel twists of fate now hold you a prisoner beneath Candlebane Hall?"

"Nevian! Lord of all power!" Drib could barely find the breath to whisper his name. He could see from the beautiful colours in the rainbow cloak that the figure standing in front of him could be none other than the Master of Magic and he was terrified. Like every other boy in the Learning Hall he had sat on the edge of his chair, enchanted by the stories of the magician, hearing how he would appear and disappear, sweeping all before him, changing things at the dry snap of his fingers. Everybody knew how he walked with kings and balanced the fate of the world in his hands.

Drib felt dizzy and faint. Wasn't he in enough trouble already without the Master of Magic suddenly appearing here in his prison? With a sinking apprehension he guessed that the King must already have heard Breakmaster's version of what had happened in the stable yard and now Nevian had come to punish him. He had vivid recollections of those stories about how he had turned thousands of Marchers into trees because they had refused to swear their loyalties to King Thane. He couldn't even begin to imagine what the Master of Magic would do to him.

Nevian laughed softly as he stopped and lifted Drib to his feet. "You have nothing to fear from me, child. Come, walk with me and tell me everything. Come," and he put his arm around the frightened boy's shoulders, drawing him into the melting, shimmering colours of his rainbow cloak.

"They . . . they accused me falsely! I mean the rough riders did . . . and Breakmaster . . . he thought I beat that pony . . . it was almost dead and . . . and . . . " Drib began to speak so fast that the words tumbled over one another in their rush to get out.

"Easy, easy, slow down, Drib, one word at a time. You go too fast for an old man's ears. Start again: let us begin from that moment when you let the brush slip through your fingers and drop back down the chimney into the flames."

Drib gasped and looked up into the Master of Magic's lined and smiling face. His eyes were round and huge with astonishment. "You know about me dropping the brush! But how could you? It only happened tonight and I haven't told anybody. How do you know?"

Nevian laughed softly, making the rainbow cloak sway from where it hung from his shoulders, its voluminous folds billowing and subsiding, the colours melting, blending together, changing from deep indigo through ultramarine to vivid jade, hot rouge and flushing pinks to cooler pale, crocus hues and azure blues. "Magic!" he whispered conspiratorially. "I am the Master of Magic and I am everywhere. I am in the wind that rustles the leaves in the trees, I am in the swirling eddies of dust at the beginning of the road beneath the Stumble Gate, I am in the noise and the bustle of the city, I am in everything where there dwells a little touch of magic."

Drib frowned, uncertainly. "Then you could have stopped that brush from falling down the chimney— or your magic could have—or you could have told my master, Sweepscuttle, that it was an accident!"

"What?" Nevian cried, looking down at the boy, his eyebrows drawn fiercely together. "You would have me squander my time and my magic running after sweeps' boys and their like, setting right every trivial wrong I stumble over?" He paused, his ancient face creasing into a smile. "No, Drib, I cannot be everywhere at once, much as I would like to set right every wrong. Remember there are many important matters that rest more heavily upon my shoulders than a ruined sweep's brush. Why, at this very moment the peace and tranquillity of Elundium lies threatened by new, strangling shadows of discontent that, with all my power, I cannot unravel. The Nightbeasts are dead, yet they haunt the Greenway's edge. Yes, Drib, there is an evil out there hiding in the wilderness of Meremire Forest and I know not how to stop it."

Nevian sighed wearily, shaking his head of flowing, white hair. "Nothing ever seems quite so clear to me now that the age of the Granite Kings has passed. Yes, we have won the daylight but the images of this new age are muddled and indistinct." He paused, glancing down to see the small, misshapen sweep's boy waiting at his side and he suddenly remembered why he had been drawn down into the dark, cold cellar beneath Candlebane Hall. "Forgive me, Drib, I have wandered a little off our path. But tell me, what happened in the stable yard tonight that Breakmaster should accuse you of such a terrible crime? Tell me of this injustice you have suffered—but be warned, keep close to the truth, because that is a quality I value above all others, and one that Breakmaster is well tried in. He, I know, would not suffer a lie easily."

Drib seized his chance to tell the truth about what

really happened but he could not help crying out as he reached the end. "Breakmaster wouldn't listen to one word I tried to say. He's so convinced that I betrayed his trust, and . . . and . . . and then everyone in the crowd cursed me and shouted that my father was a coward and a traitor before he died. They say that he was the one who let the shadow warriors into the city in the great siege. And . . . and they accuse my mother of lying with Krulshards . . . " Drib choked back his sobs, unable to repeat those last vile, untruths they had shouted and that would now be forever engraved in his memory.

Anger burnt hotly in the magician's eyes as he heard the cruel lies and injustices the boy had suffered. He cast his rainbow cloak over Drib's head so that he would know the truth. The colours beneath the cloak faded and starlight lit the frosty sky, thick streaks of smoke billowed overhead and Drib could see fires raging unchecked through the lower circles of the city. He could see the silhouette of the great gates of the city ahead of him in the flickering light of the fires and the black shadow rats overrunning the walls and pouring through every sewer and culvert, biting the defenders' heels and ankles and swarming up their legs before pulling them down onto the cold, winter cobbles. Everywhere the hideous shadow warriors followed in their wake, maiming and killing, driving the defenders back step by step. In the smoke and confusion Drib saw the Border Runners snarling and hurling the foul, brittle-spined shadow rats high into the air, Warhorses reared and plunged, crushing and killing every shadow figure that rushed to overwhelm them and stoops of owls hooted and dropped out of the battle-torn sky but they could not stop the howling black tide that poured relentlessly in over the walls, driving the city's defenders back step by step.

Drib suddenly caught his breath as he spotted a familiar figure in the smoke. It was his father in the thick of the battle, fighting to hold the great gates shut. Drib wanted so much to run and help but Nevian held his arm, whispering that he could only watch and be shown the truth. His father had been bitten a dozen times by the shadow rats and his body had become twisted and deformed; his helm was riven and bloody and his shield-arm hung lifeless, the splintered bones showing through the thin, leather jerkin that was his only armour against the shadow warriors' swords and spears, but still he fought on, refusing to retreat, building a wall of Nightmare dead around where he stood, but with each sweep of his sword he grew weaker, staggering and stumbling to his knees with exhaustion. Drib watched him crying out the King's name in defiance, swearing his love of the sunlight as a ring of shadow warriors closed in, driving their spears through his heart before they trampled his broken body into the dirt and threw the great gate open for Kruel's shadow army of terror to swarm up through the city.

It grew darker and the images beneath the cloak began to merge. Drib looked up as the Master of Magic drew back the folds of shifting colour, only now there were tears of pride shining in his eyes.

"You see, child, your father wasn't a coward: in fact he was amongst the bravest of men who spent their lives to bring your king those few precious moments to give him the time to retreat up through the city into the highest circles behind the walls that are protected by Swanwater and Candlebane Hall. One daylight it will come to pass that your King will honour him. But to know the truth is not enough: you have been sorely wronged by those riders. Here, give me your hand, it is only fitting that you should be the one to sow these seeds of doubt."

Nevian searched beneath his cloak as the bright colours changed and blended before he brought forth the small, sky-blue pouch that hung from a belt of silver strands woven through with black ebony. "Ah, here it is. Now, hold out your hand and keep it still," he laughed, shaking out a few tiny, iridescent grains of doubt into the palm of Drib's hand. They burned hotly and their weight made him stagger. "Take care, do not scatter them yet!" Nevian cried in alarm. "Wait until I tell you!"

"But what are they?" Drib asked suspiciously, trying to keep his trembling hand still.

The Master of Magic put his fingers together and tilted his head to one side as if listening, trying to catch some far-off sound. "Breakmaster is a good and honest man. He served both King Holbian, the last Granite King, and King Thane and he has always had a true heart. He fears nothing that moves in the shadows and it was his great skill as a horseman that prepared Beaconlight to carry King Holbian against the Nightbeasts in his last battle on the Causeway Fields. But if he has a fault it is that he quickens to anger all too easily in his dealings with men and sometimes it clouds his reasoning and shrouds the truth. That is why you will be the one to sow the seeds of doubt in his mind."

Nevian paused, his senses sharpening. "Yes, now, go and cast them away into the darkness. Now is the moment, they will take root and grow. Go, go on!"

The boy hesitated, unsure of what he was supposed to do. "Scatter the seeds, cast them away from you: Breakmaster is pacing his room, dwelling on the incident, at this very moment searching for the truth. Go, cast the seed away from you now!" Nevian threw his hands up in exasperation, "They'll do you no good if you keep them stifled in the palm of your hand: the moment will be lost and the truth passed over!"

"But doubt? What will doubt do now? How will it work?" Drib stared down at the tiny, insignificant grains of dust that lay so heavily in the palm of his hand.

Nevian threw back his head and laughed: there was so much innocence about this child. "What will doubt do? Well, my young Drib, in the fullness of time it might just change everything if it falls on fertile ground. But you'll never know, you'll never find out if you don't cast it to the winds now!"

Drib lifted his hand, but he hesitated as he looked past the glowing colours of the rainbow cloak into the dank, stagnant air in the cellar. "But there isn't even a draught. They'll fall on the floor and be lost amongst the straw and . . . "

Nevian cried out in exasperation. "Questions! Always questions, what am I to do with you? If you really believed in magic you would do as I ask—any sensible boy would!"

Drib nodded his head silently, afraid to utter another word as he shook his hand, casting away the seeds of doubt. As they left his palm he felt a cool breath of wind ghost his dirty cheek and ruffle his hair, catching up the tiny, shimmering seeds before they touched the floor, swirling them around and lifting them up. They vanished in an instant through the gaps in the grille high above his head.

"Yes, that should do the trick, despite all the time you wasted with those questions!" Nevian murmured as he began to gather up the flowing hems of his rainbow cloak. "You shall have the truth, Drib, just as I promised you," he called out as his image began to fade.

"But will I ever be allowed near the horses again? Dare I hope for that?" Drib tried to clutch at the melting, vanishing colours as he heard the magician's laughing voice recede into echoes.

"Fear not, Drib, it could be sooner than you think. Keep the flame of truth burning in your heart."

Drib suddenly felt all alone as the cold, gloomy darkness gathered in around him. He shivered, listening, aware that the sounds of the rats gnawing through the rubbish that littered the floor were drawing closer. He searched around anxiously for something to defend himself with, but there was nothing.

Suddenly he could hear a faint noise at the grille above his head and he looked up to see the moon and starlight blotted out, he could hear the low hoot of an owl as it beat its wings to hover. It shrieked as it saw the rats and raked its talons across the rusty, iron grille to make them scuttle away across the floor.

"You've come back!" Drib cried out in surprise as he caught a glimpse of the owl through the railings. It had to be the same one who had flown to him on the rooftops and offered to show him the way down—the one Esteron had sent to keep an eye on him. There couldn't be two owls in the whole of Elundium who would come to help him. A thought suddenly occurred to Drib as the owl hooted his name; if Esteron had sent the owl to watch over him then he must know he wasn't guilty!

He stood awkwardly on tiptoe and clutched at the cold, damp brick wall for support. "Is the pony going to be all right? Has he told Esteron that it wasn't me who beat him? Has he told him that I am innocent?"

"Patience, sweep's boy, patience. The seeds of doubt have been sown!"

"Patient! How can I be patient when those evil monsters who hurt Fleet are still roaming free?"

"Stay alert!" warned the owl, sternly. "I will leave now and bring you back a stick to beat the rats off with." So saying, he spread his great wings and silently disappeared.

Drib sighed and started to limp in a small circle, clapping his hands and stamping his sore, crooked feet in an effort to keep the advancing rats at bay. Then he paused, tilting his head to one side. He was sure he could hear voices on the winding steps that led down to the cellar and he grinned. It must have worked! The seeds of doubt must have changed Breakmaster's mind and they were coming to set him free. But the smile faded from his face as the voices grew louder and more distinct. Somebody was shouting, protesting their innocence as they were being manhandled down towards the cellar, and the other voices were those of the guards who had brought him down earlier. He recognized their snarling, cursing voices.

The door burst open and lamplight flooded the cellar. Silhouetted against it Drib saw a tall, thin fellow wrestling with four guards who were trying to push him in through the door. "Get in there, you thief! You're a disgrace to your father's good name! A disgrace to all of us!"

The youth stumbled and tripped over the threshold before landing in a sprawling heap, but he was on his feet before Drib could blink, facing the door, his right fist raised, the first two fingers held upright in the Archer's gesture of defiance just as the door was slammed in his face.

"I'm innocent—and you know it!" he shouted angrily. "You won't keep me in here for long: there isn't a dungeon strong enough in all Elundium to hold me!"

"Tell it at your judgement! See how many people believe you then!" sneered one of the gaolers as the clatter of their armoured boots receded on the stairs.

"You're no better than that sneak of a Loremaster—it's him you should be locking up down here—he's the thief, not me! He's the one stealing people's hearts, poisoning them against the King—I know, I heard him whispering, conspiring, weaving treachery—but you won't listen to me, will you! You ignorant pigs! Call yourselves King's men!"

The boy was angry, hammering on the door with his fists. "Elders!" he cried, letting his hand fall to his side as he turned to inspect the prison. "They always think they're so right. I wish I'd burnt that Learning Hall down while I had the chance, if only . . . " he paused, knuckling his fists and raising them defensively as he spotted a small, shadowy figure almost hidden in the gloomy corner of the cellar. "Who's there? Come out where I can see you!"

Drib limped forward as quickly as he could. He had recognized Eider the moment the cellar door had been thrown open: he was Captain Gray Goose's son and almost old enough to be a man. Drib had learned early on to keep well out of his way in the Learning Hall; not because he had ever hurt him or indulged in the bullying he'd had to suffer at the hands of the other boys but because he had an ugly temper and there was a scent of danger and recklessness about him. More than once he had stood up to the Loremaster and challenged his truth in the stories he told them. He would laugh and sneer, boasting that he wasn't going to wait around to step into his father's shoes, he was sick of living in his shadow, listening to all the nonsense about honour and winning the daylight—he was going to take what he wanted and make his own way. He cared nothing for tradition.

Drib had heard the wild rumours about how he had stolen from the merchants purely for fun, scattering their barter and goods on the cobbles and challenging them to catch him if they could. Once he had thrown all the Loremaster's scrolls and parchments out into the street and accused him of conspiring with the Chancellors. Not that anybody believed him, but he had laughed in his father's face and snatched the flail out of his hand when he had tried to beat him in public, and he had broken it in two before running off. Drib had a secret admiration for him but he would never have dared to do anything like that when Sweepscuttle had beaten *him*.

"It's . . . it's only me, Drib, the sweep's boy," he offered timidly.

Eider looked down dismissively. The boy was so small and so dirty it was difficult to see where he ended and the shadows began. "Is that all? Isn't there anybody else here?" he muttered, searching the furthest corners of the dank and dingy cellar.

"There's only the rats—hundreds of them. The owl

said I had to make a lot of noise to keep them from attacking me until he returns with a stick for me to beat them with."

Eider's lip curled back in a sneer of ridicule. He remembered how everybody, especially the mason boys, had taunted the little cripple for his day-dreaming in the Learning Hall. They had laughed at the way he made up stories of how the King had let him ride his horse. The other boys had hated him for stories like that but he had never joined in with the bullying: he didn't care much one way or another. What did it bother him what nonsense the boy filled his head with? But he wasn't going to put up with having to listen to it down here: he had more important things to worry about.

"Owls don't talk to the likes of you or me—and they won't go around carrying sticks for a sweep's boy. That's all stuff and nonsense from the Learning Hall. Wake up, Drib, and I'll show you what to do with the rats!" Eider stared almost casually around him but his eyes were sharp and suddenly he dived onto the ground, rolling over, his quick, agile hands snaking up through the mounds of refuse on the floor, his fingers finding and pinching shut on two long, rats' tails. The rats squealed and shrieked, their claws scratching helplessly as he swung them up high into the air. With a laugh and a quick flick of the wrist he snapped their spines and threw them dead onto the floor. All around them the grey-spined rodents that had been silently advancing through the rubbish fled, scuttling for their holes.

Drib stared down at the two dead rats at his feet. "How did you do that? Where did you learn it?"

Eider laughed and kicked their fat bodies aside. "It's easy, the power's in the flick of the wrist. Rubel taught me how to kill them with my bare hands when I accompanied my father to the Wayhouse at Woodsedge. Rubel's father, Tombel, was dead against it but he showed me anyway." Eider started to inspect the door to see if he could pick the lock.

"You met *Lord* Rubel—the Queen's brother—the one warrior in all Elundium who dared to journey deep into the City of Night? He was the one who retrieved the sword of Durondel, the sword the King used to kill Krulshards, piercing it through his black heart. Rubel carried the sword back to the great battle on the Rising, didn't he? He wrapped a piece of Krulshards' black malice around it and delivered it into the King's hand in the nick of time just as Nevian, the Master of Magic had commanded him. It's one of the best stories . . . "

"Yes, yes, I've heard it a dozen times and each time it's a little more embroidered. Magicians! Black malices! All stuff and nonsense! Now be quiet, I can't think with you rattling on worse than a barrel with loose staves. Stop asking these useless questions and telling these stupid stories all the time!" Eider turned angrily away: he was beginning to see why the other boys had persecuted this sweep's lad—he never stopped talking.

"But . . . but Rubel made Nevian a cloak from the skins of the shadow rats and it hid him during the shadowlight. I met Nevian only tonight—here in the cellar. He . . . he said . . . " Drib stuttered to a halt as Eider advanced on him.

"Don't you ever stop?" he cried in exasperation, raising his fist only to let it fall to his side and stare up at the grille set high in the wall. His mouth fell open in surprise as he heard the low hoot of an owl and then saw a long stick rattle through the bars and drop to the ground.

"There! I told you the owl would bring it, didn't I! I wasn't making it up!" Drib cried triumphantly, limping around the archer and making a stooping, lurching grab for the stick before Eider got there, calling out a thanks to the owl as it began to rise and fly away.

"Wait, call it back, don't let it escape!" Eider

hissed, gripping at Drib's shoulder so hard that puffs of soot and grime erupted in a cloud from his ragged coat.

Eider's mind was alive, crowded with possibilities. A tame, talking owl—he had never believed that a half of those tales of Battle Owls, Warhorses and Border Runners were true. He wasn't even sure how many of the stories about the Master of Nightmares, Krulshards, were fairy stories meant to frighten small children and make them be good. An owl was a bird, a Border Runner a wild dog who scavenged for its food in the forest, nothing more. Warhorses were the rogues that were difficult to break: after all a horse was a horse, a beast of burden. He knew the King and many of the Marchers and Gallopers kept owls to hunt vermin and to fly up and warn them of an enemy's approach, but the rest of it was just tales told in the Learning Hall, the close weave of fantasy dressed up by the Loremaster to fill the empty heads of boys like Drib. None of it had ever really happened. Or had it?

"Drib, call that owl back! Ask it how many guards are patrolling the doors of Candlebane Hall! Ask it if it can lift the keys to the door of our prison—or bring a bow, a quiver full of arrows. Ask it . . ."

The owl shrieked and vanished from the barred window in a swirl of feathers.

"Now look what you've done—you've scared him away," Drib accused, stepping angrily towards Eider, ignoring the fact that the other boy was twice his size. "He didn't come here to do your fetching and carrying, you know. Esteron, the King's horse, sent him to watch over me."

"Yes, yes, you're right, I shouldn't have called out like that. Perhaps you had better speak for me next time. Tell the owl I meant no offence," Eider answered thoughtfully, putting an arm around Drib's shoulder and searching out the most comfortable spot amongst the rubbish for them to sit. He could see now that there was more to Crooked Drib than had first met the eye, a lot more, that with a little careful coaxing he might just be able to use to his advantage.

"So tell me, Drib," he started, "if you're so friendly with Esteron, this magician and the owls, what on earth are you doing locked up beneath Candlebane Hall? You're not down here for your health, that's for sure!"

Drib wasn't altogether happy about telling Eider anything. He preferred the wild, reckless boy who had passed him by without a glance to this sudden attention.

"Come on, tell me, and I'll help you out of here," Eider pressed.

"I don't see how any of it will help you," Drib muttered, but he took a deep, reluctant breath and told the bigger boy everything that had happened from the moment earlier in the evening when he had dropped the brush down the chimney to the appearance of Nevian. Eider's ears seemed to prick up with interest when he told him how he had seen Grout whispering to Hinch and that group of horsemen in the inn and how they had left hurriedly before he had walked down to the stable yards. Drib had fully expected the Archer to laugh and tell him he was making it up, that Nevian wasn't real, but instead he leaned closer, his face very serious.

"I wouldn't be at all surprised to discover that Grout was at the bottom of this. There's a smell of treachery in the folds of that Loremaster's cloak: I should know, I've overheard him whispering to some very shadowy figures in the alleyways behind the Learning Hall. I know he's up to no good, but nobody listens to me!"

Eider paused and angrily struck the floor with the heel of his boot before turning to glare across at Drib. "You don't suppose you could call that magician back, do you? I bet he could open this door in an instant."

"Don't be silly!" Drib frowned, shaking his head. "It's more than I would dare do, even if I knew how he would probably be so cross at me disturbing him that he would turn me into something awful."

A sudden noise at the grille and urgent hoots made them stop and look up at the clattering sound of a bow and two arrows being hastily pushed through the rusty bars. It brought both of them to their feet, talk of the magician forgotten.

"The owl listened to me after all! Thank you!" Eider laughed, hardly able to believe his luck as he picked up the bow, testing the string and pushing the two arrows through his belt. He paused and glanced up, aware that the owl was still making a lot of noise and that Drib was listening intently to what it was saying.

"What's the matter? What's happening out there? Tell me!" he demanded, but Drib lifted his hand for silence and he had to wait until the owl had subsided into watchful silence before Drib turned round.

"They've caught those tunnellers and the two Marchers, the wild men who were causing all the trouble in Meremire Forest, and they're bringing them into the city, in chains—tonight! The candles are being lit in Candlebane Hall this very moment ready for the King to judge them. But . . . " Drib hesitated, not sure that he had understood the rest of what the owl had told him.

"But what?" Eider prompted him impatiently.

"I don't know, I'm not at all sure," Drib frowned, "the owl said something about the rumour on the Greenway's edge is that they are innocent, that they've been caught up in a lie that's weaving itself tighter and tighter around them and now there's such a lot of clamour against them that nobody's listening to their side of it."

"Well I, for one, know exactly what that feels like! They'll get no justice from this King and that's for sure!" Eider muttered with feeling, wetting his finger and testing the keen edge on each arrow's blade. "But why did the owl bring me the bow and arrows?"

"That's a terrible thing to say about the King," Drib retorted angrily, raising his fist to Eider. "Why, he stopped once and lifted me up out of the gutter with his own hands and sat me on Esteron's back when those masons' boys had beaten me up!"

"That may be so, little Drib." Eider laughed, pushing him easily away. "They say he's good with beggars and cripples but that isn't kingship, is it, not real kingship. He doesn't know how to govern. He doesn't know how to plot against those who are plotting against him. Haven't you heard the way they laugh and sneer at him as they curse his name in the narrow back lanes and dark alleyways? Oh, he's full of grand ideas, like giving those tunnellers the freedom to wander and garden, tidying up the wilderness, but who really pays? The innkeepers and the villagers, not the King and that's for sure! Take morninglight in the Learning Halls that you're forced to attend, who pays for that? Well, tell me, who?"

Drib shrugged: he had never really given it a thought.

"Why, the people whose chimneys you sweep, you fool. The barter's double now to make up for the time you waste listening to Grout, otherwise your master would only have half the barter, wouldn't he, and then you'd all starve to death! Remember, somebody's always got to pay: you know the saying, don't you, 'change is always for the worse'."

"Is that why you steal from the merchants and cause all that trouble? Is it because you hate change?" Drib asked in a small voice and from the glare of anger in Eider's eye he immediately wished he hadn't. The question had obviously cut him to the quick.

"Yes . . . yes . . . I mean no! I don't know! It was so frustrating having all those stories of glory and honour and having to grow up in my father's shadow.

Have you any idea what it's like having a hero for a father? Can you imagine what it's like to see him saluted by everybody and told what a brilliant example he is, told that you could never be half as good? And the worst of it is knowing you will never get the chance to prove it one way or another because all the battles are over and transformed into neat little fairy stories that the likes of you idolize!"

Drib lowered his eyes and looked away, sensing the rage pent up inside the young archer. They had led such different lives. Eider suddenly laughed, his voice softening, and it made Drib look quickly back at him.

"And you saw the Master of Magic tonight you say, right here in the cellar? Perhaps we're on the edge of some great adventure after all."

Eider paused and slowly paced across the floor deep in thought, "But I wish I knew what it was."

# 7

# The Honourable Company of Murderers

LOREMASTER GROUT PACED BACKWARDS AND FOR-wards, frantic with worry as he wandered through the darkened, empty halls of the Learning Hall, tripping over unseen books and scrolls that lay scattered on the floor, discarded in his haste to find anything that might incriminate him. His footsteps echoed his despair and his long, thin shadow followed him erratically as he passed beneath each feeble, flickering, untrimmed lamp. What was he to do if the King called him to account? How much had he unwittingly revealed of his secret longing to have the Chancellors back in power to the wretched urchins who crowded his Learning Hall?

Grout suddenly laughed, a tight, nervous sound, and dabbed at the trickles of sweat that were oozing from his high, bony forehead. He wasn't a brave man: he would deny everything they accused him of and blame it all on malicious gossip; after all, children couldn't be trusted, especially the wretched, filthy creatures that he was forced to put up with.

He paused, keeping to the thick shadows beside the window, afraid to show himself as he peered out into the crowded street. He listened with sharp ears to the city that was alive with the news about the rebellious tunnellers and how they had been captured near the Rising. The dust from the Galloper's horses and the echo of their shouts as they informed the prison master that the captives would be arriving, bound in chains, before the midnight bell was struck had barely settled and faded before all the lamps in Candlebane Hall were lit, blazing out like an accusing beacon in the highest circle of the city.

Grout wrung his hands anxiously. He'd heard whispers from trusted friends that the Chancellors themselves were behind this revolt and that it was they who were stirring up the trouble and unrest throughout Meremire Forest. He had even sent them word by secret messenger, pledging his help when the time was ripe to overthrow the King. What if some of the Chancellors had been captured and were being brought into the city this very night? What if his secret correspondence had already fallen into the King's hands?

"Fools, you moved too quickly, you ignored all the lessons I taught you, all the cunning and politics that are necessary to bring something like this about," he muttered to himself as he saw all those fragile hopes collapsing into catastrophe while he waited for the dreaded knock upon the door that would summon him to be judged in Candlebane Hall.

"Fools! You impatient fools!" he repeated to himself, turning away from the noise and bustle in the street and slowly pacing back through the empty, echoing halls, trying to riddle out what he should do—what he should say.

A faint, persistent noise grew louder as he reached the scullery. Somebody was scratching and tapping on the back door that opened into Blackbone Alley. He caught the sound of a voice whispering urgently, calling out his name, and it made him pause as he clutched at the throat of his gown and broke out into a cold sweat. His shallow breathing quickened: they had come for him so quickly.

"Grout, Grout, open the door!" the muffled voice hissed.

Grout took a leaden, hesitant step and stopped, his worst fears pressing in around him, but then he glanced back over his shoulder; surely if the guards were to come for him they would hammer loudly on the front door of the hall. They would bring flaming torches to illuminate his disgrace as the crowds watched and jeered. They wouldn't come with whispering, furtive voices at the back entrance. But who could it be at this hour? He took down one of the flickering lamps to light his way and his footsteps quickened with curiosity as he marched up to the low, arched door. Cautiously he drew the bolts and opened it a finger's span as he peered out into the darkness.

"Who pesters the Loremaster at this hour?" he demanded, but a strong hand pushed hard against the door, flinging it open and almost knocking Grout backwards as he was pushed off-balance.

"Quiet, you old fool! Would you rather that everyone in the city were here?" a voice snapped at him as more than a dozen shadowy figures all dressed in black cloaks and carrying large sacks across their shoulders hurried in out of the alleyway from where they had been hiding. They barged past him as they crowded into the scullery.

"Old fool! Old fool!" a harsh voice squeaked as a magpie flew in through the closing door and settled on the shoulder of one of the group.

The Loremaster almost dropped his lantern in surprise as he watched them begin to throw back the hoods that hid their faces. "Snatch, Kush, Huxort—is that you? But . . . but I thought you had been captured. The tunnellers—the tunnellers are being brought into the city loaded down with chains. I was afraid the riders had caught you: I had word that you were behind the tunnellers' revolt. Candlebane Hall is ablaze with light for the judgement. I was so afraid . . . "

"Shut up, you babbling fool! The only thing you were worried about was being found out. You were afraid we would incriminate you, afraid of what might happen to your precious skin if they found those letters you sent my father offering help to over-throw the King!" Snatch hissed, silencing the Loremaster before sending three of the others to check that the Learning Hall was empty and all the doors were securely locked and bolted.

The white magpie hopped across to Snatch's other shoulder and stared accusingly at Grout with its sharp, beady-black eyes. "Shut up, shut up," it imitated in a harsh, mocking squawk, bobbing its head rapidly up and down.

"Your father, Ironpurse, showed you the letter?" Grout whispered in alarm despite being hissed into silence.

Snatch glanced irritably back to the thin, nervous face of the Loremaster and sneered. "Our fathers don't know the half of what we do, nor do they have the will or the stomach to perform it themselves. Now be quick, there will be time for questions later!"

One by one the others hurried back into the scullery, whispering that the hall was empty and all the doors were securely locked. Snatch let out a sigh of relief.

"We're safe now, boys, in the very place no one would think to look for us."

"It's good to be back in the city: now let's eat! Grout, bring us some food."

Groaning with relief, they let the heavy sacks they were carrying slip to the floor and sat down at the long, scrubbed, wooden table. Grout came to a sudden stop and cried out in horror as the contents of one of the sacks spilled out in front of him. A wave of terror knotted up inside him; as he stared down, unable to tear his eyes away from the vile strips of scaly, Nightbeast armour and curved blackened claws and feet. Amongst the stinking mess, the hideous, snarling mask of one of the creatures stared back at him. Snatch watched as the terror of the things possessed him. Being close to the carcasses of the dead creatures had affected them all like that in the beginning but seeing the Loremaster so frightened made him sneer.

"Do you remember, Grout, how you used to terrify us with tales of these creatures when we were very young? How you used to weave stories of the Master of Darkness around us and fill our imaginations with his beasts who roamed through the night? I haven't forgotten how well you fed our nightmares before you sent us to bed."

The Loremaster nodded, too frightened to speak, guessing what the boy was going to do as he bent down and retrieved the head of the Nightbeast from where it lay at his feet and thrust it into the Loremaster's trembling hands with a laugh. "Now take a good, careful look, Loremaster Grout, and make sure you miss nothing out. That should make telling those stories even better shouldn't it?"

A roar of laughter erupted around the scullery table at the look of revulsion that spread across Grout's grey, sweating face. His fingers barely touched the double ridge of spines that rose across the crown of the head or the thick, snarling lips that hardly covered the jagged teeth, or the leathery scales that clung to the high cheekbones. There was something so menacing in its empty eye-sockets that he had to tear his gaze away.

"It . . . it . . . it feels so real! It's almost as if it's alive," his voice was nothing but a choked whisper as he hastily put it down and stepped back.

Snatch's grin widened as he picked up the severed head and pulled it down over his own. His laughter deepened and became harsher and crueller as it echoed out of the creature's mouth and his eyes took on a ruthless, bloodthirsty sheen through the scaly sockets. "It *is* real, Grout. We've given these Nightbeasts new life. We've stripped them of their armour to clothe ourselves and we've hollowed out their heads to wear as masks, digging out their crumbling bones and rotten flesh with sharpened spoons.

Those rumours you heard were not idle gossip: we are the new Nightbeasts roaming through Meremire Forest! We are those creatures that everyone fears."

Snatch pulled off the head and tossed it casually aside, wiping away the loose particles of flesh that had clung to his hair and face. Grout shuddered with horror and stared quickly around the sea of grinning faces of boys who were almost ready to become men. He could remember each one of them from their time in the Learning Hall; studious, clever boys, quick and cunning just like their fathers. But what had happened? What kind of monsters had he fashioned during those last, proud daylights of the Granite Kings? Surely he hadn't schooled them to defile the dead, to animate those vile Nightbeast carcasses and bring them back to life? No, it wasn't possible. He had taught them the skills of politics, ruthless skills though they may be; he had given them the strength to crush any whisper of dissent in the common people and all the other arts and virtues of good government. He didn't understand what had gone wrong.

Snatch laughed at the confusion and disapproval he could see so clearly in the Loremaster's eyes and drew him down onto the wooden bench beside him. "Listen to me, Grout, and listen well. Times are changing and we have to change with them. If we don't we'll be pushed aside and forgotten, trodden under the dust of history just like the Granite Kings. You remember that saying don't you—*change is always for the worse*. Well, it's wrong: we have to change, we have got to use anything we can to seize back what our fathers have lost—anything!"

"But I don't understand. What can you possibly hope to achieve by resurrecting these Nightbeast carcasses to frighten travellers and stirring up the tunnellers to revolt? Surely you must be able to see it goes against everything that I have ever taught you? How can you animate those foul creatures of the night when it goes against the very things the Granite Kings fought to rid us all of? It is a violation of everything—everything! Where is your honour? Where is your integrity?" Grout cried and stuttered to a halt, raking his fingers through the lank locks of his hair in bewilderment. He didn't know what to think or what to say next, these boys had become violent, dangerous young men.

"Honour! Integrity!" Kush snarled, bringing his fist crashing down upon the table and making the jugs and platters jump and the flames dance madly in the lamps. "There can be no true honour while we are forced to live in exile beneath the yoke of this cursed tyrant of a King! Or have you forgotten so easily, Grout, how he has stripped all vestige of honour and tradition from our people and reduced us to little more than scavengers on the Greenway's edge?"

"We have a new honour, you old fool!" Thoragrasp sneered, making the Loremaster twist round. "And we do more than merely frighten those travellers and merchants who are foolish enough to travel on their own. We have become the Honourable Company of Murderers, Loremaster, a most secret society dedicated to spreading fear, chaos and despair at the state of things throughout all Elundium!" A wicked grin spread across his face as he relished Grout's discomfort.

"Yes, but you need not be afraid of us: it is not your throat we're after!" Kush laughed. "We are pledged to bring this King and all who follow him to their knees. That is our purpose!"

"But . . . but . . . I never taught you to murder anybody! I know I didn't . . . " Grout gasped, looking nervously from face to face, fingering the loose folds of skin that hung beneath his chin.

"Exile is a hard teacher, Grout: it sharpens the perception and strengthens the resolve far quicker than idling away the daylights here in the comfort of the Learning Hall," Snatch insisted, gripping the Loremaster's sleeve and pulling him close. His face hardened and his eyes became narrow, glittering slits. "This is the only way. For too long we have sat idly listening to our fathers muttering about their lost dignity, waiting for them to rebel, while all they were doing was becoming weak, embittered old men, hatching empty plots that they could not fulfill. Nobody feared them any more, nobody respected the name of Chancellor. Our birthright is sinking into obscurity and we are being forced to haggle—to barter with the common man. You have no idea, Grout, what it is like scratching a living in the wilderness of Meremire Forest! That is why the time is long overdue for us to act. We are using the very things that this King has changed in this better world of his to bring him down!"

"But how?" Grout frowned. "How can dressing up as Nightbeasts and murdering innocent travellers, even creating a tunnellers' rebellion, hope to bring about the downfall of the King?"

Snatch laughed suddenly, letting go of the Loremaster's sleeve to drink deeply from a jug of stale ale that was standing at his elbow. He spat at the floor, wiping at the dribble escaping down his chin with the back of his hand as Squark, the magpie, imitated the laugh and Snatch petted him, letting him drink some of the beer from the corner of his mouth before he continued.

"The answer is simple, Grout: people hate change. There are a lot of people in the villages scattered through Meremire and out across all Elundium who don't really believe this precious King has killed the Nightbeasts and brought us all the peace and safety he's so fond of telling us about. They would like to, but the shadow of doubt hangs thickly over them. In their eyes nobody could be that powerful. Well, each time we dress up and murder some helpless merchant, stealing all his goods and making sure that somebody always sees us and lives to tell the tale, we strengthen their belief. They are convinced that the King is a liar! They know he could not have done what he said and they are beginning to think him a fool for disbanding the Gallopers and Marchers so quickly after his victory at the Rising. They are beginning to feel that he has left them defenceless against their greatest fear. And remember, Grout, fear is the greatest power of all. In their minds the creatures we are creating are really alive and fear of the Nightbeasts will put a stranglehold on the merchants and bring all trade to a halt. Soon nobody will travel without our protection. We will seize power through the very people we pretend to protect. Already we are charging a small barter to escort groups of travellers along the wildest roads—and, of course, they are always safe with us! But if some bold fool shuns our help and protection and tries to travel alone it is strange the way creatures almost always seem to waylay him!"

Laughter echoed around the table but Snatch frowned them into silence.

"Elders in some of the outlying villages are beginning to look to us for advice and for us to tell them about ways to defend themselves against the Nightbeasts and the tunnellers. We are not slow to remind them that our families once held control of all Elundium in safer daylights!"

"And the tunnellers—how did you get them to rebel? Surely they are the King's friends: he gave them the right to wander wherever they pleased and to live off the fat of the land." Grout's interest was sharpening.

"We didn't!" Girrolt laughed, motioning to two of the smallest members of the group to come forward. "Go on, show Grout our secret."

Anasgrasp, Thoragrasp's younger brother, and Ort rummaged in their sacks and pulled on grotesque hollowed-out masks then shrieked with laughter as they cavorted around the room, leaping up to pull painfully at Grout's hair or pinch his arms and legs, sending jugs and plates smashing to the ground.

"Enough! Enough!" Grout cried. "Stop it this instant, do you hear!"

Snatch laughed and ordered them to stop, grabbing at their flailing arms to restrain them.

"Remarkable, quite remarkable!" Grout exclaimed after he regained his composure. "They look exactly like two tunnellers. At a distance it would be impossible to distinguish them from the real ones."

"It all started quite by accident one evening in an inn at Deepling," Snatch grinned. "I had been eavesdropping on a group of merchants and listening to one of them telling the others how he had got lost and stumbled into a Nightbeasts' camp. He swore they were alive and that they fled into the forest. Imagine it, Nightbeasts fleeing from a fat merchant, how ridiculous! Anyway, a small group of tunnellers came in out of the rain; I don't know why, but that night I was suddenly aware of a hostile atmosphere: I could see looks of hatred in everybody's eyes. Nobody wanted them in there but they had to put up with them because the King had made that ridiculous proclamation. Anyway, I heard the whispers of anger growing in the dark corners of the inn, echoing in the crackling flames of the fire and gathering momentum. "What right had the King to let those ugly, misshapen creatures with their bulging eyes and shell-shaped ears wander wherever they pleased?" "What right had they to live off the fat of the land? "What right had they to come and go wherever the fancy took them, draining the barter from the pockets of honest folk? It's not natural, it's not right!"

"You know the things people say: well, anyway, those whispers fuelled my anger and I struck one of them down—a girl, I think, but they're so ugly they all look the same to me. Her singing was beginning to give me a headache. But before I really knew what was happening the crowd were cheering and urging me on so I struck another. Then the whole crowd shouted and proclaimed me a hero, carrying me about the inn on their shoulders, praising me for driving the ugly creatures back out into the rain. Well . . . "

"But didn't anybody come to their aid: surely they have some friends?" Grout interrupted in amazement.

"Yes, yes, of course they did. There were two sour-faced old Marchers sitting at their table, people that nobody like anyway. They tried to intervene but the crowd chased them out!" Snatch answered dismissively. "And it took no more than a moment to convince everyone, including the landlord, Masterwort, that they were as bad as the tunnellers, reminding them that they were two of the Marchers who had been beguiled by bad magic. It didn't take long to persuade them that the Marchers couldn't be trusted and the village was best rid of them."

Snatch paused and drank deeply from the ale jug before he continued. "Everybody marched through the village to one of their hovels and burnt it to the ground. They chased away the lot of them—they were hiding in the rat-hole the Marchers call a home—and they fled into the forest!"

The grin on his wet lips became a sneer and he held Grout's startled gaze with his cunning, ruthless eyes. "My father was beside himself with fear, begging me to remember that I was a Chancellor's son and not to act so recklessly; telling me that a squadron of Gallopers would be there by morning, that I would bring disgrace and dishonour on everybody. He sounded like you, Grout: he accused me of having no honour—but he was wrong! You're all wrong for clinging onto the old ways. I did something that night that everybody in the crowd had wanted to do for a long time: only nobody else had the courage."

Snatch laughed and leaned closer. "You see, Grout, even if the Gallopers had come, nobody would have given me away. I was the hero, I was the one who had struck out against the miserable changes the King had forced us to live with. That night was the beginning, that night was the first time any of us had stood up for ourselves since our fathers fled into exile. After that it was easy to create havoc in the surrounding villages during the dead of night: everybody was only too eager to blame it on the tunnellers, especially after we started dressing up a few of the smaller boys and girls and letting the villagers catch a glimpse of them."

"You mean that *you* are responsible for all that damage?" Grout stared from face to face.

"Yes, everything!" Kush laughed. "We guessed those wretched creatures would make for the Rising once we had chased them out of the inn in Deepling: we knew the villages that they would pass through so we shadowed them, wrecking everything we could lay our hands on, making sure there wasn't anywhere they could stop for food or shelter and stirring up the people against them. Why, even their own Lord Willow thinks they are guilty. The whole countryside is in uproar at the King for giving them the freedom to wander wherever they please and with the help of these Nightbeasts we have resurrected, and a little murdering everybody is too afraid to travel alone. And from what we've seen tonight the King hasn't kept enough Marchers and Gallopers in his service to defend this city let alone send out riders to escort people along the Greenways!"

"But why have you come here tonight? Surely it is very dangerous for you to come into the city? What if someone were to recognize you? What would have happened if one of the gate wardens had challenged you?" Grout asked, suddenly clutching at the throat of his gown as another thought suddenly occurred to him, making his face pale to a deathly white. "You didn't come here tonight to murder anybody did you? Not near the Learning Hall I hope—no, no, that wouldn't do at all: people might suspect that I'm involved, there are eyes everywhere. Oh dear no . . . "

Snatch looked at the trembling Loremaster with

disgust, wondering how he could have ever been afraid of him during his Learning Hall daylights or why his father held him in such high esteem. He had been told that this was the one person the Chancellors had been able to trust in the whole of the Granite City. "No, murder is not our main purpose here, my good Loremaster, but we might indulge in a little if it becomes necessary. We have become very good at slitting throats and we never get caught because Squark is a good lookout, better than any owl!" He grinned at Grout's obvious discomfort and fear.

"Lookout! Lookout!" the magpie screeched, ducking its head up and down.

"We have come here to set those tunnellers free," he announced quietly.

"What?" Grout cried, rising from his seat in shock. "Why set them free? The King will judge them tonight and have them flayed alive and their skins hung up on the Stumble Gate by morning. Rumour in the street says that he has to judge them guilty and have them punished to set an example to all the other tunnellers. The ordinary, decent people are incensed by what they have done and they'll riot if he doesn't."

"Oh no . . . no, no, no, that wouldn't do at all," Snatch answered impatiently. "Captured or dead those tunnellers aren't any good to us at all: we need them to be free and on the run. We can't carry on destroying things in their name if their whereabouts can be accounted for, especially when they're dead. I'm sure their leader, Lord Willow, knows exactly how many tunnellers there are breeding in their dark rat-holes near the Rising: we have to be very careful what we do since this small group gave themselves up."

Thoragrasp laughed and caressed the leering, snarling Nightbeast's head that he had just pulled out of his sack. "Without these pretty toys to disguise ourselves with, our plans to bring the King to his knees would have come to nothing by now, but the common

folk are so stupid they believe the Nightbeasts and the
tunnellers have formed an alliance to terrorize and
murder them. Wherever we go we hear rumours that
the tunnellers are stirring up the Nightbeasts from
deep within the forest and, of course, we fuel these
rumours with whispers of our own."

"But that's ridiculous! I thought everybody would
know the tunnellers were Krulshards' slaves, buried
for suns beyond counting in his darkness, cruelly
beaten and tortured by the Nightbeasts. The King
made enough fuss about that when he gave them the
freedom to live off the rest of us. They have a thousand more reasons to hate them than we do."

"Who cares what anybody thinks as long as it serves
our purpose? Now, Grout, you've got to help us to
free those wretched tunnellers before the new daylight
dawns or they're brought before the King for judgement. Dead or judged innocent are the last things we
want. We need some plans of the citadel and
Candlebane Hall—and the corridors and stairways that
lead down to the dungeons: everything's changed so
much since we fled into exile before the great siege.
There are so many new lanes and alleyways, different
buildings: we almost got lost finding the Learning
Hall. No—better still—find us somebody we can trust
who can show us the way!" Snatch hissed urgently.

"No, that's impossible. There are so many guards, I
wouldn't know who to trust, who to ask. It's utter
madness, you'll never get . . . "

"Quiet! Enough of your snivelling excuses: we
haven't journeyed this far to be put off by your spine-
less whining. To think my father valued you, Grout,
and told me you were the one man in the whole city I
could turn to for help. Why even in those parchments
you dispatched to my father you proclaimed your will-
ingness to help, or had you forgotten?" Snatch
paused, fingering something that he had hidden
secretly in the lining of his leather jerkin that made

the distinctive rustle and crackle of parchment as he touched it. Snatch lowered his voice to a menacing whisper, "Perhaps I should send this correspondence to the King. You would obviously rather serve him than us. Yes, perhaps I should inform him of all those secret treacheries you've plotted against him: I'm sure he'll understand how much you regret it now."

"No . . . no, please don't do that, I mean yes . . . yes . . . of course I'll help you, I was only concerned for your safety. I'll find somebody to guide you to the cellars beneath Candlebane Hall. Yes, I know the very person—Hinch—I overheard him cursing his master and the King earlier tonight, and I helped him plot his revenge on that miserable, sweep's boy and get the crooked creature thrown into the cellar to await the King's judgement tomorrowlight. Yes, yes, he'll help us, I'm sure of it. I'll draw you a map of the city: I'll do anything you want." Grout's voice was tight and frantic, he didn't doubt for one moment that Snatch would unmask him if he didn't fulfil all his wild demands. There was a ruthless, murdering madness in his eyes that terrified Grout.

"Cellars?" Girrolt frowned. "It's the dungeons we need to get into—where the prisoners will be taken, not the cellars, you stupid old man!"

"There aren't any dungeons in this city now. The King had them all filled in when the city was rebuilt after the siege. He proclaimed that everybody, even a criminal, had the right to the sunlight, so if anybody's held before judgement now it's in the cellars beneath Candlebane Hall."

"That will make it even easier to get those tunnellers out!" Kush laughed.

"No, I'm afraid it won't," Grout intervened in a nervous voice. "The walls are very thick and although there's a window set high on the south side it has iron bars fixed across it and they're set deep into the granite. It would take a mason a dozen daylights to hack them loose. And the door, I've heard tell, is a full handspan thick and made of ironwood. It's as secure as any dungeon, in fact . . . "

"Shut up!" Snatch hissed, leaping to his feet and running to the nearest window as a great, angry shout echoed up through the city. "The prisoners have arrived at the Stumble Gate. Listen to the people cursing them! Come on, there's no time to lose: take us to this Hinch," Snatch ordered as he shouldered his heavy sack and strode out to the door that led into Blackbone Alley.

"But, surely, if they're innocent and you set them free they'll only come straight back and give themselves up again and throw themselves on the King's mercy as they protest their innocence?" Grout cried as he was jostled and hurried towards the door.

Snatch paused in the door as he opened it a crack and grinned, his eyes half-closed, his lips thinning into that distinctive, murderous smile that Grout had come so quickly to dread. "I never said anything about letting them roam around free after we help them escape did I?" And with a slow, deliberate movement he brought the middle finger of his right hand silently across his throat in the sign of the Honourable Company of Murderers.

Berioss felt a knot of dread and despair tighten in his stomach as the slow, lumbering prison cart with its escort of silent, grim-faced Gallopers bumped and lurched its way over the rough ground to reach the crown of the last of the rolling hills and began the long descent towards the lights of the Granite City. He had never felt so ashamed and so humiliated by the people that he had once risked his life to defend against the darkness, people he had once called his friends and shared a stirrup-cup with. They had turned against him so easily with no more evidence than suspicion and rumour. It had been a long, tortuous ride from the Rising as he knelt cramped and uncomfortable in the low, wooden cage beside Ustant and the company of tunnellers.

Suddenly he had to grip at the bars to keep himself from falling backwards on top of Oaktangle who lay huddled behind him when the carter carelessly let one of the crude, wooden wheels of the cart ride up over a rock. The cart rocked violently, tossing the occupants of the cage to one side. The wooden bars creaked and groaned as the whole contraption that was already perched precariously between the axles threatened to overturn.

"Hold on tight all of you!" Ustant shouted in warning as the floor buckled beneath him.

The cart swayed and settled back onto the road as the carter swore and glanced round, a sneer splitting his face, clear to see in the light of the Gallopers' staysafe lamps that hung from their saddles. "Serves you right, you miserable creatures! I wouldn't care if it broke your arms and legs!" he spat.

Berioss bit back the reply that was on the edge of his tongue and winced as he loosened his grip on the bars. The raw wounds on his knuckles and along his arms caused by the constant stoning they had suffered in every village they had passed through on the journey had opened up as he had clung to the bars and fresh, warm blood was trickling between his fingers. "Take no notice," he murmured softly to the others.

The tunnellers were such a kind, gentle people and Berioss had been quick to see that they had been reduced to huddling, terrified, on the floor of their moving prison by the brutal attacks they suffered on the journey. They had been prodded through the bars with blunt staves and threshing sticks until they were bruised black and blue; they had been cursed and spat upon and stoned at every opportunity. He couldn't imagine what would have happened to them if he and Ustant hadn't used their bodies to protect them as best

they could and he had made each one of them, even the
smallest, tell a story of how their people had won their
freedom over the darkness. He kept their pride alive
and made them sing those enchanting, haunting songs
about the beauty and the sunlight they treasured so
much. He constantly whispered to them how King
Thane was a great King and how he was certain they
would be judged innocent. He had done everything he
could to keep their spirits up but now, as the lights of
the city drew nearer with each, slow, measured hoof-
beat of the two draught-horses yoked to their prison
cart and the slow rumble of its wooden wheels over the
loose stones and pebbles that littered the Greenway followed on deliberately, his own courage was failing.

The walls of the city were covered with thousands
of lamps and every niche and window arch from the
soaring turrets down to the dark, invisible culverts
that drained into the great ditch were filled with thin,
flickering candle flames. Lights thronged the Stumble
Gate and spilled out in a surging mass for half a
league along the Greenway towards them, vanishing
up into the city, a dense, winding ribbon of lanterns
that followed the road, curving up, appearing and disappearing between the crowded houses, until it
reached the harsh, accusing blaze of light that shone
out of the tall windows and doors of Candlebane Hall.

"I always said that bad news travels fastest, didn't
I!" Ustant muttered under his breath, leaning across
above the heads of the tunnellers who were beginning to sit up and stare ahead at the lights. "I fear the
last part of the journey is going to be the hardest."

"Yes, and we had better get ready to protect the
others as best we can. But I don't know what we can
do against a mob like that," Berioss whispered, brac-
ing himself for the first barrage of stones.

"That noise! What is that noise I can hear? It
sounds like angry hornets!" Sloeberry asked anxiously, raising herself onto her knees.

"I think it's the people of the city," Mistletoe answered in a frightened whisper as he cowered on the floor of the cage.

"What sound? I don't hear anything but the creak of the cart and the hoofbeats of our escort," Ustant frowned, peering ahead through the bars, straining his ears and turning his head from side to side, afraid to face the awful reality of journey's end, yet knowing that with every shallow breath he took it was growing closer and ever more inevitable.

And then he heard the sound the tunnellers' sharp ears had already caught. At first it was no more than a rising, persistent whisper borne to them on the still, frosty night air but with each moment it grew louder. It seemed to imitate the soft, sighing swell of the sea breaking on a shingle beach; but no sooner had it subsided than it rose again, an angry buzz, a thunderous roar, that overwhelmed the swaying creak of the wheels of the cart. It was the crowd cursing and shouting for their blood. There was a rage and a violence in the mob that made Ustant begin to shrink back amongst the tunnellers. His head sank forward and his hands began to tremble with a fear he had never felt before, and for the first time in all his marching days he was truly afraid. His courage was failing him; his spirit lay crumbling and broken as hot tears of shame began to trickle down his cheeks.

Suddenly through the misery of his despair he felt Berioss's hand on his arm, strong steady fingers that made him look up.

"Hold your head up high, old friend," Berioss whispered with bright tears in his own eyes. "And remember better daylights when we stood shoulder to shoulder against all the foul creatures of the night who battered on the doors of this city. How we stood firm when these very people who now curse us had fled in terror. Remember when all hope had perished and we had nothing left but our own courage to protect us and yet still we held the great gate shut against the darkest shadows and sang as we waited for the dawn. Remember, Ustant, remember."

Ustant nodded bleakly as the memories of that moment came flooding back, how he had felt a surge of joy as daylight had dawned and the shadows had fled before the new sun. Berioss's words brought small comfort, but it was enough to stir the spark of his pride and fan the flame of his courage.

"Remember!" Berioss whispered fiercely. "The tunnellers are not Marcher-born as we are: we must do everything we can to protect them. Remember, we are pledged to it!"

"Yes, to the last breath!" Ustant answered, rubbing away at the tears that had wet his cheeks. There was the light of war in his eyes once again as he reached across and gripped Berioss's hand in silent thanks for sharing out that last, precious fragment of his courage and making the cruel, deafening roar of the crowds that assaulted them change in his ears to the thunder and crash of old battles. "We will sing of the sun breaking free from the shadows of World's End and tell of all the beauty of a new morning!" he cried, bravely taking his place at the front of the cage, spreading out his arms to protect the others who were huddling down on the floor, their arms drawn up over their heads.

A movement in the dark, starry, night sky above their prison caught Oaktangle's attention. He glimpsed the flutter of silent wings and sharp eyes in the uncertain, flickering light of the Gallopers' staysafe lanterns as Gorass commanded the escort to draw in around their prison cart in close order. Oaktangle looked up to see the owl, Silverthorn, stoop and perch for a moment upon the bars immediately above his head.

"I judged you too harshly in the hut above Deepling," the owl hooted softly, so low that none but the tunneller heard him.

"Then if you know we haven't done these terrible

things they are accusing us of who is doing them?" Oaktangle asked in an urgent whisper, clutching at the bars beside the owl's talons.

"Nobody knows. Only a white magpie is ever seen where the damage is done. The attackers seem to have warning of when the Warhorses or the Border Runners are near and they vanish from sight." The owl watched the crowds as they approached the gates, lifting off from the top of the cage only moments before the first barrage of missiles began to rain down on the helpless prisoners.

"Now you know we are innocent can't you tell the King? Tell Lord Willow! Can't you make somebody listen?" Oaktangle cried out as Silverthorn vanished.

Gorass was quick to see the power in the fury and violent hatred of the surging crowd as they closed in around them. "Gallop, man, gallop," he shouted to the carter, bringing his whip arm down across the flanks of the draught-horses. Sparks flew from their hooves as they cantered through the Stumble Gate.

"Lower your lances; let nobody close to the cage. The King alone shall judge them!" he called out to the Gallopers as the rage and anger of the mob rose to a screaming pitch as they saw the prisoners quickly taken beyond their reach.


Far above the seething, howling mob that pursued the prison cart beneath the archway of the Stumble Gate into the city, King Thane watched in despair, clutching at the cold stone casement of the high window in the towers of granite. "Look, Breakmaster, look, Errant, just look at them! Is that frenzied mob the new Elundium? Is this the new world we fought so hard to create? Where have they all come from? The whole city must be out there."

Bewilderment and despair began to harden into anger and he stabbed a quivering finger down at the surging crowd who were fighting and trampling upon one another in their effort to reach the prisoners as the frightened carter whipped his horses into a white lather in his effort to escape.

"Get back to your homes all of you—get back at once!" he shouted, but his voice was lost in the roaring shouts of the crowd.

"I have never seen such a bloodthirsty mob, my Lord. I fear nothing will stop them, even my best Gallopers would be hard-pressed to halt and turn such a tide of hatred. If Gorass's escort falters or if the mob overwhelm that cart the prisoners are in will be torn to pieces while we look on helplessly."

"The Nighthorses are ready-saddled, my lord, I could lead them out to help those Gallopers defend their prisoners," Errant offered, turning towards the door of the chamber.

"No, I fear that more Gallopers on the streets will only inflame the crowds even further," Thane answered sadly.

Breakmaster hovered anxiously at the King's side, his fingers worrying the hem of his cloak. His real fear was for the safety of his horses and their riders as they tried to protect those prisoners mixed up in that frantic, surging crush of bodies in the narrow streets below. He knew only too well that if one of them slipped or stumbled on the uneven cobbles the sheer weight of the crowd would trample them to death.

"But what possesses them with such a murderous rage against those tunnellers? What harm have they ever done to whip up so much hatred? It is I who should judge them, not the people!"

"From the rumours I hear in the streets, my lord, it is because they are different, but perhaps there is more to it than that . . . " Breakmaster paused, summoning up the courage to speak plainly. "Lord, I fear for us if you find those prisoners innocent. The people are on the edge of riot: I cannot tell what they might do if they disagree with your findings."

"And what would you have me do—bow to the wishes of a mob? Would you . . . " Thane began to speak when a neighing scream from one of the horses below had all three of them crowding the casement searching the seething mob who had reached the third circle of the city, passing beneath the gilded emblems of the Honourable Masters of Barter, the Haberdashers and Cloth Merchants.

"I see the horse, my Lord, he's trapped, hemmed in by the crowd in the mouth of an alleyway between the barter storehouses! It's too narrow in there to swing a sword or use a lance—he'll be overwhelmed unless he can force his way out!"

"Yes, yes, I see it now!" Thane answered anxiously, unable to do anything but stand and watch while he remembered that long, terrible, dark night when he and a handful of the riders of Underfall had been trapped by all the foul creatures of the night, forced beyond the safety of the great doors of the fortress at World's End. He looked up suddenly, remembering how the Battle Owls had helped then, and he called for Mulcade to come down from his perch upon the kingpost beam; they sent him with urgent whispers to help the stricken rider.

"Spread your shadow over the people and frighten them back away from him," he called out as the owl stooped down towards the milling mob.

"Have courage and a steady heart. Remember all I have taught you—your life depends on it now!" Breakmaster shouted, although he knew the horseman would never hear him above the roar of the crowd. He willed him to hold his nerve and have the sense to cast his lance aside and draw his sword.

The rider loosed his reins to keep his balance and turned his spurs into his horse's sweating flanks. Corrinwold responded to his rider's touch immediately and, blowing hard, crouched back on his hocks. His neck was arched, showing the battle plaits that had been woven into his mane as they sparkled like jewels of fire in the flickering light of the hundreds of lamps that the mob carried as they choked the mouth of the alleyway. The horse reared and Urk, his rider, hurled the lance at the mob and drew his long, Galloper's sword, sweeping it out at the crowd, making them duck and cower away. The horse thrashed at the air in front of him and his forelegs crushed heads and smashed chests. The roar of the mob turned to screams of terror as Mulcade's shadow passed over them and they fought with each other to escape the flailing, lethal hooves and the threat of the Battle Owl's talons. Step by step, Corrinwold forced a passage back into the centre of the lane, sparks dancing around his hooves as he cantered free and caught up with the beleaguered escort surrounding the prison cart. But Urk's arm had grown numb in that desperate rush to break free and the hilt of his sword was wet with blood from the cuts he had been forced to make on the hands and arms that had clawed at him as they tried to pull him down.

"There is a wild madness in the mob. I fear for all our lives!" he shouted across to Gorass.

"Faster, man, faster!" Gorass shouted to the carter.

Breakmaster barely had the time to breath a sigh of relief when he saw that one of the wheels of the cart was wobbling dangerously loose as it climbed the steep, cobbled street into the fourth circle of the city.

"Lord, that cart is about to founder and lose a wheel. Those prisoners will never reach Candlebane Hall unless we do something to stop that mob!"

"Errant, go quickly: the Nighthorses! Now is the time to gallop to the prisoners' rescue," Thane called out as Errant ran for the door.

"Breakmaster, go to the gates of the upper circle— see to it that they are slammed shut and sealed once that cart has passed through them. Go now, run as fast as you can!"

Breakmaster turned and ran after Errant, leaping down the steps two at a time, his sword drawn. "I will overwatch the sealing of the upper circle, my Lord. I will call on every Archer and Marcher I can muster."

Breakmaster barely had a moment, the bloodthirsty mob had driven thoughts about Drib out of his mind. He paused at the first twist in the stairs and shouted back to Thane, "I will see that the prisoners are brought straight into Candlebane Hall. The sooner they are judged and punished the quicker the mob will disperse."

"No, see to it that they are locked securely in the cellar for the rest of the night. Give them something to eat and some bedding to sleep upon. I will not be dictated to by a rampaging mob. Send out criers to tell the people that the tunnellers will be judged fairly by their King in the light of a new daylight. That is my final word on it!" Thane answered angrily.

"Thane, what is happening? What is all that noise in the streets, the shouting and the sound of hoofbeats? It looks as though the whole city is in uproar. Are we under attack?" Elionbel asked anxiously, clutching hold of Krann's hand as he ran to her from his own sleeping chamber, his eyes wild and frightened. She whispered and soothed his fears as she hurried into the room, crossing to where Thane stood close to the open window. Elionbel shivered, her thin, silk-spun sleeping gown was little protection against the chill, frosty night air that was drifting into the chamber with the noise and turmoil from the streets below.

"I don't know, my love. I don't understand this: despite everything my counsellors have told me there is no sense, no foundation to the people's hatred of the tunnellers, or none that I can see," he answered, smiling at her and quickly casting his cloak around her shoulders as he saw her shiver.

"It has brought back memories of black times and rekindled bad dreams." Elionbel took his hand and held it tight.

"I listened to the others at the table yesterlight: they were talking of Nightbeasts and shadow warriors," Krann said, twisting around to look up at Thane. "And they kept on whispering about someone called Kruel. They kept staring at me—why? What did they mean? Who are the Nightbeasts?"

A shadow of concern crossed Thane's eyes. He picked the child up and laughed softly to disguise his fears, ruffling the downy white-blond hair that curled across Krann's forehead as he swung him around. "It is nothing: it is just silly talk, nothing for you to worry about, just old folk tales and empty-headed gossip. Now go back to bed and let your dreams carry the night away because when the sun of the new morning melts the frost upon the Greenway we shall climb to the top of the towers of granite to watch the swans return."

Krann cried out with delight, the dark whispers he had overheard forgotten in an instant. "Ogion and Ousious—are they coming back tomorrowlight? Can't I stay up and watch for the grey hours just in case they arrive early? They might come before the city wakes up. Please let me stay up."

Thane laughed and shook his head, "You know, if I let you do that you'll be so tired by tomorrowlight you will fall asleep and miss their arrival." He beckoned to Krann's nurse at the threshold of the chamber and handed him over to her so that the child could be taken back to bed.

Krann had brought them so much joy and laughter: there wasn't a single daylight that had gone past since the Battle of the Rising that he had regretted sparing the child's life. Elionbel had been right: nothing of Kruel had survived when he had plunged the broken blade of Durondel's sword with the shadowy fragment of Krulshards' black malice into his footprints. The memory of that frantic moment had never faded in his mind. He would always be able to see Kruel stumbling backwards away from him in the snow, tearing at the dreadlocks of his hair, trying to shed his skin and escape from his shadow, digging his nails into the hard, bony ridge of his brow. But with each footprint he left in the snow the shadow had grown stronger and darker and his body had shrunk until it had become that of an innocent baby.

"Sleep soundly, Krann, and before you know it tomorrowlight will have arrived," he smiled, calling out softly as the child left the room wrapped in his nurse's arms.

"I'll never be able to sleep, I know I won't," the child murmured but his eyelids were fluttering shut even before he was carried down the corridor.

The moment Thane heard the click of the latch on the door of Krann's sleeping chamber, he turned to Elionbel with a worried frown. "We stand on the edge of troubled times, I fear. I don't know what to do: a dark shadow of discontent is spreading across everything that we have done to make a better world. Breakmaster says it is because the people hate change but I don't know: where have we gone wrong? They are crying out for revenge on that group of tunnellers who have just been brought into the city and all because they are jealous of the freedom I gave them. But it can't really be the freedom they are jealous of, since they are all free, every one of them. In truth the only reason they can hate them as much as they do is because they are different. And then there are these black rumours everywhere about the Nightbeasts: they are saying that they have awoken in Meremire Forest. It's impossible: utterly impossible, but I'm told that good, honest merchants and journeymen actually believe they have seen them on the Greenways. What am I to do? How can I send out Gallopers to search for something that I know cannot be there?"

Thane let his hands fall helplessly to his sides and then glanced over to the door and lowered his voice, "I think it is best if we keep Krann close to us for the time being. We mustn't let him wander out of the tower alone while these wild rumours about the Nightbeasts persist. He is far too young to learn the truth of his beginnings from idle gossip. Whatever he learns that way will only be about the evil Kruel and not the innocent child he became."

"But I had always hoped . . ." Elionbel's words faltered as bright tears brimmed in her eyes and the bleak reality crowded in on her. No matter how deeply she wanted to protect Krann, to bury those terrible memories, the jagged pieces of the past would always be there to prick her soul and make it bleed. The echo of Krulshards' hatred would never completely fade or those hideous images of him that haunted the silent darkness before the grey hours stole away the night vanish. In unguarded moments she still saw the grey, bloodless strips of flesh that hung about his face in mockery of skin, the pitiless, burning eyes and the dead locks of tangled hair that streamed out from his bony crown.

She still shuddered at the memory of the touch of those black-boned, grasping fingers. It was so vivid still, all concealed just beneath the surface, waiting to fill her with despair. She clasped Thane's hands, remembering the violent rage that had possessed the Master of Nightmares on the uppermost ramparts of the ruined city when he had realized that his victory could never be complete while the last Granite King lived to name his heir. She remembered how he had turned that fury against her and her mother, Martbel, his helpless prisoners; how, in hatred of Thane, he had dragged her mother into the black, smothering folds of his malice that hung about his shoulders and raped her, violating her without mercy.

"One daylight we will have to tell Krann—there is

no other choice. You know in your heart we cannot hide it forever," Thane whispered. He felt her despair and saw it in her eyes as he held her tightly.

She nodded, "Yes, yes, I know but . . . " she paused, her shoulders trembling; "Sometimes I feel so alone, so empty with regret. I am so afraid for Krann . . . " She broke free from Thane's embrace and cried out as she ran from the room. "I must go to him: I must watch over him through the dark hours of the night and protect him from the nightmares that scratch at the windows and whisper through the gaps beneath the doors, just in case there is a grain of truth in the rumours."

Thane took a step to follow her, his hand outstretched in love, but he hesitated and let the words that would deny any truth in those rumours about the Nightbeasts' awakening dissolve on his tongue. Nothing he said would make any difference: she knew in her heart that they could never come back to life: she had seen Krulshards' severed head brought, victorious, from the City of Night. She had watched the last two living beasts crumble into dust as Kruel was reduced to an innocent baby. Yet believing it, really believing those nightmares had gone forever after so much tragedy had scarred her, was so difficult. Thane sighed with relief as he turned slowly back to the window and saw that the Nighthorses were riding through the streets below and the prisoners' cart was safely within the upper circle of the city. Nevian, the Master of Magic, had confided to him once that time would eventually heal the black wounds in her heart, but how much time? How much time would it need to truly banish those poisonous shadows, he wondered as he looked down at the restless crowds who still thronged the streets. He could tell by the shouts and curses that floated up to his window as they gradually dispersed back to their houses that they felt cheated and angry now that the prisoners were securely beyond their reach. He could see the empty prison cart lying, half on its side with one of its wheels broken beside the door that led down to the cellars beneath Candlebane Hall.

"Tomorrowlight I will do whatever I have to do to bring peace," he muttered, turning away from the window.

A sudden commotion from beyond the window ledge made him turn back and look out, searching for the source of the noise.

Mulcade was screeching, beating his wings at two other owls, preventing them from entering the chamber. "What is it? What is the matter?" Thane cried, raising his arms to protect his face from the razor-sharp beaks and talons as he tried to intervene.

"I am Chief Loftmaster and none shall enter or leave without my consent!" Mulcade hooted defiantly, driving the smaller of the two owls off and sending him spinning towards the rooftops below.

"The boy is innocent—innocent!" the small owl hooted as it flew away to perch on a chimneypot.

The Third owl, Silverthorn, tried to settle on the stone casement only to be driven back into the cold night air, his cries telling of rumours that were growing along the Greenways, rumours that told of innocent tunnellers accused of crimes that were not theirs.

"Stop it, Mulcade! Nobody's denying that you are Chief Loftmaster but please let those owls speak. What news do they bring?" Thane's attempt to intervene only upset Mulcade who flew silently to his perch on the kingpost beam, his feathers ruffled and puffed up as he turned his back and refused to answer.

Thane frowned up at the owl, his patience almost at a breaking point. He already had enough to contend with that night: the city was close to riot, Krann had heard painful rumours and Elionbel was in tears. "I thought we were friends, after all we have been through together! But have it your own way, I'll find out for myself what news they bring," he called up to

Mulcade before leaning out of the window and calling to the owls to come back, telling them that he welcomed them and they had nothing to fear from beak or claw.

Three times he called, searching in the thickening darkness as the lamps and torches were extinguished in the emptying streets below. He was about to give up when they both suddenly reappeared and settled on his shoulders, hooting and screeching together so fast that he couldn't understand more than a word here and there.

"Rumours? What rumours are they? You have seen the Nightbeasts? The tunnellers are innocent? I don't understand . . . " he frowned. "Speak more clearly," he said, turning his head from one to the other.

Mulcade screeched and stooped down and Silverthorn and the smaller owl—Silkstone—wary of his beak and talons despite the King's assurances, vanished in a whir of feathers. The Chief Loftmaster owl settled jealously on Thane's shoulder, making soft noises from deep inside his throat, nibbling at his ear and pulling at a stray strand of hair that had fallen carelessly across his forehead.

"It's no good being jealous: I need to know what those messages were. I need to know what news those owls brought!" Thane smiled. He found it difficult to be cross with Mulcade for more than a moment and he caressed the soft feathers on the owl's chest, letting his fingers run lightly over the horny skin of his talons where they pressed into the soft leather and velvet fluting on the shoulders of his coat. Reluctantly Mulcade related the messages the other owls had brought.

"There is a rumour growing along the Greenway's edge that the tunnellers are innocent and, have been wrongly accused. And all that is ever seen where the damage has been done or the Nightbeasts have robbed and murdered is a white magpie. And about that boy accused of beating a pony—he didn't do it!"

More than that Mulcade would not, or could not, repeat.

Thane didn't have the slightest idea what the story of the boy beating the pony was all about but he could easily believe that the tunnellers were innocent. But who could be doing all the damage? Who could be attacking the villagers and stirring up all this discontent in Meremire Forest and why were they doing it? It didn't make any sense: there could be nothing to gain from having the tunnellers banished.

This latest piece of news had put Thane into a real quandary. Much as he had hated the idea of finding the tunnellers guilty with nothing more than rumour and gossip to go on, he had been turning it over in his mind, if only to appease the mood of the people and to avert a riot. But what was he to do now? If the owls said they were innocent then they clearly were wrongly accused but if he released them then the people would stone them to death long before they reached the Stumble Gate. If he didn't keep them locked up, the people would extract the judgement they wanted. And he couldn't keep them locked up in the cellar forever; he couldn't even keep them here in the Towers of Granite: he didn't have enough Gallopers, Marchers and Archers to stop the people if they decided to take the law into their own hands. Gorass's escort had had enough trouble fighting their way into the upper circle of the city.

"What on earth am I to do?" he frowned, wishing that his friend, Kyot from Stumble Hill, were with him to support his decision. He gripped the cold, stone casement as he looked out over the weathered rooftops and chimneypots of the city and towards the dark, distant horizon.

Mulcade hooted softly and he looked around. Pale, watery colours, no brighter than a candle flame, began to grow and fill the room with a soft light, blending and melting together, shifting through turquoise, azure and lilac into deep mulberry and shades of indigo. A voice whispered behind Thane, breaking into the turmoil that filled his mind.

"Kings have no simple tasks: for all the threads of fate hang from their fingertips and as the master puppeteer they move us all to chase that fate."

"Nevian! Nevian! Is that you? I never thought to see you again after the Battle of the Rising: there was something so final in the way the colours of your cloak melted into the sunlight, as though, with the Granite Kings, an age was coming to an end and we stood there on the threshold of a new beginning. I thought you had left us forever."

Thane spun round but the sudden hope and joy, the laughter on his lips, faltered and faded as he searched the elusive, thin, shifting patterns of the rainbow of colours that were glowing in the chamber. "Nevian?" he called again, uncertain this time as he reached out tentatively to touch the translucent glow, barely able to see the transparent image of the Master of Magic who was forming in the centre of the kaleidoscopic arc of light.

"Nevian, are you there?" he asked urgently. "Is that you, Nevian? I need your wisdom to guide me, I need your sharp eyes to penetrate this shadow of discontent that is spreading along the Greenways. It is eating into the heart of the people. I need your help to search out the root of it, to uncover the poison that is filling them with greed and jealousy."

A soft sigh of laughter, no more than the slightest breeze that couldn't even flutter the candle flames in the tall, fluted lamps that were set about the chamber, spread from the glowing colours.

"Yes, Thane, I am here, but my eyes are weak and I cannot delve deeply into the ways of men. My great task was to prepare the threshold of the new Elundium, not to stop this canker. This is beyond my power."

"But you are here!" Thane frowned. "I would know

that voice anywhere and I can just make out the shape of your face. It looks older, more frail, as if you would be blown away by the first puff of wind. Why have you come back? Is it because there is some truth in the wild rumours of the Nightbeasts stirring deep in Meremire Forest or is it because the tunnellers have been falsely accused? Or perhaps it is to give me wisdom?"

Again the Master of Magic laughed, and there was a hint of warmth in his voice that made Thane want to reach out to embrace his old friend. Mulcade hooted and stooped from Thane's shoulder towards the magician but the colours of the rainbow cloak melted and swirled about the room as his talons sank into the translucent image. Then all trace of Nevian vanished and Mulcade beat his wings with a startled shriek to fly back to Thane's shoulder. His feathers were ruffled, his talons wet with bright colours.

"Nevian, wait! There is so much I need to ask you, Nevian!" Thane cried, but the magician had truly gone and only his voice echoed in the lamplight.

"I cannot give you the counsel you call for, Thane. The images you ask me to perceive beyond the threshold are confused and muddled with the deceits and treacheries of man. But I would warn you to beware of false friends and be slow to judge those who are brought in chains before you."

"Nevian, who are you talking about? Do you mean the tunnellers are indeed innocent? Who are the ones who are false? Nevian, Nevian . . . "

# 8

# Mock Armour for Mock Warriors

SLOEBERRY HUDDLED IN TERROR AMONGST THE other tunnellers on the floor of the prison cart, squeezed in between the two old Marchers, Berioss and Ustant, for what little protection they could give from the blood-hungry mob who crowded in on either side of the road. She pressed her long, thin, delicate fingers over her shell-shaped ears and shut her eyes tightly to try and block out the sea of snarling, angry faces, the knuckled fists with the sticks and staves raised to beat them and the continuous roar of hatred that pursued them from the Stumble Gate up through the narrow, winding streets of each circle of the city to Candlebane Hall.

"Sing—sing all of you! Hold your heads up high! Don't forget for one instant that we are innocent: show them we are not afraid!" Berioss cried above the shouts and screams of the crowd as the cart lurched and swayed violently over the uneven cobbles.

But she couldn't do it, she couldn't raise her head to face all that hatred and she huddled lower, bursting into tears. Through her terror and misery she heard the carter curse and the desperate shouts of their escort as they pressed in around them to gallop with the wind as the crowd threatened to overwhelm the cart. She glimpsed the blur of angry faces on either side and a blaze of bright sparks between the shod hooves and heard the carter's whip crack down savagely across the sweating flanks of the horses as they surged forward.

The rumble of the wooden wheels and the clatter of hoofbeats grew faster and faster. The cart jolted and juddered, bouncing erratically over the cobbles. Bolsters and couplings began to crack and splinter, hasps and strakes to break apart. The prison cage swayed and creaked from side to side, the leather bindings snapping one by one. The axle on the near side worked itself loose, making the wheel wobble dangerously and bind on the pole-brace. Berioss saw the wheel beginning to break loose and he shouted to the others to get across to the opposite side of the cage and hang onto the bars to brace themselves as the cart careered wildly across the cobbles to hit the seething mob. Shouts and curses of anger turned into screams of pain as the cart ploughed through the crowd, crushing arms and legs and sending bodies flying backwards. The cart shuddered and slewed sideways back into the centre of the road, its wheels riding up over a mass of people who were caught beneath it and couldn't escape.

The horses shrieked and tossed their heads in panic. Their eyes were white and wild with terror, their nostrils flared, their lathered chests straining against their harness in their efforts to break free from the noise and crowds that pressed in around them. Their iron-shod hooves churned up a shower of sparks and broken cobblestones as they pushed forward, dragging the broken cart behind them through the high, stone archway of the upper circle of the city.

The lights of Candlebane Hall were so bright they almost blinded the prisoners as the ruined cart skidded to a halt. The huge gates of the upper circle scraped across the cobbles as they were slammed shut and locked behind them in the faces of the swarming mob. The gates shook and rattled violently on their hinges as the crowd pounded and hammered on them angrily with their fists and wooden staves, but they held fast. Sloeberry and the other tunnellers lay trembling on the floor of the cart, too dazed and terrified by their ordeal to move.

"Out! Out! Get out, you treacherous creatures!" the door warden of Candlebane Hall shouted as the door of the cage was wrenched open and he began to grab hold of their tunics and heave them out roughly.

"But we are innocent—innocent do you hear! We are innocent until we are judged by the King and you should treat us so!" Berioss cried out defiantly, only to have the hard edge of a spear shaft brought down across his knuckles as he was prodded and pushed out of the cage and forced through the door that led to the cellar like a wild animal.

"You are guilty, no matter what the King says. And your miserable, treacherous skin will be flayed off your back by morning and hung on the Stumble Gate for everyone to see. Now, get going!" The warden gave him a final prod that sent him tumbling down the gloomy stairs.

The noise of the crowds hammering on the locked gates rose into a roar of fury as they realized that their quarry had escaped. They threw themselves against the gates, threatening to smash the locks as they cursed the tunnellers they had seen huddled in the cage with the two treacherous Marchers and howled for their blood. They cried out against the King for all the troubles he had brought down upon them by allowing those miserable creatures to wander wherever they pleased, to live off the backs of honest people's labours, lying, cheating and stealing wherever they went, stirring up the sleeping Nightbeasts in the depths of the forest and murdering folks in their beds. They cursed the escort of Gallopers and the guards and wardens for protecting them, threatening to stone them if they ever dared to show their faces in the city again.

A hail of sharp stones, sticks and anything else the city folk could lay their hands on, were hurled over the high wall that encircled Candlebane Hall and the Towers of Granite to land in the inner courtyard around the prison cart. A small company of guards, panicked by the ugly mood of the mob outside, ran across the courtyard to the cart and shouted at the prisoners, ordering them to get down into the cellar as fast as they could. They began to beat them and drag them towards the open doorway, cursing their slowness.

"We are going as fast as we can: our legs are numb and cramped from the journey!" Oaktangle cried out against the sudden onslaught, raising his arm to protect Sloeberry and Mistletoe only to be knocked senseless to the ground.

Sloeberry cried out in horror as blood gushed from a wound on the side of Oaktangle's head and she fell to her knees beside him. Rough hands grabbed at her arms, tearing her clothes and bruising her skin as she and Mistletoe were dragged away from Oaktangle and sent stumbling through the doorway where they both collided with Damask and fell down the steep, stone steps that led to the cellar, cutting and grazing their shins.

"Leave the tunnellers alone, you brutes, and try picking on somebody your own size—if you're brave enough! But remember, I am Marcher-born and I've stood too often in the shadows of death fighting for my King to be frightened by the likes of you!"

There was menace in Ustant's voice as he climbed stiffly out of the cart and his fists were clenched ready, his face darkened and set with anger. Ten, twenty guards: he didn't care, they were innocent of everything they had been falsely accused of and he would not take another step while he had to watch his friends treated like common criminals. There was a pride and the light of old battles in his eyes, a determination that made the wardens hesitate and lower their spear-blades into a circle around the old Marcher, but none of them moved to stab or jostle him towards the doorway.

"I know you!" sneered one of the guards standing behind him. "You're one of those Marchers blackened by magic. You spent more time being a tree, being eaten away by woodworm, than by defending your King! Marcher-born indeed, you're nothing but a traitor—a warrior gone bad! It's probably you and your friend who made those tunnellers get up to all that mischief! Now get along, move before I run you through!"

He prodded the spear hard at Ustant's back, cutting through his clothes, piercing his skin and making him gasp with pain as he stumbled forward. But Ustant only took one faltering step before he halted and turned around, grabbing at the spear-blade with his right hand. Blood ran wetly between his fingers but he wouldn't let go.

"You're not so brave now, are you? Not so brave now you have looked me in the eyes!"

The guard's hands trembled where they gripped the spear-shaft. He was a coward who hid behind his size and strength and Ustant's words had cut him to the quick as they exposed his weakness, but he dared not let the other guards see it. He spat in Ustant's face and opened his mouth to curse as he prepared to run the blade through the Marcher, when Breakmaster's voice froze him to the spot.

"How dare you lift a spear against these prisoners or attempt to strip them of their dignity? They are not guilty until the King judges them so in the light of the new daylight. Now, get out of my sight and bring fresh bedding and food for all the prisoners! Do it now before I horsewhip you for disobedience myself!"

The guard's eyes narrowed with fear and hatred as

they kept darting from the sounds of the mob hammering on the gates back to where Ustant stood. Reluctantly, he let go of the spear and retreated, only to stop and stab an accusing finger at the old Marcher's chest before turning towards the gates. "Listen to them!" he cried, fearfully. "Tomorrowlight will be too late: we'll all be dead by then if the people don't have their way. Are you deaf, Breakmaster? Can't you hear the people clamouring for the lives of these wretched traitors? They're nothing to us: they're guilty. I say let the people have the justice they want before we all get trampled underfoot when the gates collapse!"

"Nothing, you say? This Marcher is nothing?" Breakmaster felt his anger rising as he advanced on the guard. "Our King will not dismiss him, nor the others who stand accused with him, so easily. Nor will he be dictated to by a bloodthirsty, ignorant mob; he won't judge any man or woman on idle rumours and gossip. Now get out of my sight!"

Breakmaster had recognized Ustant the moment he had hurried into the courtyard and stopped the guard from stabbing him in the back. He remembered how once he had carried the emblem of the owl tattooed upon his arm, placed there by the Master of Magic in his youth as a sign of his love and loyalty to King Holbian at the Battle of the Causeway Fields before the gates of Underfall. He had almost lost his life defending the gates of the city in the great siege against Krulshards and had come to King Thane's aid at the Battle of the Rising, taking his place bravely in the front rank to take the full brunt of Kruel's shadow army. It had come as a shock to see him as one of the prisoners, and it made him doubt everything he had heard.

The snap of the spear-shaft breaking across Ustant's knee made the horseman stop and turn towards him. "At last, a man with enough honour not to believe all the gossip he has heard. Greetings, Breakmaster. We're innocent, you know: not a word of those accusations are true." Ustant smiled, gathering up the dusty tail of his cloak to wrap around his hand and staunch the flow of blood before stretching it out in greeting.

Breakmaster frowned and stepped back, refusing to take his hand. He was afraid to listen to him. It wasn't his place to make judgements and he knew how easily he could be swayed. Glancing anxiously at the gate, splintering and groaning beneath the frenzied assault of the mob outside, he ushered Ustant towards the door that led down into the cellar.

"Tomorrowlight we will talk on old times—after the judgement," he muttered, softly enough so that nobody else could hear as Ustant descended the stairway.


"What's all that noise? What's going on out there? It's just my luck to be locked up down here when something exciting is going on!" Eider cried as he caught the echo of the mobs rampaging through the streets, chasing the prison cart up towards Candlebane Hall. The noise grew louder and the pounding of all those feet upon the cobbles sent tremors through the floor beneath his feet and dust and mortar fell from the vaulted ceiling in a fine rain. The rats hiding in the rubbish in the darkest corners were squealing as they ran backwards and forwards across the floor before vanishing into their holes.

Drib scrambled awkwardly to his feet, frightened by the sudden commotion amongst the rats and the growing roar of sound. Suddenly he remembered a snatch of conversation that he had overheard when he was scrambling up the chimney of the Prancing Warhorse Inn earlier that evening: "It might be those prisoners who are being brought into the city. I heard rumour that they were arriving tonight, and there was talk of people wanting to take the law into their own hands and flay them alive for what they've done in Meremire. The people are fed up with the way . . . "

"Shut up! Don't you ever stop talking?" Eider snapped at him irritably. He stared up at the barred window and muttered, "I'm not interested in your rotten rumours: I want to know what's going on out there!"

On a sudden impulse he reached down and grabbed hold of Drib's collar, hoisting him up onto his shoulders before he could protest or cry out. He moved across the cellar to stand directly beneath the window. "Now mind out where you're putting your filthy feet on my clothes and reach up and grab at the bars. Pull yourself up and listen, tell me what's going on!" he demanded.

Drib stretched his arm up above his head and found the lowest iron bar that was fixed across the window. Gripping it he pulled himself up and looked out across the city. Lights blazed everywhere and the shouts of the crowds became clearer. Something pricked his fingers: he was about to cry out and let go when he heard the soft voice of Silkstone and saw the silhouette of the owl on the other side of the bars.

"What's happening out there? What's all that noise?" he asked softly.

"The prisoners are being brought into the city for judgement, but their escorts fear for their lives if the mob overwhelms them. They are innocent—innocent!" The owl repeated, vanishing before Drib could ask him who the prisoners were. He twisted round and called down to Eider, telling him what the owl had said.

"Prisoners! Is that all?" Eider muttered in disgust.

A sudden commotion on the stairway that led down to the cellar, the sound of cursing voices and iron-shod boots, caught Eider's attention and, forgetting Drib, he ran to where he had hidden his bow beneath the straw and snatched it up, nocking one of the arrows onto the string in readiness.

Drib cried out as he let go of the bars and fell backwards, landing in a heap and sprawling amongst the litter of rubbish behind where Eider stood.

"Get up, you fool, you are a disgrace!" Eider hissed at him as the sounds of angry voices outside the door grew closer.

"Listen, this might be our only chance to get out of here. The moment the guard opens that door, I shoot him and you make a grab for his sword or dagger. When you've got it you just stab anybody else who gets in our way!"

Drib barely had time to scramble to his feet or utter a cry of protest before the key grated in the lock and the door of their prison was thrown open. He had never hurt anybody in his life and he couldn't imagine finding the courage or the nerve to do what Eider wanted him to do.

"Ready?" Eider whispered, drawing back the arrow until the feathered flight touched his cheek lightly, but he hesitated as a huge, ancient, grim-looking Marcher, beaten and bruised, was roughly pushed through the doorway to stumble and fall to his knees at his feet. The man was immediately followed by a group of tunnellers, half-dragging and supporting one of their kind with blood oozing from an ugly wound on the side of his neck. They huddled together, crouching down, too frightened to move, their large eyes blinking nervously as they searched the farthest corners of the gloomy cellar.

"All right, all right, there's no need to keep on prodding us, we're not wild animals, the King hasn't judged us yet. I keep on telling you, we're not guilty of anything!"

Another ancient Marcher was shouting as he filled the doorway, retreating into the cell, a clenched and bloody fist raised defiantly at the guards who crowded the stairs above him. They took no notice as they herded him roughly into the cellar.

"There'll be no judging: you are guilty—everyone knows it. Your miserable hides will be hanging on the Stumble Gate to greet the new sun, mark my words," sneered one of the guards as he gave the Marcher one final, brutal push that sent him stumbling backwards to fall amongst the rubbish.

"You'll get no pity from us!" added another guard as he reached for the iron handle of the door, slamming it shut and relocking it before Eider had a clear view of him or a chance to loose the arrow.

Cursing under his breath, Eider eased the arrow off the bowstring, but he made sure he didn't show the relief he felt. He wasn't sure he could have killed the guard—he wasn't sure he actually had the courage to do something like that in cold blood, not deep down. Despite all his boasting and recklessness in front of his friends he didn't think he could actually hurt someone deliberately. He thrust the arrow back through his belt and slipped the bow over his shoulder. Somehow he had to get out of there, the feeling of being trapped, the oppression of all that granite pressing down on the vaulted roof above his head was beginning to make him feel panicky and short of breath. Soon desperation would overshadow any compassion or doubts about his courage.

Eider put his hands on his hips and looked down critically at the wretched group of tunnellers who were huddled together near the door and then at the two old Marchers who were climbing stiffly to their feet. He felt a sense of disappointment: they didn't look as if they were capable of causing all that trouble in Meremire.

"It's the first time I've seen an armed prisoner. What are you doing here? What's your name?" Berioss scowled at the youth as he brushed the broken scraps of straw from his torn cloak. He reminded him of somebody, somebody he had once known, but who?

"Eider. Eider Goose—and any weapon I carry is my business. But tell me what's your name—and why is everybody in the city ready to flay you alive?"

His initial disappointment was turning into curiosity. Despite their ragged looks there was something about the two old Marchers that stirred up the image of what he wanted to be. He sensed the honour and glory of the great battles that had vanished with the passing of the last Granite King, to be lost in the dust of history forever. There was a wild pride in their stature and a light in their eyes that time had not dimmed. A scent of things his father dismissed with a careful, measured gesture as the bad, violent times that were better gone and forgotten.

"Goose, you say, Goose—yes, there is an uncanny likeness. You must be Archer Gray Goose's boy: you even carry your bow the same way. But what on earth are you doing locked up down here? Surely you are not in some kind of trouble?"

Eider tried to laugh harshly. "I . . . I'm nothing like my father! I don't want to shuffle about the Towers of Granite in the King's footsteps, buried in government. I want adventure! I want to . . . "

"Be like us you mean!" Ustant's words cut him short. "Wandering vagrants living on memories—is that what you want? There is no call for warriors these daylights: we could have been famous huntsmen if we were younger but the people shun warriors once the killing's over."

"Nobody can blame you for wanting life to be more exciting, Archer, but . . . " Berioss sighed and quickly told the boy how they had become the cruel victims of the malicious lies and rumours that had started in the village of Deepling. He was protesting their innocence and had begun introducing the rest of the company when he paused suddenly as a movement in the gloom behind the youth caught his attention.

"Who else is there?" he asked, pointing uncertainly at Drib.

Eider glanced back over his shoulder and shrugged. "Oh, that's nobody special: it's only Crooked Drib, the sweep's boy. He's been put down here for beating a pony or something. But you mustn't worry about him—he's so dirty from sweeping those chimneys it's difficult to see where the shadows end and he begins. Drib, come here and show yourself. Come forward!"

"I didn't beat Fleet! I couldn't ever hurt any of the horses—it's a lie! Anyway, Nevian and the owl know I didn't do it even if nobody else believes me!" Drib cried out angrily. He had been excited about meeting these two Marchers and seeing what the tunnellers really looked like, for he had never met any before, but now he hesitated to come forward and show himself. His cheeks flushed hot with embarrassment and humiliation beneath the layer of ingrained soot and dirt that clung to his face. Why, oh why did Eider have to go and tell them about the pony? They were bound to think the worst of him now: nobody ever seemed to take his side when it came to the truth. And why had he told them he was a cripple? It would be obvious enough once he moved closer without having it pointed out at the first opportunity. He wouldn't have dreamt of introducing Eider as a thief or a rebel or anything like that. He wished the floor would open up and swallow him.

Berioss frowned as he heard the hurt and anger in the boy's denial. "We have all been wrongly accused, Drib, but if the Master of Magic and an owl both say you are innocent then it must be the truth beyond any doubt. Come forward, boy: you have nothing to be ashamed of: you are amongst friends. Come and meet Ustant, my Marcher friend, and the company of tunnellers we have done our best to protect, meet Oaktangle, Sloeberry . . . "

Drib smiled in the gloom and shuffled awkwardly forward as Berioss announced each of the tunnellers' names. There was something so gentle and yet so strong in the Marcher's deep voice, and when he reached out to grasp his hand in greeting he didn't seem to notice the dirt, there wasn't a flicker of movement in those penetrating, sea-grey eyes towards his crippled legs.

"Well met, young Drib: now come and meet the others," he had laughed softly, pulling him past Eider.

"You have met Nevian, the Master of Magic then. What did he look like?" Oaktangle asked with interest, remembering his own meeting with the magician beside the river and the visions he had seen after they had fled from the village of Larach. He felt there was something familiar about the crippled boy: he knew he had never met him before, but there was something about the way he moved . . .

"Was he wearing a cloak made up with lots of colours? What did he say?" Sloeberry asked, her soft voice full of interest.

Drib looked up sharply and turned toward her, catching his breath as he saw her slender face with its large, round eyes. In that half-light he could just see the delicate tips of her ears through silken strands of dark hair that fell to her shoulders. She was so beautiful and her voice touched memories of skylarks on the wind high above the fields that surrounded the city; or perhaps the musical whisper of windbells ruffled by the evening breeze.

"Co . . . col . . . colours—lots of colours . . . " his stammering voice faltered and died away as she smiled at him. He felt completely tongue-tied, his cheeks burning scarlet as he foolishly tried to rake his fingers through the tangle of hair that fell across his forehead.

He knew he was grinning but he couldn't help it; he wanted to laugh, or to cry, to tell her everything he knew, all the stories he had learned in the Learning Hall. He wanted to take her hand in his and show her all the things he loved, to show her Esteron. He had never felt so much like running and dancing. His whirlwind of thoughts suddenly collapsed as he saw her eyes travelling down to his crooked legs and he flinched inwardly and shrank back into himself as he waited for that look of disgust, or pity; or perhaps the brief, cold glance of dismissal that would tell him that he didn't count for anything. But to his joy and surprise it didn't come: her eyes were full of smiles and warmth as she looked up, seeking his eyes again.

Sloeberry had sensed something about him that she hadn't felt for anybody before, a confusing flush of emotions and attraction that she couldn't explain or understand. She found herself wanting to take a step towards him to know more.

"Tell us what he said," she asked eagerly, resisting the urge to touch his hand, to hold it, and she felt her cheek blush with heat.

Berioss smiled to himself. Amongst all this tragedy and hatred he had never expected to see the fragile spark of love kindle, especially between one of the city folk and one of the tunnellers. The startled looks of surprise painted on their faces, the innocence and magic of the moment, gave him new hope, and he knew it would be a moment that neither of them would ever forget.

"We should be working out a way to escape—not listening to Drib running on about the colour of the magician's cloaks, owls and all that nonsense! I warned you about encouraging him to chatter," Eider complained impatiently, almost knocking Drib aside as he pushed his way in amongst the tunnellers. "Now, the way I see it . . . " he continued, "we've got to somehow break down that door. I've heard my father talk about lots of old tunnels that used to go down from the upper circle near Candlebane Hall into the city before the great siege. If we can find one . . . "

"Escape?" interrupted Ustant, shaking his head. "Why should we try to escape? The King is going to judge us tomorrowlight and he has to find us innocent. All the accusations are false: Breakmaster implied as much as I was being jostled down the stairs from the cart. He has even ordered fresh bedding and food for us. Listen: that sounds like it being brought down now." He glanced towards the door as he heard faint voices and a scuffle of footsteps at the stairhead.

"We haven't done anything wrong: none of it is true, the King's got to believe us!" Mistletoe cried out, but the hope was fading from his voice.

"Innocent or guilty—it doesn't matter one jot!" Eider sneered in the young tunneller's face. "Somebody's got to be punished for all that trouble in Meremire, and for awakening the Nightbeasts. You must be really stupid, or stone deaf, if you didn't hear the mob howling for your blood when that escort brought you up through the city. You don't think they'll settle for less than your hides nailed up above the Stumble Gate, do you? Listen, they're still shouting and hammering on the gates, trying to break in and get at you: they don't care about verdicts of innocent or guilty—you're already guilty in their eyes just because you're tunn . . . " Eider looked up at Berioss and let the sentence go unfinished as he shrank back from the cold, hard glare in the Marcher's eyes.

"They hate us because we're different, don't they? Just because we don't look like them, all because of that they want us dead," Sloeberry whispered in a small, frightened voice, all thought of the magician paling into insignificance against the anger and fury of the crowds she could hear beyond their prison.

"I won't let anybody hurt you—I'll defend you with my life!" Drib cried, taking a step towards her.

Sloeberry smiled at him and touched his hand in silent thanks. She felt a strange, tingling sensation go through her, an inexplicable surge of joy and warmth. Her eyelashes fluttered in confusion as she quickly took her hand away, but the smile lingered on her lips. Nobody had ever said anything like that to her before.

"I don't care what happens to you either way. I don't make up the rules: I'm just telling you what will happen if the mob gets hold of you for your own good. I'm only locked up down here because that miserable excuse for a Loremaster, Grout, got me into trouble. He told the wardens a pack of lies about me stealing from him. But my father will see to it I get off, he always does." There was a degree of anger and a hint of disgust in the young archer's voice that revealed the frustration he felt about living in his father's shadow.

"He could be right," Ustant frowned with half an ear on the sounds coming from the stairway. There was something about the muffled shouts and hurried whispers that didn't sound quite right. "One of those guards who dragged me out of the cart was so afraid that the mob were about to break in and kill everybody that he wanted to hand us over to them there and then before we were even locked up. And I don't think it would have taken much to persuade the others to give us up to the mob. We were lucky Breakmaster appeared when he did!"

"There, I told you the verdict doesn't matter. There isn't going to be any judgement for you lot!" Eider hissed, quickly nocking the arrow back onto the bowstring as something thumped against the doorway and the key rattled in the lock.

"No! Put that arrow away!" Berioss snapped, reaching out to grasp the shaft, but the young Archer was too quick for him as he jumped back. "Now just stop it: it would be madness to try and escape: it would prove to the King and to everybody else that we're guilty. We've got to stay here and be judged— there's no other way to prove our innocence."

Oaktangle half-rose, stretching out his arm protectively to shield the other tunnellers, watching helplessly as Eider drew the bow string back towards his cheek and the door of the cellar began to swing slowly open.

"You're all fools, stupid fools! The judgement will prove nothing if you're already dead. Now, get out of my way: I'm not going to die with you, I'm not going to stay cooped up down here to be caught like a rat in a trap for anybody!" Eider snarled, moving around Berioss to get a clear aim at the guard who was beginning to push open the door.

There was no room for doubts now: he had to get out before the mob broke down the gates and overran Candlebane Hall to find the entrance to their prison. He knew they wouldn't bother to count heads: they'd just kill everybody in there, even Crippled Drib.

Eider took a deep breath and held it. His bow-arm trembled slightly: he knew he would have to kill the guard—there would be no second chance if he only wounded him. He would have to make his dash for freedom, retrieving the arrow as he ran through the door to loose it at the next guard. He didn't have a quiver full of sharp spines, only the one other precious arrow the owl had brought him which was still safely thrust through his belt. He had to hope his aim was true and that the arrowhead wouldn't bury itself too deeply in the body for him to pull it loose. He had to hope, too, that he wouldn't find too many guards crowding the stairway and blocking his escape.

The door creaked fully open and Eider stared in

shocked surprise, accidentally loosing the arrow which struck harmlessly on the wall beside it. Ustant stepped backwards, catching his breath and Berioss cursed, his eyes narrowing suspiciously. Sloeberry screamed, hiding her head in her hands at the gruesome sight. The guard that Eider was so carefully aiming at was certainly there but he was already dead, lifted up a good handspan above the floor and skewered to the timbers by his own spear. His head hung forward limply and his hands were gripping at the broken, wooden shaft; they glistened wetly with his blood in the uncertain, smoky light that shone from the guttering torch in its iron basket set high beside the doorway.

"By all the shadows that move who could have killed him?" Berioss gasped in alarm as Ustant ran to the door and took a step across the threshold, searching carefully to the left and right before peering up the stairway.

"There's another guard lying in a pool of blood at the first twist in the stairs. From the straw and loaves of dry bread that have been scattered around him it looks as though he was the one who was bringing down our food and bedding," he answered softly, retreating back into the cellar, unsure of what they should do.

"What's happening? I don't understand—has the crowd overpowered the guards?" Oaktangle asked in a frightened whisper, shuddering as he stared up at the guard, unable to tear his eyes away.

The sudden violence was reflected in the twisted face and his blind, staring eyes, his mouth open in a silent scream that distorted his features. Beads of wet saliva and blood clung to his stretched lips. At any moment he expected him to blink or cough.

"No, it can't be the crowd assaulting the gates, the stairway's far too quiet. If the mob had done this, I'm sure they would have burst in here and attacked us the moment they killed the guard."

Berioss frowned, his hand instinctively reaching for his sword, forgetting that he had surrendered it up to Gorass at the Rising. He cursed silently under his breath as his fingers closed on the soft folds of the lining of his cloak and the empty scabbard. He felt naked and vulnerable without it and now, with the murder of the guard, they didn't even know who their enemy was.

"Nobody move or make a sound!" he whispered, motioning to Ustant to move in beside him to protect the tunnellers.

The shock of seeing the guard skewered to the door made Drib feel dizzy and sick and he was very grateful when the two old Marchers blocked his view of the body. Death was an inescapable reality: there wasn't a daylight that went past in the crowded city when he didn't come across it or step hastily back at the sound of the buriers' bell to let the cart go past. But death had been the occasional glimpse of a limp hand or a foot left carelessly dangling over the side of the cart, or perhaps a quick, stolen glance beneath the winding shrouds at the still, waxy, shrunken face. There had always been a simplicity about death before, despite the faint, sickly-sweet smell of decay and the hum and buzz of the flies that hung in a persistent, dirty cloud about the cart, and the slow rumble of its wheels, the mournful sound of its bell were things engraved in his memory long after the procession had passed by. Death was not this sudden, senseless violence.

He felt a hand upon his shoulder and Eider's voice whispering in his ear made him jump with fright. "Get ready to make a dash for it the moment those two old fools move out of the way. There's no need for either of us to stay down here, is there?"

Drib looked up at Eider and saw that he had knocked the other arrow onto his bow. "No," he whispered. "I'm going to stay with them."

"Suit yourself," Eider shrugged. "But don't blame me if somebody slits your throat."

He moved away from the boy and begun to crouch down, ready to make a run for it, but then he hesitated and stood up, and there was anger and frustration in his face as he realized that it would be madness to try and escape on his own. Somehow he had to convince those two stupid Marchers that they had to get out of there.

"Now, listen to me, all of you!" he hissed urgently, moving closer to Berioss. "Everybody's going to think that we killed those guards."

"But that's impossible: we've been locked up in here!" Ustant interrupted.

"Nobody's going to stop and work that one out. The key is in the door isn't it? They won't care how it got there: they'll probably say we had a duplicate or something. We've got to make a run for it while we have the chance: it's madness to stay. You can sort out the innocent bit when we're safe somewhere leagues away from the city."

Berioss turned angrily on the young Archer. He could see the sense in his argument but to run now would only compound the guilt that had already been stacked against them. They would never be free of it, and anyway he didn't believe they had the slightest chance of escaping with their lives.

"He's right, you know, we'll never get a free trial now," Oaktangle agreed.

"But we can't go rushing up those stairs: we don't know who killed those guards—or why. There could be twenty or thirty heavily-armed guards, or warriors who have taken the law into their own hands just waiting out there for us to show our faces. And they would be praised for killing us if we tried to escape, wouldn't they?"

"I can't be sure but I don't think there are more than a dozen, maybe fifteen of them at the most,"

Sloeberry whispered, making the others turn to stare at her. "It didn't seem to be important at the time," she continued quietly, "but as I was dragged out of the cart I caught a glimpse of a group of men keeping back in the shadows near a half-open grating in the cobbles beside the Candlehall. I assumed they were guards or something: there was a glint of lamplight on their weapons which were partly concealed beneath their cloaks. But the odd thing about them was that some of them were quite small, not like the guards or the escort: they were no taller than we are, and they were carrying heavy sacks slung across their shoulders. And . . . " Sloeberry paused, glancing anxiously at the open doorway. "The tallest one of them looked remarkably like that boy who attacked us in Deepling."

"Snatchpurse! That evil Chancellor's boy! So that's who is behind all this treachery: that's who has stirred up all the hatred and anger against us!" Ustant's knuckles were whitening as he clenched his fists, a rage of anger against the injustice was boiling up inside him. "I'll teach that wretched creature a lesson!" he cried, starting towards the door.

"Wait!" Berioss whispered, grabbing his arm and restraining him. "Knowing who it might be behind this doesn't tell us why. Sloeberry only thinks it might be him, and she didn't recognize anybody else. There's no sense in running headlong up those stairs: whoever killed those guards didn't want us dead as well or they would have just burst in and killed us here in the cellar. Now think, man, think—you are a Marcher: we must form a plan of escape."

A muffled, indistinct voice suddenly called out from the stairhead, beckoning them to escape. It was telling them that the coast was clear and urging them to run for their lives. Eider scrambled to his feet, quickly followed by Drib and half the tunnellers.

"Stop! Get back, all of you! Think hard and try to

remember the layout of the courtyard above this cellar," Berioss hissed, blocking the doorway before any of them could squeeze past him.

"If only we could find one of those secret passageways my father talked about," Eider muttered impatiently.

Ustant laughed harshly. "If you had seen the ruin that this city was reduced to during the great siege you would put all thoughts of ever finding them out of your head."

"No, the boy might be onto something," Berioss frowned. "That gang of traitors must have got into this upper circle somehow—you said they were standing close to a half-open grating?" he asked, looking at Sloeberry.

"Yes, and I think there was another on the far side of the courtyard, beside a wall and close to the gates. But I can't be sure."

"There was an old doorway on the right near the top of the stairs: I fell against it and grabbed hold of its rusty handle when I was pushed down the steps. It didn't look as though it had been used for ages: the latch was all clogged up with dust and cobwebs. Could that be an entrance to one of the tunnels?" Damask asked.

"It wouldn't matter if it was. We haven't got anything to batter it down with or the time to do it in," Ustant answered, shaking his head.

"I bet I could pick the lock if it's not too rusty. All I need is a dagger or a strong piece of barter-wire," Eider whispered, grinning and passing his bow to Drib for him to look after.

"I have never in my life plundered the dead but need drives the desperate," Berioss muttered grimly as he rifled the dead guard's uniform. Removing the dagger he passed it to Eider then unsheathed the sword and gave it to Ustant. With this done he used both hands to wrench the spear out of the man's chest and carefully laid his body on the floor, covering the face with the tails of his cloak.

"Ustant and I will guard the stairhead while Eider tries to pick that lock. The rest of you wait on the stairs."

"Can I come with you?" Drib asked, holding up the bow and looking up at Berioss.

Berioss was about to shake his head and tell him to wait with the others on the steps below the door while Eider tried to pick the lock. Defending the upper doorway into the courtyard was much too dangerous and the lad wasn't much bigger than most of the tunnellers and he didn't know how fast he would be able to move with those crippled legs if push came to shove. He didn't want him getting hurt. But there was something in the chimney boy's eyes that told him that he had always been overlooked and pushed aside and it had left him with a longing to be like everybody else in spite of his disabilities.

"Can you use that bow?" the Marcher asked.

Drib didn't need to be asked twice: his face split into an infectious grin of delight. He had never been allowed to do anything as important as this before: the only exciting thing that had ever happened to him was when the King had lifted him up out of the gutter to sit on Esteron, and that was different because he knew the King had felt sorry for him.

"Yes, yes, of course I can!" he lied, stooping down to avoid the old Marcher's penetrating, questioning gaze and picking up the spent arrow that Eider had loosed at the dead guard. He had often watched the young Archers practicing on the great wall above the river and he would have loved to have joined in but they had always chased him away. Still, he wasn't going to give up this one chance to prove that he could do something really important. It couldn't be *that* difficult could it—using a bow? He fumbled with an arrow, trying to nock it onto the bowstring.

"Look sharp and keep close to my heels, boy, and don't get under my feet if we're attacked. At the first sign of trouble I want you back down those stairs in double-quick time. Have you got that?" Berioss frowned. Seeing the way Drib was holding the bow had given him second thoughts about letting him come with them and he was about to tell him that he had changed his mind when Eider muttered at Drib loudly enough for everybody to hear, "You're the most useless excuse for a boy I've ever met! Can't you even hold the bow properly? Come here, let me show you!"

Berioss watched as Drib's cheeks flushed with shame and embarrassment, but there was a tell-tale hint of jealously in Eider's voice: it was clear that he resented Drib being allowed to help them defend the stairs. Berioss smiled to himself and changed the boy's hold on the arrow-shaft himself, showing him how to nock it onto the string. The young Archer's arrogant attitude towards Drib had pushed all Berioss' doubts aside.

"Keep close to us!" he whispered at Drib as he and Ustant ran up the first flight of steps, pausing and crouching at the bend, pressing themselves against the wall as they checked that the way ahead was clear before beckoning to the others to follow.

Drib hurried after them, picking his way through the tunnellers who were crowding uncertainly in the cellar doorway. He paused a moment beside Sloeberry. "I want you to know, I really didn't hurt that pony."

"I knew you couldn't have done anything like that," she smiled, briefly squeezing his hand before Eider jostled and pushed Drib up the stairs.

"Watch out! Watch what you're doing with that bow! Can't you go any faster?" Eider's contemptuous voice hissed down his collar.

Drib was scrambling up the steep stone steps as fast as he could but Eider was climbing them behind him two at a time, eager to pick the lock and escape. Drib barely noticed the old, wormy door with its rusty latch as he hurried up the last half a dozen steps and crouched down beside Berioss; behind him he heard Eider curse under his breath and the sharp scrape of the dagger blade entering the lock. Slowly the keys began to tumble one by one and he could hear the soft, anxious voices of the tunnellers as they huddled below him on the stairs. The sounds of the crowds hammering on the gates and crying out for their blood had almost completely died away and the mob had gradually dispersed and returned to their homes. The cold night wind ruffled Drib's hair and made him shiver as he looked out into the darkened courtyard. The sheer granite walls of Candlebane Hall and the two Towers of Granite glittered with hore-frost and high up beyond them the sky was strewn with a canopy of sparkling stars that cast a pale light across the frozen cobbles.

"There's someone over there, hiding in the shadows: look, beneath the wall of the Candlehall," he whispered, touching Berioss's arm and pointing across the courtyard.

Berioss nodded. "Yes, I can see them, but there's more than one."

"Half a dozen at least," Ustant agreed, changing his grip on the hilt of the dead guard's sword.


"At last the rats are crawling out of their cage," Snatch hissed as he saw the dark, bulky shape of the two Marchers appear and position themselves defensively in the doorway that led down to the cellar. "Remember, we want them alive, all of them. Capture them one by one as they come out into the courtyard. Gag and bind them securely; we'll only kill them once we're safely away from here."

He beckoned to Kush who was buckling on his

Nightbeast armour. "We must make sure that some of the guards and the city folk catch a glimpse of us, it will feed the rumours that those tunnellers have awakened the Nightbeasts. They'll believe that they've broken into the city to set them free!"

"We'll strike terror into their miserable hearts!" Kush sneered as he pulled the grotesque, snarling head of the beast down over his own. "Death and dishonour to all who do not follow us!" he snarled, half-crawling, half-running as he mimicked the Nightbeast gait, the heavy strips of armour rattling together as he crossed to his position near the door.

Snatch tightened the straps of his own Nightbeast armour across his chest and then glanced round at a noise that came from behind him. "Keep quiet, you old fool, or I'll slit your throat!" he hissed at Grout, pulling him away from the half-open grating and the winding stairway that would take them down into the next circle of the city and safety. He quietly dropped the grating back in place and made Hinch, the horseman who had led them up through the city, stand on it to prevent him from escaping. Grout muttered and whispered constantly to himself, rubbing and twisting his long, thin fingers together. He was terrified that they would all be caught and his secret treacheries and longings to have the Chancellors back in power would be revealed. "Keep an eye on him in case he calls out and betrays us. Kill him if you have to." Snatch ordered Hinch.

"You had better be quick with this business. If we stay too long I'll be missed in my quarters: my master will become suspicious, he might put two and two together," Hinch muttered darkly. He was wishing he hadn't become involved, but the Loremaster had been so persuasive, it had seemed such a little thing to do guiding some of his friends up into the upper circle of the city to get the best view of the judging. He'd had his doubts about Snatch and the others from the first moment he had set eyes on them but it wasn't until they had murdered the two guards that he really realized what he had got himself into. And he was too deep in it now, he knew too much for them to let him back out.

"Don't even think of running out on us: we'll find you wherever you try to hide!" Snatch looked into his eyes with a cruel, pitiless gaze. "Watch him carefully, Hinch, and remember, don't let him utter a sound."

Snatch drew his finger slowly across his throat in the sign of the Honourable Company of Murderers and then pulled his Nightbeast mask down over his head and quickly moved across to where Kush and Girrolt were waiting to seize the tunnellers as they entered the courtyard.

"What's taking them so long? Why haven't they come out yet? Why haven't those two Marchers moved?" Huxort frowned anxiously.

They were wasting too much time: new guards could appear at any moment. Snatch ran back to Hinch and grabbed his collar, thrusting his face into his. "Tell me, are there any more secret passages or tunnels that lead into that cellar? Could they escape any other way?"

"I . . . I don't know," Hinch gasped, struggling to get away from Snatch's powerful grip and the terrifying, leering Nightbeast mask he wore. "This part of the city was riddled with secret ways, passages and stairs. The tallow-makers, weavers, armourers—every craft, even the buriers, had their own secret roads to Candlebane Hall and the Towers of Granite in the daylights of the Granite Kings before the great siege. It's impossible to know how many of them survived or even where they are."

Snatch swore at the horseman and fought to overcome the urge to strangle him, to crush and snap his useless neck with the armoured claws that covered his hands. He pushed him roughly back against the wall beside Grout and **whispered** to Squark who was perching on his shoulder, scratching the white magpie beneath its beak with a claw. "Go, my pretty watcher, search and spy for me, find out what those miserable creatures are up to."

Squark ruffled his feathers and picked at the bristly scales on the Nightbeast's mask near Snatch's ear. "Spy, spy," it mimicked, launching in a long, gliding flutter towards the door of the cellar.

Snatch moved back across the courtyard, careful not to reveal himself and keeping to the deepest shadows near where Kush and the others were positioned near the doorway.

"There's a chance that those tunnellers have found another way out of that rat-hole. I've sent Squark to see what they're up to."

Huxort glanced anxiously around the courtyard and whispered back, "Those two Marchers are armed: I'm sure I saw the flash of bright metal. That one nearest the threshold must have a sword. We can't afford to wait much longer, especially if it comes to a fight: the guards beyond the gate will hear us now that the crowds have dispersed."

"We were fools not to strip the guards of their weapons once we killed them. But give Squark a few moments longer and then we'll attack," Snatch hissed. "We'll kill those Marchers and it will be easy to make it look as though they died trying to overpower the guards."


"Look out! What's that?" Drib cried, ducking his head in surprise and almost losing his balance as a strange, ghostly-white bird flew over his head, its long tail-feathers stroking coldly against his cheek as it vanished down the stairs. With a shrieking cry it reappeared and Berioss made a grab for it as it flew between them. One of its claws scratched his neck and its harsh voice repeated, "Escape, escape!" as it rose out of their reach in a blur of white feathers.

A rush of footsteps and unearthly cries sounded in the cobbled yard on either side of the doorway. Berioss barely had time to call down the stairway, "Eider, Eider, have you managed to pick that lock? Eider—we're under attack!"

Suddenly half a dozen huge, misshapen figures—Nightbeasts, he was sure—swarmed towards them. Drib shrank down beside Berioss, terrified of the monstrous creatures that were rushing at them. They were more horrible than anything that had ever haunted his worst nightmares: he knew he had to draw back the bow and loose the arrow, but he couldn't: he was paralyzed with fear. Eider heard Berioss's urgent call and the howls of attack filling the doorway above him and his fingers trembled with haste as they gripped the hilt of the dagger and turned the blade in the lock. With a final click the latch lifted and he let out a pent-up breath of relief as he gave the door a push. The rusty hinges creaked as the door opened a crack and then stopped. Eider cursed and gave it a harder push, pitting his shoulder against it forcefully, but it wouldn't move.

"It's stuck! Oaktangle, Damask—everybody—come and help: there's something behind it, something's stopping it from opening."

Ustant looked desperately from left to right, his sword motionless in his hand. Old fears crowded his mind as he saw the Nightbeasts rush at him, swords and spears held in their claws, snarls and howls echoing from their mouths. Reason told him they couldn't be real, he had watched the last beast: Kerzolde, die and crumple to nothing in the Battle of the Rising.

"No! No! No!" he cried. "You cannot exist!" and he raised his sword: but it was too late—the first spear struck his chest. Snatch snarled triumphantly as he drove the blade deeper, forcing Ustant back over the threshold and down onto his knees. Kush brought his sword down on Ustant's sword hand, severing his fingers and sending out sparks as metal cut into metal. Ustant screamed out as the blood-stained sword flew across the cobbles. Behind him, Berioss thrust at the mass of creatures with his spear, trying to drive them away from his friend, but the broken spear was too short and he was hampered by the narrowness of the doorway. His attacker laughed and sneered at him, goading him to step out. Ustant clutched desperately at the spear-shaft piercing his chest but the creature towering over him possessed an overwhelming strength. He heard the splintering crack of his own ribs and through the searing pain he felt the sharp stab of the blade pierce his heart.

"Berioss . . . go . . . get the others to safety . . . go!" he gasped, choking as blood welled up to fill his mouth.

Drib watched, horrified, trapped by his own fear. Shame and helplessness filled him: he was too weak, a worthless cripple who had betrayed Berioss's trust. He should have stayed where he belonged, huddling in the dirt on the cellar floor. Suddenly the images of his father's death, the pictures of his courage that the magician had painted so vividly beneath the swirling colours of the rainbow cloak filled his mind, only now he saw the fear and doubt that his father had overcome. He saw that it was no easy journey that had brought him to his knees in the shadow of the great gate, the riven helm, the spears driven through his heart. In a blink he saw it all and understood, and it kindled the tiny, fragile spark of courage that had always dwelt deep down inside him.

On trembling, crooked legs he rose, and tears of anger blurred his eyes and his heart pounded in his chest, but his arm was steady as he drew the arrow back. "Get back, get back, you foul demon of the night!" he shouted defiantly.

His small voice was lost in the snarls and howls of their attackers and nobody saw him, but the song of the arrow was loud as it left the bow and cut through their wild voices, silencing them so that they could hear the thud as it hit Snatch's armour square in the centre of his chest, shearing through it and piercing his skin, sending him tumbling backwards. His snarls of triumph turned to a grunting gasp of surprise. He tore at the arrow-shaft as he struggled to his knees, snapping the shaft as he searched the darkness in the doorway. He couldn't understand it: none of the guards they had murdered on the steps that led down to the cellar had had a bow; he was sure of it. And even if the tunnellers had found a bow and a quiver lying in the cellar, they were cowards: they hadn't the stomach to stand and fight.

Doubt and fear made Snatch scramble backwards away from the stricken Marcher when he caught the glint of starlight on Drib's second arrow-head as he nocked it onto the bowstring and emerged from the doorway with the feathered flight drawn back tightly against his dirty cheek.

"Back! Get back, you foul demon beast!" Drib cried. His courage was beginning to fail him and his bow-hand had begun to tremble. He loosed the arrow too early before taking proper aim and although it sang through the frosty air, it glanced off the creature's armoured shoulder sending up a shower of bright sparks as it went spinning harmlessly away into the shadows on the far side of the courtyard. But there was enough force in the spine to make Snatch cry out and it sent him tumbling over across the cobbles.

The Company of Murderers hesitated and for a moment drew back in confusion. Ustant heard the sweet music of the arrows singing through the dark veil of pain that was folding over him. "Drib, Drib, run, escape while you can!" he called out weakly, reaching up with his blood-soaked hand towards the dim, deformed figure who stood protectively over him.

Drib dropped to his knees and clutched Ustant's hand. "I won't let them hurt you any more."

"No warrior could have asked for a better friend but you must go, get away while you still have the chance. You must escape."

The words gurgled in his throat and his head began to sink forward onto his chest as death towered over him. "Tell the King I was no traitor . . . tell him I loved and honoured him to the last breath . . . tell him . . . " With a soft sigh his head slipped sideways and his fingers went limp in Drib's tight grip.

"I promise, I promise," Drib wept, his head bowed in grief as he cradled Ustant's head in his arms, unaware of the renewed attack that surged towards them or Eider's voice calling to them from the bottom of the stairway. Suddenly he felt a strong arm around his waist and he was lifted up.

"We're coming: we can do no more here."

He heard Berioss call out and he was carried down the stairs. He hadn't realized that he still had hold of the bow until it scaped against the walls and was torn from his grip. "The bow!" he cried, trying to retrieve it, but it clattered out of reach as Berioss ran headlong down the stairs.

"There's something behind the door stopping it. We've only managed to force it open this far," Eider spoke breathlessly as he and the tunnellers flung their shoulders against the door again and again, staggering and reeling backwards, exhausted by their fruitless efforts.

The sounds of pursuit filled the doorway above them and Berioss glanced back over his shoulder, then he pushed the broken spear-blade into Drib's hands and set him down on one of the higher steps. "I know you will guard us well while I force the door open," he smiled grimly. Then he turned and threw all his strength against the door.

The ancient door shuddered from top to bottom. Dust and splinters erupted from its wormy surface and the hinges creaked and groaned as he tried again and again. "Come on! Come on! By all the shadows!" he cried.

Suddenly it moved. Something was jammed beneath the bottom crossbars and it broke apart with the crack of old bones splintering and grating noisily across the flagstones as Berioss, with Eider and Oaktangle beside him, began to force it open enough for them all to squeeze through. Stale, musty air that seethed and boiled with Nightshapes that had not been disturbed since the great siege wafted out around them.

"Quiet, everybody. Mistletoe, Damask, Sloeberry, Eider, get into the passageway!" Berioss shouted as the tunnellers crowded around him. He looked up to where he had sent Drib to defend the stairway. "Drib, come down. Jump, I'll catch you," he called, seeing the danger the boy was in.

Nightbeasts filled the stairs above Drib, snarling and reaching down with their claws, trying to grab him as he stabbed and prodded at their hideous, armoured hides. Drib half-turned his head as he heard Berioss shout. He was distracted for a mere second but his guard was down long enough for one of his attacker's claws to hook into his collar. He cried out for help but he was brutally jerked off his feet. The snarling creatures' voices grew louder as he was hoisted up. Frantically he stabbed with the spear at the mass of waving arms and claws that reached out to catch hold of him. He twisted and turned in desperation to break free and suddenly he felt two strong hands grip him around the waist and pull him down towards the open doorway. The thin, threadbare fabric of his collar tore free of the claws and Berioss almost tumbled to his knees.

"Run! Escape while you can!" the Marcher gasped, carrying him to the doorway and pushing him through the dark opening.

Drib sprawled over the threshold and collided with Eider who was huddled against the wall, crying and trembling, refusing to move despite Oaktangle and Mistletoe who were trying to pull him forward. Berioss leapt through the doorway and knocked Eider far enough out of his way to slam the door shut and throw his weight against it in a desperate attempt to stop their attackers from following them. Eider screamed in terror as the door slammed shut and total darkness closed in around them. He collapsed, burying his head in his hands and wept.

"Go on, run, run for your lives! I don't know how long I can keep this door shut!" Berioss shouted, feeling for the latch, hoping beyond hope that he could somehow wedge it shut as furious hammer blows rained down on the other side of the door threatening at any moment to force it open.

"There's a thick bolster—a wooden bar—just behind where you are standing; it must slide through those two iron hoops that have been set into the wall on either side of the door. We'll get it!" Oaktangle called out as he and Damask lifted and dragged the heavy bolster of ironwood to the door and between them they positioned one end of it through the iron hoop on the right hand wall where the door opened. Taking Berioss's left hand they guided it to the bar and slowly, between the three of them, slid it through the other hoop.

Berioss stepped back, rubbing his hands together. "It would take an army to break it down now! But how did you know about it?" he frowned, feeling in his pocket for his spark and crackling it alight so that he could inspect the door and the walls and low roof of the passageway. He glanced down and gasped, almost dropping the spark as he saw the partly-clothed skeleton of a warrior lying on the floor close to the wall.

"You forget: our people were born in shadow, slaves in the City of Night for suns beyond counting. We can see in the dark: it holds no fear for us. I think that warrior died trying to get out of here—it was the bones of his hand lying on the flagstones that became jammed beneath the door as we tried to open it." Oaktangle answered.

Berioss knelt beside the skeleton and examined it in the fragile light of his spark. It was still bound together by blackened sinews and hardened strips of muscle and bone were visible beneath the rotting clothes. He had once been a guard: that much was clear from the emblem on his cloak-tails, and a chilling thought entered Berioss's mind as he covered the blind, staring skull. Had the man died there all alone because he was trapped? Was there no other way out? Berioss looked across at Eider as he huddled down, pressed against the wall, weeping. He had seen this fear before. Whole companies of Marchers had been struck down by it, squadrons of Gallopers, strikes of Archers all suddenly possessed by it. They had been driven mad, reduced to shaking with fear, helpless with the terror of the dark. And braver men than this young Archer, too, battle-hardened warriors had been forced to cry out for a light, for a spark, a candle flame or the steady light of the moon and stars to guide them through the darker reaches of the night.

Berioss frowned, knowing how infectious this fear was and sensing his own fear creeping up on him as he imagined the millions of Nightshapes pressing in around them, deadening all sound, making the darkness so thick that you could touch it. Panic began to tighten itself around his throat, making it difficult for him to swallow. The thin blue light of his spark weakened and shrank to a tiny point of light.

Anxiously he crackled it between his fingers, reviving the light. It had to last to the end of the passageway: he would be completely lost without it.

"Eider's afraid of the dark isn't he?" Drib whispered beside him, almost making Berioss jump.

"Why, yes—yes he is, aren't you afraid as well? Light your spark," the old Marcher whispered back, fighting the panic in his voice as he rifled quickly through the dead guard's pockets, feeling around until his fingers found the man's spark. Breathing a sigh of relief he crackled it between his fingers but it was so worn out it lit once and then crumbled into dust.

"I haven't got a spark. I have never had enough barter to buy one. But it doesn't matter to me: I'm not afraid, I've had to climb up too many black chimneys to be afraid of the dark," Drib laughed, putting his arm around Eider's shoulders to comfort him.

"Could you stay with Eider then and help him along. Talk to him, search in his pockets and see if he's got a spark and light it for him. I must go ahead with Oaktangle and search out the end of this road."

"I will stay with you and help you guide him," Sloeberry's soft, musical voice sounded in the darkness close to Drib and made him smile. He felt the gentle touch of her fingers in his as he searched for Eider's spark in his jerkin pocket and pressed it into his hands, making it crackle alight.

"The bow! What happened to the bow?" Eider suddenly asked as the blue-white flame of the spark gave him courage.

Berioss paused for a moment and let the tunnellers go on ahead of him. His fear of the darkness seemed to have temporarily receded and he extinguished the spark and squatted down, resting his tired back against the wall as he mopped his forehead with the tail of his cloak. It was hot, exhausting work picking their way over the mounds of rubble and stone-choke that in places almost blocked the steeply-sloping passageway and was evidence of the severe pounding the city had taken during the great siege. It felt as if they had been walking forever, that they must be leagues below the city, but Berioss knew that time and distance were deceptive in darkness as thick as this. They had come upon the gruesome remains of another two bodies when they had to clear a way through a fall of masonry. It looked as though they had been killed by the roof of the passageway collapsing. By the look of their full-length hauberks, their leather aprons and large pockets filled with hundreds of chainmail links and iron rivets, and the blemishing hammers, crimps and fishtail snubs that had once hung from their belts Berioss guessed that they must have been armourers on their way up to the Towers of Granite in the middle of the great siege. It was becoming clear that the passage might lead them down to the old armoury.

Faint voices in the darkness from further back along the passageway made him half-turn his head as he caught the sound of Drib telling Eider and Sloeberry one of the stories he had heard about the Warhorses in the Learning Hall. He was painting it with such vivid detail that he was making the young archer quite forget his fear of the dark. There was an irresistible enthusiasm in the little sweep's boy that made Berioss smile and remember how he had found the courage to use that bow against the Nightbeasts where braver men's hearts would have failed. Berioss frowned and crackled the spark alight. He hadn't had a moment to reflect on the brief battle in that doorway but now, when he came to think about it, there was something wrong about those Nightbeasts. Something he couldn't quite put his finger on. He reached up to touch the festering scratch that the strange white bird had made upon his neck as it flew through the doorway back into the courtyard and wondered about it, puzzled about it befriending the Nightbeasts: he had never known of such a thing happening before.

"How much further do we have to travel in this infernal darkness? It presses in so heavily I can hardly breathe. Drib, stop your constant chattering: it's giving me a headache!" Eider cursed, holding on tightly to Drib's arm as the three of them rounded a curve in the passageway and came upon Berioss.

The old Marcher laughed, putting aside his fears and doubts. He was glad to see that Drib had coaxed Eider along the passageway and he climbed wearily to his feet and prepared to move forward. "You certainly sound a lot better now than you did when we first forced our way into this secret road, Eider!"

"You haven't had to listen to Drib running on and on endlessly about Warhorses and Battle Owls and what a great king Thane is, have you! It's enough to drive anybody mad!"

The laughter died away from Berioss's face. "No, boy, I haven't, but you should count yourself lucky that Drib and Sloeberry took the trouble to stay behind and help you overcome your terror of the darkness. Or would you rather they had left you whining and dribbling, too helpless, too frightened to move?"

Eider shuffled his feet and looked down, his cheeks flushed hot and scarlet. "I'm sorry, I didn't think."

"Is it much further?" Drib asked. "Only those creatures didn't try very hard to follow us: they only hammered on that door for a little while after you secured it. You don't think they'll find the other end of this passageway before we do and be waiting for us do you?"

"No, I don't think so. I have a feeling this passageway will lead us to the old armoury. But . . . " Berioss paused, afraid that if he revealed his fear that the end of the passage might be blocked there would be panic.

"But? But what?" Eider asked with fear in his voice.

Berioss laughed and shook his head. "It's nothing, nothing for you to worry about, except we have to slip unnoticed through the armoury so keep quiet all of you, there's no knowing how far our voices will travel through rock and stone."

Eider let out a sigh of relief and fell into step with Drib's awkward, dragging gait as they followed in Berioss's footsteps. After what seemed an age of shuffling along in the dark with his spark long-burned the silence became oppressive, he began to imagine all manner of creatures gliding around him, reaching out to touch him, and he gripped Drib's arm harder as his courage faltered. Gradually he became aware that the floor was beginning to level out and ahead in the weak glow of the light from Berioss's spark he saw Oaktangle and the other tunnellers examining a heavily-studded door.

Berioss beckoned them forward and Eider had to fight the urge to break into a run. "What's the matter? Why is it locked against us? Do you want me to pick the lock?" he asked, breathlessly as they reached the others.

Berioss frowned and shook his head, pointing to the ornate, rusty key that still protruded from the lock all these suns after the great siege. He looked back along the tunnel and wondered about the guard. Had he panicked in the darkness when the roof had collapsed and buried the two armourers? Had he thought, in the terror and confusion of the choking dust, that the whole passageway had been blocked? He had died a slow, starving death clawing at the back of the door ignorant of the fact that the way was clear, that safety lay just beyond the rock fall.

"I can't hear any sign of movement or voices the other side. Shall I turn the key?" Oaktangle asked, removing his ear from the grainy wood, his fingers already on the shank of the key.

Berioss motioned the others to stand well back and nodded. Oaktangle twisted the key and it slowly turned with a grating, rasping sound. One by one the tumblers fell into place. Using his other hand he lifted the latch and pushed against the door. It opened a crack and he stopped. The soft, flickering glow of a lamplight appeared along the stile close to the lock and Oaktangle glanced back at Berioss.

"There's something resting against the door: it's heavy and it's stopping it from opening. What shall I do?"

Berioss moved closer to the door, running his hands over the wood, doubtful about what to do. The door must have been locked by those two armourers moments before they had been killed when the roof collapsed, but why hadn't someone broken it down to find out what had happened to them? Why had it remained locked and forgotten for so long? Then he remembered the stories he had heard of those last moments during the great siege when Breakmaster had given King Holbian the last steelsilver battle-coat in all Elundium to wear about his shoulders as he led the city folk to escape by a secret road deep in the bowels of the earth. He remembered how Arachatt, the master mason, had brought the tower above the armoury crashing down to seal off their secret passage and prevent the Nightbeasts from following them. Berioss hesitated as he wondered what lay on the other side of the door. Was it the new armoury? Could there be piles of armoured boots and battle-gloves, metal shirts and helms stacked up against the forgotten door that would prevent their escape?

"What are you waiting for?" Eider was breathless and growing frantic with impatience, his fear was pressing in on him again, making him repeatedly try to brush the nightshapes away from his face. That thin glimmer of light he could see through the open gap was so tantalizingly close. "You were quick enough to force your way into this infernal blackness!"

Suddenly he could wait no longer and he pushed his way through the others before Berioss could turn and stop him. "Here, I'll show you!" he gasped, throwing his weight against the door.

The door juddered from the force of his attack and swung open, striking a spear-stand that had been leaning against it. The tall spears swayed and rattled against one another and then slowly toppled over, crashing noisily to the floor. Drib flinched and cowered back as the tunnellers put their hands over their ears. Berioss grabbed Eider by his collar, almost lifting him off his feet in anger and preventing him from rushing into the armoury.

"You stupid fool! Now look at what your impatience has done—it will alert the whole city to our whereabouts!"

"I . . . I . . . I didn't mean to. It was an accident. My fear of the darkness made me do it, I couldn't breathe, I had to open the door—I had to!" Eider cried out, trying to break free from the Marcher's grip and reach the light that was streaming through the open doorway.

"You were right, Berioss, this passageway does lead to the armoury, only the doorway is set up the wall, well above the level of the floor!" Drib whispered, peering over the threshold, his eyes round and wide with wonder as he saw the flickering flames of the lamps set high in the walls reflected and mirrored in the rows of polished, armoured battle-plates, ranks of chainmail shirts, shields and battle-helms. Wherever he looked there were whole forests of spears and siege-hooks marching away into the darkest corners of the room and row upon row of swords, their entwined and hammered ornamental hilts catching the light. There were banks of arrow-stands and hundreds of oiled bows of black ebony lined one whole wall. Battle-coats for horses and chainmail bridles and war-saddles lined another wall while piles of armoured boots and battle-gloves, spurs, gambesons and surcoats filled every available space upon the floor.

"It's all so wonderful—the glitter and polish, the smell of leather . . . " Drib sighed behind Eider who struggled free and leapt past the boy, pushing him roughly aside as he jumped down onto the spear-shafts, rolling them noisily under his feet as he ran towards the light.

"Wait! Not so fast! Keep back, you fool!" Berioss cursed, climbing down and helping the tunnellers and Drib before picking a path through the fallen spears and hurrying after the young Archer. He paused and stopped to listen now that the echo of those falling spears had finally faded away, fully expecting to hear the rush of footsteps and angry voices alerted by the noise they had made.

Eider looked around anxiously, for a moment listening to the silence, and then shrugged dismissively. "I knew there was nothing to worry about: nobody's going to hear anything in here. When they rebuilt the armoury after the great siege they made the walls so thick you can't even hear the armourers working at their anvils from the courtyard outside. I should know: I've been in here often enough with my father. There's never anybody in here during the night."

Berioss glanced irritably at the boy. His self-assured, cocky attitude was returning far too quickly for Berioss's liking now they were out of the dark passageway but he was relieved to hear that the armoury wasn't being guarded during the night at least. But they had to get away from there before morning. He hadn't had a moment to think about what they were going to do next—how they would get out of the city or where they would go. Hiding the tunnellers wasn't going to be easy: they would be recognized wherever they went. He felt very alone without Ustant to help him decide. What was he to do?

"All the weapons are exactly the way the Loremaster described them in his stories, only I never imagined there would be so many," Drib murmured in awe as he slowly followed the others over the threshold. There was so much to see that he didn't know where to look first, but he was careful not to touch anything, even the fallen spears, in case he made them dirty.

Berioss laughed softly. "This is nothing, lad, nothing to the arms and battle-coats that were stored here before the great siege. Why, there was enough to clothe an army. But, come on, we have got to think of a way out of here."

"That small doorway over there behind the racks of chainmail shirts opens into the riveters' yard," Eider informed them. "And on the far side of the yard Pot Kettle Lane should take you into an old Archers' track, the ones they used for taking the arrows to the Archers on the walls in times of attack. It will take you directly down towards Stumble Gate avoiding the main thoroughfare and leads you to the top of Tallow Finger Alleyway. From there you are almost out of the city."

"That's almost opposite the Breaking Yards . . . " Drib interrupted, only to be hushed into silence.

"But what will we do once we get out of the city? Winter is almost upon us and we don't have any food or warm clothing. With nowhere to go and no way of defending ourselves what are we to do?" Oaktangle asked, helplessly spreading his hands.

"Why can't we stay here? Why don't we give ourselves up and let the King judge us? We are innocent: he's got to see that, hasn't he? Then we can go back to the Rising!" Mistletoe cried.

"Innocent!" Eider laughed. "Whatever chance you had of being judged innocent died with those guards who were murdered while they guarded you in the cellar. The only chance you've got of staying alive is to run, escape while you can. It's all right for Drib and me: we're not in half the trouble you are. My father will get me off, he always does, and Drib here will just have to do his punishment, whatever it is, and that will be the end of it."

"No, no, I'm innocent, I've already told you. Even the magician and the owl believe me!" Drib cried out hotly as a smug, knowing smile appeared on Eider's face.

"Nobody's going to care what that magician says, he's just a figment of your imagination. Just believe me, Drib, it's in your best interests to say you're sorry and take the punishment. It will go all the worse for you if you don't."

Drib shook his head defiantly. "No, I'm not staying here if nobody's going to listen to my side of what really happened. I'm fed up with being punished for things I didn't do. I would rather stay with Berioss, Oaktangle and the rest of the tunnellers if they let me."

Berioss smiled to himself. He admired the little crippled boy's pluck but he didn't want to hazard a guess at how long he would survive in the wilds beyond the safety of the city he had grown up in. Nor did he really want to burden himself with the responsibility of looking after him: he had enough to contend with already.

"Wait! Think for a moment, boy, before you do something rash," he frowned, squatting down in front of him. "If we do manage to get out of the city and let you come with us, how do you think you're going to survive the winter in those ragged clothes? You will freeze to death in the first snows: you haven't even got shoes to put on your feet. Do you have any idea what it's like beyond the city gates?

You won't be able to keep up with us and how are you going to defend yourself against the wild beasts that roam in the forest if you fall behind? And what will you eat? It will be a hard enough road for us and we're used to travelling the Greenways, always hiding, avoiding the comfort of the villages, living from moment to moment."

Huge tears were brimming in Drib's eyes. There had been brief moments when he had fought beside Berioss in the doorway and helped Eider through the darkness of the passageway when he had felt normal, just like the others, not the ragged, useless cripple everybody made him out to be. He had never owned a pair of shoes and had always survived on the leftovers from his master's table so there would be no hardship for him. It was clear that they didn't want him with them. Slowly he began to turn away and hide his shame, especially from Sloeberry.

"But why shouldn't he come with us if he wants to, Berioss? He didn't hesitate to leap to our defence in the cellar, and it would be unfair if we left him behind and he was punished for helping us, wouldn't it?" Oaktangle intervened.

Berioss sucked in his cheeks, his frown deepening. Eventually he nodded. "Oh, very well, but we're going to have to do something about his clothes: it's no good if he freezes to death before we've travelled a league from the city is it?"

"I'll make sure he's not left on his own if he drops behind: you needn't worry about that," Sloeberry added. She smiled and touched his hand, making Drib look up. "What we harvest from the forest we will gladly share with you."

Drib quickly rubbed his sleeve across his eyes to hide the tears and sniffed as a grin widened across his face. There was a warmth in her eyes that he had never found in anybody before. "You mean I can come with you? You really don't mind?"

"No, of course we don't mind. And I want you to come," she whispered, squeezing his hand.

"I don't see what all the fuss is about or why Berioss picked on Drib. None of us are properly dressed to travel through winter weather but since we are being forced to flee because nobody in this city will listen to the truth then I don't see why we don't borrow some of these fine clothes from the armoury, if we can find any that fit. Perhaps while we're at it we could borrow some of the weapons and armour to defend ourselves and bring to justice whoever it is who is getting us accused of these dreadful things."

There was a mischievous grin on Mistletoe's face as he picked up a burnished helm with a wide chain-mail apron that hung down at the back to protect its wearer's neck and put it on. The helm was much too large and almost came down to his chin which made the others laugh, but Oaktangle stared at him as a cold shiver ran up is spine. Fragments of the pictures the magician had painted in the water were beginning to come true: it was all happening around him whether he wanted it to or not.

"Running away are you, Drib?" Eider suddenly accused, but there was an edge of regret in his voice that Oaktangle noticed.

"There's nothing to stop you coming with us, if you want to!"

"Yes, a good Archer's eye will be useful when we're hunting game in the forest," Berioss agreed as he began to sift through the piles of thick woollen leggings and warm gambebons.

Eider stood staring at Drib, consumed with envy. He could not understand what made him hesitate to join Berioss and the tunnellers: he had just been offered all the danger and adventure he had always longed for and yet something inside, some unknown fear, was whispering for him to stay, was telling him that the life he professed to hate so much wasn't really all that bad. He knew he had to make up his mind there and then, that he would never get another chance like this.

"But it would be stealing, wouldn't it, to take what doesn't belong to us?" Drib frowned, reluctant to touch the padded jerkins or to try on the heavy marching boots that the tunnellers were sorting through.

"No, lad, borrowing's different from stealing. We'll give it all back to the King one daylight, after this trouble's over. Now, hurry!" Berioss insisted, buckling on a pair of fleece-lined breeches and stamping his feet into a new pair of boots. Time was pressing and he was beginning to worry that the grey hours would creep across the sky, heralding the new morning before they had a chance to make good their escape.

"Now what's the matter?" he asked in exasperation as Drib still hesitated.

"I . . . I . . . I'm so dirty with all the soot from the chimneys. I'm afraid of spoiling everything."

Eider suddenly made up his mind. "Come with me," he said, grabbing Drib's hand and almost pulling him off his crooked feet as he hurried him into a small, dark washroom at the rear of the armoury where the linen undershirts and fleeces were washed. A cauldron of warm water simmered over the embers of a fire in the hearth and eddies of steam ghosted its rippling surface.

"Strip!" Eider commanded, wrestling off the boy's ragged jerkin and throwing it aside, hardly waiting until Drib had removed his breeches before picking him up and immersing him in the warm water.

"Now scrub, quickly: we haven't time to waste," he ordered, thrusting a bar of oily soap and a coarse scrubbing brush into his hands.

He picked up another in readiness to help and then

put his hand upon Drib's head and pushed firmly. The boy gasped and choked as he was immersed in the water, rivulets of soot, tar and dirt oozed out of his hair and ran down his cheeks as he rose spluttering to the surface. Eider worked fast, instructing the boy how to wash himself and being none too gentle in his scrubbing but in no time at all he had Drib pink, raw and shivering standing on the flagstone again, wrapped in a large Marcher's cloak.

"Now, quickly dry yourself and then go and find some proper clothes to wear," Eider grinned, gathering up Drib's filthy sweep's rags into a bundle and pushing them into the embers of the fire before Drib could get to them.

The sweep's lad cried out in protest: all he had ever owned was in that bundle, even the few crumbs of sugar he had been saving for Esteron and a treasured button he had once found in the gutter with a sandstone pebble. A spark from the embers touched the threadbare, sooty rags and they burst into greedy flames which licked up and rapidly consumed the rags, reducing them to nothing but ash and leaving Drib to begin his new life.

"But nothing fits—it's all far too big, even the smallest of these leather jerkins comes right down to my feet!" Damask complained.

Berioss had quickly found everything he needed, including a thick, fleece-lined Marcher's cloak and a metal helm engraved with the symbol of the sun. He crossed to the doorway that opened into the riveters' yard and opened it a crack, peering anxiously up to the dark, night sky. "Be quick, all of you, the grey hours are almost upon us!"

Sloeberry stopped searching for a warmer cloak and looked up, catching her breath in surprise as Drib emerged from the wash-house wrapped in the Marcher's cloak. He was far more handsome than she had thought. Beneath the layers of dirt his hair was the colour of autumn gold and there were freckles on his cheeks and a dimple on his chin. His eyes looked a deeper blue than they had against the grime and the embarrassed smile that widened across his face and the flush of colour it brought to his cheeks as he realized that she was looking at him made her laugh softly and quickly return to rummaging through the clothes. Eider could see at a glance that the tunnellers and Drib would find nothing to fit them no matter how hard they looked.

"Come on: there's no time to be fussy, take anything that will keep you warm," Berioss urged, keeping a watchful eye on the sky and the guards patrolling through the courtyards that surrounded the armoury.

"No, wait! I think I know where there are clothes to fit the tunnellers—and armour and weapons forged small enough for them to use. Come on, all of you, follow me—Drib, you too!" Eider called out, crossing the armoury between the harness racks and saddle-horses to fling open the double doors that led into the apprentices' hall.

Drib gasped in surprise, almost letting the cloak fall from his shoulders to reveal his nakedness. Even in the gloomy, shifting light cast by the two lamps that had been left burning in their hanging baskets he could see the heaps of old-fashioned armour stacked up against the walls. There were piles of helms emblazoned with the emblem of the owl in blue and gold, thick leather jerkins, mail-shirts, battle-gloves and breeches thrown and stacked in chaotic disorder away from the long, wooden work benches that were littered with armourers' tools, needles, lasts, glazing irons, burnishers, awls, pricking irons and cramps. Beyond the cluttered benches, looms, spinning-wheels and saddlers' clamps crowded around the huge, water-driven polishing mill and there was a forge where a single, thin spiral of smoke curled up the chimney.

"The apprentices make all this stuff in miniature to learn their crafts. It isn't much use to anybody because it's so small. A lot of it has been lying around here, forgotten since the age of the Granite Kings, but you might find something to fit." Eider swept his hand across the room before he ran back into the main armoury to select the warmest Archers' clothes he could find, high leather boots and a thick, lined cloak, but he paused before the bows and arrow-stands. He carefully chose two of the best bows, tied a dozen spare bow strings around his waist and filled two quivers with the finest new-forged arrows.

Drib laughed with pure delight. The linen shirt felt so crisp, so clean against his skin and a pair of fleece-lined breeches and a leather jerkin made him feel hot; but the pair of boots that Sloeberry had selected for him felt strange on his feet and he tottered and almost fell as he tried to walk in them.

"Here, Drib, put these on," Mistletoe laughed, thrusting a chainmail shirt and a battle-helm engraved with the owl symbol into Drib's hands. Drib staggered beneath their weight and could hardly lift his arms once he had taken the sword and shield that Blackthorn had offered him and fastened the fur-lined Gallopers' cloak around his throat.

"Are you ever going to be ready?" Berioss called in exasperation and Oaktangle made the others hurry after him out of the apprentices' hall.

Drib struggled to keep up, stumbling and tripping over every irregularity in the flagstones, unused to the boots he was wearing. Berioss smiled and momentarily forgot his impatience as he suppressed a gale of laughter that was rising in his throat as the tunnellers appeared. They were the most ill-assorted company of knights he had ever seen, but he could see from their choice of arms they were at least think-ing about defending themselves which was definitely a step in the right direction.

"Mock armour for mock warriors," he smiled. Suddenly the smile dissolved into a frown as he saw the difficulty that Drib was having crossing the armoury floor.

"We have to think of something to help Drib— quickly! He must be able to keep up or we'll never get out of the city before it gets light!" he muttered to Eider, as the young Archer passed each of the tunnellers an extra fur-lined cloak rolled up and secured with a leather strap ready for them to carry.

Berioss slipped out of the armoury, his breath ghosting white in the frosty air as he listened to the city that was wrapped in the silence of the dead hours below them. Faintly he could hear the guards shouting in the upper circles but below them nothing moved except the nightshapes gliding and drifting around the occasional lamps that still flickered in the darkness.

"It's all right, leave me alone, I'll keep up, I've got to get used to these boots!" Drib hissed at Eider, shaking off his helping hand and gritting his teeth against the pain in his crooked feet as he struggled to cross the riveters' yard, wishing he had never put them on.

"I'll stay with him: you go on ahead with the others, I'll make sure he catches up," Sloeberry whispered to Eider before dropping back and slipping her arm through Drib's.

Her voice was no louder than the murmur of hummingbirds' wings as she sang to him of all the beauties of the wild forest, of the morning dew that sparkled on the Greenway, of the great Warhorses and the border runners that moved through the leafy shadows, of the wind combing in flowing waves through the tall, summer grasses and of the leaves whispering in the branches above their heads.

Sloeberry was so intent on trying to keep Drib's mind off the pain and Drib himself was concentrating so hard to move each foot without crying out that neither of them saw the shadowy creatures break away from the far side of the riveters' yard and begin to follow them. They were moving stealthily from alley to alley, watching them, waiting for an opportunity to pounce. Nor did they see Silkstone, the owl, stoop down from one of the armoury chimney-pots to hover in the darkness above them, beating the frosty air beneath his wings as he listened to Drib's strangled sobs of pain and Sloeberry's sweet, whispering voice encouraging him forwards step by step. The owl rose hooting in alarm as he spotted their pursuers closing in but Berioss and the others were too far ahead to help them: they had already crossed from Tallow Finger Alley and were hurrying down the Oddhollows Steps towards the Stumble Gate.

Silkstone stooped sure and fast, the speed stripping feathers from his wings before he landed in the breaking yards. "Drib is in great danger! There are Nightbeasts in the city surrounding them in the old Arrow Way!" The owl shrieked and hooted as he told Esteron everything he had seen as he alighted on the kingpost beam in his stable.

Esteron's ears flattened along the side of his head and the muscles across his neck and shoulders tensed and rippled as he lifted his head and roared out a challenge that was answered immediately from where the Nighthorses were picketed, ready-saddled and bridled as was the custom in the fortress of Underfall. The horses reared and plunged, breaking the picket line and their hoofbeats became a roll of thunder in the darkness as they followed Esteron through the high-arched gateway. Their bit-rings jingled wildly and their names streamed out as they cantered up Tallow Finger Alley.

# 9

## Escape!

SNATCH CURSED. HE WAS CONSUMED WITH FURY AS the dirty little cripple who had already dared to wound him with an arrow slipped from his grasp on the crowded stairway. Suddenly their plan to capture the tunnellers and murder them secretly outside the city while making it look as though they had escaped evaporated in a rush of fleeing footsteps as all of them, even the old Marcher, had unexpectedly vanished through an ancient doorway that none of the Company of Murderers had known existed. Kush and Huxort had leapt after them, throwing their weight against the door as it slammed shut, but they were too late to force it open and their spears and axes made little impression on the grainy ironwood.

Girrolt had called down urgently from the stairhead to tell them that new guards were spilling out into the courtyard and Snatch ran up the stairs followed by the others. "Don't stop to fight—you have to run for that iron grate where Grout and Hinch are waiting. The guards will probably be too surprised, too terrified of the Nightbeast armour to attack. Now run!" he hissed, snarling and roaring as he ran out into the starlit courtyard towards the startled guards.

The guards cried out in terror as the huge, misshapen Nightbeasts lumbered towards them and they threw down their weapons and fled. Kush snarled and stabbed at them as they scattered, possessed with a killing lust and the urge to taste their blood, but Snatch had grabbed at his scaly armour and roughly pushed him down the steep steps into the secret road that would lead them out of the upper circle. They followed on Grout's heels and Hinch pulled the iron grating shut behind them, locking it as they ran down into the city.

"Where could that door have led them to? Where will it come out? I must know!" Snatch hissed, struggling to control his rage as his breath came ragged and fast. His clawed, armoured fingers were tightening around the Loremaster's throat as he pinned him against the cold, wet granite wall of the alleyway where they were hiding.

"It . . . it . . . it could have come out anywhere— the Breaking Yards, the armoury—anywhere!" Grout stuttered in terror.

"I think it used to lead to the old armoury but the other end was probably blocked with rubble when the old armoury collapsed in the great siege. A lot of those old secret roads are dangerous if you try to disturb them. My bet is that they will try to force a way through and the rest of the roof will cave in on top of them. They'll never get out alive, never—that's the last you'll see of them!" Hinch was anxious to get away from Snatch and his murderous friends and was keeping half an ear on the growing commotion he could hear coming from the guards in the upper circle of the city.

"No, we're not leaving anything to chance. Take us down to the armoury. If they do find a way out we'll capture them there and I want to skin that dirty cripple myself. How dare he loose an arrow at me!" Snatch let go of Grout's throat and thrust him aside to follow Hinch.

Grout gasped for breath and staggered, catching hold of Hinch's arm for support as they hurried down towards the armoury.

"It must have been Drib who fired that arrow: though I've no idea where he could have got the bow from," Hinch whispered as they reached the armoury. "I don't think we had better tell Snatch we had him locked him up earlier tonight, do you?"

Grout's eyes widened in fright as he rubbed at the sore bruises on his neck. "Oh no, oh dear no!" he muttered in dismay.

"Quiet, you babbling fool! Do you want to wake the city?" Snatch hissed, prodding Grout in the ribs.

"You were right, they must have found a way out of the armoury, look, there's somebody crossing the riveters' yard, I can hear their voices," Hinch whispered, hurrying forward with Snatch beside him.

They were just in time to see two small figures, one twisted and deformed, disappear into a dark alleyway on the far side of the yard.

Snatch's lips thinned into a snarl and he touched the wound in his chest as he saw Drib and Sloeberry disappear from sight. He couldn't remember any of the tunnellers having crooked legs in the inn at Deepling but it didn't matter: he'd straighten them when he caught them. He would crack the crooked bones one by one.

"They're going down towards Stumble Gate, down the old Arrow Way. We can intercept them further down in Tallow Finger Alley before they reach the Breaking Yards. The others must be somewhere ahead of them: we can catch them up in no time," Hinch whispered, ducking into the dark, low entrance of Cryers' Lane.

Snatch glanced up with hatred in his eyes as an owl hooted from somewhere high above his head in the starry darkness. "Fly, Squark, peck out its prying eyes, silence it before it warns the whole city!" he hissed, but Squark shrank down, hiding between the rotting folds of the Nightbeast armour, afraid of the owl's beak and talons in the dark. Snatch cursed the bird

and felt on the ground between his feet with his
armoured claws to find a stone which he threw up in
the air. But his hatred of owls couldn't keep him
there: he had to catch up with the others down Cryer
Lane and he was with them when they moved
stealthily into Tallow Finger Alley.

"They are only a footstep ahead of us now," Hinch
murmured, pointing at the two small figures moving
slowly down the alley.

Snatch laughed as he saw with the glint of starlight
that Drib held a shield and that a small sword hung from
his belt beneath a mail-shirt. "They'll be easy in the taking, despite those silly weapons!" he sneered, motioning
to the others to spread out and surround them.

"You won't escape us this time!" he snarled, rushing towards Drib and Sloeberry, his spear drawn
back ready to stab and thrust.

The hideous Nightbeast's shadow swarmed across
the cobbles and seemed to smother them. Drib spun
round awkwardly and instinctively he raised his
shield to protect Sloeberry and ward off the first
spear-thrust. The metal point of the spear-blade skidded off the shield and struck the wall beside his head.
The Nightbeasts towered over them and in desperation he swept his sword out of its scabbard to make a
last, defiant stand.

"Get back! Get back, you foul demons of night!"

Sloeberry drew the dagger she had taken from the
armoury and stood close beside him.

"Run, Sloeberry, escape—duck down and slip
between the monster's legs. Run! Run for your life:
I'll hold them off for as long as I can!" Drib urged as
another vicious spear-thrust struck his shield so hard
that it numbed his arm and almost drove him to his
knees.

"No! I will not desert you, Drib. I'm staying here at
your side!" Sloeberry answered defiantly, raising her
dagger to ward off another spear.

For the briefest moment their eyes met as the shadows of the beasts engulfed them. Drib had never expected her to stay and a surge of joy coursed through his veins as he realized that she wanted to be with him. "They will not kill us easily!" he cried as a clear image of his father defending the Stumble Gate filled his mind and he heard him cry out as the dark, hopeless shadows of despair swarmed all around him, heard him shouting his love of the sunlight and it gave Drib courage.

"Sing, Sloeberry: let your voice rise above these foul creatures snarling voices as we build a wall of Nightbeast dead. Sing of all the beautiful things you have told me of, let your voice soar to the bright stars in the night sky above our heads. Sing!" he called out to her as he raised his sword-arm.

A sudden rumble of thunder and a rush of iron-shod hooves shook the cobblestones and the wall of the Arrow Way. The attacking Nightbeasts hesitated, their snarls of triumph as they prepared to make the killing stroke turning to cries of terror as the Arrow Way filled with the dark, galloping shapes of the Nighthorses, led by Esteron. The wild whites of their eyes and their flowing manes reflected in the starlight and sparks danced beneath their flying hooves. Reins flapped, stirrups swung and bit-rings jingled madly as they converged on Drib and Sloeberry's attackers.

Snatch had stopped at the first sound of the horses and as soon as he heard the sound of their hooves pounding on the cobbles he shouted, "Run! Run for your lives!" and threw down his spear before jumping into a narrow gap between two overhanging buildings, pulling the startled and terrified Loremaster after him. The Company of Murderers scattered in confusion, dropping their weapons in their haste to escape, diving into every dark hole, lane and alley to escape. The echo of their footsteps quickly vanishing into the darkness.

"Esteron! Esteron!" Drib cried in complete surprise, lowering his sword and shield and stepping forward as the great warhorse stopped in front of them.

Esteron arched his neck and snorted as he brushed
his velvet, soft muzzle across Drib's cheek in greeting.

"I . . . I . . . I never expected you to come to our
rescue—and you brought the Nighthorses! There
were Nightbeasts—dozens of them, all around us!"
Drib's words were a breathless, excited jumble and
he quickly reached out for Sloeberry's hand and drew
her close to him while the Nighthorses milled around
them in a tightening, defensive circle, their iron-shod
hooves kicking up a blaze of sparks from the cobbles.
The moving circle of horses suddenly parted and
Fleetfoot trotted up to him, his broken halter-rope
hanging down from his headcollar. The pony whinnied and nuzzled the boy's neck.

Amid the noise and confusion Silkstone alighted
on Drib's shoulder, urgently pressing his talons
through the mail-shirt to get his attention. "Be quick,
both of you, mount two of the Nighthorses: they will
take you out of the city to safety. But you must hurry!
Esteron knows you were falsely accused of attacking
Fleetfoot and will not have you punished. Now,
quickly, mount!"

The noise of the Nightbeasts' attack, the thunder
of the horses' hooves, had awoken the city. Lamps
were being lit, doors and windows thrown open,
voices were crying out, demanding to know what all
the commotion was about. The guards had recovered
from their terror of seeing the Nightbeasts in the
courtyard near Candlebane Hall and had discovered
that their prisoners had escaped. The clatter of their
armoured boots and their shouts that the city was
under attack and the prisoners gone were getting
louder, drawing a huge, angry crowd out of their
houses behind them as they raced down towards the
Stumble Gate to seal the great doors.

Dawnrise neighed fiercely and Sparkfire and Dragonshill, two of the Nighthorses, turned in from the moving circle of horses and stopped in front of Drib and Sloeberry, snorting and high-blowing, their necks arched as they waited for them to mount. Sloeberry grapped at the reins and reached up for the stirrup that hung down above her head. Dragonshill looked around at her and, seeing how small she was, bent his front legs and knelt for her to mount. Drib took the reins of Sparkfire but hesitated as the horse knelt for him.

"You must go now, Drib, before the gates are sealed or you will never escape! The people will stone you to death if you stay in the city," Silkstone urged, pecking painfully at his ear.

"But . . . but . . . I cannot ride—my legs . . . even if I could, what about the others: Berioss, Eider, Oaktangle and the rest of the tunnellers—we can't leave them behind!"

Esteron neighed impatiently: he could hear the guards followed by the angry crowd already at the end of Tallow Finger Alley. He gripped Drib's collar in his teeth and lifted him up roughly, laying him across Sparkfire's saddle. The owl flapped his wings, his feathers ruffled, but he managed to keep his shoulder perch as Drib grasped hold of the pommel of the saddle just before Sparkfire surged forward and followed Dragonshill and the Nighthorses down the Oddhollows Steps in huge leaps and bounds. They scattered the startled, converging crowds as they flew past them in the dark, narrow alley.

"Hold on tight—the Nighthorses are sure-footed and will not slip or stumble: they won't let you fall. Hold on tight!" Silkstone screeched as they cantered out into the broad causeway that led to Stumble Gate.

Through flying strands of mane Drib saw the others running through the shadows, keeping close to the houses and making for the open gate. The four door wardens, disturbed by all the noise and commotion, were beginning to drag the great doors closed and the bottom rails were rumbling and grinding slowly across the cobbles.

"Quickly, mount the horses: it's our only way to escape!" Drib shouted from his uncomfortable position on the saddle as the Nighthorses came to a sudden halt close to where Berioss and the others had ducked back into a low archway to hide until the horses had cantered past.

"Drib? Sloeberry? Is that you? What on earth are you doing on those horses? How...?" Oaktangle began uncertainly as he emerged from the archway and stared at the dapple-grey horse that had stopped in front of him.

"There's no time to explain now—mount up, all of you: the horses won't hurt you. But hurry or the gates will be sealed and we'll never get out of the city!" Sloeberry cried, glancing anxiously from the closing doors back to the mass of people who were spilling out from the bottom of the Oddhollows Steps.

Word of their escape aided by the Nightbeasts was spreading faster than quickfire through dry kindling. Rage and anger were fuelling the mob and they were screaming for the tunnellers' blood, demanding revenge for awakening the creatures of the night and resurrecting all their old fears. Berioss didn't need to be urged twice: he could see the danger they were in.

"Hang on tight, all of you!" he shouted, uncertain of his own ability to stay in the saddle as they scrambled up onto the horses and surged forward in a thunder of hoofbeats.

The wardens were struggling to prevent their escape and cried out in terror, scattering as the horses bore down on them and burst through the narrow gap between the doors in single file. Drib had a brief impression of flickering lamplight illuminating frightened, upturned faces through the flying strands of mane that were wrapping themselves around his face. One of his outstretched, twisted, armoured boots struck the ironwood doors and almost dislodged him from the saddle, but he hung on through the pain, refusing to let go. In the next instant they were cantering free on the greenway and the noise and roar of pursuit was quickly fading behind them.

"Hold on! Hold on tight!" Silkstone hooted as he flew away into the dark to watch for any who may follow them.

For what seemed an age, the Nighthorses kept up their relentless pace and for Drib it became a blur of agony. His hands were cut and bleeding from gripping the mane and the pommel of the saddle and the armoured stirrups bruised his twisted legs with each bounding stride, but he was determined not to fall off. Throughout it all, while the wind tugged at his hair and he was shaken and jolted from side to side, he smiled: this was his wildest dream, the impossible had come true, he was riding!

Somewhere amongst the wild jingle of harness and the thunder of hooves he was aware of Esteron and Dawnrise as they took the riderless horses away and return to the city. Silkstone suddenly reappeared, hooting softly and settling onto his shoulder as the Nighthorses eased their pace and eventually came to a halt. Berioss dismounted stiffly and patted his horse's neck, whispering his thanks for rescuing them before helping the others down.

"There's more to you, Drib, than meets the eye—much more!" he smiled, keeping a careful watch on the owl and being careful not to touch its beak or talons as he lifted Drib down from the saddle.

"So, what now? What do we do now we've escaped?" Eider muttered, looking anxiously at the dark, indistinct shapes of the trees and bushes on either side of the Greenway, his fingers lightly tapping an arrowhead, every muscle in his body prepared to act at the slightest sign of trouble. Away in the distance, no more than a shimmering dot on the horizon, he could see the city and a part of him already regretted leaving its familiarity. There was something so unsettling, almost frightening about the unknown.

"I don't know," Berioss frowned. "I hadn't really thought that far ahead."

"We can't go back to the Rising, that's for sure!" Mistletoe added.

"We'll have to find food and shelter pretty quickly, Damask warned, wrapping her warm fleece-lined cloak more snuggly around her shoulders.

"But I thought you said you tunnellers were used to living rough in the forest? I thought you said you could always find plenty to eat!" There was a hint of anger and betrayal in Eider's voice.

"Well, yes, normally we do," Oaktangle agreed quickly. "But there are signs of early frost and the scent of snow is in the wind. There was an abundance of wild berries on the trees that forewarned of a cruel, hard winter. We'll need more than a crude roof of woven branches and a thin covering of leaves and earth to keep us warm, and we'll need to eat something more substantial than roots and berries if we are to survive."

Silkstone listened to the company's dilemma, his head tilted slightly to one side, his feathers ruffled against the bitter dawn chill that was blowing along the Greenway. He lifted silently from Drib's shoulder and settled onto the high cantle of Sparkfire's saddle to speak softly and urgently to the horse before flying back to Drib's shoulder and whispering in his ear.

"Silkstone says we should go to Cawdor. He says we will be safe there," Drib suddenly interrupted Berioss who had just proposed that they try and make a camp somewhere on the old, disused road above Notley Marsh before the snows came.

"Cawdor?" Eider laughed dismissively. "Cawdor doesn't really exist, you fool: it's only a part of the Loremaster's stories, a fragment of the myths and legends that originated from the time of the first Granite Kings. It isn't a real place, Drib, now be quiet!"

Drib felt his cheek flush hotly despite the chill wind. "But it is!" he cried, clenching his fists, determined that they should listen as the owl hooted to him again. "Silkstone says it is where the Nighthorses came from, beyond the wildness of Underfall on the dark side of morning. The Nighthorses will take us there if we ride them on a loose rein and let them find the way. Esteron has pledged them to carry us to safety, if you don't believe me then ask the owl!"

Eider took an angry step towards Drib. "Nobody but you can understand anything it says—if it says anything at all. We don't know if you are telling the truth or just making up another of your stories!"

Berioss gripped Eider's arm and pulled him back. "No, wait, you're forgetting the owl brought you that bow, and he brought Esteron and the Nighthorses to our rescue. Think for a moment, what if Cawdor really exists? There has to be a foundation to all those old myths, doesn't there? The Nighthorses are different from the Errant horses and the Warhorses. They must have come from somewhere, mustn't they? And it would be the only place in all Elundium where we won't be hunted, where we could find proper shelter for the winter." He turned to Oaktangle and asked him if he had ever heard of Cawdor or the dark side of morning.

Oaktangle felt a shiver of apprehension prickle the back of his neck. That was the place he had seen in the vision. He waved his hand in the general direction of World's End, almost afraid to answer. "I don't know: there are winter fireside stories that the elders tell of the times of the first Granite Kings, of great

palaces and fortresses and how all that is left of them
are wild, untrodden places shrouded in mist and
emptiness beyond Underfall. It is rumoured that
there was once a great forest carved from living stone
and that it dwelt on the dark side of morning; there
were towers and archways and sheer walls that rose
from swirling mists."

"Where the wind cried with a thousand voices and
the tang of salt stung every warrior's lips!" Drib
interrupted.

"Salt on your lips! Whoever heard of such nonsense—I'm telling you, he's embroidering the
Loremaster's stories: you're mad if you want to follow him," Eider muttered.

"I don't know what lies beyond Underfall. I don't
think any of our people have ever travelled towards
the dark side of morning: there is so much to see in
Elundium without ever taking that bleak road,"
Oaktangle continued, reluctantly. There was a part of
him that was afraid of being drawn further and further into that vision, of having to learn to use the
weapons they had taken: he was terrified of becoming a warrior.

"And yet fate can show us no better road to take
now," Berioss murmured, returning his attention to
Drib and looking long and hard at the owl perched
on the boy's shoulders. In his battle days he would
have followed the owl's advice without question, so
why did he now hesitate? Why was he now so unde-
cided? Was it because the bird spoke through a crippled sweep's boy instead of a Marcher or a Galloper
captain—a boy whose head barely reached his belt?

"Cawdor! Cawdor!" the owl shrieked, spreading its
wings as the Nighthorses stamped their feet, impatient for the road as they fretted and pulled at their
bridles.

Berioss walked away from the others and looked
back towards the city. He crouched down and

pressed his ear to the frozen ground and faintly heard the sounds of pursuit. "We have argued for too long," he cried, running to his horse. "The King has sent out Gallopers to capture us. We must ride like the wind!"

"But where to?" Eider asked, quickly mounting and gathering up the reins.

"To the dark side of morning. Nobody will ever think of searching for us on that forgotten road. Let the horses have their heads and carry us to our fate. Quickly, mount up all of you!" Berioss cried, his mind made up.

He turned stiffly in the saddle, urging the others to make haste, masking a smile as he saw Drib sitting twisted in the saddle, one foot sticking out to the side, the other knee drawn up close to the pommel. Sloeberry was riding close by him, helping him to keep his balance. Oaktangle urged his mount forward and close to Berioss as he saw the dark smudge of their pursuers spill out of Stumble Gate onto the Greenway in the strengthening sunlight.

"They'll overtake us in no time once they get moving," he warned, pointing back to the squadron of Gallopers gathering around the King.

Berioss shook his head, "No, the Nighthorses are fleeter of foot than the ones they ride. Now, go all of you and let the horses have their heads."

Drib laughed with delight as he clung on to Sparkfire and surged forward, cantering past the others. "Silkstone, go back, go back and tell the King we didn't steal these horses!" he cried.

They were riding to Cawdor: they were heading for the dark side of morning and the new sun was breaking free of World's End, wreathed in smoke and fire. Blackbirds were singing in the hedgerows and the trees and fields were crisp and glistening with white hoar frost. His wildest dreams had come true: he was free and riding into a beautiful morning!

# 10

## Myths and Ancient Legends

"NIGHTBEASTS IN THE UPPER CIRCLE OF THE city? In the courtyard of Candlebane Hall? But . . . but that's impossible! How did they get into the heart of the city? Quickly, seal the Stumble Gate: they must not escape. They must be caught and killed!" Thane cried in dismay, looking from Breakmaster to Errant who crowded the threshold of his chamber, and then out of the window where the renewed sounds of the uproar in the city below were floating up.

"We must catch them! Mulcade fly. Fly high and search them out! Mulcade, where are you?" Thane cursed angrily, seeing that the owl wasn't on his usual perch. He snatched up his sword from where it lay upon the linen chest close to the door, pushed past Breakmaster and ran along the corridor towards the stairhead that would lead him down into the inner courtyard.

"It's already too late, my Lord, they've gone!" Breakmaster called through laboured breaths as he chased after him.

"They've gone, but not before killing the guards who were watching over those prisoners you were going to judge in the light of the new sun!" Errant cried in anger. "The Nightbeasts freed those prisoners and took them with them—and the worst of it is they have all escaped on the Nighthorses—got clean away before anybody could stop them!"

Thane came to an abrupt halt and turned to stare
at Errant. The rising tide of noise and pandemonium,
the shouts for candlemen to light the lamps, the rush
of armoured boots on the stairs and in the courtyards
below all faded in his mind. The creak and rattle of
door-latches being thrown open along the corridor,
the sea of startled, anxious faces crowding in behind
the first Captain of the Nighthorses seemed to shrink
into insignificance. "Nightbeasts in the city—that is
impossible—they're all dead, shrivelled away to nothing. The Nighthorses would never, never have let
them put a clawed foot in the stirrup. They have been
sworn enemies, just like the tunnellers, since the time
of the first Granite Kings. I must be dreaming: this
can't be real."

Errant stood, transfixed with rage, his sword trembling in his hand. "Lord, it is a catastrophe, a disaster. We must pursue them—but there are no horses
fast enough in the stables—none."

Thane felt a tug on his arm and blinked as he
looked down to see Krann in his sleeping-gown,
holding onto him, his eyes wide and full of fear, his
hair tousled from sleep. "I heard voices calling in the
dark: howling, angry voices, and then there was the
sound of hoofbeats . . . " he cried in a small, confused, frightened voice.

A frown clouded Thane's eyes as he reached down
and lifted Krann up to comfort him. Had he been
wrong to think he had destroyed the last Nightbeast
in the Battle of the Rising? Had some of those vile
creatures survived the seeding of Kruel's shadow and
lain hidden in a dark, forgotten hole somewhere,
waiting until they were strong enough to come and
seek out Krann and claim him as their own? Was this
raid and the capture of the tunnellers merely a cover
for their real purpose or . . . ? Elionbel's voice cut
through his troubled speculations as she ran to him.

"Thane, what's wrong? The people are going mad

in the streets again: they are claiming that the city's being attacked!"

"I don't know. Breakmaster has brought word that the prisoners have escaped, that . . . " Thane paused to glance at Errant before looking closely at Krann. He hesitated to speak openly in front of the boy about the Nightbeasts. Suddenly he smiled and set Krann down on his feet close to Elionbel; there was an innocence in the child that no beast could overshadow.

"It was a dream, Krann, nothing more. Now go back to bed and forget all about it."

Straightening up, he whispered to Elionbel, "Keep Krann with you and bolt the door of your chamber: there are wild rumours of Nightbeasts in the city."

Thane saw a flicker of the old fears that had once haunted Elionbel as they crossed her face and she instinctively touched the hilt of the dagger that was always hidden beneath her sleeping-robe and then she took Krann's hand and hurried him back to her chamber.


Thane listened to the excited voices of the guards relating what they had witnessed in the inner courtyard as he bent to examine Ustant's body where it lay with a spear protruding from its chest in the doorway that led down to the cellar and he wondered who could possibly have killed the old Marcher. Why hadn't he escaped with the others? What had made him stand and defend the doorway?

"There were dozens of Nightbeasts screaming and howling as they swarmed across the courtyard toward us . . . " one of the guards shouted in a frightened voice.

"Where did they come from—and where did they go? What happened then?" Thane asked, stooping to retrieve the spent arrow that Drib had loosed at

Snatch, examining the blood-stained tip in the uncertain, flickering light from the torches that two of the guards were holding.

"I . . . I don't know, my Lord, they seemed to appear so suddenly from that doorway—but it all happened so fast: we scattered in surprise as they rushed towards us. The next moment they just vanished," another of the guards muttered darkly, reluctant to admit to his fear of the monstrous creatures.

"Nightbeasts don't just vanish: they must have got out of here somehow!" Errant replied angrily, striding across the courtyard. He stopped when he reached the metal grating set in the cobbles and squatted down. He looked closely and found that a short, metal spike had been jammed in it to prevent it being opened from the courtyard but there was something caught in the grating. "Here, my Lord, here: I think they escaped down through this grating."

"Where does this lead to?" Thane asked as he hurried across and watched Errant reach down to work loose the object he had spotted and bring it up to the light. There was a short intake of breath as he saw what it was and quickly passed it to Thane. "Nightbeast armour!"

Thane shuddered as he took it and his face grew grave with worry. "Yes, it's Nightbeast armour all right!" he muttered grimly as two of the guards struggled to force open the iron grating. "But wait, look again both of you: something's wrong with it."

And he passed it to Breakmaster who turned it over slowly, examining it carefully.

"It's an old passageway that the candlemen used to travel along, my lord, but nobody's used it for an age," one of the guards answered as the grating came loose and the secret road opened up before them.

"You are right, my Lord, there is something very strange about this," Breakmaster agreed as they hurried down the passage that was black with the soot of countless flames. "This armoured scale is withered and rotting—and there's hardly any strength in it. I could probably snap it in two if I tried hard enough. It's as if it comes from a beast that has been dead for a long time."

Thane nodded. "Yes, I have come across such creatures lying rotting on the battle-field and you could easily thrust your spear-blade right through their mouldering hides."

"But they can't be dead, my Lord, not if they killed those guards and released the prisoners—and then they all escaped on my horses. They must be alive and real—mustn't they?" Errant replied angrily.

"I don't know: none of this makes any sense. The Nighthorses would never have let the Nightbeasts ride upon their backs, and I'm not sure they were true creatures of the night at all: look at that arrow— I found it in the courtyard and there's blood on the blade, but that's not Nightbeast blood, I swear my life on it. Nightbeast blood would blacken and eat away at the blade in no time: ask any Archer who fought on the Causeway Fields beneath the walls of Underfall."

Thane frowned as the horseman crouched down to examine the ground. "They went this way, down towards Tallow Finger Alley. Look, there are claw-marks all over the ground."

A sudden commotion in the riveters' yard and shouts from the armoury brought Thane and the company of guards running. They found the master armourer standing in the centre of the armoury, the doors wide open. He was gazing at the fallen spear-stand and the chaos that had been caused.

"My Lord, I don't know what has been going on— everything's been turned upside-down: it's as if somebody was searching for something, but hardly anything of any real value has been stolen—except two of the best ebony bows and two quivers of new-forged arrows. A suit of marching clothes has disappeared which would fit a large, well-built man, and a set of archer's clothes, and there are a half a dozen fleece-lined, winter cloaks missing, and . . . oh yes, and . . . " The armourer shook his head and laughed harshly. "You won't believe this, sire, but whoever broke in here and made all this mess has ransacked the apprentices' hall and taken enough of that miniature mock armour—boots, helms, swords and shields and all the clothes to wear beneath it—for at least half a dozen people. Although where you'd find that many midgets to wear it I don't know. They were worthless, practice pieces the apprentices made to learn their craft. Some of them must have been as old as the Granite Kings: I can't imagine why anyone would want to take them."

Thane couldn't help noticing that the door on the far side of the armoury that was usually hidden by the tall spear-stands was now lying on its side with hundreds of spears scattered haphazardly across the floor. He asked the armourer where it led.

"Why, nowhere, my Lord: the door has been locked and the key lost since the great siege. I keep meaning to get the masons to block it up but I've been run off my feet and I keep forgetting. There's a rumour that there used to be a passageway that led under Candlebane Hall, but it fell into disuse when the old armoury was destroyed in the siege."

Thane quickly crossed the stone floor, picking his way through the fallen spears to try the handle of the door. It was securely locked, but there wasn't any dirt on the latch: somebody must have touched it very recently. He frowned and turned back, wrapped in thought. It made him wonder: what if Breakmaster and the guards had jumped to the wrong conclusion? What if these Nightbeasts, or whatever they really were, were trying to attack the prisoners rather than set them free? What if the prisoners had managed to escape from the cellar and open the door of that old, disused passageway and had somehow found their way into the armoury? They were certainly of the right stature to wear all that stolen armour. But why had they taken it? It didn't make sense: they weren't fighting people, so why burden themselves with something they would never be able to use—unless to defend themselves? And why take the bows? The tunnellers were not archers: they wouldn't be able to use them.

"Were there any other prisoners locked up in that cellar?" Thane asked on impulse, retracing his steps to the doors of the armoury.

Breakmaster thought for a moment. "Yes, there was that sweep's boy, Drib, the one you befriended, sire, although I have my doubts now that he was guilty of anything. He should be praised for going to Fleetfoot's aid when he did."

"And there's my son!" Gray Goose called out in a shamed voice. "Eider was locked up earlier tonight for breaking into the Learning Hall and destroying many of the Loremaster's scrolls. I was going to plead for him in the morning, my Lord."

A faint smile tugged at the corners of Thane's lips. He was well aware of Eider's recklessness and it explained who might have taken the bows, but he still couldn't comprehend how the Nighthorses would ever allow such creatures as the guards described anywhere near them.

"There aren't any claw-marks on the floor or the walls of the armoury, my lord. I don't think the Nightbeasts could have come in here."

Thane beckoned Errant and Breakmaster to follow him out of the smoky lamplight and into the frosty, night air. "How did the Nightbeasts get into the Breaking Yards? Did they kill the wardens who guarded the gates?"

Breakmaster frowned and shook his head. "No, my Lord, I don't think so. The duty grooms were awakened by an owl shrieking in Esteron's stable and then there was a terrible commotion as the Nighthorses broke free of their picket lines and, with Esteron at their head, stampeded out of the stable yards into Tallow Finger Alley."

"The noise was enough to wake the dead—nobody could have stopped them!" Errant added.

Breakmaster looked up from the ground. "From what the guards tell me it happened a short while after the Nightbeasts vanished from the upper circle of the city. I can show you where the creatures mounted the horses before cantering at breakneck speed down the Oddhollows Steps and out of Stumble Gate onto the Greenway."

Thane hurriedly followed the other two down the Arrow Way and crouched down to run his fingers over the mass of hoofprints that had chipped and scarred the cobblestones. It was easy to see the Nightbeasts' claw-marks amongst them.

"They must have mounted the horses here, my Lord, because there aren't any more claw-scrapes on the ground beyond this point," Errant informed him with disgust.

Mulcade flew to Thane's shoulder, momentarily distracting him with his screeching warnings about Nightbeasts in the city and Nighthorses galloping onto the Greenway.

"Yes, yes, we know, the prisoners have escaped and the city is in uproar. Will you fly up to the Towers of Granite and watch over Elionbel and Krann: see no harm comes to them."

Mulcade hooted softly and rose into the lightening sky. The grey hours were at an end and the new sun was breaking free of World's End.

"We must hurry, my Lord: we must pursue the Nighthorses even if there are none fast enough to catch them we must at least try. Their trail grows colder with every moment we linger here," Errant warned.

"No, wait, look more closely at the ground: there's something odd about the pattern of scuffs and chips in the cobbles. Look, you can see them better now it's growing light."

Errant and Breakmaster moved impatiently into the centre of the Arrow Way and looked down at the ground. Slowly they turned around, their eyebrows raised in surprise. "Yes, you're right, my Lord, the Nighthorses were running in a defensive circle here: it's as if they were protecting somebody. And those Nightbeast claw-marks are scattered, as though they were fleeing."

Errant paused as his eyes followed a set of claw-scrapes through a narrow gap between two of the horses that dropped sharply away into Winders Lane. "There are discarded weapons scattered everywhere and the claw-marks suddenly vanish after a few paces. I wonder—what on earth happened to the beasts?" he frowned and hurried back to where Thane and Breakmaster stood.

"I'm not sure now what was happening here. It seems that the Nightbeasts were chasing those tunnellers—perhaps those creatures didn't escape on the Nighthorses at all. No, my guess is that Silkstone warned Esteron and he and the Nighthorses came to their rescue, snatching them away to safety in the nick of time. But why?"

"It just doesn't seem possible for anybody, especially the tunnellers after all their people suffered, to throw their lot in with the Nightbeasts. But then the creatures broke into the city to set them free. What I don't understand is why were they chasing them if they had just set them free?" Breakmaster frowned.

"Perhaps they didn't . . . " Thane answered slowly, searching the ground as they moved towards the Oddhollows Steps. "Perhaps we have been jumping to the wrong conclusions, perhaps they're not even really Nightbeasts at all."

Thane paused and threw up his hands helplessly. "I don't really know what to make of it all, but something inside, some instinct, has been telling me that the tunnellers and those two Marchers would never have done the things they're accused of. And there's something about those Nightbeasts that isn't . . . " he paused again, "isn't real. I'm getting the feeling that somebody or something wants us to think that the tunnellers have become treacherous rebels, that they've awoken the creatures of our fears, but I don't think that's the case."

"But who would want to do such a thing? And why would they? What purpose would it serve?" Breakmaster asked in bewilderment.

Thane shook his head and was about to follow the hoofmarks down the broad, winding steps towards Stumble Gate when he heard a shout from the guards on the walls telling him that Esteron and Dawnrise with the remaining Nighthorses were cantering back towards the city. "I don't know: there's much more to this riddle than lies on the surface for us to see, that much I am sure of. If those beasts are still in the city then we must find them quickly. Send as many men as you can to comb through every house, lane and alleyway: leave no doorway closed or hidey-hole unsearched. Breakmaster, organize a search—Errant, come with me: we will ride in pursuit as soon as Esteron reaches Stumble Gate."

Morning was breaking across the frozen countryside as Thane and Errant waited impatiently for the horses to return. Breakmaster spoke urgently to the guards and then ran out beneath Stumble Gate to join them. The rays of a new sun touched the tall Towers of Granite and the weather-bleached roof of Candlebane Hall making the hoar-frost that the night air had painted glitter and sparkle in the strengthening light. Long, sharp-etched shadows from the trees and their tracery of bare, winter branches stretched across the crisp, white grass at Thane's feet as he stood upon the Greenway.

"Where will the tunnellers flee, Errant? Where will the Nighthorses take them? Winter is almost upon us and I fear they will find little welcome in the villages that lie beside the Greenway's edge. How will they survive without food or shelter?"

Errant stamped his feet against the cold and frowned. "The Nighthorses are fleet of foot, my Lord, and they know all the wild places. They will look after the tunnellers, I am sure of it, and if we don't overtake them I doubt if a whole army of Gallopers will ever find them. They have a greater start than even Esteron and Dawnrise can match."

"Lord, you should stay here," Breakmaster suddenly interrupted. "The people are close to riot and only your voice can calm them. Let me go in your place. I can have Beaconlight saddled in no time at all." The old horseman sounded anxious as the thunder of the horses grew louder on the Greenway.

Thane shook his head as Esteron approached. The horse had his neck arched and his nostrils flared and a sheen of sweat glistened on his coat, for he was breathing hard. Thane took the reins and reached for the stirrup that was swinging free as he prepared to mount. "The only thing that will stop me from riding in pursuit is if I knew for sure where the prisoners were and I could be sure that none of those creatures were amongst them."

Esteron whinnied, tossing his head and moving sideways, preventing Thane from mounting as the rest of the Nighthorses milled around Errant. A shadow passed briefly over the low, morning sun. Thane looked up as Silkstone stooped to perch briefly on the high cantle of the saddle, shrieking and spreading his wings in agitation. "Cawdor . . .

Cawdor" the owl cried, lifting up on the chill, morning air as it rose and flew away, repeating the same piercing call again and again.

"Only ten of the Nighthorses are missing, Lord," Errant cried as Thane heard the owl's words and caught hold of the pommel, springing into the saddle and pirouetting Esteron, sending ice sparks dancing between his feet as he shaded his eyes against the dawn and watched the owl vanish into the distance.

"Cawdor? Where is Cawdor? Which road do we take, Errant?" he cried, as Errant vaulted into Dawnrise's saddle and the riders of the Nighthorses streamed out of Stumble Gate ready to ride with their King.

"No! Wait my Lord," Breakmaster called, grabbing at Esteron's bridle as he risked Thane's anger. "The owl must have come as a sign, an omen—you must stay here. Only the prisoners escaped on the Nighthorses, none of those creatures—all the other horses are accounted for. Remember your promise."

"Cawdor is the place where the Nighthorses were first found, gathered from the dark side of morning in the time of the Granite Kings, somewhere in the wild lands. None know for sure where it lies. That must be where they are going now!" Errant cried out.

"Then there's no time to lose: we must overtake them before they leave the Greenways. Get out of my way!" Thane hissed. There was anger in his eyes as he spurred Esteron forward, threatening to trample on the old horseman. But Breakmaster stubbornly stood his ground.

"Remember your promise—you said you would stay, my Lord. It is more important to stop the people from rioting. Let Errant go after them."

Thane hesitated, wondering if fate had meant the prisoners to escape. Perhaps they had been mounted on the Nighthorses so that they may find a safe haven at Cawdor. He frowned. What chance did he have of finding their road, a road that had been long-forgotten and lost in history. He doubted their guilt now even more strongly than before. He would have the city searched until they found those creatures who had clearly attacked them: they were probably at the bottom of this unrest and the troubles that had spread through the countryside.

"But we must go after them or the city folk will think we have deliberately allowed them to escape. We must find them and bring them to the hearing even though we know they are innocent. Let my Gallopers follow them!" Errant cried.

"Wait!" Thane drew his mount in close beside Dawnrise. "Yes, pursue them: that will appease the city folk for now, but do not attempt to capture them or do more than mark the path they take beyond Underfall. I want them safely out of the way until I get to the bottom of this. If you bring them back to the city I cannot be sure what will happen to them. Now ride, but slowly, and mark their path well."

Thane turned to Breakmaster and lowered his voice. "Where will I find knowledge of the dark side of morning?"

"I am sure there must be much written about it in the Lore of Elundium. The Loremaster probably has many dusty old scrolls that refer to it."

Thane nodded, holding Esteron back as Errant led the riders out to gallop along the Greenway.

"Remember, mark the path well!" he called out to them.


Grout shrank back into the shadows of the Learning Hall, trying to hide amongst the clutter of books and scrolls, frantic with panic. His long, bony fingers were clutching at the throat of his gown, his lips dribbling and trembling uncontrollably as he believed all his secret plots and treacheries had been uncovered.

The King, Breakmaster and a company of guards were mounting the steps of the Learning Hall and at any moment he would hear them pounding on the door. Curious onlookers, spiteful people whom he knew would revel in his disgrace were beginning to gather, to crowd the wide steps behind the King's guard. Their voices were growing louder as they chanted his name. Suddenly they were on the threshold. Grout jumped and whimpered with each echoing, hammering knock.

"Open up! In the name of the King open up, Loremaster Grout: the King has need of your wisdom!"

Grout glanced wildly around the Learning Hall, past the tiers of shelves and dark cubby-holes piled high with dusty scrolls and old manuscripts of lore, past the mountainous books about the daylights of the Granite Kings, past the litter of history that filled his life towards the small, arched doorway that led to the scullery. He half-rose, intent on escape, when he felt the sharp prick of a dagger-blade in the small of his back.

"Answer that door, Grout: your precious King calls for you. Remember, one false move—one careless word—and I'll slit your throat from ear to ear and pull your useless, babbling tongue out through the hole!" Snatch's voice hissed out from where he was hiding amongst the books.

"But we are found out, unmasked! I knew no good would come of such foolishness: I will be publicly flogged, disgraced," the Loremaster whined.

"Shut up! You stupid fool, do you think that the King would bother to knock if he had the slightest idea of what you were doing during the night? Answer that door and be quick about it—and keep your wits about you. Remember—one false word and you die!"

Grout opened the door nervously, bowing and mumbling anxiously as he twisted his fingers

together. "Oh what an honour, my Lord, an honour
that you should grace this humble Learning Hall with
your presence, that you should spare a moment in
these troubled times to visit one so unworthy. It is
such a pity that the children are not here to see you.
But have you called to hear what that wretched
Archer's son did when he broke in here yesterlight?
He is a dreadful boy, my Lord, and he deserves the
severest punishment. He did no end of damage!"

Thane smiled coldly and shook his head. There was
something about the Loremaster's ingratiating manner and his cunning, furtive look that filled him with
distrust of every word and gesture. It was as if he had
something he wished to hide. Or was it the place
itself that filled him with such misgivings? He could
choke on the childhood smell of chalk and vellum
that the airless, dusty gloom harboured. Memories
came flooding back, memories of his school days
when the Chancellors' sons, egged on by Loremaster
Pinchface, had chased him from the Learning Hall
while howling for his blood.

"No . . . no . . . I will deal with Eider's punishment
at a later date. There is a more pressing matter than I
bring to you . . . " Thane hesitated. Something
warned him to be wise and stay silent about Cawdor,
to take his question elsewhere. But before he could
dismiss the Loremaster and turn away Breakmaster
cleared his throat and asked.

"It is the way to Cawdor that we seek. The place
where the Nighthorses were gathered on the dark
side of the morning. We think those prisoners who
escaped during the night may be heading for it."

Thane cursed Breakmaster inwardly but it was too
late.

"Cawdor?" Grout exclaimed, his nervous manner
turning to a startled look of surprise. His cunning
eyes darted a glance back to the shadows and Thane
thought he heard a short, sharp intake of breath from

somewhere in the gloomy depths of the Learning Hall. He took a step forward, searching the piles of dusty lore that littered the back of the hall.

"Who's there? Who lurks in the shadows? I command you to come out!" he demanded, his fingers curling around the hilt of his sword, wishing he had Mulcade on his shoulder so that his sharp eyes could penetrate the deep shadows.

"There is nobody there, my Lord, only the rats. They are such a nuisance: I have to spend endless hours chasing them out with my flail as I try to prevent them making their nests in the piles of older scrolls. They gnaw at the parchment and vellum, you know." Then he rushed past the King and his guards and rushed backwards and forwards, beating his flail at the books and scrolls. "The vermin have fled, my Lord, there are no eavesdroppers in my Learning Hall, none, none at all!" he cried, hurrying back, all bows and smiles.

Grout knew that he must not give the King the slightest excuse to search the hall or for one moment doubt his loyalty. He swallowed and breathlessly licked at his thin, bloodless lips, wringing his hands together in an effort to mask his nervousness. It didn't matter what he told the King about Cawdor: anybody with an ounce of common sense knew it didn't really exist beyond the myths and fairy tales of the Granite Kings. They were just stories that he told to the unruly, filthy brats that filled his Learning Hall to keep them quiet.

"The place of Cawdor, my Lord, is wreathed in mystery. Its ancient origins are buried so deep in the legends of the first Granite King that nobody knows for sure where it lies save that it must be somewhere beyond the last lamp that burns at World's End in the fortress of Underfall. It lies behind the distant heights of the Emerall Mountains and it is shrouded by the dark side of morning where there are endless wild grasslands. It is where all the legends say the Nighthorses came from, beyond the great petrified forest of living stone where there stands a citadel so strong, so powerful that it has the power to guard the very margin of the world. Stories tell that frozen orchids climb the towers and trail in blazing colour from every archway, that there are carvings of the purest black marble veined with silver rising sheer and terrible above the swirling mist where the wind cries with a thousand restless voices as it combs through the darkness and the sharp tang of salt wets every warrior's lips and stings their eyes."

"Salt on their lips! How ridiculous! It is the way to it we want to know, not to hear this drivel!" Breakmaster had never liked the Loremaster or the tales he wove so easily with his silken, soothing tongue but there was no one else in the city that was so learned, no one else they could ask.

"A way to the dark side of morning? You wish to pursue those prisoners to the forgotten citadel of Cawdor? Why, my Lord, there are many tales of that ancient road but I fear time must have overgrown it with wildness, it has long been lost and fallen into disuse."

"The way—where will the Nighthorses go then? Which direction? Which Greenway will they take? We haven't got all day to listen to your fairy stories!" Breakmaster prodded the Loremaster's chest with an impatient finger, sensing that Thane was growing restless.

Grout's eyes narrowed with hate at the way the horseman bullied him but he would get his own back: he would send them searching for a road they would never find, a road that didn't exist beyond the stories he wove out of the ancient myths about the Granite Kings. He would have them scouring the steep, inhospitable shoulders of the Emerall Mountains for an age of daylights while Snatch and his murderous friends seized back everything the Chancellors had lost. He would teach this new King a lesson, he would lose him forever in the wastelands beyond the Fortress of Underfall. He would soon learn how dangerous it was to try to change everything.

"Oh yes," he smiled. "There are legends of a high pass only three daylights' ride beyond the great lamp of Underfall. It is due west of the old road that rises from Notley Marsh, and it skirts the heather meadows and passes close to the gates of Night before entering a deep ravine. But it is a wild, dangerous path, my Lord: the stories tell that once you have journeyed through the mouth of the ravine, giant spires of ice and jumbled, twisted, wind-cracked cliffs of emerald stone overshadow the narrow road. It was rumoured in King Holgranos's daylights that the way was guarded by many-headed serpents and armoured, hump-backed beasts that spat boiling steam and fire from their mouths."

Grout paused for breath and laughed. "But I doubt there's more than old, forgotten bones now littering that road, and certainly nothing to bother so great a King who rules us now. That, my Lord, is all I know of the road you seek."

"Many-headed serpents and armoured beasts? What stuff and nonsense you tell: but at least we know enough now to find the road in the spring, if it exists at all after all this time!" Breakmaster muttered, casting a last, glowering look at the Loremaster as he followed Thane out of the Learning Hall.

Snatch rose silently from the shadows with a triumphant leer thinning and stretching his lips as the doors of the hall were slammed shut and the clatter of the guards' armoured boots faded and merged with the noise and bustle from the street outside. "So you think I'm vermin, do you, Grout?" There was a menace in Snatch's voice that made the Loremaster cower as he advanced on him.

"No . . . no . . . of course not, you will be the great-est, the most powerful Chancellor—it was the only thing I could think of to stop the King searching my room . . ." Grout's voice choked in terror but Snatch merely laughed at him and pushed him aside.

"Relax, you stupid old fool. You did well and you shall be rewarded. Now we know where the King thinks those wretched, slippery tunnellers are head-ing for and we can follow leisurely in their hoofprints causing all manner of chaos and damage in their name!"

"But . . . but . . . those tunnellers will never survive the winter. There is no point following them. I thought you would stay here and spread fear and ter-ror through the people of the city, make them hate the King and rise up to overthrow him!" Grout cried in dismay.

Snatch shook his head. "You're forgetting, old fool: we have made it look as though the Nightbeasts and the tunnellers are allies, we have even convinced the King that they have escaped together on the Nighthorses, to stay here and do as you say would only expose their innocence. No, there will be much more profit in spreading terror along the Greenway's edge—and rich pickings from lonely travellers and isolated villages with which to line our pockets. We will not return until our power in the very place he drove us to in exile has grown enough to topple the King. We must find the bodies of those tunnellers and bury them or follow them to the dark side of morning. If they're lucky enough to survive the jour-ney then we must kill them. Nobody must know what really happened to them, that way we can keep their evil deeds going forever." Snatch laughed, picking up the heavy sack of Nightbeast armour and throwing it easily across his shoulder before beckoning to Kush, Huxort and the others to follow him out of the scullery door. He paused on the threshold and grinned at the Loremaster, slowly drawing his middle finger on his right hand across his throat.

"Watch out for us, Grout: watch for us in the dead hours of the night. Listen for us scratching at your door because the Honourable Company of Murderers will return, I promise."

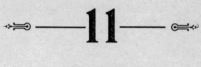

# 11

## Cawdor

DRIB SHIVERED UNCONTROLLABLY IN SPARKFIRE'S saddle, huddled forward against the weather as the snow flurries stung his cheeks. He had never been so cold before. The bitter winds and howling blizzards they had endured as they rode through the high passes of the Emerall Mountains had found its way through every fold, every gap and button-hole in the warm, winter clothes he had taken from the armoury and frozen him to the bone. Frost had even settled to stiffen his breeches beneath the heavy, fleece-lined cloak that he wore and kept pulled up high around his ears to stop them burning with the cold. His hands and feet were numb: he couldn't feel his toes inside his stout, armoured boots or his fingers where they gripped the pommel of the saddle and the tip of his nose was also numb.

But all the discomfort, all the cold, the saddle-sores and aching limbs, even the gnawing hunger of that desperate ride to reach Cawdor before winter finally closed all the roads and left them stranded and sure to die had been worth it. For Drib it had been the most wonderful adventure: there had been so much to see and wonder at that he hardly dared to blink. It had all been so much more beautiful, more magical than he could have ever have imagined from those stories Grout had told them in the Learning Hall and yet everything had been in its place exactly as he had been taught. The dark, forbidding forests, the endless sweep of hills marching away to the edge of sight, the steep mist-shrouded skirts of the Emerall Mountains, the distant rush of waterfalls cascading into hidden gullies, the eerie cry of the wolves at night and the roar of the great, antlered mountain stags: everything had been there, just waiting. Sloeberry had ridden beside him whenever the narrow paths allowed pointing out and telling him about the plants and the trees as they passed but now even Sloeberry had fallen silent and each one of the company sat huddled in their own frozen misery, clinging to the fragile, fading hope that the path they had followed into the dark, silent, stone forest two daylights ago really would lead them to Cawdor before they perished.

Silkstone hooted softly and moved inside Drib's cloak where he had sought shelter during the worst of the storms. The owl pecked impatiently at the frozen folds of the cloak and emerged blinking his large eyes and ruffling his feathers as he scented the air before flying ahead through the tangled and seemingly endless archway of petrified branches that shut out most of the daylight overhead. The branches were festooned with an interlacing tracery of frost-glittering vines and creepers of the deepest shade of indigo, their still flowerheads and petals glowing softly in the gloomy darkness like a million hanging lanterns that changed from bright saffron and cadmium through hues of marble rust as they rode past.

Drib sensed something was different and he blinked away the film of ice and snowflakes that had clung to his eyelashes and straightened up painfully in the saddle, his face burning with cold. He looked about him and realized that the gloom beneath the silent, gnarled trees of the stone forest was beginning to brighten and he could see light ahead. The swirling snowstorm that had been filtering down on them through the branches had stopped but there was something else—an odd sound, the faintest whisper on the still air. He twisted and turned his head as he tried to catch it.

"Sloeberry—that noise—listen, can you hear it? What is it?" he called, turning awkwardly in the saddle towards her. He licked his lips as he spoke and frowned as he tasted the sharp tang of salt.

"I don't know: it sounds really strange, as if there are voices crying in torment," she answered with an edge of apprehension in her voice, fearing what might be lying beyond the trees.

"It must be Cawdor!" Drib whispered in excitement. "Remember what the Loremaster said, "the wind cries with a thousand restless voices".

"But there isn't any wind: the air is perfectly still. Drib, I'm afraid. What if there is an army of warriors who guard the dark side of morning? What if they hate us as much as the people of the Granite City? Listen to them: their voices are growing louder with every step we take, how do they know we are here in the forest?"

Drib cried out in fear and hung on tightly as Sparkfire snatched at the bit and cantered free of the trees. The horse snorted and whinnied, calling out to the other Nighthorses to follow as it sensed the closeness of its ancient home. It carried Drib out at breakneck speed across a bleak, empty, windswept headland towards the vast ruins of a once-great citadel that still perched precariously in its dereliction upon the margin of the world, guarding the dark side of morning and surrounded by a restless, shadowy sea. The tide surged and thundered in grey-green waves against the tumbled rocks and sheer, marble cliffs, breaking in huge, icy plumes of spray that froze and glistened on everything it touched. Above the crumbling towers and battlements thousands upon thousands of wheeling, crying sea-birds darkened the sky.

Sparkfire cantered up the steep causeway followed by the other Nighthorses and halted before the broken doors. One by one the company dismounted and stared up at the ruins that once were Cawdor. Each one of them felt overwhelmed with despair when they saw the dereliction of the place.

"So this is journey's end!" Berioss muttered bitterly, leading his mount into the inner gloomy courtyard and listening to the horse's hooves echoing in the emptiness.

"I've seen this place before—it was in that vision. It's exactly the same as the place I saw when I was beside the river and saw the Master of Magic in the water; only there was summer ivy on the battlements and sun-shadows beneath the archways and . . . oh yes, Drib was in the picture, dressed in armour—yes, I remember now!" Oaktangle cried out in excitement as he looked around him.

"Well, if this is to be our future then we must do our best to weather out the winter here, we must survive, somehow, and make it happen. Let us search for firewood and see if any of those towers still have a roof to give us shelter. I'm near frozen to death," Mistletoe began to gather anything that looked as though it might burn.

"There may well be enough wood and rubbish to burn all winter and keep us warm but what are we going to eat?" Berioss frowned as he returned to the others.

"I'm sure I saw animal tracks in the snow, large ones, on the edge of the forest," Damask offered.

"Drib, you can use a bow, if the way you aimed at that Nightbeast in the doorway was anything to go by. Come with me and we'll hunt for supper!" Eider grinned, passing one of the ebony bows and the second precious quiver of arrows across to Drib before remounting his horse.

"Don't venture too far into that forest and get

THE KNIGHTS OF CAWDOR     343

yourselves lost—and stay together whatever you do!" Berioss warned them as they rode away.

Drib glanced back to the gaunt ruins of Cawdor silhouetted against the restless waves as they followed the animal spoor beneath the eaves of the eerie, silent, stone forest.

It wasn't anything like he had expected it to be. A thick cloud of sea-birds were crying as they spiralled and circled around the whispy ribbon of blue smoke that was rising from one of the towers and he could see Berioss standing with his hands on his hips watching them from between the broken doors. He raised his hand to wave as Silkstone stooped down to perch on his shoulder and he reached up to caress the owl's chest feathers.

"Nobody in the Learning Halls will ever believe that we actually reached the dark side of morning will they? And to think the sound of all those voices crying in the wind was only birds! And . . . "

"Shut up and pay attention if you want any supper: your infernal chattering is enough to frighten away the deafest animal!" Eider hissed, suddenly slipping the reins.

His heartbeats quickened as he reached for an arrow and nocked it onto his bow-string. There was something moving between the trees: he heard a muffled, snuffling snort and thought he glimpsed the enormous shape of a Nightboar moving clumsily through the undergrowth.

Berioss frowned as he watched them vanish into the dark forest. He should have gone with them and led the hunt instead of standing here worrying. He was sure that the creatures who had attacked them in the Granite City would pursue them and their tracks through the mountain pass would be easy to follow. "Cawdor," he muttered. These derelict ruins wouldn't give them much protection against the weather, let alone from an attack.

A noise in the courtyard behind him, soft laughter and singing voices, made him glance round quickly to see Sloeberry and Damask manhandling a large, old, fire-scalded caldron that they had discovered in the ruins, pulling it towards the tower where Mistletoe had built a fire. Oaktangle and Blackthorn were kneeling, trying to repair the broken pulley of the well, talking softly as they worked. Berioss smiled and rubbed at the frost that still clung to his beard: the tunnellers were such an inventive, hard-working people who seemed to thrive on adversity. His fears of not surviving the winter began to fade. He looked back at the silent, stone forest that pressed in around the ruins of Cawdor and on towards the distant peaks of the mountain that was now completely wrapped in storms. Perhaps fate had been kind to them: perhaps winter had already closed the pass behind them. He sighed, wishing Ustant was with them as he examined the riven doors, running his cold fingers over the ancient, wormy wood. Perhaps they could somehow fortify the ruins. Perhaps he had until the spring melted the snows to teach Oaktangle and the others how to defend themselves; after all they had taken all that mock armour from the armoury, it would be silly not to put it to some use.

A faint movement in the darkest shadows beneath the gate arch, a swirling glow of soft rainbow colours against the wind-smoothed stone, made Berioss step hastily backwards and gasp in fear as the fragile, translucent figure of the Master of Magic began to appear. The last time the magic had appeared before him on the Causeway Field it had turned him into a tree.

"Fear me not," Nevian smiled, reaching out and warming the old Marcher's hands with his touch.

"What? What do you want from me?" Berioss's lips were trembling so much he could hardly speak.

"Marcher Berioss, you have learned, through a

long, hard life, to hold honour and justice above all things. I pledge you now to use those virtues and make this company strong. Forge them into the Knights of Cawdor. Prepare them to ride out in the name of justice and honour in the dark daylights that lie ahead, for their King will have great need of them. Prepare them well, for they know nothing of the shock and sway of battle."

"Nevian! Nevian wait, tell me, who are the creatures who are pursuing us the ones who attacked us in the Granite City? How much time do we have? Nevian!" Berioss cried out, trying to hold onto the melting colours of the rainbow cloak as the magician's voice faded and blended with the mournful cry of the sea-birds that wheeled overhead.

He looked down at his gnarled, old fingers where the soft colours of the cloak were infusing into his skin, smoothing and strengthening his hands and he laughed, feeling proud that the Master of Magic had entrusted him with such a task. He drew his sword and strode out between the broken doors.

"They will be ready, you have my pledge on it!" he shouted against the thunder of the surf as the sea boiled against the rocks below. He swept his sword in a glittering arch that reflected the low, winter sun and lightened up the dark side of morning.

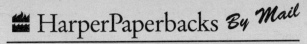